GUNS OF HORSE PRAIRIE

When they had him thrown in jail, Tubac Jones was almost ready to call it quits. Laying claim to the abandoned Holeman rangeland wasn't easy...especially when the most important man in Horse Prairie had it in mind for himself.

At first, Tubac wasn't going to let them get away with it. He had a number of clever ideas as to how to hang on to his squatter's claim. But now here they had him all locked up and it looked as if they were set to throw the key away. Unless, of course, he could get them to dancing first to the tune of his trusty old six-gun.

WILDCATS OF TONTO BASIN

Had the man who arrived in Tonto Basin on the night Juke Ronstadt was murdered been an ordinary puncher, the forces out to smash a ranch and grab the cattle empire very likely would have killed him and thereafter plumb forgotten him. But he as not an ordinary puncher. He was Bufe Telldane, ex-lawman and outlaw—and about the deadliest man with a gun in that whole stretch of the country.

NELSON NYE

GUNS OF HORSE PRAIRIE/WILDCATS OF TONTO BASIN

LEISURE BOOKS **L** NEW YORK CITY

A LEISURE BOOK®

October 1991

Published by

Dorchester Publishing Co., Inc.
276 Fifth Avenue
New York, NY 10001

GUNS OF HORSE PRAIRIE

I

IRONED OUT

WITHOUT CARE for the clerks or the wide-eyed customers, ignoring the shouts of the shotgun guard, the tall gaunt stranger in the brush-clawed chaps strode through the last gate and stopped by the desk with a hard, brash grin.

Behind the desk's satiny finish the honey-haired girl showed conflicting emotions as her glance swept over his trail-dusty garb and finally came up to his face with a frown. "Do you have an appointment with Mr. Haines?"

It was not an encouraging start by considerable, but the tall stranger dragged off his hat with a flourish. He showed her another half inch of white teeth. "If I ain't," he said, "don't blame it on me. I've sure wore a groove in your doorstep tryin'—"

"I'm sorry," declared the honey-haired girl, "but Mr. Haines sees no one without an appointment." She picked up her pencil and held it poised suggestively. "If you'll give me your name—"

"Jones—" said the stranger—"Tubac Jones."

At that the girl shrank back in astounded dismay. "How did you get in here?" she gasped.

"Seems like I musta walked in, ma'am—I don't recollect nobody carryin' me." He gave her his toothy grin again and, as though she were viewing the devil, she took fevered stock of the rest of him—the battered black hat and the dusty black hair curling out of its shadow, the worn pinto vest, the checked flannel shirt, the sporty checked trousers shoved into scuffed range boots. Three things held her notice longest—the big .44 poked into his waistband, his grin, and the tough, fighter's face of him.

She recalled the frantic instructions that had been slammed out of the inner sanctums at her at least twenty times in the last five days. She gulped back her fright and recovered her poise. Once more she became the cool and polite but inflexible secretary of the great Mr. Haines, profound and scintillating head of the Stockmen's Bank & Mortgage Loan.

"I'm sorry," she said, "but—"

"That's quite all right, ma'am. You just trot on in an' tell that swivel-eyed Mormon pirate either he's comin' out here or else I'm comin' in, pronto. I ain't figurin' to be stood off no longer! You tell him, ma'am, if him an' me ain't passin' chin-gab inside o' five seconds, I'm goin' to pull this temple o' Mammon down an' spank him with the splinters!"

"Mr. Jones' black scowl looked so ferocious, Honey Hair had jumped up and was reaching for the door when the shotgun guard put his oar in. It was not a well-advised interruption; but if the guard had been smart he'd have been something other than a gun packer. He jabbed the snout of his shotgun into Mr. Jones' back and, as tough as the panting difficulty he had in breathing would let him be, said: "All right, *you!* Git a wiggle on—pronto!"

And the Jones from Tubac certainly did.

He reared around like a clout-stung grizzly, yanked the weapon from the startled guard's hands and with one quick blow broke its back on the gate rail. With a testy scowl he heaved both pieces through the nearest window.

The guard let out an infuriated howl. "That gun cost—"

"Go away," Jones said, "before I hurt you," and dusted his hands on what he found handy. That it happened to be Mr. Haines' new white coat, carefully hung on the hat-tree alongside the door, appeared completely to slip Jones' notice. He flipped a reassuring wink at the horrified girl. "Go right along in, Miss, an' tell 'im I'm waitin'."

But she was saved the trouble. The door banged violently open, and an angry face framed in mutton-chop whiskers peered furiously into the outer defenses. "What in—"

The falsetto squeak ran off key and stopped; the gimlet mouth stayed open, gaping; the astounded eyes nearly popped from their sockets. With a bleated oath the man grabbed for the door, but Tubac Jones put a boot in the way of it.

"Well, well!" he drawled with vast satisfaction. "If it ain't the great 'Hi Grab' in person—galluses, yaller shoes, mutton chops'n ever'thing! Plumb overflowin' with the milk o' human kindness! As benevolent a sinner as ever—"

A strangled sound gulped out of Haines' throat. "Come in! Come in!" he spluttered hoarsely as his wilted stare caught the grins of customers. "Don't stand there braying—"

"Your education, I'm scared, has been plumb neglected. Nobody brays but a jackass or banker—an' while we're on the subject, why don't you throw out some of these gun dummies an' hire a few guys that've been to third grade?

7

This yap—" Jones jerked a contemptuous thumb at the glowering guard—"ain't got enough savvy to drop sand down a rat hole! He's been claimin' all week that you an' the other big guns of this highbindin' outfit—"

Haines, fairly frothing with spleen, grabbed Jones' arm and yanked him into the office. Somebody kicked the door shut. The banker was just about fit to be tied. By his look you'd have said he was kin to Vesuvius, and was hunting quick cover to get out of the ashes. But Tubac Jones appeared no more alarmed than a tramp would have been of a seam squirrel. He walked coolly over to the banker's chair, brushed some papers off the desk and cocked his boots on it. He took a cigar from an open box and scratched a match on the banker's shirtfront as Haines hovered over him, spluttering with rage.

"Well, gents," he said, looking round with a grin, "I see wer'e all here. Let's get down to brass tacks an' put our cards on the table. The first thing I want's a written agreement; a hands-off policy with all your names on it—"

"You'll get a *bouquet* with all our names on it," growled a copper-cheeked man who was short one finger, "if you don't make a dust for other parts pronto!"

"That's kid talk, Lot," Jones said, "an' you know it. You ain't got a leg—"

Lot Deckerman snorted. "For the last time, Jones, I'm servin' you warnin'. As general manager an' superintendent of the Stampede Hog an' Cattle Company, I'm orderin' you off the Holeman grant. Be off it before sunup tomorrow, or I'll see you facin' a jail sentence—get me?"

"Hoo, hoo!" jeered Jones. "You an' your jail sentences make me laff! Jail sentence for *what?*"

"For illegally preempting a valuable property this institution is holding in trust—"

But Jones' loud whoop cut the rest of Haines' words off.

"The only trust you can find in this bank is the trust that's bleedin' this country—"

"Have a care!" Haines shouted. "There's such a thing as libel—"

"You're golrammed tootin'!" Jones flung back at him. "I'm *li'ble* to put this bank on the dung heap if it don't quit stickin' its nose in my business! The way you—"

"If you come here huntin' trouble, Tubac, you'll get a bigger dose than you bargained for!"

Jones looked down his nose. He made an impolite sound. "Aw, go pick up yer knittin', Percy," he growled at the banker, and turned a sly glance on Lot Deckerman. "You know as well as I do," he said, "that the Holeman range has been layin' empty for goin' on six years."

"Well, it ain't empty now—"

"Sure it ain't! Your damn range-grabbin' syndicate's got cattle runnin' all over the place—I've a good mind to pen 'em up for trespass!"

"You lay a hand on them cattle," Deckerman choked, "an' we'll string you up higher'n Hamen!"

"Never heard of 'im," Jones scoffed. Then a steely glint came into his unblinking eyes, and he slapped the desk with a big-knuckled fist.

"I come into this hog waller plumb gentle as Mary's lamb. I knowed about this Holeman grant; for six years hand-runnin' I been watchin' that grass come belly-high to a full growed hoss, an' nary one hoss to eat it! So I says, by Jinks, I'll fall heir to that place, an' over I come without a care in the world—"

"If gall was dollars—"

"Never mind antagonizin' me—I'm plumb riled up a'ready —an' damn good reason fer bein' so! No sooner do I get settled cozy than up comes this range-hoggin' Deckerman an' starts throwin' cattle onto my grazin' grounds like a country kid heavin' corn to a grist mill. Trampin' my waterholes, gobblin' my grass, pullin' down my fences what I paid good money to Jim Brown t' send me—an' a hell-tearin' freight bill gettin' 'em here! It's enough to—"

"You hadn't no right to go stringin' fence—"

"Who says so?" Jones glowered at Haines with such intensity that the banker made haste to put the desk between them. "Who says so? I got a sight more right on that grant than Deckerman—or anyone else, if it comes to that!"

"That's a damn lie!" Deckerman surged forward angrily, doubling his fists. "The Stampede Hog—"

"I'll stampede your hogs if you don't git the dang critters off'n it!" Jones blared. "You're so good as servin' warnin's— here's one you can play on your mouth harp: Startin' to-morrow mornin' I am to salivate any stray stock I catch on the place! Go smoke that with your chawin' terbacco!"

They were all on their feet now, glaring, hands bunched into fists, hate and turbulence making their faces savage, when the door was flung open and a scar-faced man in loose-fitting store garb strode in silently and shut the door back of him. Dark eyes judged the scene with one quick glance.

"Ike!" Banker Haines shrilled squeakily: "I demand you arrest this man immediate—this instant! Do you understand?"

The newcomer looked at Jones mildly. "What's the charge?"

"*Charge!* Great jugs to Bacchus! Did you say what *charge?*"

The newcomer nodded. "I can't arrest a man without some definite charge against him—"

Lot Deckerman said: "You get him under lock an' key. We'll figger out the charges later—"

But Haines had dragged a pistol from his pocket and, bolstered by the sheriff's presence, was waving it wildly in the direction of Jones. "Put your bracelets on him! Put 'em on 'im, I say! Right now, Sheriff, if you want this bank to back your election! I'll give you all the charges you want—illegal entry, threats an' intimidation, fradulent possession, disturbin' the peace, upsetting business—"

"Just a minute," the sheriff said. "Let's take this in order. Now, illegal entry—"

"Never mind that," Lot Deckerman growled. "You've got a sure-fire case on fradulent possession. He's squattin' on the Holeman grant, he refuses to budge, an' he's threatened to kill off stock owned by my company." He grinned at Tubac coldly. "I guess that'll do for a starter."

Jones gave the Stampede boss a look of contempt, then turned to the sheriff. "If you expect to hold down your office much longer, you better not back no hand like that. I've filed due claim on the Holeman grant; an' whats' more, I got possession, to boot. This range hog ain't got a leg to stand on, Sheriff. I been usin' that place for the last three months an' no one said: 'Boo!' till a fortnight back when a bunch of his waddies shoved a big herd of cattle—"

"That's a stinkin' lie!" the banker shouted. "I say it's a *lie!* The Holeman grant is a property held in trust by this bank for the lawful heirs of Sam Holeman—as you should know, Sheriff! In the interests of the aforesaid heirs, this bank has been leasing the property to the Stampede Hog an' Cattle—"

"Since when?" Jones jeered.

"For the last six years!"

Jones' mouth dropped open and he stared at the banker through a startled silence. Then his jaw snapped shut, and he said through his teeth: "If that's the truth, why ain't they been usin' it?"

"We been holdin' the stock off to build up the grass—"

"For six *years?*"

"Why not?" Deckerman grinned at him smugly. "Holeman

11

over-grazed that range. It's took us six years to bring it back—"

"I'd like to see this precious lease," Jones said grimly; and Hi Grab Haines stamped his fist on a button.

Honey Hair's white face peeked timidly in from the doorway. "Let me have those papers on the Holeman grant—*all* of them," Haines snapped. And when she brought them he spit on his thumb and leafed hurriedly through them till, near the bottom, he found what he wanted. "There you are, Mister Shallet," he smirked.

The sheriff passed it back. "I guess that settles it," he said to Haines. But Jones insisted on having a look for himself, and after he had it he still wasn't satisfied, though everything appeared to be properly in order.

His sultry scowl raked the banker suspiciously. "There's a polecat smell about this business." He swung broad shoulders and faced the sheriff. "You lettin' 'em take you in like that?"

Ike Shallet's chubby face looked dubious. "How d'you mean?"

"Why the ink ain't hardly dry on them papers—that ink look six years old to you? It's a frame-up!" Jones said with withering scorn. "A child could see *that* much! What's more, there wasn't nothin' said about no bank or lease when I filed on the place three months ago! How—"

The sheriff shook his head. "You'll not get far on that line, stranger. I had occasion to consult the land-office records only yesterday. Your name's Jones, ain't it? Well, I'll take my oath there's no 'Jones' signature any place in the book—"

"By Jinks!" Jones snarled, striding forward angrily. "Are *you* in this, too?"

"Sit down," growled Deckerman, and started to push him. Jones' fist exploded against Deckerman's jaw, and Deckerman, staggering, went three strides backward and sat down in a waste-basket; and it took the combined efforts of the sheriff and Haines to work his seat loose and get him afoot again.

"No more of that!" the sheriff warned sternly; and Hi Haines waggled his pistol dangerously. "Put him in jail 'fore he kills somebody! I say it's your bounden duty—"

"I know my duty!" the sheriff snapped. "Hand over that gun, Jones!"

Jones scowled, but did so. "Things has come to a pretty pass—"

"I think so myself," the sheriff said grimly. "I'm goin' to see you across the county line. If you're smart as you look, you'll keep on going—"

Lot Deckerman said: "He'll keep going, all right!"

II

X MARKS THE SPOT

AND so he did. But not a fearful great ways. He kept going until the upthrust brow of a sugarloaf hill cut off all view of the grinning escort; and after that he flopped down in the dappled shade of some wolf's candle and pulled off his boots with a doleful groan. *That* had been Lot Deckerman's notion, unhorsing him at the boundary and sending him off on shanks' mare. "*An',*" the Stampede boss said wickedly, "don't show up again or we'll *bury* you!"

"Fine kettle of fish!" growled Tubac bitterly, gingerly inspecting his blistered feet. That he'd been paid for the horse was small consolation. The most malicious insult devised by man was to leave a waddy afoot in that country; and Tubac Jones was never the man to forgive or forget an injury. He could nurse hate like an Indian; and he was waxing fairly eloquent on what he would do to Lot Deckerman when he saw a cloud of dust coming up the trail. He broke off a curse at the second syllable and yanked the returned gun out of his belt and glared down the trail like a broken-back scorpion.

He did not, however, bother getting up—not even when a horse herd broke round the bend.

It was a band of fuzzies and willow-tails, and Jones' lip curled at the sight of them. Ordinarily he would not have given such crowbaits a second look, but their advent had caught him in the lap of adversity, and beggars, he reminded himself, were in no condition to be particular. A horse was a horse, and Jones raised his voice in a lurid hail.

The saddle stiff trailing along behind them looked to Jones like a nester. He was either a nester or a two-bit range thief, for no man with a smidgin of self-respect would have dared show his face in such rummage-sale garb. His brush-clawed miner's shirt looked as if the butterflies had taken it over. His bony knees showed through the rents of frazzled corduroy pants that were a good foot short of their proper length, and the run-over boots that hid his feet were cracked from the weather in forty places. A battered Chihuahua hat covered his head and a scraggle of whiskers matted his cheeks; but Jones, in his need, hailed him anyway.

The rider angled over to where Jones was hunkered, and a saturnine grin showed his snaggled teeth as leering eyes took in Jones' situation.

"Never mind laughin'," Tubac growled, and let the rider have a squint at his gun. "Cut me out one of them shad-bellied plugs—"

"You mean one of these here racin' thoroughbreds?"

"I don't care what you call 'em. Just cut me out one an' quit gassin'."

"Money talks—"

"So does this smoke-pole!"

"Say—what is this? A stick-up?"

"Jest call it a loan. I got some urgent business that demands my presence a considerable ways hence at a very near moment—"

"Lemme sell you one, pilgrim—I'll make 'er real cheap."

"Where'd you steal 'em?"

The tattered horseman scowled resentfully. "If I was goin' to steal—"

"Okay," Jones said. "I'll buy one." And the rider lost his scowl in a hurry.

"What'll you give me for the entire herd?"

"I ain't no circus man," Jones came back dryly.

"You don't know what you're passin' up, friend. Why, with this remuda you could open a stable—"

"You mean a glue factory, don'tcha?" Jones started to pull on his boots, but his feet had swollen and he quit with an oath. "I'll want a bill of sale—"

"Tut, tut," said the rider. "Ol' Snaggle-Tooth Potter wouldn't gyp nobody—"

"You *have* got an open face," Jones said, "but I'll take your John Henry just the same."

"As you please," Potter growled. "Just dig out your roll an' we'll git down to business; but you better take 'em all while you've got the chance. Two of these plugs is national champions, an' one— Well, I'm warnin' you, pardner, horses like these ain't come by on *every* bush—"

"How much you want?"

"How much you got?"

"I got a smoke-pole here with five ca'tridges in it—"

"We-el, in that case," Potter shrugged philosophically, "make it twenty-five dollars—"

"For the bunch?"

"For the—Say! What the hell you take me for?"

"Okay," Jones said, and got out his wallet. Potter's face registered surprise, disbelief and finally plain downright anger when he caught the edges of some of the bills as Tubac thumbed through them in search of a small one.

"Of all the cheapskate pikers," Potter was growling, when

17

Jones coolly tossed him a greenback sporting three figures, the first one being a five. Potter's eyes bulged until they nearly popped from his noggin. He said, "What bank you been doin' business with, friend?"

"If I told you that," Tubac grunted, "you'd know 'most as much as I do. Gimme a bill o' sale for the bunch; an' look —" he added, putting his wallet away—"how about loanin' me that shirt an' hat for a bit?"

Potter looked as if he were certain now that he was dealing with a dimwit. He grinned. "Make it *two* bits an' I'll do it, friend. What do they call you, if I might ask?"

"You're lookin' at Tubac Jones, boss an' owner of the T Bar J."

"Never heard of it. Where you located?"

"Squattin' on the Holeman grant."

"You're—the—*what!*" Potter clutched wildly for the horn of his saddle. "Did you say *Holeman* grant? H-O-L-E—"

"Nothin' wrong with your hearin'."

"Great shades of Morgan!" Potter gulped. "You better take these broncs an' head fer Alaska—an' brother, don't git off to pick no posies! The *Holeman* grant! Great grief a-flappin'! I thought *I* was soundin' the depths of iniquity when I lifted this here cavvy; my friend, you're in a class by yourself. The *Holeman* grant! Hell's wishbone!"

"I can see," Jones said, "you've heard of it."

Potter grabbed off his hat and fanned himself. He mopped his bald head with a shirtsleeve. "Mister, when the Stampede Hog an' Ca—"

"They already know about it." Jones grinned sourly. "That's how come I'm over here without no horse," he said; and told him the story.

Potter whistled. "An' you're allowin' t' go back for more?"

Jones scowled. "I'm goin' back all right. You watch my

smoke! No whoppy-jawed this-an'-that can treat Yours Truly like Deckerman done an' expect—"

"You don't know what you're bitin' off, pardner!" Potter tapped his left palm with a gnarled trigger finger. "Why, guys've been killed around here for less damn hell than you've raised already."

"Humph! I ain't even got started yet." Jones glared, and then got gingerly up on his feet. "Gimme that hat an' shirt."

"What for?"

"To go to town, of course."

"Are you *loco?*"

"Not so's you could notice it. I got pressin' business—"

"You'll get a shutter if you go back there!"

"If you'd put a shutter on your jaw fer a spell an' hand me them duds, I'd get there faster."

Potter said: "It'd be plain suicide. The whole town's got their hooks in that grant. You ain't jest fightin' Haines an' Lot Deckerman—"

"For a guy with a tied-down holster, you sure sling a lot of gab," Jones said. "You goin' to lend me that stuff or ain'tcha?"

"Oh, you can have the stuff an' welcome," Potter growled. "But you're a golrammed fool t' go rampin' back there. If there's somethin' you're needin'—"

"I got a batch of goods bought at McGillis' store an'—"

"D'you know who ol' man McGillis *is?* Lemme tell you, brother! Archie McGillis, among other things, is boss director of the Stampede Hog an' Cattle Company, an' the minute he sees your mug in town—"

"I'll take care of that when I meet it," Jones scowled. "It ain't your funeral anyhow. Peel outa that shirt an' hand it—"

Potter said: "How about sellin' me some chips in this game?" and Tubac Jones stared suspiciously.

"What's the big idea?"

19

"I owe that outfit a smack or two. They done me outa my spread a while back; these broncs are all I could save from the slaughter. The bank run in a forged note an' foreclosed me."

"Well, the dirty dogs!" Jones said, and scowled. "So that's the stripe of polecat Haines is."

"Hell, he's slicker'n slobbers. But about this town trip—you better let me—"

"They mightn't give 'em to you."

"I could buy some more. They won't be expectin' to see *me*—"

Jones said grimly: "They won't be expectin' to see *me*, neither!"

It was crowding toward dusk when Tubac Jones, in the battered Chihuahua and moth-eaten miner's shirt, with Potter's saddle strapped on a bay horse, rode back to the scene of his recent defeat. The lamps of Stockton spilled pools of light through the felted shadows and from one of its honkytonks came the scrape of a fiddle as Jones kneed the bay through the hock-deep dust.

He'd more urgent reasons for coming back than the supplies he'd mentioned to Potter. The first and foremost of these was his white-stockinged roan, Calliope. He had raised the horse himself from a colt, and it could do everything but talk. It had, on three separate occasions, actually saved Jones' life—not a thing to be passed over lightly.

It was hardly likely, he thought, that Deckerman had given the horse a second look—or the sheriff, either, for that matter. Their main idea had been to set him afoot as a hint that the going would be rough if he ever had the nerve to come back there. A sly man, Lot, and fresh as they came—but Jones aimed to be a mite fresher.

It was a pretty safe bet, he told himself, that they had put

Calliope in some public corral or feed barn. He found the horse at the first one he tackled. He flipped the stableman a couple of silver dollars and stooped down to lift up his saddle.

"Hold on there!"

Jones gave him a mackerel-eyed stare; and the man said, "What in thunder you think you're doin'?"

"I'm gettin' ready to saddle my horse."

"Well, you kin jest put that saddle back down on the floor. The sheriff brought that critter in here, an' here he stays till Ike Shallet says diff'rent!"

Jones did some quick thinking. The last thing he wanted was a row. "Didn't he tell you I'd be comin' after it?"

"He didn't tell me nothin'!"

"Humph—danged funny. Ne'mind; I'll have him gimme a note to you. Just get the nag saddled. I'll be back in a jiffy," Jones said, and wheeled out of the stable and around the corner, where he tore a page from his tally book. "Give bearer the white-stockinged roan," he wrote with a grin, and signed Shallet's name with a flourish. Then he went back into the stable.

The hostler stood just where Jones had left him. "Ike Shallet never wrote that, mister."

"How the hell," Jones scowled, "do you make that out? You ain't even taken a look at it."

"I don't have to look at it," the stableman said; and then Jones saw the sheriff.

III

"NOT IF HER TEETH WAS PAVED WITH GOLD!"

HE WAS STANDING back in the shadows coolly twirling a gun by the trigger guard. "Howdy," he said; and a wolfish grin spread apart his wide lips. "I'd an idee you'd be back again." He looked Tubac over and chuckled. "Where's the fancy-dress ball at, compadre?"

Jones, caught flat-footed, could do nothing but glare.

The stableman lounged against a feed bin and spat. "Yah," he sneered. "Another damn lamb in wolf's clothing!"

Ike Shallet said: "Lot Deckerman opined we was all through with you; but I been around some, bucko, and I had you figgered right down to the ground. It takes a smart guy to fool Ike, boy. I'd jest as leaf've been fooled in you, though —they'll put you over the road this time. Well," he said, shrugging philosophically, "you shoulda thought of that 'fore you came back here. Pass Tobie your iron."

"What for?"

"You're a smart fella, Jones—got a lot of gall, too. But you cut your string a mite too short when you come in here to buck the Stampede crowd. You're the kind of fresh egg us Stockton folks like to put away in cold storage."

"You aimin' to arrest me?" Tubac asked at last.

"Brother, you called the turn," Shallet said. "Jest toss that Peacemaker over to Tobie."

"Just a second," Jones said. "I've a cussin' acquaintance with the law myself. What're you figurin' to take me up for?"

"Plenty!" Shallet grinned. "You're a smart boy, Jones, but you can't buck the law. I could arrest you for forgin' my name to that note."

"Yes! Go right ahead, you ol' walloper! I'll laff you plumb outa court!"

But the sheriff just grinned his amused little grin. "You might at that; but you won't get the chance. I'm arrestin' you for horse-stealin', bucko."

"Horse-stealin'! You need to have your head examined! That horse is mine, hand-raised from a colt."

"It may've been hand-raised from a elephant, but it sure ain't yours by a jugful. You sold the nag to Lot Deckerman, an' Deckerman sold him to me."

"He's a damn horse-thief then!" declared Tubac; and the sheriff's grin folded into a frown.

"What're you tryin' to put on here, anyway? I saw you write him a bill of sale."

"You better get fitted for glasses!" Jones sneered. "Where is this famous bill o' sale? Have sour-puss over there read it for you."

With a scowl the sheriff fished a folded paper from his pocket. Keeping stare and gun hard focused on Tubac, he tossed it over to the stableman. "Never mind the writin' on the back—that's Lot's; jest read out what's on the face of the thing."

"By grab!" muttered Tobie, and with a grudging admiration read: "This is to certify that one Lot Deckerman, at the point of a gun, took this white-stockinged roan—"

The rest was lost in the sheriff's bitter curse. "Don't say you never been stung!" Jones jeered, and began backing off, still chuckling.

"Stop right there!" Shallet roared. "Another step an' I'll let daylight through you! There ain't nobody goin' to make a fool of *me*."

"I wouldn't presume to improve on Gawd's handiwork."

"That's enough of your lip! You been a sight too smart for your britches! Tobie—" Shallet snarled—"git his iron—"

"Go right ahead!" Jones grinned at him, and the stableman fell back with a scowl.

The sheriff swelled up like a chuckwalla. "What in seven hells are you scared of? I got him covered."

"Sure you have," Tubac grinned. "Come on, Tobie. Don't be bashful—it's only a little pussy-cat."

And then Shallet saw the small striped animal that was rubbing its head on Tubac's ankle the while it gracefully waved its beautiful tail. "Goddlemighty!" he said. "Where'd that pole-cat come from?"

"Perky," Jones grinned, "say 'hello' to the sheriff." And pronto, the skunk started to cross the stable. The stableman went through the nearest window.

But Shallet was made of sterner stuff. He stood like a rock. "Call it off, by God, or I'll kill the critter—"

"Not tonight," Jones drawled; and with an upwheeling stare the sheriff cursed. The byplay with Perky had lost him the drop. There was a gun in Jones' hand, and the look in Jones' eyes said he'd just as lief use it.

"Throw your pea-shooter up in the loft, Ike."

Shallet spluttered like a hooch-drunk squaw. "That's a stinkin' trick—"

"It ain't stunk yet—" Jones said— "but it can."

Short minutes later Tubac stepped from the saddle in front of a squat frame building. Great red letters painted across its face proclaimed it to be McGILLIS GEN'L STORE & MEN'S HABERDASHERY. Jones tied Potter's bay to the hitchrack, but left Calliope, a gentleman's horse, on grounded reins. He gave the big roan's neck an affectionate pat and left it munching on a hunk of hard sugar.

His spurs clanked a tune as he strode up the steps, and he flicked a brash grin at the barrel-seat loungers; but no one appeared to recognize him. He was about to pass into the lamplighted store when a face he remembered started out from behind bundles; Jones dragged off his hat with a flourish. "An' whose lucky calendar did *you* step out of?" he hailed the apparition; and Honey Hair caught her breath sharply.

"Oh!" she cried, very obviously startled. "Is it really you? They told me you'd left Horse Prairie—"

"They were a little previous," Tubac grinned. "No," he said, "I'm still browsin' round—Say! how'd you like to have a *good* job, Bright Eyes?"

"I've got a good job."

"Excuse *me!* You don't call workin' for that widow-robbin' banker any kind of a job for a nice young girl!"

"What's the matter with it?" Honey Hair's chin came up coldly.

"Well, but don't you *see?*" Tubac grumbled. "It's the *principle* of the thing—just like bummin' around with the hangman's son—"

"And you think working for you would be an improvement?"

"Couldn't help bein'. No comparison a-tall," Tubac boasted. "Heck, that dang o' reprobate's jest *usin'* you! Hirin' you jest like he bought all that gold paint an' marble—tryin' to make his gyp bank look respectable! How much business do you reckon he'd get if you wasn't round to bring the suckers in? He'd curl up like a leaf quick's you walked out the door!"

Honey Hair looked at him queerly. But Jones had got his steam up now. This looked to him like a first-class chance to put the skids under Hi Grab Haines; and when he observed the watching loungers' interest, he rushed on full tilt, never pausing to consider how the girl might be taking it.

"It's plain as pain what the danged skunk's up to; he's out to grab this whole durn country—an' he'll do it, too, if you keep on frontin' for 'im. Your face is his fortune—anyone could see that! No one'd ever think a nice girl like you could be mixed up in such danged skulduggery. Some rancher gits short. He remembers the bank. He talks to Haines, an' Haines lends him some money on a short-time note. Right off the dumb rancher steps into hard luck. His wells go dry or his windmill breaks—or mebbe somebody starts stealin' his cattle. First thing he knows his note's come due an' Haines steps in an' takes him over."

"By grab," one of the loungers growled, "you sure said a mouthful that time, mister—that's jest how he got my Crazy 3 outfit!"

Jones beamed at the man, then looked down at Honey Hair. "See?" he said. "Jest as easy as packin' your pipe with tobacco. I tell you, ma'am, it'll be jest like stealin' your neighbors' hearth rugs! That walloper aims to skin this country, an' don't give a dang how he does it!"

"But aren't you overrating my importance?"

"Not a bit of it! Not by a danged sight!" Jones assured her. "That whoppy-jawed sidewinder would lift the ribs right out of a corpse if he thought he could find a market for 'em!"

"Oh!" exclaimed Honey Hair, and went suddenly tense. She gazed around and sniffed suspiciously. "Do I *smell* something?"

"Polecat, prob'ly—I been talkin' to the sheriff. Anyone sticks around Haines close as *he* does is bound t' git smellin' like him sooner or later. But like I was sayin', ma'am—"

"By Gawd!" bleated one of the loungers, hopping up as if a bee had stung him. "*I* smell it, too! Must be a skunk got under this porch."

But Jones ignored him. "Like I was sayin', ma'am, if you'll quit Haines an' come out to the ranch—"

"Well—" began Honey Hair, and again broke her words off. She wheeled half around and peered at Tubac closely. There was agitation in her quickened breathing, and her eyes, could he but have read them, had gone soft with pleasurable interest. "Are you, by any chance, trying to *propose* to me?"

"Pro— Hell *no!*" Jones scowled. "Not by a danged sight —'scusin' my English. I wouldn't marry the best danged female in forty-five states—not t' mention Canada an' the Territories! No *sir*—I mean ma'am! Not if her pockets was loaded with diamonds an' all 'er teeth was paved with gold! Not on your tintype! I got too many friends has made that mistake—"

He broke off, gaping, astounded, as Honey Hair, chin up and eyes flashing, went past him as if he were a buffalo chip.

IV

DESPOILING THE PHILISTINES

BUT HE LAMMED around like a sprinkled cat when one of the loungers started nickering. He said: "You wouldn't be laffin' at *me*, would you?" and the man shut his face in a hurry.

Jones snorted and went into the store. Women were all alike. No matter how young or good-looking you found them, all they ever thought about was getting their hooks in you. Give 'em an inch and they'd grab ten miles! All you had to do was smile and the bells for the wedding would shout the tidings! Lord! Tryin' to grab her a man right there on the doorstep!

It made Jones blush just to think of it! And she was such a sweet-seeming filly, too! It just went to show a man wasn't safe till the grave-digger's dirt rattled down on his coffin.

With which sour conviction Jones stepped up to the counter. A trio of hard-faced hombres were lounging against it when Tubac got out his wallet. Giving them barely a glance, he said: "Got that stuff I ordered fixed up for me yet?"

"Ye got nothin' here."

"I'm aware of that," Jones said, giving McGillis a slanchways stare. "But I ordered a whole bunch of stuff. This mornin'—yes! By grab, an' paid for it, too!"

McGillis was Scotch and dour as they come. Tall, stoopshouldered, with lined roan cheeks on a bony face and bigknuckled hands criss-crossed with blue veins. He wore tight pants held up over his ribs by bright yellow galluses. He looked Tubac over unfavorably.

"Ye may've ordered them, mon—but not o' McGillis."

Tubac Jones hitched up his belt and laid his six-shooter down on the counter. "I shoulda known better'n to trust a Scotchman with an Irishman's handle. You got one chance, McGillis. This is it. Pony up them things an' be quick about it."

You could see by Jones' eyes that he meant it. McGillis hesitated, and shot a quick look at the loungers. But they had no eyes for McGillis; all their attention was bent on Jones' wallet. McGillis said: "Ye didna come, so I put them away."

"You can go fetch 'em out again."

McGillis put the flats of his big-knuckled hands on the counter. "Goods put up and nae called for are confiscated—"

Tubac's stare flashed cold as a gun bore. "In about two seconds I'll confiscate *you!*"

"How about a little stud-hoss poker?" suggested one of the loungers as McGillis tramped off.

"Yeah—jest a friendly game."

The third man said: "You can quit any time you feel like it."

Jones said, yawning: "I'm too damn tired, boys. Some other night."

"Okay said the paunchy man, scowling.

The one called "Sugar Dip" sneered. "Whatcha scared of?"

"You guys look like professionals to me."

"You reckon he's kiddin' us, Yellowstone?"

The thin-lipped man with the mole on his chin said: "Lord, he mus' be! Nobody but a blin' man would ever pick *me* for a card shark!"

Kettle Belly announced: "I'll go git Ike Shallet—*he'll* play."

"Here—wait! Hold on!" grunted Tubac hastily. "If you're cravin' to play cards that bad, I'll take a hand."

"That's the talk!" Yellowstone approved; and Kettle Belly patted Tubac's shoulder jovially. "Come on, sport. Mac's got a first-class lamp in the back room here . . ."

"Lemme peel off a couple centuries," Jones interrupted. "I'll leave the rest of my roll with McGil—"

"What's the matter?" Yellowstone said. "Don't you trust us?"

"Well, sure," Jones grumbled, and limped along after them. The back room, he guessed, would be as safe as any place, and he had left Ike Shallet pretty well tied up in one of the feed bins with some hay pulled over him. The stableman might go back at any moment, but if he didn't go poking around too close, or if Ike didn't work his gag loose, Jones guessed he could play for an hour or so, anyway.

Yellowstone produced a greasy deck of cards. Kettle Belly riffled them. Sugar Dip shoved them at Jones for the cut. Jones rapped the table. Kettle Belly dealt.

Jones picked up his cards. Three queens and a pair. "I thought we were goin' to play stud-hoss," he said.

"Dealer's choice," Kettle Belly told him, and opened the pot for a hundred dollars. Sugar Dip asked: "How many?"

"Gimme two," Jones grunted. He got the fourth queen and

31

kicked the pot for another two hundred. Kettle Belly called and Jones raked in the pot.

Yellowstone dealt. Jones looked at his cards and scowled. "How many you goin' to take?" he asked.

Yellowstone winked. "Tag along an' see."

"Nope—too rich for my blood." Tubac tossed four kings in the discard, twiddled his thumbs and stared at the ceiling. Yellowstone, scowling, bet ten dollars. Nobody called. The deal came to Jones. Yellowstone cut. Tubac grinned.

Kettle Belly said: "Deal me out this time."

"What's the matter?" Jones jeered. "Can't your aunt wait a minute?"

The paunchy man shrugged, and settled back in his chair. Jones gave him four tens and a deuce. Sugar Dip blinked at four jacks and a tray. Yellowstone muttered when he picked up four kings.

Kettle Belly opened for two hundred dollars. Sugar Dip set up a yowl for McGillis. "How's my credit?"

"What credit?" Jones jeered, but the lanky Scot frittered in for a look, and when he spied the pat four jacks swallowed his Adam's apple.

"Make up your mind," Jones growled at him.

" 'Tis nae ma mind needs making up—'tis ma conscience, mon. 'Tis loath I am to take such an unfair advantage—"

"Sing or get off the pot," Jones said; and McGillis blew out his cheeks.

"Bid yer hand," he dourly bade Sugar Dip, and the muscular puncher met all bets on the table and showed his teeth in a feline grin. "I'll just kick that five," he said softly.

"Five what?" said Yellowstone, eyeing four kings; and when Sugar Dip told him, "Five hundred," Yellowstone heaved in his hand.

Jones tugged off his boots and waggled his toes luxuriously. But there was a glint in his eye as he looked at

Sugar Dip. "Never mind the pictures, Sheep-Dip. In God we trust—all others pay cash." And he laid his gun on the table.

"What do you mean 'cash'?" Sugar Dip scowled.

"Just what I said—*cash*. You can save your I.O.U.'s for the suckers. White money talks. Put up or shut up."

The place got awfully still for a second; then Yellowstone said: "I small skunk—"

"Don't look at *my* feet," Jones cut back at him. "I'm a guy that bathes once every month—regular. If it's skunk you smell it must be McGillis." He said impatiently: "Come on, Dip! Bid or chuck in your hand."

"You tryin' to freeze me out?"

"I'm tryin' to keep the game moderately honest," Jones told him. "Either put up the money or go roll your hoop."

Sugar Dip's look got ugly. McGillis groaned but signalled his agreement. "Go on, mon. I'll gi' the money—"

"Go get it now, then." Jones sat back and folded his arms. The others glowered at him, until McGillis came back with a bulging sack and plopped it down on the table.

"Count in your five hundred," Jones told Sugar Dip; and, when the man had done so, said: "I'll jest tack five onto that!" and tossed a thousand-dollar bill in the pot.

McGillis' cheeks turned as pale as a milk pan.

There were just the two of them in the game now—Jones and Sugar Dip. Sugar Dip met Jones' raise and was reaching his hand to the sack for more when McGillis put his foot down. "Hae a care, mon, whose gude money ye're wastin'!" he snarled, and snatched his sack out of Sugar Dip's reach.

"How many?" Jones said; and Sugar Dip grinned. "I've got all the cards I'm needin', bucko."

But his grin became considerably warped when he **saw**

Jones throw his whole hand in and proceed to deal himself a new one.

"Hey!" he yelled, kicking back his chair. "The dealer can't—"

"The dealer," Jones stated, "can do as he pleases. You said so yourself—dealer's choice."

There were some hard looks passed, but Sugar Dip finally sat down in his chair. Maybe it was something McGillis whispered, or it might have been he'd thought to take stock of the chances. They were certainly strongly in his favor. The likelihood of Jones beating four jacks with a brand-new hand was not worth getting up a sweat about.

Sugar Dip sneered. "Where the hell did you learn to play poker?"

Tubac said: "What you bettin', sonny?"

"I'm checking the bet to the barefoot mogul."

"Okay," Jones said. "I'll bet a dollar."

Sugar Dip broke from his stare with a fleering guffaw. "You ort to 've kept the old ones, Gran'paw."

Archie McGillis drew a long, relieved breath and plopped his sack on the table again. Sugar Dip asked: "How much you got in that wallet, pilgrim?"

Tubac frowned, and sighed a doleful sigh. "As a pers'nal favor—"

"Aah—" the stocky puncher's lip curled insultingly—"I like a *man's* kind of man. You sizzle-pants pikers make my guts ache! If you'd got anythin' in that bran-new hand you've bid your damn head off! Here's your dollar, Hazel—an' fourteen hundred more bucks on it!"

Tubac Jones eyed his cards in a disgruntled manner. "That's a hell of a lot of money," he said; and McGillis showed a dour Scot's grin.

"If you want to hear the owl hoot," Sugar Dip crowed,

"you better shake the butterflies outa that wallet. C'mon, sport—put up or shut up!"

They figured they had Jones right where they wanted him; and by the look on his face they were figuring right. "Worms is awful diet," he mourned.

"Come on, you fourflush," Sugar Dip sneered. "Sing or git off the pot!"

Jones licked his lips, finally reached for his wallet. With hesitant fingers he thumbed through his bank notes. "There's your fourteen hundred," he said at last; and Sugar Dip scoffed.

"Well, of all the swivel-eyed tinhorns! Ain't you goin' to raise it?"

"Nope," Jones said, "I'm too tender-hearted. What you got?"

"Four jacks!" whooped Sugar Dip, and reached for the pot.

"That's tough," Jones said. "I got four aces."

Came a startled instant of complete and utter silence. Then the rasp of someone's hard breathing cracked it, and Sugar Dip roared: "I don't believe it!"

"Take a look," Jones grinned, and tossed the cards face up in front of him.

Sugar Dip's eyes looked like holes in a blanket.

Jones picked his gun up and was looking for trouble when he saw the gangrenous look of the glaring McGillis. The lank Scot's eyes were like bugs on a stick, and his spatulate fingers kept opening and closing as he stood there swaying like a pole-axed steer.

Sugar Dip bellowed: "It's an onery damn trick!"

Jones made an uncouth noise and laughed at him. "Hoo, hoo!" he jeered. "I like a *man's* kind of man!" And he thrust his wallet inside his shirt front. Then he reached a big hand out to rake in the pot.

"Don't you *dare* touch that money!" Sugar Dip shrilled. "That deal was crooked! I'll hev the law on you! You cheat—"

"Cheat?" echoed Tubac; and suddenly his eyes went cold as a well chain. "You're a great one to talk about cheatin'! You bunch of two-by-four spittoon-trammers—"

That was where he was when he saw Ike Shallet.

V

BLACKWATER BILL

HE WAS CROUCHED in the doorway like the skeleton at the feast; and something in his wolfish grin stirred chills along Jones' back as he tipped his shotgun's barrel so it covered Tubac's stomach.

But if Tubac was perturbed, no one else in the place would have guessed it. He gave the sheriff a knowing wink. "Come right in. Don't be bashful, Ike—you're jest in time to tell these cheapskates—"

"I'm tellin' *you*," Ike Shallet rasped, "to git your hand off that hogleg pronto!"

"Now listen, Ikey; that was all in fun."

"Oh—fun, was it? Well, this'll be fun, too!" growled Shallet. "You get them dew claws over your head an' be gol-rammed quick about it!"

"Well, but—" Jones began, and then with a sudden shrug put his hands up.

Just as if it were a signal, Jones' shirt tail popped up out of his pants and a ball of fur bounced onto the floor, came apart, bounced upright and arched its back like an angry cat.

It was only Perky, Jones' pet skunk, but consternation became at once apparent on the contorted faces of Tubac's enemies. Perky was only a runt, stunted perhaps by the coffee Jones fed him; but he didn't like being dropped that way. There was a malignant glint in his bright little eyes. He was only pint-sized, but a pint of some things is more than plenty —as McGillis' screech gave ample testimony.

He danced about like a sprite in the welkin. Perky, nervous and irritated by such wild gyrations, turned half around and got his tail up.

"Grup him, mon! Dina stand sat gowkit! Grup him swithe an' fling him oot!"

But Sheriff Ike Shallet knew well the better part of valor, and when to leave well enough alone. He would as soon have hugged the devil as have established a contact with the volatile Perky. He had notions of his own, and jerked up his shotgun.

"Dinna shoot him in here! Dinna shoot, ye latherin' penny wheep! Put him oot, ye clatty frampler!"

McGillis was almost beside himself. There were tears of rage running down his cheeks. "Gang awa'!" he cried, flapping his apron at Perky. "Gang awa', ye unsicker kitlin!"

But Perky was in no rush to be off. The glint in his eye said he was going to enjoy this. He seemed to be gauging the range, for he backed off a bit and took sight again. Then up sprang his tail like a flag to the masthead.

It was at this precise and fateful moment that Sheriff Ike let go with both barrels. So did Perky.

It was like kicking the lid off the top of hell.

What happened is not quite clear even yet. Reports were contradictory; the evidence, offered in damage suits, is even more garbled and libelous; and Tubac Jones, it has been definitely ascertained, was nowhere around at the time Ike Shallet squeezed the triggers of his shotgun. There emerge, however, several concrete facts. These are backed by sufficient profane testimony to insure their being at least *reasonably* reliable. The clothes the sheriff wore that night were never again seen on his person subsequently. The McGILLIS GEN'L STORE & MEN'S HABERDASHERY remained closed for a week—for "remolding," the sign said; and when it re-opened there were many evidences of vigorous cleansing, and paint shone brightly all about the place, and a lot of fresh stock filled shelves that had not been there on the night of the blast. And the court records show that a lot of the neighbors made complaint concerning vile smells; also, the STOCKTON BILLIARD HALL & LIQUORS swore out a writ against "person or persons unknown" charged with heaving a "dead cat" through their back window.

As for Tubac Jones, he was well away from the place by the time the excitement reached its "crescendo." Mounted on the faithful Calliope, with his sacked supplies tied back of the cantle, he was humming a tune as he rode down the Charleston trail, quite pleased with himself and headed for the ranch.

He picked up Potter and the broomtail cavvy a couple of miles out; and even by the light of a clouded moon he could tell that Potter was not too happy about the long time Jones had forced him to wait. He eyed Tubac without much favor. "A guy would think—"

"No recriminations, Potter. If you work for me, you got to learn to put up—"

"I been 'put up' with these fuzz tails f' more'n eight hours; an' who the hell said I was workin' for you?"

"Well, I thought that was the general idea."

Potter scowled at him testily. " 'F you had anything to

think with you'd be bustin' a gut to get outa this country. Gimme back my shirt an' hat!"

"Okay," Jones grunted, and tossed him the hat. "I thought," he said, peeling out of the shirt, "you was huntin' a chance to get back at—"

"I ain't huntin' no chance to get put in no grave!"

Jones tossed him his shirt and got into his own. "I'm sort of disappointed in you, Potter. I figured you for a man's kinda man—the sort that would pitch in an' help a guy."

"The biggest help I could ever give *you* would be to show you the quickest trail outa this country."

"Horse Prairie," Jones said, "suits me down to the ground. By the way, I got them cartridges."

"Ca'tridges! Is *that* what you went back after?"

"What'd you expect to fight that crowd with—cream puffs?"

Potter squinched up his jaws and spat again. "I never said I was expectin' to fight 'em."

Jones looked at him. "You're 'bout as reliable as a woman's watch! Last time I saw you you was champin' the bit to git even with—"

"That was eight hours ago. I was mad then."

"Reckon you could stay mad for a hundred a month?"

"Humph! Pistol-pusher pay!" Potter snorted. "You tryin' to git me killed?"

"I'm tryin'," Jones said, "to hire me some help."

"Hell! You don't ackshully think you can *lick* 'em, do you?"

"I'm managin' pretty well *so* far."

"You ort to have your head looked at," Potter growled. "You ort t' be bored for the simples." He spat and went on: "That crowd ain't even got started yet!" He peeled back his lips in a scornful laugh. "Just to show what a nitwitted fool you are, them horses I sold you was stolen!"

"I guessed they was when I bought 'em," Jones grinned. "You looked over that money I give you for 'em yet?"

"Huh?" Potter glared suspiciously. "What's the matter with it?"

"Live an' learn," Jones said with a leer. "An' now that I come to think of it, I dunno as I want to hire you anyway. You're a heap too uncertain to suit *my taste*. Just turn that nag round an' point back towards town—"

"What's the big idea?" Potter blustered.

"The idea," Jones said, "is that this gun is apt to mess you up proper if you don't git clear of here pronto! Hell's hinges!" he scoffed. "Did you think you could take me in with that line? You ain't over-bright—nor the Stampede crowd for sendin' you. You go back to town an' tell Hi Grab Haines he better think up somethin' better than *you* if he expects to get me out of Horse Prairie. An' you can leave them horses right where they are."

"Them horses," Potter snarled, "belongs to the Stampede—"

"Aint' that jest too bad?" Jones commiserated. "Mebbe you can explain how come you sold 'em."

"They'll hev the law—"

"The law," Jones grinned, "has knocked off for a while. But send Shallet out any time you feel like. I've got your John Henry on that bill of sale."

Snaggle Tooth Potter guffawed. "Ho, ho!" he jeered. "That's one on you! I signed my name in fadin' ink!"

"Yes," Jones said, "it was right thoughtful of you. But I been weaned two-three days myself. I had a carbon under that bill. I reckon your name won't fade off'n that!"

Dawn was not far off when Tubac Jones came in sight of the cabins Sam Holeman had erected on his Horse Prairie grant. Lampglow made pale cracks of light around the

41

drawn shades of the ranch house windows, and Jones, cutting a wide circle around the place, threw his cavvy of broomtails into a pasture he'd recently fenced and, dismounted, approached the house cautiously. A horse stood on dropped reins alongside the porch.

There was a menacing glint in Tubac's eyes as he jerked out his gun and kicked open the door. But the fellow inside was a stranger. He was a tall, gaunt man with a sharply aquiline nose, an expressive mouth and a lean face, handsomely contoured, with heavy blond eyebrows and military mustache. He was not a young man nor, despite his pale, anemic leanness, did he appear particularly old. His eyes were a cold and dancing blue with more than a touch of sour humor in them as they came to an inquiring rest on Tubac. He was dressed in the garb of a riverboat gambler, with a black frock coat and black string tie with its ends tucked into a flowered silk vest that must, Jones thought, have cost him upwards of a hundred dollars. His crossed legs were encased in tight buff trousers, and a huge white hat reposed on the table beside him. He met Jones' regard with one considerably cooler and offered neither to get up nor speak.

"Well," Tubac said sarcastically, "nothing like makin' yourself at home! I trust you find the place comfortable."

"Quite," replied the stranger coolly. "Are you, by any chance, the owner of this ranch?"

"I'll pass for the owner till some tougher buck shows. You cravin' to try your luck, are you?"

The man shrugged his shoulders and shook the blond hair that curled at his temples, and a kind of vague twinkle looked out of his stare. "No," he said in his cool, precise English. "Not at all—pray allow me, sir." He got up with a bow that was graceful and smooth. "Blackwater Bill, at your service, Sir. A gambling man rather down on his luck."

"Yeah," Jones said. "Never mind the spiel—I know the rest of that line by heart. You find yourself 'temporarily' strapped—"

"I'm afraid," said the stranger with quiet dignity, "you've rather jumped to conclusions, sir. I am not without funds. I can still pay my way. What I need is a rest."

"Then you better keep right on ridin', mister, because you'll get no rest around here," Jones said.

"But this seems ideal, the very kind of a place I've been looking for."

"Looks is deceivin'. This place is known as the Holeman grant. It takes in the whole of Horse Prairie, an' there's a good many guys that would like to have it, an' some of 'em," Jones said grimly, "ain't above cuttin' notches to get it! In other words, mister, there's a range feud brewin'."

"Then perhaps I could·be of some assistance to you. In my younger days I studied for the bar."

"Nothin' doin'," Jones said with finality. "There ain't no use arguin'. I don't want to seem inhospitable, mister, but there's apt t' be a lot of lead flyin' round."

"I'd welcome the chance to risk that, sir." A faint, knowing smile curved Blackwater's lips, and Tubac stared at him sharply.

"Just what the hell are you up to?"

The gambler said: "I could be quite a help to you, Jones, if you'd let me."

"So you know my name, do you?" Tubac growled. "What else do you know?"

The gambler sat back down in his chair and stared at his finger tips thoughtfully. "I know Haines' bank's got you in a cleft stick and is just about fixed to stamp your rattles off."

"Oh! Is that so!"

"Well," Blackwater grinned, "isn't it? What about that

43

lease of Lot Deckerman's that Hi Grab claims is six years old? How are you figuring to get around that?"

Jones' mouth dropped open and he eyed the man, startled. "How'n blue lightnin' did you know about that?"

"The fact at issue," the gambler said with a chuckle, "is that you just plain *can't* get around it—unless I help you."

"Unless you help me, eh?"

Blackwater Bill nodded coolly. "Unless I help you you're sunk. Right now."

Tubac rested a hip on the table. "I guess you don't know so damn much at that. I've filed on this place."

"And that page has been cut from the book," smiled the gambler. "So your filing don't amount to a row of bent pins. You've got just one chance to beat that lease. If you want to play this smart, I'll make a deal with you."

VI

"I'LL TAKE IT OUT OF YOUR HIDE!"

"OH, A DEAL, is it?" Jones inquired thinly. He twisted up his forehead in a corrugated frown, but the gambler continued to sit there and grin until Tubac grew vaguely uneasy. Plainly this was no ordinary tinhorn and, if sounded right, might reveal a few things Jones could use in his business. So he dragged out a smile that was bland as the gambler's. "What kind of a deal?" he asked, and Blackwater Bill chuckled slyly.

"Just a deal," he said, "that'll put the skids under that slick banker, Haines. We'll fold that bank up like an accordion."

"Well, it sounds good," Tubac admitted. "But how you figurin' to do it? That whoppy jawed hypothecator cut his eye-teeth on—"

"He never cut no teeth on this one," Blackwater Bill said grimly. "It's just the kind of dumb play he loves, and he'll gulp it down hook, line and sinker."

Jones said: "It must be gold, the way you're guardin' it!"

Blackwater Bill grinned broadly. "Dead center, Mr. Jones; I can see you're a man of perception. You've called the turn.

45

Gold it is. When you bait your hook for a banker, gold's the only thing you can use."

"Okay—okay!" Tubac grunted. "Don't make a story out of it! Just give me the works an' get a wiggle on."

"Hm. Great notions aren't hatched in a moment. And, besides, I said a 'deal.'"

"I heard you the first time. What is it you want for this brainstorm?"

Blackwater Bill leaned forward. "I want a half interest in this ranch."

"Well, you ain't no piker—that's sure!" An admiring glint brightened Tubac's stare. "If nerve was dollars, you'd have Haines' bank."

"You can have that bank any time you want it."

"Just like that, eh?"

"Just like that."

"Talk's cheap," Jones scoffed.

But Blackwater Bill grinned coolly. "Just say the word and I'll show you."

"Well—a quarter interest," Tubac temporized; but Blackwater Bill stood firm.

"A full half or nothing. There are other spreads round here. I expect I can interest—"

"Okay—okay," Jones grumbled. "I'll give you a half—if the deal comes off. Go ahead. Spill it—an' it better be good!"

The gambler chuckled. "It's good all right, and simple—that's the beauty of it. It's just the sort of fool stunt you'd do."

"Oh! It is, is it?" Jones blared fiercely. "Well—"

"Now look—" said Blackwater suavely—"the first thing to do is for you to take all that money you won at McGillis' and—"

"Here—wait!" Tubac growled. "How'd you know about that?"

"I have my ways of finding things out. Now quit interrupting and listen to what I say. The first thing is to get that money in the bank—"

"In the *bank!*" Jones cried, and looked the gambler hard in the eye. "You must think I'm green."

"You want to bust that bank or don't you?"

"Sure I—but—well, go on," muttered Tubac dubiously. "I put my money in the bank. What then?"

"You leave it."

"Yeah," Tubac said sarcastically. "I'll leave it all right if that wall-eyed Mormon ever gets his mitts on it!"

"If you'd stop interrupting and pay attention for a minute—"

"Go on," Tubac sighed. "Go ahead. Git it over."

"You put all that money in the bank—every penny you can get your hands on. I've got a few hundred that I'll chuck in, too. As you've so rightly suspicioned, under normal circumstances we'd never see a cent of it again. Hi Grab Haines would stage a robbery or some other dido, and that would be the last we'd hear of it. But—" and Blackwater Bill smiled thinly—"the circumstances aren't going to *be* normal. Before Haines gets around to pulling anything, we'll yank our money out again and leave his bank with crepe on the door!"

Jones shook his head. "Mebbe I'm just a iggerant saddle bum, but that play don't look very bright to me. Even if we're lucky enough to git our mazuma out o' his clutches, how's that goin' to bust his bank? He'll still have as much as he had before—as he's got right now."

"Will he? I guess you're forgetting. I said the circumstances won't be normal. When we pull that money out of there, we'll start a run that'll clean Haines out like the Augean stables."

"Never heard of 'em," Jones growled. "And anyhow, what's a stable got to do with Haines' bank? You musta been smokin' rattleweed to think up anything as harebrained as that! No, thank you, Mister Blackwater Bill. My money's a heap safer right in my pocket!"

"You talk like a fool," declared the gambler scornfully. "I tell you this is a sure-fire thing. It *can't* miss! You put your money in the bank—"

"You said all that before."

"I supposed I was talking to a man with *brains*. Since it's plain I'm not, I'll endeavor to couch the plan in language even a child could absorb. First, we put the money in the bank. After an interval we take it out—whether we get it or not makes little difference. We present our receipts and demand the money. Have you got that digested?"

Jones regarded the gambler like a prodded steer; but he finally nodded.

"Fine," said Blackwater and, leaning forward, tapped Jones' chest with a rigid finger. "Now here's the joker. After we deposit our money, and before we go back to draw it out, we arrange matters in such a way that Haines has a need for his ready cash elsewhere. Quick's he's used it we ask for our money. Is it plain to you now?"

"It's plain," Jones said, "that I'll lose my money."

"You might. I don't think you will, but you might. Even so, what's two or three thousand? Ain't it worth that much to bust Haines flat—and maybe that Stampede crowd along with him?"

"Sure!" Tubac scowled. "But I still don't see—"

There was a glint in Blackwater's eyes as he said: "I happen to know Haines has put considerable money into X & L Mines—bought all the stock he could get, on margin. If the market fluctuates—"

"It won't," Jones predicted. "I know them mines. They're at Pearce an' sound as a rock!"

"As a matter of fact, they're sounder," smiled Blackwater. "But the stock and the mines are two different things."

Jones eyed him sharply. "So that's your game, is it?"

."There's no game in it! Stocks—"

"I know all about stocks!" Jones cut in grimly. "I learned about stocks from an expert! But it takes hard cash to force stock—"

"We don't have to force it up. All we're got to do is sell Haines the *impression* it's being forced up."

"An' how are you goin' to do that?"

"There are ways—just you leave it to me. Once Haines is convinced someone's monkeying with that stock, he'll move heaven and earth to save his shares. *He* knows those mines are good as well as you do! That's what I'm counting on. He'll not want to see his shares wiped out, even if it means he's got to dip into his bank for the money to save them. And when he dips—"

Blackwater Bill spread his hands and smiled.

Tubac smiled too. Then he remembered the telegraph. "Hell," he said with a scowl. "It's a good idea, but the first thing he'll do if we scare him is wire—"

"Haven't you heard?" Blackwater's smile became almost sinister as he contemplated Tubac. "The telegraph people have been having trouble with that line; they *might* have more trouble about the time Haines needs it."

Jones, staring bug-eyed, suddenly laughed. "By grab, you're a genius!" he cried, slapping his thigh. "I believe it'll work."

"It will work all right—have no qualms on that score. Now the first thing to do," said Blackwater briskly, "is to get our deposit money into the bank. How much of a stake have you got altogether?"

49

Tubac got out his wallet and thumbed through his pile. "Forty-five hundred, eighty-seven dollars an' fifty-four cents."

"And mine tots up to fourteen hundred. I'll put in a thousand, and with forty-five hundred from you we'll have a grand investment total of fifty-five hundred dollars. *That* should be enough to cook him. Here you are," said Blackwater, smiling. "You better grab a bite and start right back."

"To *town?*" asked Jones incredulously.

"Certainly!" Blackwater eyed him impatiently. "You will be in no danger whatever. They won't be expecting you back so soon; and the sheriff will be too busy disinfecting himself to worry about you for a while. And *should* anything befall you—"

"I'll take it out of your hide!" Tubac said; and Blackwater Bill stopped beaming.

VII

BEGGARS AND BANKERS

THE BRIGHT desert sun was smashing down in full fury as Jones, atop the best of Potter's broomtails, once again rode into Stockton's main street and saw the gesticulating group that was gathered in front of McGillis' closed store. There was a strong smell of skunk coming out of the place, and Tubac rode by without stopping.

All the way in from the ranch he'd been trying to think up some really slick way of keeping Deckerman from seizing his ranch, but nothing that had crossed his mind was half so cute as Blackwater Bill's plan for humbling Hi Grab Haines. He had thought a great deal about Blackwater too; but now he had to keep his eyes skinned. There were wolves in the land, and this was their lair, and woe be unto the man who got careless!

He pulled up his bronc in front of the bank and tossed his reins across the hitch rail. It was pretty near noon, and the first man he spied when he stepped through the door was banker Hi Grab Haines—in person.

Haines was halfway down the lobby, going out, and he jumped as if a pin had stuck him. But you had to hand it to the old pot-walloper—he hadn't any more courage than a country mouse, but he sure knew when to turn the charm on. He'd been all set to yowl for his guard, but, instead, he grinned at Jones heartily.

"Well, well! Glad to see you, Mister Jones," he said, pumping Tubac's hand just as if they were *buen amigos*. "And what can we do for you this morning? Perhaps you could use a little loan?"

"Loan?" Tubac said. "Hell no—excusin' my English. I've rode in to make a deposit."

"A—a *deposit* did you say?"

"Oh, jest a little one. I expect you can use it, can't you?"

Hi Grab's rabbit nose started twitching, and he looked at Jones as though the sky were falling. "Well—yes," he said. "Of course. This is a bank—er—naturally. But I thought—"

"You thought I was just a grub-line drifter! Tut, tut. Never judge a man by the clothes he wears."

"Yes—of course. Ha, ha!" Hi Grab looked round at the gawking customers and beckoned a clerk over hurriedly. "This is Mister Jones," he said. "He wants to open an account with our bank. Wulson, I want you to show Mister Jones every courtesy—he's a personal friend of mine. Understand?"

"Certainly, sir. Right this way, Mr. Jones." And Tubac followed the clerk to the grille and passed in his fifty-five hundred.

"Never mind makin' out no pass-book," he said. "I'll just take a receipt, *if you please*." And when he turned round, after putting away the paper, there was Hi Grab still waiting.

"Perhaps we had better have a little chat, if you could spare me five or ten minutes, Mister Jones. I'd like to settle our difficulties amicably."

"If you're wantin' to bury the hatchet," Jones said, "I

ain't the guy to stick a stone in your way. Lead on, Mac-Duff—an' don't try no damn monkey-business!"

A pained look crossed the banker's face. "We may have had our little differences, but I'm not the man to hold a grudge. Live and let live is my motto."

"Glad to hear you've seen the light," Jones chuckled; and winked at Honey Hair as he followed the banker into his private office.

"Ah—please see that we're not disturbed, Miss Lambert," the great man said as he shut the door. Then he got out a bottle from the drawer in his desk and a pair of clean glasses from a cabinet. "Say when, Mister Jones," he invited, pouring.

"Good stuff," pronounced Tubac, smacking his lips. "Best I ever sampled."

"Try one of these cigars," urged the banker, beaming, and pushed his private box across, from which Jones filled his pocket.

"Nice shop you got here," Tubac drawled, lighting up and blowing a few smoke rings expansively. "Must've taken a good many widows' mites to outfit a—"

"Now see here," Haines snapped. "We agreed to let bygones be bygones."

"Who agreed? Not *me!*" Jones said. "You an' that high-binder, Deckerman, think you're pretty flossy, shovin' me round like the way you done yesterday. But I'll learn you! Just keep on agg'avatin' me an' you'll find a buzz-saw tame by comparison. You think—"

"Just a moment!" cried the banker, flushing. "We'll get no good from this talk, Jones, if you insist on taking that attitude. I can overlook much—"

"Hoo, hoo!" jeered Jones with a guffaw. "Hi Grab Haines —the great overlooker! Now look here, you thievin' chinch bug; we're all alone here, so why not admit you're jest a cheap crook that would skin a flea for its hide an' tallow?"

"This is insufferable!" the banker spluttered, and reached a shaking hand toward the row of buttons that shone brightly on his desk top.

But Tubac was not to be caught napping—not by any penny-wheep banker. With a hard, sure grin he whipped out his gun and gave the great man a look down its barrel. "Go right ahead!" he invited. "Thump all of them buttons you want to—but remember this: The first interruption what knocks on that door is goin' to put *you* on a *shutter!*"

Hi Grab jerked his hand from the buttons and with a kind of parched smile subsided. "You're fooling, of course—but after all, Mister Jones, you should never point firearms around that way. That thing might be loaded."

"You bet your boots it's loaded!" Tubac growled, fiercely squinting through slitted lids. "An' if you want to keep your health intact, you better stretch your mule ears an' do what I tell you. I'm all fed up with bein' shoved around by you an' your crew of plug-uglies! From here on out I'm crackin' the whip! You got paper around here, ain't you?"

Pale as a bed sheet, the banker nodded.

"Get hold of some then—an' don't try no tricks or I'll scatter your teeth on the carpet."

Shaking like a leaf in the wind the great Hi Grab, with his pop-eyes bulging, got a handful of stationery out of the cabinet.

"Sit down at that desk now an' write what I tell you," Jones ordered; and waited till the banker picked up his pen. Then he said with a cold-jawed grin: "Write this: 'I, Hi Grab Haines, on behalf of the Stockman's Bank & Mortgage Company, and on behalf of our client, the Stampede Hog & Cattle Company, do hereby waive, bequeath an' deed to Mr. T. Jones, his heirs and assigns forever, any and all rights and

54

interests we may have in the property known as the Holeman grant.' "

The scratching of the banker's pen came to a stop finally, and Jones looked over his shoulder to make sure he had written as directed.

"Fine!" he approved. "Now sign your name—an' don't forget the flourish."

Haines signed. Then he put down his pen as if its touch had scorched him and ran a finger around the inside of his collar. There was sweat on his face and a vein stood out on his forehead. "Well, you've won," he said with a grimace. "I admit I've been whipped."

"By an expert," Jones grinned. "Now trot out one of your pretty red seals an' plaster it under your signature."

"On a document of this sort I'm afraid a seal would look out of place. It is not customary."

"I'll be the judge of that!" Jones said; and with a shrug Haines affixed a seal to the paper.

"Now get out your bank stamp an' put that on, too."

Again the banker seemed about to protest. But the protest died a-borning when he caught the glint in Jones' frosty stare. With a nervous bleat he snatched out his pad and stamped it.

Jones picked up the paper and carefully read it. Then his pleased grin faded and a thoughtful scowl came between his eyes. "It strikes me we've left out somethin'. Here—" he thrust the paper back in front of Haines—"add this: 'All the above is attested voluntarily in exchange for the sum of one dollar and other valuable considerations.' Now put your John Henry on there again an' call in somebody to notarize it—I aim for this to be done up legal."

"No point in wasting your money on notary fees."

"I'll consider the money well spent," Jones grinned; and with a shrug Haines summoned his secretary.

Honey Hair came in with her pencil and notebook. But she had her chin up and would not deign to give Tubac a glance. "Get your notary seal," Haines grumbled, and Honey Hair came right back with it.

But she got no chance to examine what she was witnessing, for Haines had folded the written part down, leaving nothing showing but his seal and signature.

"That will be all, Miss Lambert," Haines growled when she finished; and she went out, brushing past Tubac without so much as a look. "Now," Haines observed, when they were alone again, "I hope this will end matters between us. You've got what you wanted; now suppose you get out."

"I aim to," grinned Tubac, folding the paper in his wallet. "I'm particular about the company I keep. Skunks is all right, but I draw the line at belly-crawlin' sidewinders an' bankers!"

But Haines refused to rise to the bait; so Jones, helping himself to some more cigars, picked up his hat. "Well, I guess I'll be running along," he began. Whereupon the banker told him the agreement called for a dollar and that notary fees came at four bits a throw.

"Much obliged for remindin' me," Tubac grinned. "Obligations is sacred with me—here's five dollars. An' you can keep the change. I'm only a iggorant saddle bum, but I always tip beggars an' bankers!"

VIII

CROSSED UP

JONES HIRED two hands before he left town and made them ride along out with him. They were not the best punchers in Arizona, either; but good hands were hard to come by in those days, and he was scared that if he left them to get sobered up they would never dare come out to work for him. Hi Grab Haines must have passed out the word, because all the loafers had fled at first sight of him. Winch Face and White-Eye he'd found drunk in an alley, and work was the last thing they'd wanted; but when he'd offered them eighty and found, with a quart of good rotgut thrown in free of charge, they'd signed on the line, and he had them.

They'd do with a deal of close watching, he thought, eying them covertly as they jogged toward Horse Prairie. Winch Face looked like a two-bit rustler—he had thirteen notches in the handle of his gun; and White-Eye was a half breed Indian.

But he'd other things more important than these two new hands to occupy his mind during the ranchward ride. Sam Holeman was prominent in his thoughts, and the cute way he had outslicked Hi Grab. *That* would be something to relate to Blackwater—with the proper pauses for emphasis.

But mostly it was Holeman, Tubac thought about.

Sam Holeman had, so the story went, come into this country on a shoestring. Late in the seventies, that had been; and he'd hung on up to six years before. He hadn't been a cowman, first off—the cows had come later after he'd built his pile. He had started as a ten-hitch freighter, working out of Tucson, and within two years owned a whole string of wagons and had every one of them filled to the guards with stuff being hauled into Tombstone. Then he sold off his teams and bought into Ed Schieffelin's Lucky Cuss Mine that was running fifteen thousand dollars to the ton; and the next year took out papers on homestead, timber and rock claims. A salty young buck he'd been in those days, who would just as lief fight as look at a man. He *had* fought with plenty, and killed them, too, if there was any truth in the tales men told. But mostly he'd got along with folks and had come to be thought right well of. When Tombstone was in its palmiest days he had run a saloon on Tough Nut Street and had been silent partner in several others—even to having a share in the Bird Cage (though that had not been generally known); and all the time he had been building up this new ranch of his south of Charleston.

The "Holeman grant" was not, and never had been, a "grant" of any kind. It had come to be called that because of its size which, in mileage, was something to write home about. He had filed on the very best water around, and when the big outfits started west from Texas he had had the foresight to fence it.

It had been a smart stunt, fencing off that water; it was all that had kept those big trail herds from eating him out of the country. But it wasn't conducive to amicable relations, and Sam's popularity took a downward dive—particularly after he conceived the lucrative notion of watering the drifters at so much per head. The trail bosses claimed they were entitled to that water and the townsmen had backed them up in it, but Ol' Sam was a plumb cultus hombre and cut back every steer not paid for.

It was a lucrative business watering those cattle at so much per head, and with the money Sam bought more land till he owned every inch of Horse Prairie. They called him Sam Holeman—the Waterhole King; but some of those outfits were pretty stiff haters, and a couple of years later three-four of those bosses drifted quietly back, and from that time on Sam's luck was out.

There were still no fences in the Cherrycow country save the cedar post ones Sam had built to protect his water. He had no more love for fences than the rest of the Cherrycow outfits, and it was this that began his unraveling. Encouraged by the townsmen—the storekeepers and saloon crowd —squatters began sifting into the country, and Sam soon had his hands full. It was discovered that, through some error or deliberate chicanery, the sections recorded in the land-office records as belonging to Holeman were hillslope claims whose only advantage was the water he'd fenced. The big lake he'd impounded down on the flats of Horse Prairie, together with his headquarters buildings, his chutes and corrals, were on public domain—land open for staking—and there were plenty of guys ready to stake it! All that kept them off was Ol' Sam's gun and the tough crew of punchers he had on his payroll.

And then, one by one, the crew started dwindling.

Sam raised their pay three times in a last-chance effort to hold them; but the Texans were putting on too much pressure. The crew was panicky. Those who stayed loyal commenced having "accidents"—two men in one week got ragged by their broncs; and another was found, smelling

violently of liquor, at the bottom of a forty-foot precipice.
Sam buried sixteen men inside of three weeks; then he got
John Slaughter made sheriff.

John was a Texan himself and knew the ways of his kind.
He never argued, did no blustering, but he was sure-fire hell
on rustlers. When he told a man to pack his roll, that man
either packed or stayed permanently. Putting the star on
John was the smartest thing Ol' Sam ever did—but it came
too late to save him. He had made too many enemies, and
these, sicked on by the ax-sharpening trail bosses, were out
to hang Sam's hide on the fence. Slaughter's coming, though
it couldn't save Sam, gave him time to consolidate his dwin-
dled acres, and for those on which he couldn't get patent he
could show quit-claim deeds from the owners. Horse Prairie
became the "Holeman grant," but Ol' Sam's days were numbered; and in the end it was his friend John Slaughter,
armed with a warrant, who took out after him. The Texas
trail bosses had dug in too deep; they had grabbed everything Sam didn't have title to, and they had fixed him up
very proper. The warrant in John Slaughter's pocket read:
*Wanted for murder in connection with attempted hold-up
of the Benson stage.* John Slaughter came back from the man
hunt alone, and the look in his eyes stopped all questions.

That was how things stood six years previously. No one
had clapped eye on Holeman since; and meantime, a new
law had been passed, designed to increase territorial revenue.
Homesteaded property was made taxable, and in four more
months Horse Prairie could be bought in for same—which
was what Grab Haines had been waiting for.

By a lucky fluke Tubac had discovered this, which was
why he had jumped Horse Prairie. He had known from the
start he wouldn't be able to file on it—you couldn't file on
anything now, and Haines knew it as well as he did. His

talk of filing had been sheer bluff, as had Shallet's little joke of a page being missing from the land-office records. Anyone mauling a page of those books would pronto have got sent to Siberia for life! By law Sam's holdings belonged to his kin, but none had come forward to claim it—nor had the bank been paying Sam's taxes. The Texas Trail bosses had been laying low, letting folks think Sam might some day come back; and all the time on the strict q.t. they'd been waiting to grab Horse Prairie for taxes.

Jones slapped his thigh with a guffaw. They must have stayed up nights, laying pipe for that place; and now, when at last they were ready to grab it, along had come Jones and squatted.

Possession, he thought might give a man some edge at the sale—and smart Lot Deckerman appeared to think so, too. Which was why that trumped-up "lease" had been rigged. But Jones had proved too slick for them. He was the "man in possession," and as long as he had Haines' conveyance safely tucked in his pocket, the Stampede crowd—lease or no lease—hadn't a leg left to stand on!

But Tubac wasn't underrating them. He had known too many damn Texans; and Lot Deckerman, the Stampede super and general manager, was one of the Texas trail bosses Ol' Sam had imposed his water tax on—while Archie McGillis was another one! They'd been the ones behind Sam's downfall, and they weren't going to take this calmly.

Alkali grit and the hot desert winds had pretty well sobered Tubac's new hands by the time they rode up to headquarters. Blackwater Bill, taking a smoke on the porch, lifted a languid hand in salute. "Hired some hands, have you?" he said, looking them over without much enthusiasm. "They don't look much to me like workers."

"Appearances is plumb deceptive," Tubac told him. "Light

down, bops, an' meet the co-owner. Winch Face an' White-Eye—my pardner, Blackwater Bill."

"I've met that Injun before," declaimed Blackwater, and White-Eye scowled at him sullenly.

"You'll have to watch this fellow," Blackwater said. "He's heap bad medicine; scalped his squaw for hiding his firewater and bushwhacked half a dozen prospectors, I'm told. He's a half-breed Apache from the Mescalero country, and the Injun police are hunting him."

"So!" exclaimed Tubac, looking him over. "Hard case, eh?"

"Black Coat lie!" grunted White-Eye. "Me good Injun—go white man's school. Heap smart!" And there was a glint in his eye like that in a rattler's.

"He's plenty foxy," Blackwater admitted, "but you'll have to keep your eye on him, and if the police catch him here we'll be in for it."

"Can you shoot?" Tubac asked; and the old scoundrel wrinkled up his face in a grin. His glittery eyes were fixed on the gambler, but Blackwater Bill kept his thoughts to himself. When they were alone he said:

"You get that money put away in the bank?"

"Sure," Jones said. "Hi Grab knocked me down to the clerk, an' I got his paper to prove it. That was a pretty slick stunt you hatched up, Bill—but Yours Truly has went you one better! Old Hi Grab nearly jumped out of his skin when he seen I had all that mazuma. Treated me just like a prince, he did. Took me right into his private office an' passed out the smokes an' rotgut like he was fattenin' me up for hog-killin' time. But you bet I showed the ol' bully-puss! I give him a squint down the snout of my six gun an' cleaned him slick as a whistle!"

"You crazy loon! If you've robbed that bank—"

"Do I look like that kind of nutty galoot?"

"Then what's all this adding up to?" Blackwater asked suspiciously; and his frosty stare combed Tubac over like a Cousin Jack hunting for color.

But Tubac swelled his chest with a chuckle. "You ain't the only slick guy in this country. You're a smart lad, Blackwater, but don't ever think you're the brains of this outfit. I laid down the law to that banker! I said: 'Git out your pen an' some paper, Hobart, an' take down a little dictation.' An' believe me he done it—wrote jest what I told him, an' signed it. I got it right here in my pocket—bank stamp, notary seal'n everything!"

"Got what?"

"Got the Holeman grant." Tubac grinned at him like a Chessycat. "Yep—our troubles is over! Hi Grab's give up all claim an' interest. On behalf of himself an' the Stampede crowd, too."

"Lemme see that paper!" snarled Blackwater, forgetting his schoolteacher English.

And Tubac, still chuckling, fetched out his wallet.

"Well, here's the receipt for our—" And then his face went blank as a bucket; and he dropped the paper as if its touch had burnt him and wildly pawed through his wallet. Suddenly he grabbed up a folded paper, fumbled it open and swore in a passion.

"What's the matter?" growled Blackwater edgily; and Tubac swore like a mule skinner, for Hi Grab had crossed them up proper!

There on the floorboards lay the receipt for their money, with the bank's stamp scarlet as an Arizona sunset; and here in his hand was the precious conveyance he had pried out of Haines at the point of a gun—bank stamp, notary seal and the sticker with its pretty blue ribbons. But Haines had loaded his pen with that cursed fading ink, and now all the writing had vanished!

IX

THE LAW—A LA BLACKWATER

"I TOLD YOU they were smart," declared Blackwater, holding his temper. "That banker's slipperier'n slobbers. An' Lot Deckerman—boy, you want to watch him every minute. He's so tough, I've heard, he has to sneak up on the dipper in order to get a drink of water. But they'll be feeling pretty chesty now. It's our move, and we better wade right into them, because once they catch their breath it's goin' to be all over but the digging."

Blackwater screwed his frosty eyes up and seemed deep-mired in complex thought. But after a moment he smiled a little, and a couple of heartbeats later he murmured reminiscently: "In the old days, so they tell me, the old duffer running this outfit used to cut back all the strays he found piled up against his water fence. I expect likely that was smart stuff then; but times has changed and grass won't grow if you stand on it. Things clever as hell ten years ago might be plumb foolish now, d'ye see?"

But Tubac at the time was too deeply bogged in the bottomless pits of humbled pride to see very much of anything—except that he had made a great fool of himself. That banker was a plumb slick actor! It made Jones writhe just to think how completely Haines had taken him in. It weren't as though it were just the money—though the loss of that had been bad enough—but in his overweening pride Tubac had ruined beyond all hope of salvage Blackwater's truly brilliant plan for hanging crepe on Haines' door! Hi Grab had snaffled their money, and they had nothing whatever to show for it. Nothing but a piece of white paper with the name of Haines' bank stamped across its bottom in beautiful scarlet letters!

It was enough to make the angels weep; and though Tubac wasn't any angel, he was almighty close to weeping.

Then something Blackwater Bill was saying abruptly caught his wide-eyed attention. "Huh?" he exclaimed, blinking owlishly. "Say—ride that trail again, pardner, will you?"

"I said," smiled Blackwater genially, "that great pride goeth before a fall. That's Scripture. You know there's a lot of sound stuff in the Good Book, Tubac—very educational, too. Got a lot of fine tips for the man with his eye peeled. I've often improved my time looking through it; and I— That horse hoofs I hear coming?"

Tubac jumped to the porch edge and stared up the trail. "Hell's fire!" he snarled. "It's that blasted Ike Shallet!"

"Here—none o' that!" said Blackwater grimly. "Put up that gun! I'll handle this!"

And when the sheriff rode up to the porch it was Blackwater Bill who said warmly: "Well, well! Mister Shallet, I believe. This *is* a pleasure—it truly is! Light down and rest your saddle, Sheriff. Jones—go scare up something to drink—"

"Hold on, you!" Shallet barked at Jones, and the light in his eyes said he wasn't fooling. "Move one more step an' I'll let you have it!"

Jones looked at the sheriff's gun and stopped.

"Who's that?" Shallet's nod was jerked at the gambler; and Blackwater said before Jones could speak:

"I beg your pardon, Sheriff. I should have introduced myself. I'd forgotten you might not remember me—you were one of John Slaughter's deputies last time I saw you. My name is Bill Nameloh. I'm Sam Holeman's nephew, and I've decided to open the ranch up again."

The sheriff raked him with a mackeral glance, then sat a moment with his thumbs whitely hooked in his braces. After which he got out his makings and, still watching Blackwater, coolly twisted himself a smoke. Then he got a match from behind his ears and scratched it on his Levis. "I thought," he said, through the cigarette smoke, "there was somethin' kind of familiar about you. So you're Ol' Sam's nephew, are you? Come out to open the ranch up again . . . Well, well. Goin' to take a deal of money, looks like." And he punched back the rim of his hat from his eyes and considered Blackwater inscrutably.

Tubac was eying Blackwater, too, and he very nearly gave the whole show away before he grasped what the gambler was up to. Then he turned and looked back toward the horse corral so the star-packer wouldn't catch the grin on his face. This Blackwater Bill was a pretty cute article.

The sheriff's thoughts may have run that way, too. "Of course," he said with a thin, wintry smile, "I am not pr'sumin' to doubt your word, but there'll be some who'll want to see proof, understand—I'm speakin' about your kinship to Sam. The Stockman's Bank an' Mortgage—"

"Yes, of course—quite naturally," Blackwater nodded. "With such a large place at stake—and due to be sold in a few weeks for taxes—it is entirely understandable that some persons might wish to prove me an interloper."

Blackwater's smile shared the thought with the sheriff. "I

expect they'll be a trifle bitter about it. But I can prove it all right. As a matter of fact, I've got Uncle Sam's will—"

"What!" gasped the sheriff. "You say you've got Sam's will?"

"Certainly." Blackwater's eyes shone blue as whetstones. "You don't imagine I'd lie about it, do you? It's a homemade will, but it's all in order. I've had my attorneys look over it, and they assure me it is quite in order."

The sheriff looked a little bit rattled, and some of the nap seemed worn off his grin. He said: "It seems rather queer—"

"That I've waited so long to come out here? Well, you must understand— But no matter! My acts are accountable to no one." Blackwater Bill straightened his bony shoulders and looked every inch the outraged gentleman. "While we're on the subject," he said dustily, "I would like to know by what rights the Stockton bank has dared meddle with my business? Jones, here, tells me they claim to have been leasing Horse Prairie to some foddlederah syndicate"

"You'll have to take that up with them," remarked Shallet hastily. "I know nothing about the matter. But I *should* like," he said, skewering a finger at Jones, "to know your connection with—"

"With Mister Jones?"

"Exactly." Some remembrance turned the sheriff's look ugly. "He come in here like a damn March gale—"

"Yes, I know," murmured Blackwater blandly. "He had the same idea that's been buzzing around in some other folks' heads—that the Holeman place would be sold for back taxes. But that's muddy water gone under the bridge. The place is not going to go. I'm paying the taxes and, incidentally, Mister Jones has agreed to stay on as my range boss."

"He's goin' to stay, all right!" Ike Shallet snapped. "He's goin' to be *locked up*—and if he ever gets out it won't be *my* fault!"

"Do I understand you intend to arrest him?"

"I *am* arrestin' him! Right here an' now! You may be all you claim to be, but this skunk-coddlin' fourflusher is goin' straightway to jail!" Shallet snarled and, sliding out of his saddle, tossed down his reins and advanced on Tubac like a sore-backed bull.

"Indeed?" said Blackwater quietly. "May I ask what for?"

The sheriff swung round with an oath. "What for! If there's anything on the calendar—"

"Let's be specific—shall we?"

The sheriff's cheeks were mottled, but with an effort he got hold of his temper. "Very well," he said grimly, "if you're hirin' him you've got a right to know, I guess. There's half a dozen charges we could bring against him, but—"

"Oh, is that so?" Tubac growled. "Name 'em!"

The sheriff whipped round and for a moment looked as if he were about to strike him. But he didn't. He said: "Horse-stealing—"

"From who?"

"From the Stampede Hog & Cattle Company."

"Who says so?"

"The company range boss, Potter."

"Better ask Potter what his name's doin' on a bill of sale."

But the sheriff was not to be sidetracked that way. "We ain't pressin' that charge," yapped Shallet, crunching his nut-crackers. "We could jail you for all that stink you made in town—for packin' concealed polecats an' disturbin' the peace an'—"

"You'd play hell provin' it," Tubac said, grinning. "Who's bringin' the charges an'—"

"We ain't pressin' that one, either. There's a little matter of trespass we could send you up for if that danged Lot Deckerman wa'n't so chicken-hearted—but he's said 'hands off' on that count, so—"

69

"Downright noble of him!" Tubac scoffed. "Musta got religion, or maybe—"

"What you're bein' arrested for," Shallet's growl cut through his gab, "is breakin' an' enterin'. Breakin'," he said, plainly pleased with himself, "an' enterin' the Stockman's Bank & Mortgage—"

"Say! What is this?" Jones demanded. "A frame-up?"

"Stick out your hands," rasped Shallet. "These bracelets is jest your size."

"Just a moment," interposed Blackwater. "Let me get the facts on this. Do you wish me to understand you're arresting my range boss for robbing—"

"I never said nothin' about robbin'," the sheriff muttered. "As a matter of fact, Mr. Haines, the bank president, invited this—this skunk-coddlin' viper into his private office. Whereupon this scoundrel drew his gun and forced Mr.—"

"Who says so?" Tubac snarled at him; and Blackwater asked:

"Do I understand you to say Mr. Haines is preferring the charges?"

The sheriff hauled up to think that over. But it looked straight enough on the surface, and, after all, Haines *had* brought the charges; so he said belligerently:

"What about it?"

"I'm afraid that's not answering my question, Sheriff."

"All right. He did. That make any grist for your mill?"

"Depends," Blackwater said darkly, "on some things I'm not at liberty to disclose just now. But I will say this much, Sheriff—and I say it in all seriousness. If I were Mr. H. G. Haines I would not press this thing any further."

The sheriff stared at him suspiciously. "What you drivin' at?"

"That's one of the things I cannot divulge. But you may take my word for it, sir. Grave misfortunes may overtake Mr.

70

Haines if he continues the attack along these lines. They have a proverb in Mississippi that fits his case rather neatly—it concerns people who live in glass houses . . ."

"Let the righteous man heave the first rock," Jones misquoted.

"*You* better keep *your* damn trap shut!" Ike Shallet snapped vindictively.

And Jones, with mock humility, said: "Pardon me for breathin', Sheriff. I'd plumb forgot Haines had to initial it."

Blackwater poured hasty oil on the waters. "If Jones did the thing you claim, he certainly ought to be jailed for it; but that poses a very pretty question, Sheriff. Did you—with your very own eyes—observe Mister Jones pull a gun on this banker?"

"I didn't come out here to bandy words," Shallet told him. "I come after this fugitive from justice. Are you givin' him up, or are you figgerin' to aid an' abet him? An' don't bother dressin' it up in a lot of fancy gab. Are you? Yes or no?"

"I will answer that when you tell me what proof of this charge Mr. Haines has brought forward."

"Proof! What do you mean 'proof'?"

"It is customary when bringing charges to offer something in—"

"Oh, *that!*" The sheriff grinned at them nastily. "The evidence—oh yes, that bank's offered plenty evidence. It seems that just before this lobo cleared out—"

"Let's not get ahead of the story," protested Blackwater. "You haven't said what Mr. Jones was threatening—"

"He wasn't stoppin' at threats! He was all fixed to force Mr. Haines to open the private vault in his office."

"Doesn't seem likely he would threaten and then fail to—"

"Mr. Haines was too smart for him. He punched one of the buttons on his desk, and Jones got scared an' hopped it. But, before he cleared out, he snatched up a coupla sheets

71

of paper, stamped the bank's name on 'em, made Mr. Haines get him a red seal with blue ribbons an'—"

"Horse feathers!" Blackwater snorted. "Why, this is ridiculous!"

"Is it? Well, this lobo won't find it—"

"I never listened to such childish twaddle in my life," scoffed Blackwater testily. "If that's all you've—"

"If this sidewinder's got them papers on him—" Shallet began; but Blackwater said:

"Don't rant, Sheriff. Have a little regard for the dignity of your office. Use your head instead of your elbow. Count ten and think this over a bit. *Anyone* could happen to have two sheets of blank paper with the Stockton bank stamp on them. Why, a—"

"One of these papers had been notarized—"

"Do you mean to say it is the bank's practice to keep blank sheets of paper prepared with—" Blackwater let his words trail off and looked at the sheriff very queerly. "Hmm. Yes, indeed," he muttered. "This looks like a case for the bank examiners. I've a friend up at Washington that I believe would be—"

"Here!" snarled the sheriff. "What're you up to? What're you doin' tryin' to twist my words—"

"I'm afraid," declared Blackwater coldly, "I've nothing more to say to you, Sheriff. Arrest my foreman if you care to. I shall get in touch with my friend right away. I'm going to have that bank looked into. Criminal negligence is the very best face I could put on it. I think I shall prefer charges. Willful intent to defraud. Misappropriation of bank clients' money. Embezzlement—"

"Wh—wh—what are you talkin' about?" The hand holding the sheriff's pistol trembled. He reached a hand to the porch post to steady himself, and his cheeks were strangely mottled and damp. "What's that you're sayin' about embezz—"

"I have nothing further to discuss with you, Sheriff. I sent Jones in with fifty-five hundred dollars to deposit, and he brings me back a blank sheet of paper with nothing on it but the bank's rubber stamp. The receipt was made out in fading ink, but my Washington friend is an expert on inks."

The sheriff said wildly: "You've got this all wrong—you've let this Shylock bamboozle you, sir! It's plain enough now why he stole the bank paper."

"You insult my intelligence," drawled Blackwater stiffly. "It happens I've a witness to the entire transaction who will swear she saw Haines' teller make out a receipt for the money my range boss deposited. Your friend, Mr. Haines, has tricked the wrong man this time, and trying to cover it up by swearing out warrants—Really, I don't think I should discuss this with you further. You will be hearing from my attorneys, Sheriff, and I should advise you to have a better story for them than this preposterous tale you've been telling me. There stands your prisoner, sir. Put your handcuffs on him and be on your way!"

"I—ah—er . . . Perhaps I had better—"

"You had better take him—in fact," declared Blackwater sternly, "I shall brook no argument, Shallet! I shall *insist*—"

But the sheriff had fled. With a bitter curse he had jumped on his horse; and now he was gone, burning up the trail in his haste to get back to Hi Grab.

X

THE CANNY LOT

With admiring oaths and uproarious guffaws Jones clouted Blackwater Bill and, snapping his fingers, danced a jig about him.

"I sure take off my hat to your gall," he grinned, wiping the laugh tears out of his eyes. "Never since Noah have I heard—"

"Make no mistake," said Blackwater grimly; "we've not seen the last of that bunch by a long shot! Those fibs I told make pretty good stage props, but the best they can do is gain us a breather. I'd like to have that bank looked into, but it would be time wasted unless—Mmmm; might work at that, but . . . Nope," sighed Blackwater, shaking his head, "they'll never risk it. They'll have the whole works covered up like a toad before we could say 'Jack Robinson.' What they'll do is forget about you and shift their attentions to me."

"They'll sure want to see your proof that you're kin to Sam."

"I'm not worried about that part," Bill said. "When it comes to faked signatures, I'm an expert—if I do say it myself."

75

"Then we've got 'em!" whooped Jones; but Blackwater looked far from satisfied.

"The trouble with that," he said, frowning, "is that I can't afford to get mixed up in a court fight. I . . . um—well, I'll tell you, Tubac. I'm one of those guys you've heard tell about that departed his past just in front of a sheriff." And he stamped back and forth across the porch for a bit, head bent and frowning stare thoughtful.

"What about the will?" Jones inquired.

"Oh, I could rig up a will with my eyes shut. It isn't *that* I'm scared of. I could ram this pose of Sam's nephew down their throats and make it stick, like enough, in the bargain. But you see, Lot Deckerman knows me—he's one of them Texans with an elephant's memory for faces, and though it's been several years since our trails crossed . . . No; it just wouldn't work. He'd remember just as quick's he clapped eyes on me."

"Who was that witness you mentioned—that 'she' what saw me deposit—"

"That was just a bluff," said Bill absently. "As a gambling man I've had considerable experience in the ancient—Ah! Wait—don't speak! Let me think a minute . . ."

He stood by a post staring out across the range with a far-off look in his gambler's eyes, and with his thumbs sagged into his flowered vest pockets. Tall and gaunt he was, with a sharp, hooked nose, and lace at his sleeves—a handsome duck, Tubac thought, faintly envious.

Blackwater had said to let him think a minute; but Tubac had been thinking, too; and abruptly he asked, squinting: "What's the connection between that bank an' that side-windin' Stampede outfit?"

The gambler looked round at him sharply. "Ain't you figured that out yet? It's quite simple, really. The Stampede Hog & Cattle Company is a syndicate made up of and controlled by the disgruntled Texas trail bosses Holeman levied his water tax on. They came in here, I've heard, with the avowed intention of whittling Sam down to their size. Since they got rid of Sam they've hatched the idea of annexing all of Sam's property. But you were asking?"

"What connection there is between that outfit an' Haines' bank," Tubac said.

"Well, Haines—" Blackwater broke off and stood there lost in some sudden idea that had come to him. He seemed to forget Tubac entirely; but just when Tubac was getting ready to shove his oar in again, Blackwater said, looking up with a grin: "Haines was just a blackleg lawyer the Stampede bunch picked out of a crib in Tombstone. He's slick all right an' about as shifty as a cup of tea; but when it comes to bank policy he does just what Deckerman tells him. Despite all his airs and paraded importance, he's nothing but an overgrown pawn in this business—just a figurehead. It's the Stampede crowd really owns that bank."

"Then we're really fightin' Lot Deckerman?"

"Every minute," nodded Blackwater grimly. "Now look— I been mulling things over, and the first thing we better do, seems like, is make a gather; comb the range and—"

"Throw 'em outside the fence?" Tubac grinned.

"On the contrary. Better have that sour-pussed rustler you hired fix up any breaks he can find in our fence. We'll hold those cattle for damages. I'll give in they're pretty much runts, but they ought to have more or less nuisance value. You and White-Eye go round them up while I auger this over in my mind a little."

It was not until several hours later, while he and White-Eye were combing the draws, that Tubac realized how neatly the gambler had changed places with him. "Damn 'f he couldn't talk ol' Gabriel outa his horn!" Tubac scowled, and pulled

Calliope up with an oath. "What a yap I am for takin' his orders! By grab, I'll have it out with him pronto!" And, leaving White-Eye orders to continue the gather, he struck out, still spluttering, for headquarters.

It was pretty nearly dark and, not being too familiar with that part of the range, Tubac was following a section of his new-strung fence where it separated Stampede land from the Holeman acres when, topping a low rise, he saw in the dusk before him a pair of stopped horsemen sitting square in his path, one on each side of the drift fence.

They were talking, but much too softly for Jones to pick up anything. And the light was too poor for him to pick out facial details. But the near horse looked like the one Winch Face had been riding when he'd left the ranch on his fence-mending tour; and Tubac kneed Calliope forward with a hand grim-wrapped round his six-shooter.

The man on the near bronc was Winch Face all right.

Just as Tubac got within hearing, Winch Face's voice said indignantly: "Nope—nothin' doin'. When I eat a guy's salt I stick by him. I'm s'prised at you, Mister Deckerman, tryin' to bribe a honest galoot like me!"—And then somebody's horse nickered, and both riders whirled and saw Jones.

"Set tight," warned Tubac ominously. "I got both you rannies covered like a tent, an' the first guy that blinks gets his light snuffed—savvy?" Then he urged Calliope forward.

"Why—it's Mister Jones!" exclaimed Deckerman. "The very man I been wantin' to see!"

"All that believe that can stand on their head," scoffed Tubac. He gave the Stampede boss a hard stare. But Deckerman shook his head in a sorrowful manner.

"No sense packin' a chip on your shoulder. I've decided to let bygones be bygones. Live an' let live is my motto, Jones. I don't like you no more'n you like me, but seein' as we're neighbors, I reckon we ought to make the best of it an'—"

"What's all this leadin' up to?"

"Shucks," said Deckerman, and met his scowl with a smile so disarming and friendly that Tubac, puzzled, found himself wondering if perhaps, after all, he had not mistaken a molehill for a mountain. "Shucks," said Deckerman. "Don't you know that kind of talk only boils up feuds an' gun-fightin'? The way to get along in this world, Mister Jones, is to meet a man halfway. Here I come bringin' olive branches—"

"What you got under 'em—" Jones jeered—"catclaw?"

"Here," grunted Deckerman, extending a hand. "Have a cigar an' let's bury the hatchet. Sorry to hear about your recent hard luck."

"What hard luck?"

"Why, about that fellow, Nameloh, showin' up. They tell me he's one of the Holeman heirs—Ol' Sam's nephew or somethin'—an' that he's figuring to restock the old place."

"What about it?"

"Must've been a disappointment for you."

"Oh. I dunno," declared Tubac. "He's offerin' to split with me fifty-fifty."

"That so? Hmmm. Reg'lar philanthropist, ain't he? Shallet was tellin' me he looks like a gambler. Never heard of a gambler playin' Santy Clause before—never saw a gambler I would trust half as far as I could heave a dead horse. But live an' learn, I always say. He *might* be on the level; but it's usually been my experience, when you come across one of these generous guys, it's time to start boardin' up the windows. Elsewise they'll git every stitch you got on you an' wind up sendin' you a bill for the launderin'. It don't seem reasonable, if this bird was really kin of Sam's—"

But Tubac snorted. "You're wastin' steam, Deckerman. Blackwater—"

"So he calls himself 'Blackwater,' does he? Ike said he looked like a T. B. to him."

"Yeah; an' Shallet smells like a skunk," grinned Tubac, "but—"

"The point is well taken," admitted Deckerman, smiling. "This fellow is probably just what he claims to be. It's my suspicious mind, I reckon. But say—try this cigar. It's a special blend I import for my friends."

"So I'm bein' elevated to the inner circle," Tubac grunted. He took the cigar and sniffed of it. "Smells like plain cabbage to me. Here, Winch Face—*you* smoke it."

But Deckerman just chuckled tolerantly. "We're a heap alike, you an' me, Tubac. We'd make a great team if we'd quit slingin' rocks at each other."

"What's all this peace talk buildin' up to?"

"You been readin' too much about the Greeks bearin' gifts," smiled Deckerman. "I come over to apologize—"

"Oh! I thought you rode over for a powwow with Winch Face. Did you reckon you'd find me waitin' by the fence?"

"Tch. Tch. Tch," clucked Deckerman. "I was trying to persuade this puncher of yours to ride over to the house an' fetch you. I'd have gone myself, but he wouldn't let me step foot—"

"Speakin' of feet—" Tubac muttered; but the Stampede boss said hastily:

"Just what I was comin' to see you about. I want to apologize for settin' you afoot the other day. I was entirely wrong an' I come to make amends—"

"Oh, you come over to rub my feet for me, did you?"

"I'm strictly in earnest—"

"So am I!" blared Jones. "An' I've heard all your lies I've a mind to! I been dry behind the ears quite a spell an' I don't have to use no peach twig to know hogwash when I hear it! Jest turn that nag of yours straight around, Mister, an' light a shuck back where you came from. The Holeman grant's in mighty good hands."

"Just a minute!" said Deckerman thinly. "I come over here to apologize an' try to bury the hatchet—"

"Yeah—I know where you wanted to bury it!" Jones jeered.

"—and to set you right on a misunderstanding," went on the Stampede boss, ignoring Jones' interruption. "Ike Shallet took too much on himself, storming out to your place like he did. I didn't know a thing about it—nor Mister Haines didn't, neither—till he come back an' admitted what a fool thing he'd done. Said he had aimed to have some fun with you— the crazy loon! As a matter of fact, he made that whole bizness up; he never had no warrant or anything. As for that invisible ink—that was a prank of Haines' clerk. Haines fired him quick as he heard of it. He wants you to know your deposit's all safe; you can have a new receipt or the money any time you want it."

"Well, isn't that just lovely!" Tubac sneered. Then he jerked up his gun and thumbed the hammer back. "Now you kick up that bone rack an' git to hell outa here! There ain't no swivel-eyed son of a Choctaw goin' to put nothin' over on *me*, by Judas! You—"

But suddenly Tubac's voice went hollow and he stopped in full tide with his jaw dropped open and his eyes gone big as teacups. A rattle of shots had rung out from the ranch; and then he saw Lot Deckerman's grin and everything became clear on the instant. The Stampede boss had been detaining Winch Face in idle gab while his men sneaked up on the ranch house to trap T. Jones and Blackwater!

"C'mon!" Jones yelled to Winch Face, and gave his horse the steel.

XI

"O, DEATH—"

Tubac had known from the start what a back-biting lobo Lot Deckerman was and had tried mighty hard to outguess him. But the Stampede boss's only purpose had been to hold Jones and Winch Face there by the fence while his men sneaked in and killed Blackwater.

Gusty and bitter were the oaths with which Tubac larruped the night as, crouched low in their saddles, he and Winch Face fogged ranchward. With quirt and spur they drove their broncs in a headlong race against time; and little by little Tubac crept ahead of the puncher, for Calliope had the heels of Pegasus and fairly flew across the rolling ground. And as he rode, Jones unlimbered his rifle and his glance raked the night for a target.

There were a good many things about Blackwater Bill that he figured would take some explaining. Particularly puzzling was the gambler's sure grasp of things even Jones wasn't certain of; and the completeness and source of the man's information was likewise bothering Tubac. But Bill had a head on his shoulders; and in some odd way, his wry, tight-lipped smile had found the crack in Jones' armor. Despite his little mysteries, Blackwater was a man to tie to, and Tubac's eyes glinted malice as he rushed his horse through the night.

Then he was topping the last bit of rolling ground, and the gaunt, weathered lines of the ranch building showed vaguely through the curdled murk. But nothing else was visible—not the faintest flash of a muzzle light—and Tubac reined in with a curse.

The raiders had gone. They had gotten their quarry and fled, he guessed, and subsequent search seemed to prove it.

A fight had been staged here—that much was certain. There was a good deal too much evidence to leave room for doubt. The house walls were pocked with bullet holes. Not one window had a whole glass in it, and the living room looked as if a cyclone had struck it, with broken stuff lying in windrows. Every stick of furniture in it was reduced to splinters and stove wood.

And there was no sign of Blackwater any place.

Stampede had struck with a vengeance, and Jones eyed the wreckage gloomily.

"They're a cold-blooded lot," muttered Winch Face. "I guess ol' man Holeman found *that* out. You heard what happened to *him*, didn't you? He brought in Slaughter to kill off the rustlers, but it was Salughter killed *him* in the end, I reckon. Shallet figured sheriffin' cramped his style, I guess; he give up his job as depity and took to drivin' the Benson stage. He come in one night with his stage boot empty an' shakin' like a weed in a norther. He had two dead men inside the coach and he swore it was Sam stuck the stage up. Lot Deckerman swore out a warrant an' told John Slaughter to serve it. He come out to the ranch here after Ol' Sam, but Sam hadn't waited. Slaughter took up the trail next mornin', an' where he went nobody's ever found out; but he was gone three weeks, an' when he come back he had Sam's hat. He give the warrant back to Lot Deckerman—I was workin' for Deckerman then an' I seen it. It had 'Cancelled' writ clean acrost it."

Tubac scowled morosely. "What happened after that?"

"Nothin'. Slaughter chucked in his star a couple months later an' went back to his ranch. Deckerman had Ike Shallet appointed to fill out the term, an' he's been fillin' it out ever since. No contest a-tall. Lot Deckerman had showed he meant business, an' nobody wanted a repeat. You an' this Blackwater pelican is the first ones that's bucked Stampede in six years, an' if you'll take my advice—"

"If you're scared for your hide, you can quit right now," Tubac snarled.

Winch Face shrugged and got out his chawin'. "When I'm ready to quit I'll tell you. This' the best pay I've drawed in forty-three years. I'll string along till they break you."

"Humph! Thanks for nothin'," scowled Tubac, and wondered what he'd better do. The suddenness of Blackwater's disappearance had kind of unsettled his stomach. He had known the Stampede outfit was plumb cultus, but he hadn't figured they'd go in for plain murder.

There was no other way to look at it, though. Either they'd murdered Bill or they'd kidnapped him.

"Might be we could trail 'em—"

"Trail right ahead," spat out Winch Face, "but don't cut *me* into such foolishness."

Tubac peeled back his lips contemptuously. "An' I thought you was a *salty* buck, a real double-actin' en-gine! Tough—"

"I'm tough," Winch Face scowled, "but I ain' plumb daffy. If you got to be a bright an' shinin' hero, it's all right with me—but I'll save *my* talents fer cattle."

"Cattle?" Tubac showed sudden interest. "Did you say—"

"Yep—that's me. I'm a re-write man from who laid the chunk. Anything you want done on cow-critters, jest send a wire to Yours Truly. But don't count me in on no rough stuff."

Tubac stood turning these remarks over a minute. "Go scare us up somethin' to eat," he said finally and, turning, tramped out to the porch. He sat down heavily on the steps to think—and that was when he saw the paper. It was neatly tucked in a crack of the step, and Tubac stared at it curiously. Then he got out his knife and worked the note loose.

Winch Face yelled at him after some while; and after they'd downed the chow he'd fixed they got out their papers and rolled up a smoke. Then Tubac remarked offhandedly: "Got a little work for you, Hotshot—cow work. Gonna give you a chance to prove up on that brag." He proceeded to talk for a long ten minutes; and before he quit the re-write man was flashing his fangs in a wolfish grin.

"By golly!" he said. "If Lot Deckerman's bunch ever git onto this, they'll string you up higher'n Haman!"

Tubac screwed up his nose and snorted. "You git your horse an' git out there—I'll show them skunks I mean business!" Then he reread the note he had pried from the step and sauntered outside, still chuckling. The note had been from Blackwater, advising Tubac to visit the bank. Some way, evidently, Bill had wriggled clear and was all set to wind up Haines' rope.

Bright and early next morning Tubac rode into Stockton. It was not quite nine by the clock on the bank, but the day was heating up nicely, and the thermometer, in the shade of Haines' door, had passed the hundred-and-thirty mark without even pausing to spit.

"Calliope," adjudged Tubac, eying it, "it may git a little

warmish today. You go hunt you some shade an' cool off your heels whilst I go in an' diddle this banker."

With which admonition he got out of the saddle and, flicking the reins loosely round the horn, left Calliope free to do as he chose.

Tubac strode through the lobby to Honey Hair's desk and took off his hat with a flourish. "See you're still chummin' round with the orphan robber." He grinned when Honey Hair lifted her chin; but she was mad clean through, and he knew it. "Tut, tut," he said with a chuckle, "I'm still keepin' that job at the ranch open for you."

"I think," she declared with biting scorn, "you're the most hateful man I've ever met! Why can't you act like a gentleman?"

But Tubac's grin was derisive. "I leave all that stuff to the bankers an' minin' stock brokers. How's the freeze-out business gettin' along these days? Foreclosed on any more suckers?"

Haines' yellow-haired secretary blushed with vexation. But a quick glance over her shoulder revealed that the lobby nearby was filling rapidly. It seemed as if everyone and his uncle wanted to get a look at the man who had squatted on the Holeman place in defiance of Haines and Lot Deckerman. So Honey Hair swallowed her pride and remembered she was Mr. Haines' secretary. "Did you come in about your deposit?"

"No," Tubac grinned, "that served me right—I sh'd've known better'n to put any money in this joint. How's Brother Haines this mornin'? Got all the eggs scraped off his chin yet?"

Honey Hair grinned then in spite of herself, and Tubac chuckled uproariously.

"You're quite a card, aren't you, Mr. Jones?"

But Tubac said: "Call me Tubac—an' look: would you mind tellin' me *your* name?"

"Sue Lambert," she said. "I thought everyone knew that. Half of this country calls me 'Sue.' But honest now, Mr. Jones, do you think that was a very nice thing—what you did to poor Mr. McGillis, I mean? That skunk and—"

"What do you s'pose my skunk thought about it? Gettin' hove through a plate glass window! I ort to *sue* that ol' reprobate!"

"Shh!" Miss Lambert said, finger to lips. "All those folks in the lobby are staring at you."

"Let 'em stare!" Jones scowled; but Honey Hair said hurriedly:

"Would you like to see Mr. Haines now? He's probably going over his mail but—"

"Tottin' up the widows' mites he's snared!"

"Why do you be so hateful? Do you *like* always to be in trouble?"

"Who—*me?*" Jones stared to see if she was pulling his leg, but the look of her seemed to be serious enough. Been hearing too many of Hi Grab's lies, he thought. "Ma'am," he declared, "if there's a more docile guy any place in this country than me, I'll *eat* him! Hide, hair an' all! You jest don't know what you're talkin' about—you got me all wrong!"

"Well . . ." She looked at him dubiously. "The sheriff said—"

"The sheriff!" he mimicked. "Hell's bells, ma'am! You don't want to pay no mind to what *that* bird tells you! Next to Haines he's the biggest danged liar—"

"What's all the racket out—Oh! So it's *you* again, is it?"

Banker Haines stood peering from the door of his office. His little pig eyes were snapping with anger, but fear had drained all the blood from his cheeks, and his hand on the door frame trembled.

"Eavesdroppin', eh?" said Jones with a sneer; and the banker's face grew mottled with fury. He straightened his whippersnap shoulders and seemed about to yell for his guard; but something must have warned him not to, for he summoned a frozen smile and stood back.

"If you've anything to say to me, it would better be said in my office."

"That suits me right down to the ground," Jones grunted, and strode past Haines, kicking the door shut after him. Then he paused and turned back and opened it, saying loudly:

"You'll oblige us by calling the sheriff, Miss Lambert," and gave the scowling Haines a quick, sour grin. "What's the matter, Haines? *You* ain't scared of him, are you?"

"Just go on with your work," Haines told Honey Hair. "If I want Ike Shallet I can call him." Then he closed the door again carefully, and his nose was twitching like a rabbit's.

"What did you want to do that for?" he bleated. "More of your grandstand plays, I presume? One of these days you'll grandstand too often."

"Don't count your chickens till they're in the pot boiling," Jones advised. "An' while I think of it, you can give me another receipt for that money I loaned you—an' make it out in pencil."

"I have one all ready for you," Haines said stiffly, and got it from his gilt filing cabinet. He pushed it across the desk at Jones. "You probably won't believe it, but that crazy ink was a prank of my clerk's—"

"Yeah," Tubac said. "It's too bad about him—an' it's goin' to be mighty bad for you if there's anything screwy about *this* one." He gave it the once-over, grunted, and put it away in his wallet.

The banker got out a little gold penknife and set industriously to work on his fingernails. "If there's nothing else, Mr. Jones—"

"Don't rush me," Jones growled, "an' quit fiddlin' around

with that dinkus. When I talk to a man I like to have his attention. What are you going to do about the Holeman grant now that I've got a pardner? One of Sam Holeman's kin, by the way—his nephew, in fact."

"I'm afraid that's a topic best left undiscussed. You'll be hearing from our attorneys."

"You bring any lawyers into this business an' I'll close up this bank like an empty box!"

Hi Grab's eyebrows jumped into his hair. "More threats?"

"Just a promise," Jones said; "an' here's another: "If anything happens to my pardner, Haines, I'm gonna hold you strictly responsible. A eye for a eye is my motto—remember it! I'm for peace at any price—if it ain't too high. But if it's war you want, just say the glad word."

"This is preposterous!" the banker sputtered. "*Preposterous!* If you can't conduct yourself like a gentleman—"

"Nope—I can't do that," Jones sneered. "My trail ain't crossed enough widows an' orphans. I'm jest a plain, brush-poppin' cowpoke—an', speakin' of cows, I got a big bunch coming. Goin' to restock Horse Prairie. I've shoved all them Stampede strays outside the fence—an' they better *stay* outside if they know what's good for 'em."

"So you're bringing in cattle, are you? Going to try and make this bluff of yours stick, eh? Aren't you afraid—"

"Not a chance," Jones grinned. "If your rustlers can work *them* critters over, they can have 'em an' welcome. Just tell 'em to drop round any time. We bar the doors to bankers an' sheriffs, but—Say!" exclaimed Tubac, suddenly leaning forward. "What'll you take for that Stampede 'lease'?"

"That lease," Haines said with a glower, "is not for sale."

"Hoo, hoo!" jeered Tubac. "Don't hand me that line! You've all got your price—C'm'on, now! What'll you take?"

But Haines drew his chin up haughtily.

"All right," said Jones. "Suit yourself, of course; but don't come cryin' to *me* when you're broke an' they've put **you** away in the poorhouse. You're jest about done in this country, Haines. My pardner has fetched out Sam Holeman's will—an' I guess you know what *that* means!"

"I refuse to be drawn into any discussion concerning the Holeman property," Haines snapped; and he looked like a harpooned codfish. "Our attorneys—"

"Yah! You an' your lawyers!" Tubac scooped up his hat. But he turned at the door for a parting shot. Before he could frame something suitable, though, someone hammered its panels frantically.

Then the door popped open and Honey Hair, white-cheeked and all of a tremble gasped: "Mr. Haines—there's a man—I think it's the bank examiner!"

She was thrust aside then, and a tall rawboned man in a flat-rimmed hat stood lounging there, cold eyes inspecting them, thumbs grimly hooked in his galluses. Had it been Simon Legree who'd stepped into the place, the effect could have been no more startling.

Jones had been expecting Blackwater, and all he could do was goggle while cold sweat came out on his forehead. Something had slipped, for the man in the door was that scourge of all crooks—Jinx Mueller, the U. S. Marshall

XII

HI HO, HI HO—

To SAY THAT Tubac was surprised would be the mildest of
understatements—he was petrified. With his mind on that
note he had pried from the steps, he'd been making small
talk while awaiting Blackwater's appearance, and when that
fist had pounded on the door he had gleefully supposed it
was Bill; but when he saw Jinx Mueller peering in you could
have knocked him down with a feather. The go-getting U. S.
Marshal was the last man he wanted to see.

But if he was shaking in his boots, no one would have
guessed it from the cool and casual look of him. With a grin
he stuck out his hand. "H'are you, Marshal? Long time no—"

But Mueller wasn't even looking at him. With an odd look
on his frosty face, he was staring intently in the direction of
Haines; and Tubac, following his glance, emitted a sudden
chuckle. The banker was squinched away down in his chair,
and in the fish-belly pallor of his mottled cheeks his little eyes
glinted like a cornered rat's.

"What's the matter with him?" Mueller demanded.

"Et green apples by the look of 'im—or mebbe he's realized

93

how his sins have done caught up with him. Well, I warned him—"

Tubac stopped as the marshal's cold blue eyes flickered over him. He knew this gun-throwing marshal's rep, and he'd a pretty good notion what the marshal thought of him. The marshal's look backed the thought up fully.

"Choke off the blat," Mueller told him curtly. "I've had all your horseplay I aim to put up with. I expect you figured to be pretty cute when you—"

"Now, Jinx," protested Tubac, "that was all a mistake—"

"You're bound to think so 'fore I git through. You slipped me once, but there ain't no crook this side of the Rockies ever put up a deal on Jinx Mueller twice!"

The marshal's stare grew cold as a gun bore. "I want a look through your wallet, Jones. Lay it down on the desk an' don't try no smart stuff."

Tubac did some quick thinking then. His hunch had been right when he'd given Jinx the slip in El Paso. Those bills had been marked! He should have guessed it; a guy like Chacon would hardly be packing any honest coin round with him.

Then abruptly, in the flicker of an eyebrow, the truth broke across him. Jinx Mueller's visit was a little too pat. It smacked a great deal too much of conjuring to be the result of blind chance. That note he had dug from the step had been phoney—Blackwater Bill hadn't left that for him. Blackwater—if he wasn't dead—must be hidden out some place with a Stampede guard watching over him. It had been slick Lot Deckerman, the ex-Texas trail boss, who had scrawled that note. No two ways about it. The whole deal was earmarked with the same cunning that had gotten Sam Holeman a too-early grave. Lot Deckerman—

Mueller said crisply: "The jig's up, Jones. Put your gun and your wallet over there on the desk. An' no tricks."

Tubac shrugged. He did as directed. "Takin' up pocket minin' these days, Marshal?"

"I'm goin' to have a squint through that wallet," Jinx said, "an' you're goin' to behave while I'm doin' it . . . or else."

"You got me all wrong," Jones protested. "Ain't nothin' fancy about me no-way. Plain Tubac Jones, run-of-the-mill cowprodder from—"

"I'll give you the *run* part," Mueller conceded. He peered at Jones dourly. "C'mon, sport—where is it? What've you done with it?"

"Done with what?" Tubac looked plumb flabbergasted. "Honest, Jinx, I dunno what you're talkin' about."

"Yeah," Mueller jeered. "Innercent like a unborn babe!" Then his face shed its habitual expression of tolerance, and Jones read the hate in his eyes. "You been shovin' 'queer,' " he spat, "an' by grab—"

"*Me?* Hell's hinges! You ain't believin' I'm counterfeitin'—"

"Look! Either you talk, or . . . Hell! I've wasted enough time—"

"I sh'd say so!" Tubac flicked a thumb at the recuperating banker. "There's the guy you're lookin' for—the Great Hi Grab. The widow's friend. The orphan's advisor. He takes care o' my money for me—every nickel I spent comes outa his vaults. Talk to him."

The marshal's hard eyes turned their grim focus on Haines. "Hmmm. Does look kind of sick, for a fact. What about this, Haines? Has—"

"This is preposterous!" Haines snarled thickly. "Utterly pre—"

"Watch out!" Jones grinned. "Remember your blood-pressure."

"Button your lip," said Mueller curtly. "You ain't out of the woods by a long shot, bucko, an' if I hear any more—"

"Make him let you look over his ready cash, Marshal."

Mueller said to Haines: "Jones got an account with you?"

"No—y-yes. Come to think of it, he opened one yesterday; but you—"

"That's only half the truth," Tubac growled. "He give me a receipt written in some kinda screwy ink, an' when I got out to the ranch all I had was a blank piece of paper."

"I explained all that," spluttered Haines, dabbing at his face with a handkerchief nervously. "It was a prank of my clerk," he assured Mueller hastily. "I fired the man quick as I learned of it."

"Yeah—I'll bet you did! Ask him," Jones jeered, "where he gets all the money to buy X & L on margin!"

Hi Grab looked about ready to swoon. "This—this is ridiculous!" he snarled. "It's nobody's business what I do with my money."

"*If*," grinned Jones very meaningly, "it's your money."

"I think," Mueller said, "I'll have a look at your books."

"You'll do nothing of the sort! You've no right—"

"Are you tryin' to tell me how to run my business?"

"It's high time somebody told you!" Hi Grab, almost beside himself with fright and anger, was in no mood to prune his language. "You monkey with this bank an' I'll have that star off your shirt so quick it'll make your head swim!"

"Oh, you will, will you?" Jinx Mueller said softly; and Tubac, on a sudden hunch, said:

"Guess I better leave you gents to iron this out by yourselves. Just a plain, garden variety home-growed, hand-spanked cowpunch—that's me. Bankers an' counterfeiters is outa my class. I'll be across the street, Marshal, feedin' my face, should you happen to need me."

And thus, like Moses, he picked up his belongings and eased himself out of the door.

XIII

THE SPARK AND THE KEG

Tubac was feeling pretty good as he pushed through the mob that was crammed like sardines in the lobby. Bug-eyed and gaping, they were all standing round for a look at him—at this two-bit nester in the brush-scarred chaps who thought he could buck Grab Haines and his backers.

Well! He was buckin' 'em, wasn't he? Doggone tootin'!

Tubac threw back his shoulders and, cuffing his hat to an arrogant angle, strode through the crowd at a saddle-bound swagger, flinging out smiles the way he'd seen Haines do; and then, by the door, he saw Archie McGillis, and Sheriff Ike Shallet was right by his side.

"Well, well!" Jones said. "Come sneakin' outa your holes again, have you? Where's the widders an' orphans Haines sent you to round up? Better ketch him some quick, 'cause he's sure goin' to need 'em!"

"Ahr—you an' your blowin'! Why'n't you rent yourself out fer a windmill?" sneered Shallet; but McGillis stretched out his hooked finger to stop him.

"Here—hold up, mon! What's a-brewin' in there?" he demanded, eying Haines' closed private office apprehensively.

"Why'n't you push in an' see?" blared Jones loudly. "Hell of a bank director *you* are—don't even know what's goin' on in the place! If this sheriff was worth a fifth part of his badge, he'd arrest you for criminal negligence! An' that reminds me," he muttered and, breaking loose of the storekeeper's hold, he hostled his way to the cashier's window and shoved Haines' receipt through the grill.

"I'll be takin' my money," he said grimly; then he noticed the others had followed him.

"You'll have to take this down to the teller's window—" began the cashier; but Jones cut him off with a bellow.

"What's the matter? Ain't it *good?* Has that damn potwalloper tricked me *ag'in?* First he gives me a receipt that ain't nothin' but a blank piece o' paper. Now he gives me another an' you won't pay—"

"Just a moment, sir—ah—er—I'm afraid I didn't understand what you wanted—"

"What're you doin' in a bank then?" Jones spluttered. "Damndest passel of imbeciles I ever stumbled onto! There's Haines' signature right on the line—*see it?* Ar'ight then! You goin' to give me my money or ain't you?"

"Pay it, mon! Pay it!" yelled McGillis, jumping up and down in his excitement. "Pay it an' git the windlestrae oot o' here!"

"Oh! So you're tryin' to gimme the bum's rush, are you?" Tubac folded his arms. "Well, go right ahead! Just roll up your sleeves—"

"Pay 'im!" snarled McGillis; and the cashier was doing his best to. Moreover, Ike Shallet was beginning to look ugly. But Jones wasn't to be hushed that way. With all this crowd looking on, it was too good a chance to be missed.

"I put fifty-five hundred dollars in this widow-robbin' joint, an' I ain't pullin' my freight till I git it! I'll stick to this place like a heel-fly in—"

"They're a-gittin' your money, you blamed idjit!" snarled Shallet, catching hold of Jones' shoulder. "Turn off your golrammed megaphone an'—"

"I'll turn it off when I get my money! What's the matter? Ain't they *got* it?"

Grabbing Jones' hand, the sheriff, spluttering like a dew-damped firecracker, slapped a thick sheaf of greenbacks into it and started him precipitately doorward.

But Jones hung back, digging in his spurred heels, and suddenly he loosed a yowl that would have done a Comanche credit. "Hey!" he shouted. "I don' want this printin'-press stuff! Gimme—"

"What's the matter with it?" Ike said, bristling.

"How do *I* know? I'm just a poor dumb igerant—Well! I *would* shut up if you'd give me back my fifty-five hundred!"

"Here!" The cashier came running with a big sack of coin, and McGillis, with his cheeks the hue of an overripe tomato, snatched it out of his trembling hands and dumped it ker-plop into Tubac's arms.

"There's your damn money!" snapped Shallet, grabbing the greenbacks. "Now take it an' git to hell outa here!"

Tubac needed no further prompting. With all this racket going on, he was going to catch hell if Jinx Mueller came out and spotted the cause of it. But just as Jones reached the huge brass-bound doors, opportunity came in like a pig on a platter.

It was Sloppy Gus, the stableman; and Tubac yelled with a hand to his mouth: "Lather it up if you're wantin' your money, Gus. The U. S. Marshal's got Haines in the office an'—"

After that it is doubtful if even an iron horse's whistle could have made itself heard.

Tubac sat down on the curb outside and had a great belly-laugh at the look he had caught on the nearest guys' faces, and at the look he knew Hi Grab Haines would be wearing when the crowd in that lobby got done with him. If this fly-by-night bank didn't get nailed up for keeps, it certainly wouldn't be *his* fault!

XIV

ATTAR OF ROSES

JONES WENT across the street to the Lone Star Hash House and ordered everything they had on the menu. *This* was an occasion that called for drinks; but the saloon, he'd heard, was run by a cousin of Ike Shallet, and you never could tell with a breed like that *what* might go into your tumbler! Tubac was taking no chances.

He ate with relish and kept an eye on the bank. "Sure doin' a land-office business over there," he remarked to the fat proprietor; but the man wasn't interested in any bank but his own, and he kept that in his pocket.

Tubac felt downright pleased with himself. Run him off of Horse Prairie, would they? Move him out of the country, eh? He guessed this would teach them a lesson! Shove him around like a mangy dog, would they? Trump up forged leases and—

But across the street the bully-puss guard, Sugar Dip Carlin, was closing the brass-bound doors of the bank, and Tubac gave over reviewing his wrongs to enjoy another good belly-laugh. The great run was on, and the street out in front of the Stockman's Bank was crammed with a mob of irate citizens, all yelling and cursing at the top of their lungs and shaking their fists and flourishing ropes and pistols. A soot-smeared hoof-shaper on the the fringe of the crowd started picking up rocks and heaving them toward the bank's ornate plate-glass windows.

When Jones' boisterous laugh was at its most zestful, someone dropped a big hand on his shoulder and, looking up, Tubac saw Mueller; and the laugh fell away from him pronto.

"Don't make no more trouble or I'll lay you out cold," the marshal purred, slipping Tubac's gun from its holster.

"What's the big idear?" Jones demanded. "You can't arrest me—"

"Can't I?"

Tubac temporized. "What I mean is—"

"Not interested," Mueller said. "Come along now—"

"But what *for?*" Tubac cried, exasperated.

"For startin' that run on the bank, that's what!"

"*I* never started it! *Haines* done that when he shut his doors—"

"Come along," Jinx Mueller growled coldly. "You can tell all that to the judge next fall when they bring you up for arraignment."

"Next *fall!* Hell's hinges!" Jones blared. "How'm I gonna hold down Horse Prairie an' keep it away from that land-hoggin' Deckerman claim-jumper—"

"You should have thought of that sooner. C'm on," Mueller grated. "Pay for your grub an' let's amble."

The Stockton jail was nothing to write home about, but it was stout—as stout as bar iron could make it; and Tubac, after one quick glance, knew he was due to spend the summer there unless somebody came to his rescue.

The marshal, he thought, was exceeding his duty, if not

acting arbitrarily and downright illegal; but there was nothing he could do about it unless outside help was forthcoming.

He stared gloomily out of the window and wished the whole push in the hot place. Fine way to treat an honest cowpoke! Lock him up in the jug just for wanting his money! And what in the devil would Blackwater do if he was depending on Tubac to aid him?

Jones stewed and fretted and tramped the floor like a cougar on display at a circus. He used up all his best cuss words and began bitterly making up new ones. But no one came near him—no one; and when suppertime came he yowled for the jailer.

"What're you chipmunks tryin' to do—*starve* me?"

"I ain't been given no orders to feed yuh."

"I'll give you some orders right damn now—" But the man had lounged out to the office again, and Tubac swore in a passion.

A hell of a situation! A *fine pass* this country was coming to when a sawed-off squirt like Jinx Mueller could throw you in jail and forget you!

Jones kicked the bars till he hurt his big toe; then he slumped on his cot in a fury. The whole damn thing was a dirty conspiracy to do him out of Horse Prairie! He had squatted on the Holeman grant, and, since all their efforts to move him had flopped, they had flung him in jail to be rid of him!

It was all that Lot Deckerman's doing—the guy with the elephant memory. He—

Jones' thoughts suddenly scattered. The jailer was coming down the corridor again and—by grab! there was somebody with him!

With a considerable effort Jones got hold of himself and smoothed the scowl off his face. Probably cold-jawed Lot Deckerman coming to offer to dicker or something. He'd grant

103

Jones his freedom, probably, in exchange for his immediate departure with all strings jerked off the Holeman place. He could go duck his head in a jug of sheep dip if he thought Tubac was falling for that kind of gaff.

But it wasn't the Stampede boss at all. It was Haines' chic secretary, Honey Hair! Jones bounced from the bunk with celerity. "Lord love us!" he cried. "Did you come to see *me?*"

Pleased surprise wreathed his face, which had a kind of calf-eyed look coming up; but if Honey Hair noticed she ignored it.

She said: "I didn't come here of my own accord, you may rest assured of that, Mister Jones. Mister Haines sent me over to ask you a question."

"Yah! Haines!" Tubac sneered. "I sh'd think you'd've had all you want of that guy after seein' the kind of cheap crook he's turned out, givin' depositors hunks of blank paper—"

"That was all a mistake, as Mister Haines told you!" flared Honey Hair, pulling her chin up. "He has dismissed the man responsible—"

"Isn't that just lovely! An' where do you think the guy'd have gotten that ink if Hi Grab hadn't give it to him?"

"I did not come over here to discuss bank clerks and ink," declaimed Honey Hair haughtily; and Tubac gave her a nasty grin.

"What *did* you come here for? No—never mind! Don't answer! I can see through a window as quick as the next; you come over here to ask me to get Haines loose of that counterfeitin' charge—to get me to say that bum money he's got was put in his bank by Yours Truly."

She stood there looking up at him from under her long, dark lashes. "Well, yes," she admitted finally. "But how did you know?"

Jones grinned down at her sourly. "Because I know Hi

Grab Haines an' his kind," he sneered. "They're all alike—tough as hell when things come their way, but when the goin' gets a little uppish they yap like a cactus-clawed coyote. They got no more sand'n a stack of hay; an' if you had any pride about you you'd've quit the old thief long ago. It fair makes me sick t' see a nice girl like you—"

"Time's up," grumped the jailer, scuffing his boots; but Honey Hair said imperiously: "Just a moment, please!" and he slunk back out of sight again.

Then Honey Hair turned her warm smile on Tubac, and when the scowl had got off his face she said: "Let's forget our differences, shall we? I'm sure we could be good friends if we tried. It seems so silly in a little place like this, everyone being on the outs all the time. You know," she said, "I just *love* to ride, but there's never anyone to ride with here; and I have to work all day at the bank . . ."

"Shucks," Jones said, "I got plenty of horses. I'll fetch you in one next time I come by."

"And you'll come to see me sometimes, when it's moonlight, and—"

"Sure! Ridin' by moonlight's my specialty! You know, Sue," Tubac said boldly, "I never thought much about girls till I met you. Seems like most of 'em's such a all-fired nuisance, allus peckin' at a man, houndin' him t' do this, that an' the other thing. All the time tryin' t' make him over jest as quick as they git their rope throwed on him. But gosh! You're *diff'rent!* You know, I could like you a heap!" he told her.

Tall and slim she looked in the dusk where she stood just beyond the door's grating. He could not be sure, but he thought she blushed; and then she said, real soft and shy-like: "I'm—I'm sure I could like you, too . . . if you wouldn't be so hateful."

"Reckon I *am* kinda mean," he nodded. "I suppose I been

brought up to it, sort of. It's a tough ol' world an' I never had no one to learn me better. Never had no mammy nor pappy; leastways, if I did I can't recollect 'em. Except I growed up pretty wild-like. But I can read an' write!" he said proudly. "Never had no one to learn me it, neither, but I've sure picked up a lot of big words—in minin' camps mostly. Some of them high-powered promoters can sling talk jest like a dictionary. I seen a fella once up at Ryolite—"

"Yes," she said, "but I'm afraid I have to go now. But we're going to be friends hereafter?"

"You bet!" Tubac said; and she gave him her hand—reached it in to him through the grating. Tubac took it in both of his own and, with the pulse in his throat beating wildly, kissed it, reverently—the way the fellows did in the books he had read.

Honey Hair gasped, and he looked up quickly. He was sure she was blushing this time; but she gave him a tremulous smile through the bars. "And you'll tell the marshal all about that money?"

Tubac let go her hand as if its touch had burnt him. "So *that's* all you come here for, is it?"

"Oh! You think—"

"Never mind!" Jones snarled. "Go on—clear out! An' you can tell the ol' thief I ain't bitin'!"

"I hope you're not going to be hateful again. After all," said Honey Hair reproachfully, "I find this just as distasteful as you do. Do you suppose I enjoy asked favors of people? If you had tried to meet Mr. Haines halfway when he wanted to patch up your troubles, none of this could have happened; but no—you had to start that run on the bank, and now they have put you in jail for it. Oh, Tubac," she cried, catching his hand again, "it's such a little I'm asking—and it's all for your own good, really."

Tubac scowled, but he let his hand stay in hers. "Well, what is it you want me to do?" he said gruffly.

"Just tell the marshal about that money—"

"An' get sent up to Siberia for life? Humph!" snorted Tubac. "I can see myself doin' it! You can tell that dang ol' widow-robber his little scheme ain't—"

"But it's not 'his scheme,' " protested Honey Hair. "It was *my* idea; and I had an awful time trying to convince him. But when I heard they had put you in jail—"

"Did you say this was *your* idea?"

"Of course! Mr. Haines didn't favor it at all, and Mr. McGillis declared you could rot in jail before he'd ever lift a hand to help you—but I finally talked them around to it."

"Well, go on," Tubac grumbled, shaking his head. "What's the deal? If you went to all that trouble for me, I guess the least I can do is hear it. But I'm not givin' up Horse Prairie. So if that's what they want—"

"Oh, but it isn't. All they want is for you to tell the marshal the truth about that money—I mean, about you're depositing it in the bank yesterday, so the marshal will withdraw that counterfeiting charge. If you'll do that, they will arrange it so you can get out on bail and not have to stay—"

"What good'll it do me to git out that way? If I admit I put bum money in the bank, they'll—"

"But you can tell the marshal how you got the money."

"Hmmm," Jones said. "But how do I know—"

"Mr. Haines is a gentleman, Tubac. His word is as good as his bond."

"I dunno as I'd put such stock in that, either," Jones sniffed; but Honey Hair said in a pet:

"Very well! If you insist on being hateful and humiliating me, after all the trouble I've been to on your behalf—"

"Okay," Tubac growled. "I'll be a s— I'll be a gentleman

if it kills me. Go tell the old thief to start layin' pipe. I'll git him off that counterfeitin' charge—but Gawd help the swivel-eyed sidewinder if he don't fix it so I can get out of here!"

XV

A RIFLE COMES VISITING

So TUBAC TOLD the marshal that he was the man who had put the bum money into Hi Grab's bank. "But how did *I* know it was bum money?" he growled. "I took it in payment of a debt—an' I supposed the guy was a gentleman."

Jinx Mueller eyed him dubiously," he said grimly. "Forty-five hundred dollars is quite a real pile of jack, an' you ain't got the look of having forty-five cents. What would a man be owin' you all that money for? Suppose you bust down and elucidate. I'm not promising anything; but if you don't come clean, by the gods, you'll stay here till hell freezes! Now what about this money? Who's the guy that owed it to you? An' when did he pay you? An' *why?*"

It was a long and, the way Tubac told it, quite an involved story. Boiled down, it summed up to just this: Two-three years before he'd had a small spread in Texas, close to the border; had been raising horses for the army—and doing well at it, too, until one night his place had been raided and half his best stock run off. Revolutionists from across the line, he'd guessed; and a couple of hours later he'd had confirmation of the opinion when a bunch of Rurales had come larruping up, hot on the trail of the bandits. They were dusty and lathered, and their uniforms of dark gray whipcord were brush-clawed and grimed from the chase.

A hard-looking outfit and eager for the kill; and their Capitan—a great ox of a man with a fierce mustachio—had demanded he give them fresh horses. Though not too keen on the notion, a number of considerations had swayed Jones. The Rurales' mounts had been pretty whipped out, but they'd been first-class broncs in anyone's language; and besides, though Jones knew the company had been out of bounds, he had wanted the horse thieves captured. So he'd nodded agreement, and the Rurales had cleaned out the last horse he'd left and gone off driving their own broncs.

"What!" exclaimed Mueller incredibly. "You let 'em clear out with nothing to prove—"

"Well, they seemed to figure they'd ought to have remounts."

"By the gods!" Mueller snorted, and looked at Jones slanchways. "You ought to be bored for the simples!"

"Aw—" Tubac said. "I ain't quite that daffy. The Capitan, he give me his note for the stock—said if they didn't git back to return it he'd send me the money mañana."

"Tomorrow, eh?" sneered the marshal. "Well, tomorrow never comes, you yap! So that's how you got shut of the horse business, was it?"

Tubac sighed lugubriously, then gave Jinx Mueller the nod. "I allus try to remember I'm a Christian—"

"Hell!" Mueller said. "You can't be a Christian an' live in this country—not long! But you still ain't explained how you got that fake currency."

"If you'd shut up a spell I could git to it. Like I was fixin' to tell you, before them Rurales galloped off with my stock, this Capitan feller he give me his note, an' when he seen me next time he paid me off for the horses he took."

"How much?" said Jinx Mueller skeptically.

"Five thousand bucks!"

Jinx whistled. "An' you expect me to believe you hung onto that money all this time?"

"Ah—hell! He only give it to me two months ago."

Mueller just stood there and gaped.

"Well, it's the truth," Tubac grumbled.

"I reckon it is—sounds a heap too loco to be a invention. Three years ago he grabs off your stock an' two months back he pays for it! You oughta collected some interest."

"I did. Five hundred bucks' worth. The deal was for forty-five hundred."

"An' you're claimin' this queer you been shovin' is the dinero this Capitan give you?"

"Honor bright," Jones muttered.

"Hmmm. What did this Rurale bird look like?"

"Well," Tubac considered, "I'd say he was tall, angular, gaunt an' some quick. Dark an' deep-set eyes. Square chin—was in need of a barber's services last time I saw him."

"An' where was that?" Jinx asked him; and his stare had gone suddenly intent.

"Across the line—below Naco."

"Below Naco, eh?" said Jinx thinly. "An' what were you doin' down there?"

"Ain't sayin'. But that's where I seen him."

"An' what'd you say his name was?"

"Chacon—" Tubac stopped short, and a startled look wrinkled his cheeks up and abruptly his eyes bugged like saucers.

"Yeah," snarled Jinx, and started swearing. "You've sure played hell all round, you have! Chacon! *Augustine Chacon!* You bonehead! That's guy's no more Rurale than *you* are! Next to Joaquin Murrieta, he's the toughest Mex who

111

ever rode a bronc! There's twelve thousand reward on that hombre's pelt, an' you give him horses to ride off on!"

"But," protested Tubac, after a long silent moment, "he was dressed like a Rurale, an' the rest of 'em called him Capitan. How was *I* to know diff'rent? An' all them others was dressed like Rurales—"

"In stolen uniforms—prob'ly stripped off their owners' carcasses," Jinx Mueller came back at him caustically. Then he glared at Tubac bitterly and finally shook his head.

"Well, I guess your yarn's straight," he said dourly. "I don't hardly guess *no* man would make up a spiel dumb as that is. They got a place for fellas like you, Jones—got the walls all padded with blankets."

But Tubac said nothing. There was nothing to say. He'd been taken in like a booby. It had probably been Chacon who had stolen his broncs, then had borrowed the rest to catch them with. The Mexican had swindled him proper!

It was a greatly sobered Tubac who, by the light of the moon, turned into the Charleston trail that night, once again headed back toward Horse Prairie. He felt lower than a centipede's belly. "They oughta feed me sheep dip," he growled; and Calliope nodded reluctantly.

But where had Chacon got hold of that counterfeit money? If reports of the wily outlaw held any truth, he had been much too busy hiding his trail from the star-packers to have any time left over for turning out counterfeit currency. So it must have been given him—or else he had stolen it from some place. There were a lot of real likable things about that Chacon; there was a lot of Robin Hood in the bandit, which made Tubac inclined to think he had worked for that money —had earned it for satisfaction rendered.

But to hit on the name of the outlaw's employer was a deal too much like hunting the proverbial needle in the haystack;

and Tubac shook his head gloomily. For all *he* knew the spurious money might well have been printed in Mexico. He rather inclined to the belief that it had been.

Of course he had thought first off it was some of Haines' work—or maybe a sideline of the Stampede crowd with Haines' bank handling the distribution.

With a scowl Tubac dismissed the whole business and turned his mind to thoughts of Honey Hair, who certainly was something to think of. That is not to say that his thoughts were *serious*. He might be the boneheaded yap Jinx had called him, but his head wasn't solid ivory! None of your frills and furbelows for *him*—there was not going to be any gal's apronstrings hitched onto Tubac Jones, by grab! Not on your mortal tintype!

But she was a danged nice critter just the same, and he guessed bee trees was plain gall beside her; however, he wasn't going to think of her seriously. Too many guys had got hooked in that fashion—and some of them right good poker players, too. Girls were all right if you just kept your head. Galin' was like eating striped candy, Jones thought, only you could take a dose of salts if you got too much candy; whereas if you got too much girl— Well, anyway, she was as handsome as an ace-full on kings, and the prospect of taking her horseback riding some night was nothing to get the creeps up about.

Which was more than you could say for some around here. Take Mrs. Ike Shallet, for instance. She was boss of the Ladies' Sewing Circle, rodded the Ladies' Uplift Society, was Chairman of the Stockton Mission for Backward Children and told Eli Clump, the new Methodist preacher, what kind of Methodism he'd better preach if he wanted any shekels in his box of a Sunday.

Which was all right, Jones guessed, if you weren't married to her. But she looked to him like a Heart and Hand product, or a Jim Brown woman sent West on approval. And such times—not often—as she'd roped Ike into taking her to town meeting, the sheriff's face had been solemnly reminiscent of a tenderfoot trapper misskinning a skunk.

Nope! Marriage was a fine institution, but for somebody else—not Tubac! No frills and flounces for him, by grab! Nobody, of course, would ever think to mention Honey Hair Lambert in the same breath with Mrs. Ike; but Honey Hair was young yet—who knew what she'd turn into by the time she got to Mrs. Ike's age! Which was where the element of chance came in, and the world was chancey enough as it was without taking on any problems like that.

After a while Jones thoughts turned to Blackwater, and he felt a twinge of conscience for having neglected his pardner this way. Of course he hadn't really neglected him, because the note he had thought Blackwater had left him was the reason he'd gone off to town in the first place. But it was uncommonly odd where the gambler had gotten to. Either the Stampede outfit had dragged him off some place for some dark purpose not yet disclosed, or else they'd plain out and out killed him and fed his remains to the buzzards.

He would have to scout around a little and see if he couldn't turn up some clue that might give him a hint to Blackwater's fate. You couldn't plan much unless you knew how things lay. And that was the trouble with this fuss. A fellow never knew from one minute to the next where he'd be, or how, in a few seconds. It was like hunting the North Pole with a pocket watch.

And then he was cresting the last low rise that lay between himself and Horse Prairie. Kneeing Calliope up the shale-strewn trail, he wondered how Winch Face and White-Eye were coming along with the chore he had set them, and if they had got all the horns off yet, and if the Stampede

114

crowd had come calling again to kidnap the rest of his outfit.

And then he was pulling up, startled.

The buildings were all in plain sight just below him. He saw no lights, but none were needed to show the strange bronc standing hitched to the porch rail—or the man's dim shape in the rocker. Moonlight showed those things well enough and, thinking perhaps it was Blackwater, Jones was gathering breath for a loud halloo when a sudden thought closed his mouth tightly.

It would be just as well to take a look around first; and he eased Calliope off the trail. In a thicket of brush he got out of the saddle and folded the stirrups up over the horn and then tied the reins to it likewise. Then he gave the wise horse strict instructions and started him off with a slap on the rump; after that, covered by the sound of its hoofbeats, he raced along below the ridge for a way and came up on the house from the back of it. He could hear Calliope entering the yard from the lane, and he examined his six shooter carefully. On tiptoe then he made for the porch, rounding the side wall's angle just as the man creaked out of the rocker. Jones saw the glint of a hiked-up rifle as the man crouched forward to peer toward Calliope, saw him stiffen, heard him curse—and knew he'd discovered the empty saddle. Then moonlight disclosed the strange rifleman's face.

It was Snaggle-Tooth Potter!

XVI

WHAT-A-MAN POTTER

"Lose somethin'?"

Potter jumped as if a scorpion had kissed him. But he didn't whirl. He knew better than to pull anything brash like that, caught as he'd been with that ready rifle. He stood as if a blight had struck him, not batting so much as an eyelash.

"What you takin' off on—the Petrified Forest?"

It seemed as if Potter must have heard the old rhyme about sticks and stones. At any rate, he was taking no further chances. He stood like a caught fence-crawler, with his face gone white as a wagon-sheet.

Jones strode round the angle of the porch and stopped just short of the Stampede foreman. "All right, coyote. Heave that blunderbuss off in the brush. Now heave that six-shooter after it. Got any Arkinsaw toothpicks hid on you? Any forest razors or cavalry sabers? If you have, you better get shucked of 'em, 'cause the first time you look at me cross-eyed I'm goin' to work you over like a fresh-skun hide."

"That's all I got," Potter muttered.

"Turn around then. I wanta see your mug. Hmmm. Could

stand a few changes. Nose needs straightenin'. Wouldn't hurt none to file them teeth."

"Now look!" Potter blurted. "I come over here t' do you a friendly turn."

"What I figured when I saw that rifle. Any time I want to get buried, I'll call in a undertaker, Potter. Start oratin'."

Snaggle-Tooth glared.

"Uncork yourself 'fore I kick a hole in you."

"You wouldn't believe me on a stack o' Bibles!"

"Somethin' in that," Jones admitted. "Better get that chin waggin' anyhow; if you don't I'm liable to unhinge it."

Potter emitted a few oaths. Then he shrugged. "Like I said, I come over here t' do you a favor. Heard your pardner'd lit out—"

"Try again."

Snaggle-Tooth bared his yellow fangs.

"You Mormon-faced old whelp," Jones said, "you talk an' talk quick or I'll give your crowd somethin' to remember me by. You won't be the first guy I've pistol-whipped—when it comes to remodelin' looks I'm a expert."

"Ahrr," sneered Potter, "you ain't got enough savvy t' git out o' the rain! Don't try to scare *me!*"

"I won't try," Tubac said, "I'll *do* it!" Flame streaked out of his six-gun, and Snaggle-Tooth Potter clapped both hands to his ears and howled as if a Paiute had scalped him.

Jones saw the blood on his fingers and grinned. "Now, you danged old lizard-eater! For the last time—you gonna talk or ain't you?"

Potter flayed the night with a rush of wild oaths, but he choked it off short when Jones lifted his pistol. "What'ya wanta know?" he snarled; and Tubac said:

"I want the name of the guy that hired you to kill me. Was it Hi Grab Haines or Lot Deckerman?"

"Who said anyone hired me?"

"Start talkin'."

"I'll hev the law on you fer this!" Potter raged, scarily patting his ears with his neckerchief. "I'll—"

"You'll wind up on a shutter, by Judas, if you don't unhobble that tongue mighty quick," Jones predicted. He thumbed back the hammer of his six-shooter. "Want me to part your hair with a bullet?"

"Here—wait!" Potter spluttered. "It was Lot—Lot Deckerman!"

"Yeah?"

"It *was*, I tell you!" wailed Potter. "It was Lot! He said: 'I've got five grand you can blow yourself on quick's you bring me that squatter's ears—'"

"Ears, eh?"

Snaggle-Tooth did not like the way Jones said that; nor the calculating glint that he saw in Jones' eyes.

"Ears . . ." repeated Tubac softly, and peeled back his lips in a wicked grin.

Potter's blood turned to water. His knees got to knocking so badly he had to catch hold of the porch rail to keep himself upright. "Wh—what're you fixin' t' do?" he gasped; and his eyes nearly popped from their sockets when Tubac fetched a knife from his belt and began vigorously to whet it on a boot sole.

"I think I'll mail him *your* ears an' collect that ransom. 'Tain't hardly likely he'll guess they're not mine, d'you reckon?"

But Snaggle-Tooth Potter, the tough Stampede foreman, had fainted dead away.

XVII

"NEXT TIME I'LL TRIM YOURS!"

HORSE PRAIRIE in the morning light lay shimmering in its dust and heat, lay rimmed and girded by its cliffs and canyons, cut and slashed by trails and gullies, with the great cloud-shadows sweeping its floor and dappling the sun's gold with cobalt. Horse Prairie, whose tawny bosom had echoed the wild tremolos of a thousand tribes, whose canyons had damned the harsh crescendos of bandit guns and owlhoot laughter, whose creeks had run with men's hot blood, and were likely to do so again by the signs.

On the railed veranda Sam Holeman had built sat Tubac Jones with his horse-thief hat pulled over his eyes, a limp cigarette in the corner of his mouth. He was thinking—very briefly—of Potter, and of how last night it had taken three brimming buckets of horse-trough water to bring the man out of his vapors. And of how, when brought to, the Stampede foreman's teeth had chattered as he'd promised, if allowed to slope, that his shadow never should darken Horse Prairie again. On that understanding Jones had let him go.

"An' good riddance!" he muttered, scowling. Then, suddenly bending forward, Tubac peered across the wind-swayed grasses. "Hmmm! Now who in hell is *that* comin'? Get rid o' one an' git stuck with another. Sure ain't Blackwater—don't ride like him nor ain't built the same. Hmmm. Comin' from town, but it ain't Ike Shallet—don't look like Jinx Mueller, neither. Now who in Tophet . . . Could it be McGillis? Don't seem like he'd be pasearin' out here; an' yet— Well, *Judas Priest!*"

Jones jumped from the rocker with a startled curse, ducked into the house and came tearing out with an extra six-gun and a .50-70 rifle. There was no mistaking that gaunt figure now. He knew that loose-shackled rider as well as he knew the palm of his hand. Yonder visitor was Augustine Chacon!

"Ah! Aha!" cried Chacon, reining up with a grin. "Did you remember me then, amigo, or were you looking for somebody else to ride by?"

With the rifle held ready in the crook of his arm, Tubac scowled up at him bitterly. "The Great Chacon!" he said with a display of his teeth; but the Mexican was not offended. In his great Chihuahua hat and crossed cartridge belts, he made an impressive figure as he lounged in the saddle, smilingly twirling a corn husk cigarro. He guffawed jovially at Tubac's black scowl. "A-a-ai-hé! You have the face of the mad dog, compadre. Is it that you bemoan those caballos you sold me?"

"It's the broncs you *stole* I'm thinkin' about, an' that wad of bum money you handed me—a fine trick to play on a poor man! I thought you robbed only hidalgos."

"That is true," Chacon nodded, and puffed a few smoke rings through which he eyed Tubac amusedly. "Only the rich and the arrogant—that the poor may have food for their bellies."

"Do I look like a rico?" snarled Tubac; and the Mexican roared with laughter.

"O-ho!" he chuckled. "Do I look like a capitan of Rurales?"

"No!" Tubac flared, and spat in the dust. "You look like that lobo, Augustine Chacon, who would steal the pennies off a dead man's eyes and pay his just debts with fake money!"

"Basta—enough!" grated Chacon, every hair of his mustachio bristling. "Do you call me a—"

"You bet your damn boots! A thief an' a swivel-eyed liar!"

"For less than that I have killed men, Gringo! Have a care with your words lest I—"

"Bah!" Tubac sneered. "You sure showed your true character when you passed me that bum money. Don't blow your chest up at *me!* You're nothin' but a rag-tail robber—a thievin' ladrone—a two-bit bandido who would sell his best friend down the river!"

Chacon, dark with anger, peeled back his lips and, swelling up like a chuckawalla, grabbed out his six-gun and cocked it; but Tubac laughed in his face.

"Go ahead!" he jeered. "You got the drop—what you waitin' on? Go on an' shoot, you pelado!"

Before matters could be carried any further, they heard a rattle of hoofs coming pounding over the ground, and a wide-eyed, quirt-slinging rider came tearing around the harness shed corner and pulled up his horse in a cloud of red dust.

It was Winch Face, trail-smeared and dripping with sweat; and he shouted:

"By God—I've found *Blackwater!*"

Like a man stumbling out of a trance, Tubac said: "What's that? You've found Blackwater? *Where?*"

"Stampede south line camp," Winch Face gasped. "They got him in a root cellar—leastways, I *guess* it's him! They've sure as hell got *someone* there!"

"Who is this Blackwater?" Chacon said, laying a hand on Jones' arm.

Tubac shook him off with an oath and started for his horse on the double. But Chacon came lumbering after him, and as he shook out his rope the Mexican said: "Señor! This Blackwater—who is she?"

"Dadblast it! I told you! Blackwater Bill Nameloh—my pardner! Can't you understand plain English?"

Chacon grunted under his breath, but he waited till Tubac had roped Calliope and was leading him out toward the kak-pole. Then he demanded: "What does she look like, this Blackwater?"

"Go 'way!" Jones said, picking up his saddle. "Anyone that would pass a guy bum money—"

"Did *I* know this money was no good?" cried Chacon, scowling. "You think I take no-good money for job if I'm knowing it? *Carajo!* I weel cut that gringo's heart out an' stuff hees damn' toes in hees gullet!"

"Go along an' do it then," grunted Tubac indifferently; and suddenly let loose of the trunk strap he'd been jerking, to whirl and eye the steeple-hatted outlaw intently. "Here— just a minute," he muttered. "Did you say a gringo had give you that money?" And Chacon ducked his head pronto.

"What gringo?"

"That no-good son of a lizard, Lot Deckerman—"

"Deckerman!" Tubac cried; and Augustine Chacon bared his teeth in an ugly smile.

"Sure! She's hire me for rustle cattle from this ranch—long time back; five-six year, mebbe. I steal the cattle, but she's no pay me. Aguacil she's got after me and I'm leave this co'ntry—*whisht!* like the whirrelwind! Not see this gringo pig long time. In Naco I see heem and she's give me—"

"Mean to say that five thousand you give me come from Deckerman?"

"Si—es verdad, amigo. She's give me ten t'ousan' pesos—Americano," Chacon nodded, with his eyes watching Tubac brightly.

"Hmmm," murmured Tubac reflectively. Then a cold grin flicked back his lips and he said: "I don't savvy what's brought you here now, but if I was you, compadre, I'd see the old rip an' make him pay me all over. That dinero he give you was fake—make-believe money—no good for hell. He took you for a dumb palado an' paid you off in fake money."

The outlaw with a scowl ran his tongue over his lips and appeared to be thinking it over. Tubac finished his saddling, got his Winchester out of the harness shed and shoved it beneath the stirrup leathers. Then he climbed up into the saddle. "You an' White-Eye git on with that work," he called out to Winch Face; "an' if anyone comes pokin' round, you give 'em a tune with your rifles."

"You goin' after Blackwater?"

"Never you mind about me," Tubac told him. "Rope yourself out a fresh bronc an' git back to your job like I told you."

He turned to Chacon. "Make yourself at home, compadre. The house is yours."

"Mil gracias, amigo," said Chacon; but Tubac could see he was still thinking how Deckerman had tricked him. The wolf look still glittered in his deep-set eyes, and the smile on his lips was a grimace.

"Well, take care of yourself," Tubac told him, and kneed his horse into the trail.

It was well after noon when he came in sight of the Stampede outfit's south line camp. The buildings shimmered in the stifling heat, but there was no sign of anyone round them. The corrals were empty and no smoke curled from the chimney.

Nevertheless Jones kept a wary eye peeled. Lot Deckerman was slippery as slobbers, and this might very well be a trap he had baited.

But the place really was deserted. There was nobody around, not even the cook; but Winch Face was right—at least partly. There were plenty of signs in the root cellar that the place had been used for a prison. One of the Stampede punchers must have seen Winch Face. They had gone to hide Blackwater elsewhere.

Jones climbed back into his saddle and sat there a while grimly scowling. He could try his luck at tracking, or he could ride on over to the Stampede's main ranch. They'd hardly chance holding Blackwater there; but on the other hand, if the prisoner was Blackwater—and it probably was—trailing this bunch held even less likelihood of profit. There were tracks of four broncs leading out of there. That meant three guards were keeping tabs on the captive. And, unless Tubac was misjudging Deckerman plenty, they would not be run-of-the-mill ranch hands; they would be Texicans—hard case hombres; hired guns who would have all the answers, and then some. No point trying to track such guys. Easier to scratch your ear with your elbow.

He might just as well drop over and pay Lot a visit. Might *better*, in fact. He'd a thing or two he wanted to show Brother Lot—something Winch Face had got him out of Chacon's saddlebags while the outlaw was watching Jones saddle.

It was close to supper time when Tubac rode into the Stampede headquarters, and the hands were all down at the horse trough giving their mugs the once-over. There were five of them, rough-looking jaspers; and every man jack stared plumb hostilely when Tubac pulled up and said howdy.

"What in thunder do *you* want?" asked a buck-toothed fellow, dropping his hand to his pistol. "Say! Ain't you that guy Jones—"

"Yours Truly," Jones grinned. "Where's Deckerman?"

"An' what would *you* be wantin' with him?"

"That's for Lot to find out. I didn't come over here to jaw with hired hands. Tell him to rustle his hocks an' git out here."

Their scowls got tougher. But one of them set up a yowl for Deckerman, and pretty soon Lot poked his head out the door.

"What the— Hmmm!" he said, as his glance fell on Jones. Then a crafty glint lit up his eyes. "Git down an' rest your saddle," he invited. "Decided to sell out, have you?"

"Not on Tuesdays," Tubac said dryly. "How d'you like the looks of your range boss now?"

"Who's that? You talkin' about Potter?"

"Ain't got more'n one, have you?"

"Hell, I fired that fool las' week," Lot said; and Tubac nodded sardonically.

"Good thing you did. Be gettin' you in trouble one of these days if you hadn't. Told me you was collectin' ears now, so I brung you over a couple. *His,*" Tubac added, and tossed Lot the package Winch Face had got him off Chacon's saddle.

Deckerman peeled back the handkerchief skeptically, then dropped the thing as if he'd grabbed a rattler, and his eyes looked like holes burned in a blanket. The punchers round him stared with slack jaws while Tubac laughed derisively.

"What's the matter?" he jeered. "Are you *scared* of 'em?"

Then he reached down a hand and tapped Deckerman's chest. "Next time you monkey with me, you danged crook, I'll come over an' trim *yours* for you—savvy?"

XVIII

LUCK TAKES A HOLIDAY

NIGHT, LIKE A black cat's overcoat, hemmed the town in a murk of shadows, but the saloons were still doing business, and the screeching of fiddles and stamping of boots came drifting out on the wind as Tubac hitched Calliope to a snorting-post fronting the largest.

He pushed his way to the crowded bar and rapped on it with his six-shooter. Some of the talk sloughed off a little, and men turned to look as the word got around. There were still a number of citizens who had not yet clapped eyes on Jones; those who had gave him cautious nods. But Tubac treated them all alike. "Step up," he said, "the drinks are on me," and tossed a handful of gold on the bar.

Then he turned his guile on the fat and aproned bartender, being careful to let enough others hear to make sure the story got round. Lugubrious of look and with husky voice, he said: "Too danged bad about Deckerman, ain't it?"

"What's that?" asked a man to the left of Jones; and the barman pricked up his ears.

"Why ain't you heard? About his trouble with Chacon?

Hell," Tubac snorted, "I s'posed it was all over the country by now."

"Chacon?" said the barman. "You mean that slat-sided Mexican bandit?"

"I don't mean his uncle," Tubac told them. "Shucks, I reckon I shouldn't of mentioned it, but I s'posed it was common gossip round here."

The bartender's eyes had a glint in them. "If it is, *I* ain't heard it. What about 'em? Deckerman didn't catch him, did he? Gor!—there's twelve thousan' bucks on that hombre's pelt . . ."

"Chicken feed!" sniffed Tubac contemptuously.

But the barman was not to be put off like that.

"But what'd you mean when you claimed it was too bad about Lot?"

"Well," Tubac drawled, "I suppose it's all of a pattern with the high jinks Banker Haines has been playin', but I was sure surprised to hear Lot had mixed up in it. Seems," he said, raising his voice a little, "Lot—five or six years back—hired Chacon to steal Sam Holeman outa the cow business. I guess he would 've done it, too, only after the first six months or so Chacon got a mite anxious to collect some of his money. But Deckerman told him to go to hell, an' to make sure he did, went an' sicked the law on Chacon, an' he had to hightail it across the Line. Coupla weeks ago Chacon come back quite sudden, an' it seems like Lot didn't want no trouble about it. He paid the Mex all the money he owed him—but he paid off the debt with *fake* money."

"Ho, ho!" laughed the barman. "That was pretty good, wasn't it?"

"You think so?" Tubac stared at him coldly. "Well, I can tell you this much: Chacon has swore to get even—an', all things considered, I expect he will do it. Wouldn't surprise me at all if he raided this place—cleaned this town out lock, stock an' barrel."

And while they were looking uneasy, Tubac played his trump. He said, looking square at the barman: "Guy that'll pass bum money around will lap sheep dip with a snake. What guarantee have you got that he won't unload some of this spurious money on *you?* Why, you prob'ly got your safe full now! By grab, if *I* was in business around this locality, I'd damn sure look mighty careful every time I took a bill off that outfit!"

And with a wave of his hand and a sour grin on his lips, Jones left them to think it over.

The night was getting on to being pretty nearly morning, and why a woman should be abroad at such an hour was neither clear nor understandable, but as Tubac was passing the mouth of Boggs' Alley a scream brought his horse up sharply.

Jones sat stiff in his saddle, eyes peeled and head canted, listening. And it was not too easy hearing, either, for there still were upwards of ten fiddles screaking, and some fool puncher in a whisky baritone was mournfully yodeling "The Dying Cowboy" out back of Cherokee's barber shop.

Then the scream came again, and there was no mistaking it this time. Tubac came out of the saddle with a six-gun gripped in each hand. The scream had come from the alley, and Tubac went plunging into it.

Muzzle flame spurted from the cloying gloom and lead shrilled whining above Tubac's head.

He drove two swift shots at the flash and jumped to the left to flatten swiftly against the wall; and that way he stood, breath held, listening hard. But all he could hear was the jouncing of his heart and the dimming echoes the guns had

131

churned up; and he concluded finally that the fellow had slipped away from him.

Still, you never could tell; so he stayed where he was, stiffly motionless, for another five or ten heartbeats while his narrowed stare searched the felted gloom. Then, easing the cramp from his muscles, he took a forward, investigating step. Took another. Took a third—and dropped flat as the hidden man's gun belched flame again.

Flat on his belly, Jones loosed three shots; and through their din he caught the diminishing clatter of the fellow's departure.

With a disgusted oath Jones jumped to his feet and, sheathing the emptied gun, got a match from his hatband and struck it.

The leaping flame in that inclosed space showed a crumpled form. A woman's! Face down she lay, not ten feet away. Holstering his extra gun, he hurried forward, hands cupping the match. Reaching her, he dropped the match and turned her over. Then, cautiously lifting her to a sitting posture, he got a knee braced behind her back and struck another match.

A startled oath burst out of him and he almost dropped the match from his hand. "Great guns!" he muttered. *"Honey Hair!"*

There was a rent in her blouse and her eyes were closed; and Jones in a panic thought she must be dead—thought perhaps he, himself, had killed her with one of the shots he had fired at her assailant. With the match gone out, he was stooping to lift her when something hard bored into his back and a cold voice told him gratingly:

"Reach—*an' reach quick!*"

XIX

STARTLING DISCLOSURES

TUBAC REACHED—but not for the stars.

That voice was the sheriff talking, and Jones was getting plumb fed up with being shoved around. From now on things would be different. Live and let live was his motto; but when that failed to get desired results, it was time for a change in tactics. He was a lazy-seeming guy, this Jones; but let him have something to hurry about, and lightning hung fire by comparison.

Tubac spun on his bootheels, and his grabbing right hand caught the sheriff's gun by the barrel. It glazed, but the slug tore into the ground; and with a sudden swift twist Jones had the gun away from him. In the next split second the butt of it took Sheriff Ike Shallet square in the face, and, with a wheezy sigh, he came down like an empty tent.

Jones didn't stop to commiserate. Heaving the sheriff's gun through a nearby pool-parlor window, he caught the swooned Honey Hair up in both arms and bolted.

He went by back alleys, cursing the clatter of kicked cans and the treacherous roll of slithering bottles, but making quick time despite all that.

He was breathing hard as he came out into the street again, not twenty yards from the front of the dark and bolted bank which was Honey Hair's daytime habitat. She came to just as he reached it, and with a moan blinked open her eyes.

"Oh—Tubac!" she cried, and hugged him tight. But Jones wasn't hunting no truck with women; and, anyhow, this was no kind of time for imitating that guy Lochinvar. He got loose of her clutch and grabbed for his breath while he took a quick squint at their chances.

One thing was certain. Shallet had very probably recognized him, and as quickly as he waked up to his hurts there was going to be proper hell to pay! He would be numbered with the loafer wolves now and be any man's meat for the shooting. It would be "Git Jones!" and no holds barred! It was high time to shift his picket pin; and he certainly would have done it, right then and there, the Holeman place notwithstanding, except that Honey Hair caught his arm with great urgency and, hysterical, half sobbing with fright and shaking like a leaf, she cried:

"Oh Tubac! *He has found me out!* What shall I do? What *can* I do? He was *wild!* He—he says I must marry that terrible Carlin or—"

"Hey—whoa up! Lemme get this straight," growled Tubac, unwrapping her arms from about his neck, his narrowed glance raking the shadows nervously. "*Who's* found you out, an' what's he found, an' why all the—"

"Oh! But you don't *understand!*" wailed Honey Hair. "It's horrible—it's just too vicious for words! He came in and found me writing my attorney and—"

"Hey! Haul up! Lemme get my breath—I can't make heads or tails of this rigmarole! Who found what an'—"

"Mister *Haines,* of course! He came up to my room at

the Breyer place—all the Breyers have gone off to Flagstaff —and he saw—"

"Mean to say you're all alone in that house?"

"Yes—and he—Oh! I'm so mixed up I— Anyway, he came straight in without so much as a knock, and the first thing I knew, there he was right behind me, reading my letter and—"

"Now look," Jones said, catching hold of her shoulder and shaking her. "I judge you're in some kind of a jam; but I can't make heads nor tails of this jumble. Git hold of yourself an' start all over. Tromp down on the soft peddle an' git a firm hold on the bridle this time. You kin count on me till hell freezes, ma'am; but I got to know what you're talkin' about."

"But of course!" She brushed the golden hair back off her face and took a long breath. "I'm acting like a silly goose! I'm afraid Mr. Gillcrist was right after all; I should have stayed home and let them handle it. But I'd thought perhaps if I was on the spot . . . But I keep forgetting—you don't know Mr. Gillcrist—"

"I'm beginnin',", Tubac mumbled, "t' think I don't know beans. Who's this Gillcrisp?"

"Gillcrist, Gillcrist & Pattersom—my *attorneys*."

"But hell's hinges! What does a nice young girl like you wants go gittin' mixed up with a bunch of danged—"

"Oh, dear!" sighed Honey Hair desperately. "I'm not telling it very well, am I?"

"Might help," Tubac grunted, "If I knew who you was wrastlin' with in that alley—"

"Oh! That horrible *Carlin!*" Honey Hair shivered. "Mr. Haines says I've got to marry him."

"Who? That ape? The hell you have! You ain't—"

"But Mr. Haines says he'll send me to State's prison—"

"Aw—no," tucked in Tubac sardonically. "Mister Haines is a *gentleman*."

Honey Hair gulped, and through her long lashes she peered up at Tubac reproachfully. "If you're going to throw that up to me—"

"Well, you can't say I didn't warn you," Jones couldn't resist reminding her; but Honey Hair's shoulders got to shaking again, so he put out an arm to steady her and was considerably amazed to find how snugly she fitted into it. Why, she wasn't any bigger than a wasp, seemed like, and—

"Say!" he muttered, remembering Ike Shallet. "We better be gettin' a wiggle on. Wait here till I get a horse for you—"

"Oh, but—"

"No buts about it! You're going out to the ranch with me, an' the quicker we get there the better!"

So they rode. They put the town far behind them, and a cool wind whooshed through the long waving grasses, and gradually Honey Hair recovered her composure so that when the dawn found them in sight of the ranch Tubac had the whole story. And an amazing tale he found it. He kept eying her slanchways and shaking his head; it was just like something in a book, he thought. It didn't seem possible somehow.

But he knew Honey Hair wouldn't lie about it.

Her name was Susan H. Lambert. She was from Wichita Falls, and her mother had been Sam Holeman's sister!

XX

THE OUTLAW CODE

It was all quite simple.

Sam had never been much of a letter-writer, and he and his sister had never got along—had been on the outs for a good many years; and though he was her own uncle, Honey Hair had never clapped eyes on him. Her mother had died a couple of years back, and since that time she had been a typist, eking out her existence as one of the tiniest cogs in the great firm of Gillcrist, Gillcrist & Pattersom; that is, up until the red-letter day when Mr. Gillcrist, Sr. had called her into his private office and, with a great many impressive throat-clearings, had carefully shut the door.

He had wanted to know if she had any relatives living in Arizona. She had shaken her head. "But that middle name of yours—Holeman . . ." And then she had remembered Uncle Sam, who lived on a ranch at Horse Prairie or some place; and Mr. Gillcrist had beamed like a Chessycat.

"Why then, if you can prove this relationship, I believe you are really in luck, my dear," he told her. "You may come in for quite a tidy sum—quite a tidy sum indeed, I think. He seems to have owned practically all of Horse

137

Prairie and, while I've no idea whether the place is a town, a ranch or just a wild stretch of river bottom, it would appear to be negotiable, else that bank would not take so much trouble."

The Stockman's Bank & Mortgage Loan, of Stockton, Arizona, had advertised for heirs of Sam Holeman, apparently deceased. Mr. Gillcrist, dexterously parting the tails of his coat, had sat himself down and written them, describing the firm as legal representatives of Sam Holeman's only surviving heir. Fortunately he had not disclosed either the name or the sex of that heir; and when the bank failed to answer the firm's third letter, Sue had taken matters into her own hands and forthwith, quite heedless of Mr. Gillcrist's expostulations, set out for Arizona.

She had felt, she said, that there must be something about the matter which was not quite aboveboard. Messrs. Gillcrist and Pattersom had wholeheartedly shared this opinion. They declared something should be done about it—through legal channels, of course; but Sue had been adamant. She intended looking into things personally; and she had packed up her grip and gone.

The bank had advertised. It had neglected to answer the firm's letters. Therefore, were there any skulduggery afoot, the bank must be mixed up in it. She put up at the Stockton House as Miss Sue Lambert, of Joplin, Missouri, and secured a position as typist and public stenographer. Within a month Mr. Haines had asked her to be his secretary; and that was how matters had stood when Tubac breezed into the picture.

"I thought you were just common riffraff," she said, blushing prettily; but Tubac tossed it off grandly.

"As one horsethief to another," he grinned, "I'll admit it—but don't call me that in public."

Until the advent of Tubac, she had not got the least bit of evidence. Then things had started happening in a hurry. Mc-

Gillis, Lot Deckerman and Sheriff Ike Shallet had closeted themselves with Haines in his private office, and the drone of heated altercation had gone on for hours; and then abruptly, the next day, the Stampede lease had appeared in the files of the Holeman Estate.

Still, although that was plainly evidence of something, it was not evidence of intention to defraud the Holeman heirs, so Sue had kept her mouth shut. The time for denouncing Hi Grab Haines and Lot Deckerman might come any day; but she mustn't step in ahead of time.

Then had come Marshal Jinx Mueller, and, with the run on the bank, the Stampede crowd had got the wind up. They'd had a big session with Haines this afternoon, and Sue guessed something was due to pop when the bank opened up the next day. Yes, they were going to open again; they had got in a big load of money from Phoenix so they could weather another run if one started. And Jinx Mueller had gone off in the stage for Tucson.

But it was the big coup hatched for the morrow that interested Tubac greatest—something to do with the Holeman Estate, though Honey Hair hadn't learned what.

"Easy as rollin' off a log," Jones said. "They aim to marry Sam's place to Carlin; then Carlin'll step out, and they'll have it!"

"But it was only tonight that they learned who I was—"

"Don't you never think it, ma'am!" declaimed Tubac. "Them polecats prob'ly been watchin' you from the start. Lay you ten to one they been into your luggage an' know all about you. How many times you written those law fellas?"

"Only twice."

"Only twice!" echoed Tubac, and groaned. "Didn't you know the first thing they'd do would be to look into who you was writin' to? You got to realize that Lot Deckerman an' Haines, between 'em, just about run this end of the country.

139

Heck! a man don't dast even spit around here without one of them two says it's all right!"

He rasped a hand across his unshaven jaw and chewed at his lip reflectively. "Go over that part again where Hi Grab Haines— Hold on! Take it from the time you was writin' that letter."

Honey Hair kind of shivered, but she pulled her chin up bravely and once more recounted the details leading up to the plight in which Tubac, fortunately, had found her.

She had been in the sitting room of the Breyer place writing to Mr. Gillcrist, setting down the salient features of local events and asking his advice, when all of a sudden she had looked up and found Hi Grab Haines staring down at her. She had tried to snatch up her letter and hide it, but Hi Grab had been too quick for her. He had already read it across her shoulder, and with a sneer he put it in his pocket.

"So you're the Holeman heir, are you?" And the malevolence in his thin, gray laugh had rooted her in the chair. "Well, well," he had cackled. "How would you like to spend a few years at Yuma? Free grub and no rent—State's prison, you know. They've a special ward for your kind of women. House of Correction they call it." And Sue had cringed from the look in his opaline eyes.

"I think you understand me," he had said in his mincing voice. "What I say in this town carries weight—a great deal of weight. I could call you a strumpet, and no amount of testimony from other sources would do you a bit of good around here. I could say you had stolen things out of the bank, or out of my private safe, for instance. Or I might say you had connived at burgling the place with that shiftless squatter—that Tubac Jones. And I could clinch it by testifying you— But the point is this: You may save yourself all this notoriety and unpleasantness by marriage. Oh no! Not with me," declaimed Hi Grab Haines fleeringly. "With Mr.

Carlin, the new Stampede foreman. I give you till morning to make up your mind."

Tubac muttered something under his breath, and it was lucky for Hi Grab he wasn't within reach. "An' then he left, eh?"

Honey Hair nodded.

"An' then you started for the livery stable?"

"Yes. I was so terrified I couldn't even move for the longest time. Then I thought of you! I was going to get a horse."

"An' where was it Carlin stopped you?"

"By the butcher shop. He was standing there under the awning. It was dark there, and I didn't see him till he put out a hand to grab me. Then I ran! I must have screamed when I realized he was chasing me. He was cursing terribly and calling me all kinds of vile names. I ran around back of the pool parlor—I was frantic! I had no idea of direction at all! He must have sneaked up that alley. Just as I came opposite the back of it, he sprang out of the shadows and caught me."

"Yeah! The dirty hound! Something's going to catch *him* right soon, or I'm a chimpanzee's gran'maw!"

Tubac scowled. "Isn't Carlin the name of that lop-eared hound what used to be Hi Grab's bank guard?" And when she nodded, Tubac snarled: "I'm goin' to make that sidewindin' son—"

"But, Tubac," cried Honey Hair, clutching him, "whatever shall I *do?* My coming out here won't stop Mr. Haines from telling those horrible lies, will it?"

"No," he growled, "I reckon it won't. But—" He broke off to raise his head and sniff. "Say, look—you wait here, will you? The ranch is just off there in the hollow an', while I don't look for any trouble, mebbe I better look around a little before I take you down there." And he reined off into the brightening light before Honey Hair could protest.

Not that he thought there was really any danger. But it was an old Jones adage that an ounce of prevention was worth a ton of cure, and he didn't aim to take any chances. Values had undergone a considerable change, and Horse Prairie couldn't rightly be regarded now as anyone's place who could grab it. The ranch was Honey Hair's heritage from Sam Holeman; it was all Ol' Sam had left her—all she had in the whole wide world. And no danged whoppy jawed sidewinder was going to take it away from her!

And then, as the bright sun flung its new-risen glory across the vermilion peaks, he came in sight of Sam's headquarters ranch and jerked his horse up with a curse.

His nose had not deceived him. Of all those grand old buildings Sam had built, nothing remained but a tottering, askew chimney and a handful of smouldering uprights. All else was a red and black bed of ashes.

In the dark of night Stampede had struck, and this was Lot Deckerman's answer!

XXI

HOT LEAD CHORUS

As Tubac sat there viewing the ruins, a loudening rumble of hoofbeats came sweeping fast from out of the west, and Tubac, bleak-eyed, yanked up his rifle and laid it across the pommel. But he saw quickly enough who the horseman was. It was Winch Face; and his pockmarked face was black as Old Nick when he stopped his big bronc on its haunches.

"We're cleaned!" Winch Face yelled. "Cleaned slick as slobbers! That Stampede crowd struck the herd not two hours back, an' there ain't enough beef left t' put in a basket! White-Eye's dead, an' all them strays we dehorned an' branded has been druv plumb over Apache Leap!"

"Over the Leap!"

"Yes!" yelped Winch Face, and cursed like a Cornish trooper.

"So they wanta play rough, do they?" Tubac snarled; and Winch Face tucked in: "Too rough for me. Just give me my time an'—"

"I'll give you somethin' all right," Jones swore, "if I catch you tryin' to run out on me! This is a finish fight an' *we're* goin' to finish it. C'm'on," he yelled, and spurred back up the trail. But when they came to where he'd left Honey Hair, there was nothing but the empty trail to greet them. It was mighty plain what had happened. Sue was gone, but there was plenty of sign to tell why she hadn't waited. She had had no choice in the matter. Four men had come spurring out of the brush and had gone, taking Honey Hair with them.

"What's the—who'd they grab?" asked Winch Face, frowning.

"Hi Grab's secretary—Honey Hair Lambert; an' I don't need to do no figgerin' to see whose Eye-talian hand's behind this! I'll make him wish he never was born!"

But saying and making were two different things, and Tubac soon began to realize that the four who had kidnapped Honey Hair were a long way from being amateurs. The trail petered out within ten horse lengths, and they quartered for a long half hour before they finally cut the men's sign again. Someone in that outfit was slicker than slick when it came to blanking out horse tracks; but Tubac had learned from experts. By the time the sun was four hours high, they were entering a country of upthrust buttes, of mesas and up-and-down canyons. By all the tokens they were getting close.

"Can't be over ten minutes ahead of us," muttered Winch Face, peering about nervously.

Tubac nodded. "Better keep your eye skinned for a ambush. Like enough they've—" The rest was lost in the racketing crash of a rifle whose slug cut the band neatly off of Jones' hat. They were in a kind of gully-like swale, and the shot had come from a flanking hogback just ahead and a bit to the right of them. You could see the smoke drifting up from the brush, and Tubac, as Winch Face jumped from his saddle, grabbed up his rifle and peppered the place. But the dry-gulch artist had moved from the spot, and his next shot ricocheted from the horn; and Tubac got off the horse pronto.

"Watch 'im!" he growled at Winch Face. "Blast hell outa the place next time he shows. When you quit he'll pop up an' I'll nail 'im!"

"Yeah, but—Hell's unholy hinges!" yelled Winch Face, squinching his belly as flat as the rough ground would let him. "Run yore eye acrost that arroyo we jest come outa!"

Jones took a quick look and cursed. Two riders were coming up out of the gulch back there. Yellowstone and Kettle Belly—his two old friends of the poker game—and they were coming hellity larrup.

"They ain't stagin' no rescue—"

"Never mind," snapped Tubac. "All the more reason why we got to wind up this—"

The sniper up front took another shot at them, and Winch Face emptied his rifle. At that last shot the drygulcher's head came above the brush and sun-glint shone from his rifle. Tubac's Spencer vomited flame.

"Well!" Winch Face said admiringly. "There's one sourpuss won't be troublin' his cook for cawffee t'morrow mornin'!"

"C'm'on," Jones muttered, swinging into his saddle. "Time to be lightin' outa here."

"Yuh know what I think?" demanded the re-write man, spurring his bronc alongside. "I think that hombre yuh jest handed a harp to, an' them two gunslicks that's larrupin' up from behind, is three of the four what run off with yore woman."

"My own idea, exactly. They've split. The fourth skunk's foggin' off with Honey Hair while these three've dropped behind to—"

"Great Caesar's ghost!" breathed Winch Face, clapping in his spurs. "Them fellas must be ridin' whirlwinds!"

A backward look showed Tubac that Kettle Belly and

Yellowstone had indeed closed the gap between them by a distance which was anything but reassuring. Also, they had come within fair rifle range, as spurts of dust all about the hoofs of their galloping broncs began to give ample testimony.

When they'd crossed the crest and put the ridge between them and the guns of the two Stampede men, Winch Face wanted to know how Jones expected to look for sign so long as the pair kept after them.

"Can't," declared Tubac curtly. "We got to knock them coyotes out of their saddles. No—wait! We'll drop the horses; that'll serve just as well. When we come to that clump of trees just ahead, we'll ride straight through, then drop back an' give 'em a tune from our rifles."

"You can," Winch Face said generously, "but me, I'm foggin' right along. There's a big dust comin' down that gulch on the right."

Tubac swore, for so there was, and this would not be a safe place to linger when the men who were making it debouched in this gully. There must have been eight or ten in the bunch; and the two friends spurred for the timber. Just beyond it, to the left, another canyon opened; and with a quick call to Winch Face, Tubac swung Calliope into it. "Look there!" he cried. "Them tracks! That'll be Honey Hair an that swivel-eyed Mormon in charge of her!"

It seemed a pretty logical conclusion. "If there's a good high rise any place in this canyon, I'll sure whittle down the odds, by grab!" Tubac muttered. And a half-hour later they saw one—a rise built just to order. They rode for it, plying both quirt and spurs, as though to give the impression they were hunting the quickest way out of the country. But after they crossed it they slowed down some while. Tubac squinted for cover. There was a rubble of boulders at the foot of the slope, and just beyond, screened from the rise by the towering rock shoulders, there was a break in the canyon wall on the right, and a trail angling up toward a plainly visible plateau, with the tracks of two horses deep-scoring it.

"There's the way that highbinder went with Honey Hair an'— But first things first," grunted Tubac, and forthwith slipped from the saddle, throwing his reins and, with his rifle, crawling back through the boulders till he found a good spot giving a view of the rise. "We ain't got no time to be messin' around. When that bunch of horsebackers skylights themselves, give e'm everything you got in the barrel," he told Winch Face. "An' don't be afraid of hurtin' 'em!"

The clatter of hoofbeats rose to a crescendo. The rise showed suddenly black with horsemen, and Tubac waited till Winch Face quit firing, not caring to waste any bullets. Two men left their saddles at Winch Face's salvo, while another swayed wildly and clutched at the horn. Then Tubac came to a knee and let go. The foremost rider—and it looked like Potter—flung his arms out and pitched head first from his horse. His hat came off and rolled down the slope, and the man rolled over four or five times, too. But Tubac wasn't watching him; he was pumping lead at men still in their saddles, firing coolly, maliciously, placing each shot to the best advantage.

All was confusion at the top of the divide. Curses and shrieks resounded wildly, mingling with the crashing echoes of saddle guns. Hoarse yells tangled with choking screams; and then, like magic, all the riders were gone—all who had managed to stay in their saddles, gone in the dust of retreating hoofs.

Tubac sprang to his feet and rejoined Winch Face, who was already nervously up in his saddle and anxious to be gone. "I got an idea buzzin' around in m' head that I reckon you'll be some interested in," he muttered as Tubac swung up beside him. "I think I know where that gopher's headin' for. There's an old abandoned mine up this way that used to be right much of a diggin's five-six years ago. It's up by Black Point, not four-five mile from where we are now. Be a first-rate place to hole up a pris'ner; an' I betcha that's where he's takin' her."

"Reckon you could find it?"

"Why, I know this country like the seat o' my pants—"

"Then what the hell are we waitin' for?"

But there weren't any horse tracks, nor any horses, showing when they reached the mouth of the old Black Point diggings.

"That don't mean nothin'," Winch Face muttered. "Nach'-rally he'd hev enough savvy t' rub out his tracks. There's a cavern, just inside a ways, where they could leave the horses. I'm bettin' we'll find 'em in there, too!"

And so it proved. They were looking over the sweaty broncs when three shots rang out so nearly instantaneously as to seem one monster roar of sound. Winch Face dove for the side of the cavern to get himself out of line with the entrance. But Tubac fired from his hip at the flash; and at once a shriek joined the gyrating echoes, and Jones went instantly dashing forward to make sure the man wasn't shamming.

He wasn't. It was Sugar Dip Carlin. He was very dead.

"Better keep our eyes peeled," Tubac muttered. "Might be another of these lobos round here some place. Where you reckon they've hid Sue?"

Winch Face was already off exploring, and his voice, a moment later, came back with a sudden shout. "By grab," he yowled, "there's a door back here in the tunnel wall—padlocked, too!"

Tubac, hurrying up, struck a match. The door was a stout affair bound with strap iron and heavy bolts. No shoulder was going to break it in. "Quick," he said. "We got to find a axe or a pick—"

"Here y'are!" Winch Face panted up with a pick, and Tubac, taking it, stepped back and swung at the door with all his strength. But the planks must have been extra thick. The pick point was embedded in the door, but the match Winch Face held in cupped palms didn't reveal any cracks.

"Well, here's for it," Tubac growled, dragging out his sixshooter. "If them lobo've been sneakin' after us, I reckon they'll jest have to hear it. We ain't got no time to play ring round the rosie. We got to be gettin' outa here before them vinegarroons trap us here. Go fetch our horses in an' pick yourself a place on the tailin's where you can keep an eye on the trail leadin' up here."

As Winch Face's bootsteps went echoing off, Tubac put the muzzle of his gun to the padlock and fired. The lock fell apart, and he yanked the heavy door open. Then with his left hand he struck a match, and all but dropped it with a startled oath as he stared astounded at what its flame disclosed to him.

Honey Hair's glad cry he had expected. But never for a moment had he thought to find Blackwater here. With an arm around Honey Hair's shaking shoulders, he sheathed his gun and shook Blackwater's silently thrust-forward hand. "By grab," he said, "I figured they'd killed you sure!"

Bill grinned in his quiet gambler's way. "They aimed to—just hadn't got around to it proper. There were a few little legalities they wanted me to fix up for them before they put a bullet through me. Real lately they've been trying the starvation program on me—I don't suppose you've got any sandwiches in your saddlebags—"

"No—but we got to be gettin' outa here," Tubac broke in, suddenly remembering the gang he'd driven to cover. They'd be getting pretty close by now; not for a second had he thought to have discouraged their pursuit except temporarily. "If they've so much as hurt one hair of your precious head," he told Sue Lambert, "I'll—"

"I'm all right," Honey Hair assured him, squeezing his arm.

"Then—"

Winch Face's shout cut into his words. "They're a-comin'! An' brother, they are comin' fast!"

They rushed to the tunnel entrance, crowding up behind Winch Face where he lay behind the mine dump. They followed his pointing hand. Tubac took one look and swore. They were trapped. The Stampede crowd was down below, and every trail was blocked.

Honey Hair looked, and her face went white. With a hardy courage she choked back the scream that rose to clamor at her lips. Lot Deckerman's bull voice shouted: "If you fellas will give up peaceful—"

"Come an' get us!"

"I can do that, too," declared Deckerman. "This's your las' chance, boys. We got dynamite down here, an' I'd jest as lief use it as not."

"Go ahead then," Tubac cried. "Won't none of *us* grab a holt on your shirt-tail. Fly at it!"

Honey Hair touched him nervously. "He'll kill us—Oh, Tubac! I'm so frightened. Don't you think perhaps we had better give up?"

"Not on your tintype! He'd kill us anyway if he got the chance. Only one thing t' do with skunks of his stripe—fight 'em to the last danged toenail!"

Blackwater, who had gone back into the mine tunnel, reappeared with an armful of rifles. Jones and Winch Face each grabbed one and examined it to make sure it was loaded. "Our trouble's going to be bullets," Tubac muttered. "Couldn't you scout up some cartridges, Bill?"

"All we've got is—" The rest was lost in the crash of Winch Face's firing. A startled curse came up from below. The battle had commenced in earnest.

Presently Blackwater Bill called Tubac aside. "They're getting closer, son. How long you reckon we can keep 'em off?"

Tubac scowled. "Not much longer—but cut out that 'son' stuff. You talk like you was Methusalem or somebody. I wish," he said, scowling around morosely, "there was some other way of gettin' outa this mess."

"Well, there is," Blackwater mentioned. "I've heard Potter and Carlin talk of it; but the trouble is we'd have to expose ourselves to reach it—to reach the start of it, I mean."

"Yeah, an' someone'd have to stay behind to keep them devils from swarmin' up here an' seein' what we was up to."

"I would deem it an honor to play that part—"

"What do you take me for?" Tubac snarled. "If anyone's goin' to—"

Winch Face cried: "Them lobos is clearin' out! What the hell d'you reckon they're up to?"

Jones and Blackwater rushed to the rim for a look. Deckerman's crowd *did* seem to be leaving. They were slithering back through the brush toward their horses, and even as Tubac looked several of them got into their saddles and spurred away. "It's a trick!"

"Wait—what's that?" demanded Blackwater pointing. "Looks like . . . I swear it *is!* It's the Stampede ranch buildings; Someone's set them afire!"

"C'm'on," Tubac muttered. "Now's our chance to make for that trail!"

"There it is," pointed Blackwater a few moments later. "Pretty steep. You reckon your young lady can make it?"

151

"Of course!" cried Tubac with a rough man's scorn, assumed, perhaps, to cover his embarrassment at hearing Honey Hair described in such fashion. "Lead on—"

"Quick!" Winch Face bellowed. "That crew's comin' back!"

They went scrambling up the perilous trail so steeply angling the almost sheer wall of the cliff-like butte that was called Black Point. And they had nearly made the top when a shout and the quick flat cracking of rifles proved that the Stampede men below had sighted them. The whine of lead was like wasps humming, and the shrill wild screams of ricochets were enough to shiver a man's grip loose—but they made it; and Tubac hustled Honey Hair back from the rim where the Stampede lead couldn't reach her.

"Them thievin' sons is right on our heels," called Winch Face, darting back from the rim. "They're swarmin' up the mine dump now." He broke off at a sudden wild crashing of rifles, went sprinting back and peered over the edge. He let out a screech. The rifle dropped from his hand with a clatter. He spun half around and dropped head first to the rocks below.

Honey Hair screamed, and even Tubac's cheeks went gray. He said: "That's what we'll get if we ain't damn careful! I think, Bill, we—" Then he saw Blackwater's face and stopped.

Blackwater said: "I guess we're done," and pointed wearily down the sloping trail they had figured to take. There were horsemen on it; they were climbing upward, the late sun flashing from the barrels of their rifles. "We're blocked behind and in front as well."

A rifle banged from the rim behind them, and Tubac felt Blackwater, at his side, suddenly stiffen. Honey Hair screamed and Tubac whirled, dropping his rifle and snatching out his belt gun. Flame spat whitely from its leveled muzzle, and Kettle Belly, who was just in the act of hooking a knee over the rim, let go all holds and dropped from sight.

Honey Hair, passing Jones, rushed to the side of the groaning Blackwater; but Tubac dared not look round to see to his partner. He had all he could handle if he was to keep that bunch below from rushing them. His only plan was to shoot each time one of the Stampede gun fighters showed—shoot until his cartridges were gone. It would not be long.

The crashing of rifle fire below the rim had risen to the loudness of a full-pitched battle. He could not understand it until he remembered Chacon. That was it—Chacon! He had told the outlaw how Deckerman had stung him with all that fake money, and Chacon had come to pay off the score!

Just as Tubac reached this comforting conclusion, the clatter of a horse's hoofs rushed from the rear. "Don't shoot!" cried Honey Hair as Tubac whirled. But Tubac, just then, was incapable of shooting. He was struck dumb and rooted by sight of the man striding toward him.

Jinx Mueller, the U. S. marshal!

"Fly at it, boys—clean 'em up," Mueller said to his men, and came over and grabbed Tubac's hand and shook it. "All is forgiven," he said with a grin. "That tip you gave me was straight from the shoulder. It was Deckerman an' his crowd that was passin' that money—I got a confession outa Haines. He gave the whole show plumb away. McGillis has pulled his freight, but I got Haines an' Shallet put away nice an' snug, an' we just caught Deckerman down below. Hear that? Firin's quit. But say! Who's this?" he said, jerking a thumb toward where Blackwater lay with his head in Honey Hair's lap.

The gambler looked up at them. His lips framed a tired, pale grin. "Just Ol' Sam Holeman, Marshal, come back to die on the ol' stampin' ground."

"Sam Holeman!" Jinx exclaimed incredulously, and Tubac

stared bug-eyed at the man who had been his pardner. "Sam Holeman's been dead—"

"A lot of folks figured so," murmured Blackwater drily, "but old John Slaughter could have told you different."

"I'm afraid," Jinx said, "if you're really Sam Holeman I'll have—"

"Don't bother," smiled the gambler tiredly. "I ain't got long enough to make no never-mind. Man don't get over a forty-five slug through his chest at my age. I'm about done, I reckon. But I'm glad I came back. McGillis, Lot Deckerman an' Ike Shallet framed me on that Benson stage deal. Been botherin' me . . . got so I couldn't sleep nights. Had to come back an' even the score. Call that pardner of mine over here."

Tubac moved round to where the old man could see him. "I'm sure sorry—"

"Nothin' to be sorry about; we all have to go sometime," Sam said. "I've had my fun. Wisht I knew who it was fired them Stampede buildin's."

"It was Chacon an' his gang. We sweat like hogs tryin' to nab 'em," Mueller grinned, "but the whole danged crew got away."

"That's what I call justice," Sam sighed. "It was Deckerman an' McGillis that was makin' that fake money Sue's been tellin' me about, Marshal. You'll find their press an' the rest of the stuff down there in the mine where they been keepin' me prisoner. Was goin' to leave me there to rot, they said, unless I signed over all my holdin's to them."

His voice was getting pretty faint. But he beckoned Tubac closer. "When you an' my niece figurin' to get hitched up?"

Honey Hair blushed. But she said defiantly: "We're not, Uncle Sam. Mister Jones wouldn't marry the best girl on earth—he's made that very plain to me. 'Not even if her teeth were paved with gold!' "

"Aw—I was jest talkin' to hear my head rattle then. Any-

154

ways, I didn't know there was any girls like *you!* Daggone, you ain't goin' to hold that ag'in me, are you?"

"Well, but—"

"C'm'on," Tubac said. "We got to talk this over."

"You'll make a mighty fine pair," Old Sam said. "Don't want you to disappoint me. I'm leavin' you each a half-interest in Horse Prairie, an' I'd sure hate to see the old ranch split."

WILDCATS
OF TONTO BASIN

For Jack Byrne
Who has turned out—
in our humble estimation—
one of the finest Westerns
we have seen in years!

CHAPTER I

THROUGHOUT that South-west country one name stood head and shoulders above all others; a cognomen as far removed from most men's names as Timbuctoo from Ararat. That name was *Bufe Telldane*, whose owner was considered an enigma—the wastelands' greatest mystery.

All across New Mexico, West Texas and the Panhandle, tales of this man's daring furnished the raw materials for after-supper yarning round the camp-fires of the cow camps. His record smacked of legend, his deeds were things oft-told in whispers; but cursed or blessed he went his way, at once a danger and a warning.

There were those who swore by Bufe Telldane; a great many more swore at him—though seldom in his hearing. The tales were contradictory, the rumours considerably more so. You might be regaled at Laughing Horse with accounts of incredible daring, with tales of an open-handed generosity wellnigh unbelievable; at Roaring Fork the accounts of this man's doings would make your stomach turn cold and crawl.

You might be told he came of a high-placed frontier family; that his father had been a ranger, his mother a Governor's daughter—yet there were those who as stoutly held him the scion of backland brush-poppers, and cursed every time he was mentioned. It was apparent that no man knew. Nor could any say with certainty which town had been his birthplace, or what his education. You could not guess by his speech or dress, for these like his manners varied.

A*

A corpse-and-cartridge occasion in a gambling dive at El Paso had first brought him into notice. The cartridges had been his—and the corpses, too! He'd departed without much leisure. And wisely; for people didn't know him then and would just as lief have swung him.

The victims had been prominent men.

He was a riddle that defied folk's solving, though all the country tried its hand and shook its head with dark scowlings. On one thing, though, most thinkers agreed—there was a woman behind him somewhere; only a woman could set a man, they said, to carving such hell-bent trail.

Concerning Telldane, however, there were a number of fundamental truths that were subject to little twisting. During the late war, as boss of transportation, with the pay and rank of a major, it was known that the man had got supplies and munitions through where no other could have done it. Five hundred mules had been dumped on him and the hardest task of the war; he had done it swiftly, ruthlessly and unforgettably, without comment, without parley. He could laugh in the face of bullets; often chuckled when there seemed no out—it were as though he invited death, defied it. Before the war, as scout under old Al Sieber—as Chief of Scouts under Crook, he had been repeatedly commended for bravery. He spoke Spanish and Apache fluently; was a crack shot, an all-round cowhand. As a deputy sheriff he had been the scourge of bad men. So much was known all across the land; the rest was garbled, uncertain. It was this rest' that kept folks talking.

It was hotter than hell's backlog and the pair in the creaking buckboard alternately cursed and mopped their faces. A wild, forbidding stretch of country, this land below the Mogollon Rim; a region of rugged, untrammelled beauty that a man might travel a right long way to find. These men had travelled a right long way—all the way from Texas—but were not come hunting beauty.

An oddly assorted pair, these two; as alike in many respects as two peas in a pod, yet different as night from day in others. They had the same kind of lean, long-fingered hands, the same coiled-spring restlessness of movement; each had a cold, gun-barrel stare—the same edgy interest in his backtrail. But one was tall and one was short; the first was burly, the other slender. One was dressed like a dude and affected a dude's polished manners; the other was dressed like a saddle bum and had no manners at all.

Guy Topock, the tall man, kept twisting his thick red neck about, hardy eyes showing the glint of approval. But the other, Andy Cooper he called himself, kept his bony face straight front, nursed the rifle in his lap and malignantly cursed the heat, the flies, and ' this goddam excuse fer a road! '

Topock chuckled. " Plenty room for your elbows round here, boy."

Cooper, unloading a stream of tobacco juice, allowed there had better be and announced himself fed up with being shoved around. " Reckon the ol' coot'll bite? How the hell much farther *is* it? "

" Three-four mile, I reckon. Great grief! Twenty mile ain't far to go to get set up in the cow business——"

" Not if he sets us up, it ain't. It's a hell of a ways to go for——"

" He's set others up. Leastways we've heard he has."

After a while Cooper said: " Hope this damn rig

holds together that long. Heat's enough to fry you!
Reckon them rims'll stay on? "

Topock sawed on the reins and took a look. Climbing back he said: " They're still on now; but was we
to run 'em through a creek———"

" Creek! " Cooper's laugh was rasping. " That's
good! 'Creek,' says you! Why, the goddam frogs
can't even swim! Where you goin' to find a creek? "

The tall man shrugged. " Reckon that's Wildcat
Hill off there? Damn 'f I don't think it is," he said,
squinting. " They said it looked like a mountain, an'
if that ain't a mountain———"

" 'Cordin' to the Payson crowd," Cooper said, " the
best graze Kerwold's got is on that hill—and," he
added, with a hand rasped across his jaw, " the on'y
strings he's got on the place is that he's always used it.
'Tain't his at all. An' it's open to filin'———"

He looked at Topock thoughtfully.

Topock grunted; then suddenly swore. " Lookit
that! Barb wire! By God, look there—goes clean
out of sight! "

Cooper eyed the wire bitterly. " Thought you said
this was free-grass country———"

" By God, I thought it was! First I ever heard of
any wire round here—must be somethin' new."

They scowled toward where the fence was building
off yonder across the hogback. Topock wheeled the
horse. " Let's go over there an'———"

" Hey! Look out fer that stump! " Cooper yelled;
but his cry was a trifle tardy.

Topock, belatedly observing and trying to avoid the
stump, swung the horse too far to the left—too far
and much too abruptly. The ruts of the road held the
wheels like a lock, and the left shaft, with the animal's
weight brought hard against it, snapped.

It fell with a clatter; and Cooper swore. "That's done it! By——"

"Aw, dry up!" Topock snarled, and got out. "There's some junk in the back of that seat there. See if you can find some wire——"

"Go find it yourself if you want it! *I* ain't fixin' no busted shaft in this heat—nor helpin', either! You busted it; go on an' fix it."

Topock's cheeks came round and his eyes jabbed a hard glance at Cooper. "All I asked——"

"I know what you asked——"

"Never mind!" Topock scowled, and looked across toward the fence-stringers. "I ain't so all-fired anxious to work up no lather, neither. There's some guys that'll do it——" He lifted his voice: "*Hey, over there—you birds by the fence! Wanta make some quick money?* That'll fetch 'em," he told Cooper and, leaning against the buckboard, rolled himself a cigarette.

They saw one of the distant men detach himself from the wire and start toward them. "You can tell," Cooper sneered, "that guy's a hired hand by the hurry he's in to get here."

Topock grinned. "Prob'ly one of Kerwold's riders. Lazy crowd, from all I hear—treated too good, I reckon."

"When Kerwold sets us up," Cooper said, "what-say we hire two-three of 'em away from him an' work the bloody hell out of 'em? Set the rest a good example an' show Sam Kerwold how a real cow outfit works——"

"Say-y! You know what?" Topock muttered, squinting across to where the new-fangled red wire was going up. "Bet that ain't none of Kerwold's bunch at all! Lay you ten to one them fellas is nesters—

betcha Kerwold don't even know about it! "

Cooper looked again and swore. " By the looks of this specimen I'd say you're right."

He referred to the man coming toward them, a heavy-set fellow with a stomach that was putting on weight. Stoop-shouldered he was, with a weathered face criss-crossed by wrinkles, with gnarled, rough hands and a four days' stubble of whiskers.

" From what I hear," Cooper muttered, " Kerwold's just the kind to lallydaddle round an' let a bunch of sod-turnin' riffraff move in on 'im."

The man from the fence came up with a good-natured, " Howdy. Havin' trouble, boys? "

" Damn shaft busted," Cooper growled, ignoring the greeting.

Topock said: " Reckon you could fix it? "

The man rasped a hand across his cheeks, eyed the broken shaft, then looked at them and nodded. " Expect I could, like enough."

" Get at it then," Cooper growled at him. " Be money in it for you if you can make it hold. This part of the Flyin' K range? "

The stoop-shouldered man looked around and nodded. " Have to go back to the wagon a minute an'——"

" How long'll it take to fix it? "

" Won't take long. You boys in a hurry? "

" Kind of," Topock answered. " How far off's the ranch? "

" Not above four mile, I reckon. Lays over behind that hill a piece."

While the fence-stringer pointed, Cooper's uncharitable glance took in his faded overalls, scuffed boots with their run-over heels, cheap shirt and sun-faded, floppy-brimmed hat. His own garb was not much better, but with an oath he spat across the single tree. "Damn nesters are comin' in everyplace."

The fence-stringer appeared to consider the remark. He said mildly, "That so?" and then, with a shrug: "Well, I'll get over an' fetch my cutters an' get you boys fixed up."

Cooper, biting off a fresh chew, copiously splattered the harness-tugs. He said loud enough for the departing man to hear: "If there's one breed of critter riles my bowels, it's the stinkin' hoeman tribe!" and spat again for good measure.

Elsewhere, and some hours later, twilight's obscuring haze bent down across the desert and concealed the backtrail of the solitary horseman who had just come jogging out of it. Peering forward into the shadows of a wooded valley, this man sat motionless as a carven image; then, afterwards, turned his blue roan into a dry-bottomed wash that went angling upward into the timber's higher reaches.

He was bronzed, this man, baked dark by the glare; a tall, high-chested hombre with a tough and rugged face harsh-whipped by wind and weather. He rode stiffly in the saddle and probed each inch of the gloom-curdled way with a reticent, careful watching. Close acquaintance with violence had bred this care deep into him, and experience had confirmed its need.

At full dark this rider sat hunkered on his boot heels high up in the green-clad hills, stare lost in the smoke of his camp-fire, a cold pipe gripped in his teeth.

From the tumbled slopes at his left a stream lifted felted melody. The night was damp with an earthy smell and chill with the down-sweeping breeze lifted off the yonder crags that, like a saw's edge, blackly etched themselves against the shine of stars.

The fire burned low. Neither blaze nor pipe was replenished.

Perhaps the rider dozed.

His chin was against his chest and all the lines of his face were loose, relaxed, when the gun's report laid its flat, sharp challenge across the night.

The man's tipped head came instantly up; the embers' glow showed his eyes alert and bright as steel's cold glinting. Like that he stayed for still, crouched moments.

Fog lay in the hollows now. It sparkled on his hat brim and was pale across his shoulders, wetly beading his rifle where it lay on the ground within quick reach of his hand.

For half a dozen heart-beats his shape held the embers' glow. Then he came, cat-soft, to his feet and eased himself back out of it. He took the rifle with him and, with features set like a mask, he got upon his saddled horse and for some further moments sat there with the track of some sombre thinking grimly re-shaping the lines of his cheeks.

This thinking determined his actions; all his impulses were subdued to its need. From out of the north that shot had ripped; it was eastward that he turned the roan. He sent it that way slowly, with a flexing of his knees.

A scant two miles lay behind him when a tightened rein stopped the horse. Indian-still, intently grim, the man eyed the wink of lights coming out of a platter-like basin. A ranch lay there, or some cross-roads hamlet.

It did not attract him, apparently, for he was turning the roan to round it when a second horse moved from the tree gloom.

A man's voice said: " If you're riding down to the

store I'll ride with you."

"An' if I ain't?"

"But you are." A cold mirth ran that answer. "Of course you are—because why should a trail-tired hombre be passin' up a store an' lodgin' at one o'clock of the mornin'?"

CHAPTER II

COLD TURKEY

IF the old man heard what Cooper said, he gave it no attention. He had reached the fence and was starting for the wagon hitched a little way beyond, when Topock growled: "You might 'a' waited till the fool got out of hearin'."

Cooper sneered. "Hell! I never seen a squatter yet with enough peck to make a dungbug hustle."

He settled himself more comfortably and commenced paring on his fingernails with a long-bladed knife from his boot top. "Trouble with you is, you worry too much. Too damn careful. Too soft—that's what the matter is with you! It's why you won't never get no place. Hell! If it hadn't been for me——"

Topock snorted.

"I'll be runnin' cattle a long time after toughness has got you planted." He grinned at Cooper wryly. "*Your* trouble's packin' that stunt too far. One of these days——"

Andy Cooper grunted. "Horse hocks!" he sneered, and eyed his nails admiringly. "Horse hocks an' sparrow dung. I'll be pavin'——"

"You'll be pavin' the road to hell," Topock said, "if you don't quit bein' so contrary."

The old man returned with his wire-cutters. He released the horse from the buckboard, led it off a little and tied it. Picking up the broken shaft he fitted it to the stump and, shaking his head a bit, grunted. Setting the broken part down he drove a square nail into the shorter piece, using his pliers for a hammer. He took a pair of short boards from his pocket and, fitting the shaft to the stump again, placed one of the boards at either side of the break like a splint on a broken arm and stood thoughtfully a while, considering it.

"We ain't got all night," Cooper hinted.

Topock dug his ribs with an elbow, but the fence-stringer seemed not to notice. After a bit more of head-shaking and eyeing his work, he put the splints back into his pocket and again laid the shaft on the ground. He removed the nail he had driven and tamped in another nail closer to the stump. To this he fastened a length of wire securely. Fitting the shaft to the stump again, he put the splints back on and bound the whole methodically with wire, afterwards driving a couple more nails clear through the entire affair and flattening their ends on the farther side.

Everything seemed quite solid.

He stood back, surveying it with a critical eye while Cooper fumed and spluttered.

The old man, looking up, smiled at Topock. "I expect that'll do it," he said, and got the horse back into the shafts.

Cooper snarled, "Give 'im 'is money an' let's git started. I'm drier'n a damn cork leg!"

"They got a right smart of water up to the ranch," the old man mentioned. "Just a minute now till I wrap this with a piece of hide so your horse won't——"

"To hell with the horse!" Cooper snarled. "Plenty

more where he comes from. Get out of the——"

"Here's your money," cut in Topock hastily, toss-ing the man a half-dollar. "Much obliged. Do you know if old Kerwold's home?"

"Why—y——" The old man shoved back his hat. He scratched a hand along the side of his head and stood eyeing them somewhat dubiously. "You boys goin' up there to see Sam Kerwold?"

"Well, yes," Topock said, cutting off Cooper's sarcasm. "We was figurin' to—got a little proposition to put up to him."

"Ain't much sense goin' way up there, then." The fence-stringer told them soberly: "I'm Sam Kerwold. What's your proposition, boys?"

Topock stared. Cooper's jaw hung slack. Topock's face got red and he said uncomfortably: "Uh—er—— Well, you see, Mister Kerwold, sir, I—we—er—— We——"

"That's all right, boys. Just tell me what you wanted."

Cooper, whose tongue was swung from the middle, said: "We heard up at Payson how you been stakin' a number of fellas to a start in the cow business an'——"

"I'm afraid not, boys." Kerwold shook his head. "Sorry—but I don't hardly guess I could. Anybody that wouldn't know how to fix a wagon-shaft wouldn't cut much figure in the cow business." He shook his head again. "No, I'm 'fraid not, boys. Runnin' cattle is pretty much work."

CHAPTER III

WARP AND WOOF

THE man who had been camped in the hills could think of several good reasons why a fellow might not care to be the recipient of the yonder store's hospitality at one o'clock in the morning, but he was careful not to mention them.

He sat with inscrutable cheeks still turned toward the shine of light and with a twisted smile at last picked up his reins and at a slow jog sent his blue roan down the trail; and when they reached the store he got indifferently out of the saddle and looked at the other man briefly.

Store light, cutting the road-front shadows, showed this second man to be garbed after the Mexican manner. He wore leg-clutching pants, short jacket and sash, with a chin-strapped sombrero for headgear. There was a mole's black spot at the right of his chin, and his stare showed bright and distrustful.

The man who had camped in the hills dryly mentioned, " We're here.   Might's well go on in, hadn't we? "

A subtle change took place in the mounted man's stare; then he shrugged and stepped out of the saddle. " Might's well," he said; and the two of them crossed the porch's warped planking and, still watchful, went into the store.

It was not the Ransome custom to stay open long

after supper; but custom, for a lot of folk, was in the discard lately. A bit of research would have disclosed this change to have coincided with the arrival of a couple of Texans, though none took time for this effort. The change had come, was accepted.

Abe Ransome usually kept the store after nightfall for the hour or two it stayed open. But he was not a well man and here just of late his ailment had made itself felt more than usual; his daughter, Holly, had taken his chores and sent him off early to bed.

The first night she had charge of the store, one of the above-mentioned Texans—Guy Topock was what the man called himself—had helped her while the time away with tales of his random travels. He had been a cattle buyer, he said, for Dallas' biggest packing-house. The work seemed to have taken him far afield; his accounts of it were fascinating.

They'd been less so on the second night. The third night, after outstaying all other customers, he'd attempted to improve their acquaintance, to put it on a considerably more personal basis. It had called up all Holly's tact and firmness to keep him in his place; by the time he'd finally left it had been nearly twelve o'clock.

But this fourth night was much the worst, she thought; it was after twelve already and Guy Topock still sat around grinning, with his hateful eyes doing things, she guessed, he'd an itch to have his hands doing for them.

About nine it had been when he'd drifted in; Juke Ronstadt had just ridden in at the time on his periodic trip for supplies. Old Juke was a kind of shiftless sort, a homesteader from over in Buck Basin. But a kind man and a husky one; and Topock had kept his jaw within bounds until after the old man left. Then the

Texan, widening his grin, had got up and crossed to the counter.

" Gets kind of lonesome round here, don't it? "

Holly said, " I haven't noticed it."

" Sho. Like enough the reason is, there ain't been nobody round man enough to show you the difference."

His grin—the glint of his eyes—was a challenge. But Holly, throttling her resentment, was intending to change the subject when, grin widening, he leaned over the counter.

" Hold on now, girl—keep your shirt-tail in; ain't no need you gettin' jittery." His hand shot out, just missing her as she backed off, stopped by the wall.

Her cheeks were white, her half-scared eyes wide and angry.

" Now what kind of way is that to act—fella'd think I was poison or somethin'."

He put the flats of his hands on the counter, firmly, as though of half a mind to jump it. She blushed suddenly and profusely at something she saw in his eyes. She was reaching behind her for something on a shelf when Topock decided to take it a little slower. After all, there wasn't any hurry; she'd keep open till he left.

He was a slick talker, this Guy Topock; bland, suave and cunning—particularly with the ladies. He prided himself on his abilities in this direction. He said: " You ever thought of marriage, Holly? "

Holly's shoulders relaxed a little, but she kept her place by the wall. She shook her head. " Not much." Even in her own ears her voice sounded kind of queer.

Guy Topock thought so too, seemed like. A gloating look got into his eyes. He took a fresh grip on the counter and the knuckles of those hands were showing white when the porch planks creaked and across his shoulder Holly saw the rawboned shape of Pecos Gann.

Topock wheeled with his big-knuckled hands gone knotted. But the oath died sullenly on his lips when he saw who was in the doorway.

Gann's glance rubbed across him knowingly. "Warm night," Gann said.

He was a slat-shaped man with a lantern jaw and squinty, close-set eyes. A cud of tobacco bulged one cheek and a hank of greyish hair hung down across a corrugated forehead whose most significant feature was a long knife-scar that began at his chin and lopped off half the left eyebrow. Gann had been a sheepman and still had a sheepman's habits, and when Holly spoke to him, asking what he wanted, his only answer was a surly grunt as he dropped down on to a nail-keg from which he continued to eye Topock knowingly.

Topock's dark glance shifted but his talk was friendly enough. "It's a damn quiet night, if that's what you mean," he grumbled. He shrugged, let go a deep breath softly. "Deadest country ever I seen— your corral posts heir to dry rot yet?"

Gann said, "Not that I know of," and turned his speculative glance on Holly. She could almost *feel* the thoughts going through his head. She was wheeling away from them, red-cheeked, angry, resentful, when Gann said gruffly: "Where's that brother of yours at?"

It stopped her short. Then remembrance came with its need and she shrugged, went across the store.

She was rearranging stock on the far wall's shelves and the two men were swopping small talk like a brace of gamecocks sparring round, when horse sound drifted in again and a rider's boots were presently knocking echoes from the porch.

It was her brother. His face was flushed, excited.

"Here's news!" he cried. "Clean your ears out, Gann. There's a hell's own smear of wagons comin' down Davenport Wash!"

All the lines of Gann's face deepened and he came half off the keg, with his black eyes showing ugly. "What's that?"

Ransome said: "Wagons! Twenty-thirty of 'em comin' down Davenport Wash!"

Gann sank back on his keg with a snorted oath. "Humph! Nothin' newsy to that," he said; but Holly noted that all expression was gone from his cheeks. His tone simulated indifference, but the look of his eyes didn't match it. "Been wagons," he said, "in that wash before. Headin' for the New River Mountains, prob'ly; goin' to stop at Ashfork for supplies. More homesteaders—that whole New River country's filled with 'em——"

"It may be," Tim Ransome growled, "but these ain't headin' that way. They're comin' down here, by grab, an'——"

"Hell!" Gann scoffed. "You better quit drinkin' that rattle juice Brill's puttin' out fer whisky."

"I'm tellin' you straight!" young Ransome scowled. He was a bony, peaked youth with the down of adolescence still satining his cheeks. Plainly the wish was in him to appear important. Resentment edged his eyes at Gann's indifference. He said: "I got it right from Lou Safford. Lou's talked to 'em—they're askin' the way to Saint Clair Mountain——"

"Don't signify a thing," Gann told him, with a wink for Topock. "That trail connects with the road that goes up Seven Springs Wash. They'll be cuttin' over at Rackensack; take the ol' Fisk Mill road——"

"They *could*," Ransome said impatiently, "but they ain't. They give out to Lou they been tipped off this is all open range down here an' every man of 'em's aimin' to file!"

Gann rose with a sudden anger. "Then by God I know who told 'em," he said blackly. "That goddam Straddle-bug Holcomb!"

Through the quiet that settled on Gann's remark came the humus-muted sound of falling hoofs. It came from the roadway yonder and drew all eyes to the door as spurs rasped across the porch planks.

Two men came in; Duarte Vargas, Kerwold's foreman, with his yellow stare sardonic, and a stranger. The stranger said to Holly: "If you've an extra bed round, ma'am, I sure could use it."

He was dark, above six feet, broad-shouldered, arrow straight. For some reason she herself could not define, Holly glanced at him again, more closely. The rim of his broad felt hat was slashways pulled across his eyes and there was a conscious power in the way he carried himself; it was not a suggestion of cockiness or arrogance, but seemed rather the result of conviction—some knowledge not shared with these others. A faint smile was edging his lips.

The smile went away. He had observed her interest.

"Why," she said, "I——"

"Never mind," Guy Topock said, and came striding over. "You've got no room for him—see?"

The stranger looked at him casually, brows lifted in polite inquiry. His question seemed a natural one. "You're the proprietor?" he asked.

"Never mind," growled Topock harshly. "There

ain't no room for you here."

Holly saw the amusement brightening Vargas' yellow stare, and wondered. Then her glance wheeled back to the stranger, found him eyeing her again. The set of his shoulders appeared to dismiss Guy Topock as of small importance. It did her good to see the look on Topock's face.

Then Topock's arm slashed out and whirled the new man round. "Damn you! " the Texan snarled. "When I'm talkin', you lis——"

He stopped like that with his stare gone wide, uncertain.

Holly stared at him wonderingly, for some of the ruddiness had gone from his cheeks and she saw no reason for it. The stranger, now that Topock's arm had fallen away from him, maintained a pose of careless ease; hipshot he stood, with thumbs hooked into his gun-belt. A lazy smile was edging his lips, disclosing the shine of white teeth.

Topock took a long deep breath and his voice sounded strangely husky. "Say—ain't I met you before some place?"

"Have you?"

Topock's odd stare held a moment longer. He said, more to himself it seemed than to the other, "I—I believe I have . . ."

To Holly it sounded like dust had got into his throat.

But the stranger appeared not to have noticed. "Well, perhaps you have," he murmured; and looking toward Holly again: "About that bed, ma'am——"

Whatever it was had bothered Topock appeared to have been shelved or forgotten. He said, cutting into the man's talk roughly: "I told you this place is full up. There's no room here—nor any place in this country——"

"You must be mistaken," the stranger said coolly. "This gentleman"—and his glance flashed at Vargas —"has invited me to stay for a while, and I've just decided I shall."

Holly's eyes followed Gann's and her brother's to Kerwold's foreman. Duarte Vargas said, grimly amused, "There was somebody killed in the hills tonight; I met this gent comin' out of 'em."

The place went queerly still. It were as though a mill had shut down and left its echo behind it.

The stranger's smile was regretfully for Holly.

"So I guess you've got a boarder, ma'am."

He leaned broad shoulders against a post and coolly shook tobacco from a sack into curled brown paper. With his teeth he drew the sack's strings shut; left hand thrust it in his pocket. A curling roll of the right hand's fingers made a perfect cylinder which his tongue's end licked while he considered their cocked expressions.

"Who was it?" Tim Ransome's voice had a shake in it.

The Flying K range boss shrugged. "I didn't notice." The polished brass of his stare stabbed its implication at the stranger.

"Why . . . I didn't notice, either," the stranger's drawl came blandly. "Never had much time for dead men—the live ones keep me too busy."

Gann said: "Tim, go get the marshal——"

Hot colour stained young Ransome's cheeks. "Go yourself! I ain't no errand boy!"

"I will," Gann said, coming off his keg. But just then boot-sound crossed the porch and stopped him; brought his head around to find the marshal framed in the doorway.

The marshal's raking stare found Vargas, and he said tightly: " Juke Ronstadt was killed in the hills to-night. What do you know about it? "

Vargas' glance hooked across to the stranger. "There's the gent you want to talk to."

" I'm talkin' to *you*! "

Duarte Vargas shrugged. Seemed to be a habit he had. "All I know," he said, " is I met this stranger comin' out."

" Whereabouts? "

" Near what's left of that corduroy road them fools——"

" How come *you* to be over there? "

Vargas met the marshal's stare brightly. "Why, I'll tell you, Lou. It ain't none of your goddam business."

Lou Safford moved a half step back and a long pale hand moved to cover his mouth as a racking cough bent and shook him. The face beneath his ash-blond curls was flushed and twisted as he pulled his head up after the coughing. The bit of cambric lifted from the breast-pocket of his Prince Albert was looked at as it came from his lips before, with a shrug, he put it away. There was no expression in the wax-pale cheeks that he turned from Vargas to the stranger. His question under the circumstances was polite. "I'd admire to know what handle you are packing, friend."

" Bufford Dane," the stranger said.

" Dane, eh . . ." The marshal's left hand drummed a barrel top. " And what were you doing in the hills, Mister Dane? "

"Camping."

" About where? "

" 'Fraid I couldn't tell you. I'm a stranger to these parts."

" Hear any shots? "

" I heard one," Mister Dane said finally, slowly, carefully.

" Mind if I look at that gun you're packing? "

" 'Fraid I do." The stranger smiled.

Lou Safford didn't. He said sharply: " I'm marshalling this locality——"

" Glad to know you."

Safford's stare flashed a little narrow. He said no more about the gun. Instead he asked: " What can you tell me about that shot, Dane? "

" Nothing."

" Didn't you investigate? "

" It occurred to me that might be an unwise thing to do."

The marshal's stare revealed a subtle change. The silence thickened. The stranger's shoulders rested easily against the post; nothing about him showed perturbation. His eyes watched the marshal with a level directness that was baffling.

" Where you from? " Gann spoke abruptly; and Holly saw Topock's glance whip an instant look to the stranger's face.

" You might say," the man drawled, " I'm from Texas." And Lou Safford's pointed mention that Texas was a " pretty large place " brought only an indifferent shrug from him.

" Pretty large."

Topock put the thing to words. He said: " What part of Texas? "

" And what might be *your* interest, friend? " Dane's shoulders came away from the post. His tone was cold as gun steel.

A ruddy colour stung Topock's cheeks and he drove a step forward with his big fists clenched and temper's warming in his eyes. "You're the one that's bein' grilled! An' you better——"

"That's right," Safford said. "I think——"

"Don't bother." Dane's eyes mocked them. "All you got to do is wait for daylight. Backtracking me will tell you all you need to know."

Topock sneered. "The wind——"

"Quit an hour ago," Dane said evenly. A cold amusement edged the stare he gave Topock.

Gann, who had been eyeing the stranger long and queerly, said abruptly: "*Jeez!* D'you know——" and without bothering to finish the thought, drove a frantic hand at his gun-butt. The thing was fast— fast and unexpected; but it wasn't quite fast enough. As the gun cleared leather light burst from the stranger's hip in a livid streak. The weapon was torn from the sheepman's hand, sent skittering across the floor, its clatter drowned in the reverberation Dane's gun slammed against the walls.

The group in the store stood frozen. No one moved but Gann, who was shaking his hand and cursing.

Safford, eyes flashing dark with anger, curtly said: "Put down that gun, Dane! I've a notion——"

"Sure," Dane smiled, "we all have," but the smile was glinting, mocking. "If notions was dollars, we'd be millionaires. The gentleman isn't hurt, you'll find. The slowness of his draw is to be commended— otherwise I might not have been able to take such deliberate aim. If all the parlour tricks are over now —and the young lady has a bed to spare—perhaps I'd better be sayin' good night. It's a little late and I'm sleepy."

CHAPTER IV

BLIND TIGER

BUFFORD DANE sat a long while upright on the bunk before he turned out the light and got into it.

This place was a kind of warehouse behind the store-room proper. Long it was and narrow and perfumed with the mingled essence of many smells, much the strongest of which were those of cheap soap and sorghum. The dirt floor was cluttered with gear and with barrels; sacked grain and ground meals had their share of its space and the broad shelves lining three walls sagged with the weight of packaged goods and boxed stuffs. There was only one window, a narrow affair nailed tight as a drumhead and further secured by thick bars. It was a little remindful of a jail-house, and Dane, connoisseur of atmospheres, permitted himself a dry smile.

But little mirth marked the indulgence and it was with a sigh—not entirely regretful—that he finally pulled off his boots and got into the bunk. His only other preparation before willing himself to sleep was the reluctant removal of gun-belt and pistol—and the pistol he kept under his hand.

The sun was three hours high and the land commencing to broil again when Dane pulled on his boots and strode out into the store. An elderly man sat behind the counter with his bent glance on a book. Sunlight showed the gentleness of wrinkled, scholarly features; hardly the kind a man would look for in country wild as this.

Crossing the room Dane leaned against the counter, getting out sack and papers. The doors stood open and in this bright light the last of a quitting breeze playfully tousled the reader's hair; rattled paper on the counter. But the man read on, as unaware of wind's idle vagaries as he appeared to be of the stranger's presence.

Dane scratched a match on his Levis and the man looked up, near-sightedly, reluctantly put aside the book and made a question of his glance. "Good morning."

"'Mornin'," Dane drawled leisurely. "Good book, that—though a little on the tame side."

"You've read it, sir?" The man's eyes brightened. "A notable piece of work, sir—yes, indeed. There's genius in that fellow's pen—you've read his other works?"

Dane shook his head. "Don't have much time for readin'," he said dryly. "Uh . . . Would there be a place around here somewhere I could get a bite of breakfast?"

"Why—why, yes. Just a moment. I'll call my daughter."

But he didn't have to call her. She came through the door as he spoke. She had a smile for Bufford Dane; a smile he was starting to return when some dark thought appeared to cross his mind, straightening his lips out bleakly.

A moment's curiosity looked out of her level eyes. After which she said, "We've—— Oh, pardon me! Father, this is Mr. Dane. Mr. Dane, my father, Abraham Ransome."

Dane reached across and shook the other man's hand; a thing he didn't often do, for shaking hands was dangerous. "Glad to know you, Ransome."

"Holly," Ransome said, "Dane has read this book of Lytton's. Thinks it rather tame." He chuckled.

But Holly's eyes, briefly touching Dane's big pistol, showed an odd, half-wondering frown. But, whatever her thought, she shook it off. She said to Dane, "I've been keeping things hot. If you'll come with me . . ."

She turned away and Dane, reluctantly it seemed, followed her to the kitchen.

While she busied herself about the stove he let himself into a chair. He put his elbows gingerly on the oilcloth-covered table and roved a glance around. The room was plain, rather scantily furnished with rude things made in the country, but some magic of this tall girl's hands had made it homey, comfortable. A grudging approval briefly coloured the stranger's stare.

He said, "About this fellow, Ronstadt . . . Have any enemies round here, did he?"

She said without looking up: "I never heard of any. He was a harmless old man. A homesteader from over in Buck Basin——"

"I see. A homesteader . . ." Dane said thoughtfully, and let his voice trail off.

Such times as Holly looked up from her work, the stranger's glance seemed always lost in consideration of some view beyond the window; but when she was not looking his regard was darkly on her, seeming to contrast her against some memory in his mind. It kind of bothered him, looked like, for the line of his face was sombre.

He ate without comment and afterwards pushed his chair back, getting out the makings and twisting himself a cigarette.

An odd stick, Holly thought of him, but somehow strangely attractive with his strong dark face and enigmatic stare. He had the look of a man who kept his horse at work. Her glance went oftenest to the big gun strapped at his hip; it seemed so much a part of him.

"What kind of jasper is this marshal—this Lou Safford?" he asked abruptly.

But she didn't get to answer.

Voice sound came from the store and on its heels the clump of boots. A deliberate, measured tread; and then Lou Safford was looking in at them, bony shoulders against the door.

He spoke with his glance on the stranger. "You'll be glad to know investigation backed you up, Dane. It don't seem hardly likely you could of had any part in Juke's killing. What are you going to do now? Figurin' to stay, or——"

"Why," Dane said, "I allow I'll stay. For a while, anyhow."

Safford nodded. "Kind of hoped you might see fit to." He paused, appeared to consider. His glance rubbed across Dane's pistol; calculation showed in the look. "Pretty fair with that gun, are you?"

Dane smiled dryly. "I expect I could make out to use it."

Safford said thoughtfully, "Be huntin' you up a job, I guess, eh?"

Dane shrugged. "Hard tellin'—ain't at all sure I'm goin' to stay, yet. Any of these outfits needin' a man?"

"I suppose Sam Kerwold might put you on." Safford said abruptly: "Sam's throwin' a party to-night—his daughter's just back from the east. Sort of birthday celebration. You might drop round; give you a chance to get acquainted——"

Dane said: "'Fraid my talents ain't along that line."

Once again the marshal appeared to be communing

with himself. He said abruptly: " I could find a use for a man like you . . ."

A quick light flashed in Dane's cold eyes. " You mean as deputy? "

Lou Safford nodded.

A wry grin parted the stranger's lips. " No, thanks," he drawled sardonically.

Lou Safford's glance was narrowed, odd. " What do you mean? "

" Trouble's buildin' up in this country——"

" Trouble? "

" Ain't a murder usually trouble? "

" Who said anything about murder? "

" A guy got killed in the hills last night. I didn't hear but one shot."

Lou Safford looked at him darkly. But all he said very quietly was: " That job will still be open to-night. You better think it over."

The bar-room at Brill's was big—long, low-ceilinged. A cluster of lamps, their yellow glare dimmed by tobacco haze, showed sections of the walls to be adorned with garish lithographs; the glass eyes of an elk's head, mounted above the back bar's mirror, leered out across Brill's bottled goods. Sweat and stale beer fumes mingled with the reek of whisky and from a rear room came the rattle of crap and chucka-luck games and the rumble of divers voices. Brill's place was known in the parlance of that day as a ' blind tiger.' It did not mark a cross-roads junction. It was crouched far back in the hills.

Apparently, though, it got its share of patronage. Any man was welcome so long as he packed no tin; and on this night the back room was pretty well filled with fellows, and a good many others were in the main room, ranged beside Brill's rough bar.

Two men, however, sat apart. Guy Topock and Andy Cooper. They had their heads together over a bottle, but they were not communing with any spirits. They were—as Cooper might have described it—'laying pipe.'

Topock was doing the talking, but every so often Cooper put in his oar—as now. "What," he said, grinning shallowly, "about this stranger, Dane?"

"What about him?"

"You don't need to wrinkle up your face at me," sneered Cooper. "Save it fer the women an' kids—they'll swaller it, mebbe." He laughed at the look in Topock's eyes. "That fella's got the Injun sign on you, boy!"

You could see that it bothered Topock. But all he said was, gruffly: "I'll take care of him when the time comes. Now quit your yappin' an' listen—you didn't leave any sign around that homesteader, did you? I mean, anything Lou Safford could use against you?"

Cooper snorted. "Yeah," he said sarcastically. "I scratched my name on his belt-buckle!"

Topock ignored this pleasantry.

He said: "We got to work this quick, Andy——"

"I thought you was goin' to *tell* me somethin'!"

Topock watched Andy Cooper, a glinting anger in his eyes. "I don't know," he said, wickedly soft, "if that would be possible!"

"Horse hocks." Cooper grinned derisively. "Get on with it."

"What time you fixed it for that bunch of sod-busters to show up here?"

"Any time after to-morrow. Figgered we ort to have things——"

" Where'd you tell 'em to locate? "

" Wildcat Hill." Cooper grinned. " You said we wanted action—that'll fetch it."

" Great Scot, man! " Topock came half out of his chair. " That's the best graze Kerwold's got! "

" Sure—all the better, ain't it? The Flyin' K will hit them fools like a ton of lead."

" But, damn it! They'll have kids an' women with 'em——"

" All right; that won't hold the ol' coot back any. If they start tearin' up that grass—hell," Cooper sneered, " he's got to smash 'em or kiss good-bye to the cow biz."

Topock looked at him a long half minute and finally shook his head. " You ought to sailed with Morgan— you'd made him a damn good mate. Ever stopped to think what's goin' to happen if any of them women or kids git hurt? They'll have the troops down here s' quick it'll make your head swim! " Topock ran a shaking hand through his hair and swore.

Cooper's lip curled. But he had the wit to keep his mouth shut. He understood Guy Topock pretty well; knew to a fraction just how far he could prod the man—knew that limit had been reached.

" Look," he said after a moment. " The plan is to get these hoemen to prod Kerwold's crew into gunplay —all right. Beddin' 'em down on Wildcat Hill will do it. He'll tear into 'em like the devil beatin' ten-bark—prob'ly burn up half their wagons for a starter. Fine! that gets the ball to rollin'. That's what we been waitin' for, ain't it? Sure! All right; we hit back at Kerwold—cut his fence, burn a couple line-camps, mebbe; kill three-four of his men. Surer'n hell he'll lay it on to them homesteaders. When the smoke clears off there won't be any Flyin' K—won't be any homesteaders, neither. We step in an' take the whole works over. What the hell would be sweeter'n that? "

Guy Topock remained without speaking so long that Cooper shifted uneasily. He poured himself another drink and when he picked the glass up it was his left hand that curled around it; his right was at the table edge, short inches from his gun.

Topock ironed the scowl from dark features, but anger still thickened his voice. He said: " You got a ridin' crew lined up? " and Cooper nodded.

" Got eight-ten fellas—all of 'em good with rifles. It wasn't no chore; these small-spread ranchers round here ain't wastin' no love on Kerwold. Been expandin' too fast—they're scared of him, 'fraid they're goin' to be gobbled. I——"

" Did you sign on Holcomb? "

Cooper said " No," reluctantly. " Wouldn't talk one way or the other." He said with his tone turned thoughtful, " May have a little trouble with him."

Topock growled, " Never mind. Can you get these boys in a hurry? "

" Any time you want 'em."

" Where's young Ransome? "

Cooper's head jerked a nod at the back room's closed door. " He's in there buckin' Brill's games. Want him? "

Topock's glance was considering. " No," he said finally, " not now. You fixed it up with Brill to take his I.O.U.s? . . . Good. I got a——"

" How you goin' to work Safford? "

Some secret thought crooked Topock's lips. He said, " Your worry's handlin' Vargas. That guy has got ambition——"

" I got a handy cure for ambition." Cooper sug

gestively patted his gun. "You goin' to Kerwold's shindig?"

"Yeah." Topock looked at his watch and got up. "Keep those fools well heeled with money." He tossed a buckskin sack on the table and ten minutes later went out.

CHAPTER V

"I WANT THAT STEALIN' STOPPED!"

THERE were five people enjoying Sam Kerwold's spiked punch in the Flying K's long living-room when Bufford Dane brought Holly into it. There was Sam Kerwold and his daughter, a neighbour rancher, Lou Safford and one of the men Dane had seen in Ransome's store the night before.

An ironic smile disturbed the set of Safford's lips as he bowed, but he vouchsafed no remark, and Holly, after returning the greetings of Sam and Sam's daughter, said to Kerwold: "Mr. Kerwold, I would like you to meet Bufford Dane who is staying at the store for a while."

Sam Kerwold held out his hand and Dane shook it, after which Kerwold said: "Like to have you meet the guest of honour, Dane—— My daughter, Jane."

Holly, looking up at Dane, saw the sudden tightening of his shoulders; observed the way the long hands, until then loose-hanging at his sides, went oddly white about the knuckles. With a catch of breath she stabbed a look at Jane.

She had known Jane rather well before the latter

had gone east to school. But someway this was not that Jane; this girl was different, not merely more mature, more dignified and graceful, but different in her habits of thought—different of mental viewpoint. Holly sensed other changes not so easily labelled.

As Holly looked at her, Jane went a half step backward, stood with cheeks gone pale, her startled gaze incredulously fixed on Dane. It was only for a second Jane stood with feelings naked, but Holly saw, and her swift, half-vexed interpretation was that these two, Jane and the stranger, had met before.

Kerwold's daughter must have recalled her surroundings then, for her chin came up and with strengthening colour she said quietly, " How do you do? " but did not offer her hand, nor, apparently, did Dane expect her to.

It seemed to Holly that Dane's bow was a trifle elaborate, and she thought to read the glint of a malicious humour in his glance as he said coolly, " I'm fine enough, thank you," and, turning to grin at Kerwold, asked: " Are we celebrating the prodigal's return? "

Kerwold had been eyeing Dane a little oddly, almost searchingly. But he chuckled at the question. " You might call it that, I reckon, though I haven't readied any fatted calf—and may not get to," he added more soberly, " if somethin' ain't soon done about these rustlers."

" Something's being done," Safford said, a little quick with his answer. " Dane, here, is figuring to help me get the deadwood on——"

" He means he *hopes* I am," Dane answered, grin showing the cold white teeth of him. " As a matter of fact, I've about decided not to take on that chore. Havin' lead thrown at you from behind every rock and pinon ain't hardly my idea of a happy life."

Lou Safford frowned. "That mean you're turning down my offer?"

"I'm afraid it does."

Lou Safford said: "I might have known a man too careful to investigate a shot, like you done in the hills last night, hadn't sufficient guts to be a deputy."

They were a little shocked, those others, by the marshal's plain-put words. Sam Kerwold looked embarrassed, but the stranger took it cool enough. His tipped-up cheeks revealed a cold amusement; but as he seemed about to comment, Guy Topock came through the door and his bold stare picked Lou Safford out immediately. "What's the latest on that hold-up, Safford? Got a line on the killer yet?"

It was a good entrance; he could not have made a play that would have grabbed attention quicker. All eyes wheeled, and Pecos Gann, who had been about to say something, stared with his mouth left open. "What hold-up?" Kerwold said, quite plainly startled. And "What killing?" Pring, the other rancher, said.

Lou Safford scowled. "It ain't generally known yet," he admitted, "but the Phœnix stage, coming west from Globe, was stopped this evening just above Horse Mesa——"

"The driver," Topock cut in, "was killed and the strong box emptied of every last nickel in it!"

"Reason I haven't mentioned it," Safford said, with a malevolent look at the Texan, "is because I didn't want to throw cold water on the party. I've got men all through the hills hunting sign——"

"Haven't heard anythin' then yet, eh?"

"Not yet," the marshal said curtly; and Kerwold stared at his boot tops gravely.

"How'd you come to hear of it?" Pring asked Topock, and the Texan grinned.

"I was there when that fool coffee-drummer come tearin' in with the stage." He laughed at a sudden memory. "His eyes was bugged out like marbles."

Plainly Safford did not care to discuss the hold-up, and presently the talk, turned into other channels, became more general. Dane brought Holly a glass of punch and dipped another for himself, and Pring, leaning forward, asked if he'd care for a riding job at sixty-five and found. Dane, without committing himself, said he'd keep the offer in mind.

Pring, Holly told him later, was owner of the Double Bar Circle. "They say Sam Kerwold helped him when he was starting six-eight years ago; they're great friends," Holly mentioned and, watching Dane carefully, said: "Gus used to be pretty much interested in Jane before she went off to school—everyone figured they'd get married sure."

But Dane showed nothing beyond polite interest; and then Guy Topock came striding over and Dane, excusing himself, said he guessed he'd go have a smoke.

Dane was not long on the veranda when a voice said from the shadows beyond the rail: "Vargas told me how he herded you into Ransome's store last night."

It was Kerwold's voice, guarded but unmistakable.

Dane did not move to join the Flying K owner, but at once dropped his unfinished smoke to the floor-boards and put a foot on it. "Yeah." He said: "Damn fortunate, as things worked out, but kind of odd."

"How you mean, odd?"

"For one thing, what was he doing there?"

"Why—ah—just what the hell you getting at?"

"Well," Dane's voice was considering. "He came out of the trees like he'd been there handy, waitin' for something."

There was a moment of silence. The wind made a lonely sound.

Kerwold said abruptly—sharply, almost: "Are you insinuating——"

"Never mind. Let it ride," Dane answered gruffly. "I can take care of myself, I reckon. Did you tell him you had sent for me?"

"Hardly." Kerwold's tone was nettled. "I didn't tell him anything."

"Good!" Dane said, and after a moment: "Don't. You know my style—a lone hand always. Only way to get anything done. Your letter didn't tell me much; what are you up against here?"

Kerwold took a long time answering. He said then grimly: "As God's my witness, Bufe, I'm damned if I know. I been expandin' a little lately; buyin' up small holdings here an' there—I need more range and the free grass days are done. Homesteaders comin' in everywhere; there's goin' to be fences, pastures, farmin'—as a matter of fact, I'm fencin' myself—got to. It isn't makin' me popular. The small-spread outfits think I'm fixin' to hog the water, and in a way they're right; man that's got water's goin' to control this country and I'm not goin' to be froze out or dictated to by no passle of weed-bendin' hoemen. I——"

"You're not fencin' open range?"

"No. But I'm buyin' it fast as I can—I've got to protect myself. I can see what's comin' all right. I don't blame these little fellers—I started that way myself——"

"Any your men filin'——?"

"Sure; every one of 'em is. Soon's they prove up, I'll take over—they'll not lose anything; I've agreed to pay them five hundred dollars apiece, over and above their wages. They wouldn't make nothing of it anyway—not cut out to be farmers. There ain't one of 'em that'll do anything he can't do from a saddle; they'd feel insulted if I asked 'em to string fence. I'm doin' all that myself—me an' the cook."

"What did you want me to do?"

Kerwold hesitated. He said suddenly, angrily: "Put the fear of God in these rustlers before they rob me blind!"

"What's the matter with Lou Safford?"

"Nothing—that I know of. But he's only one man; he can't cope with everything."

Dane might have pointed out that he, too, was only one man. But instead he said, "You looked kind of funny when that guy Topock was blowing off about the stage hold-up—have anything on it?"

Kerwold swore, quietly but with undoubted warmth. "Two thousand dollars cash comin' from the bank at Globe!"

Dane pursed his lips in a soundless whistle. "What was the big idea?"

"The Government Land Agent at Prescott has announced that a big jag of land just east of here, startin' at Wildcat Hill, is goin' to be let on a five-year lease——"

"You mean this land's to be bid on?" Dane interrupted.

"Yeah," Sam Kerwold said morosely. "Wednesday, at Fort McDowell——"

"Why there?"

"Don't ask me—some kind of politics, like as not.

But you ain't got the picture yet. This land's goin'
to be bid on Wednesday *if an' providing that no*
homesteads have been taken up on it in the meantime. If one homesteader stakes a claim, the bidding's
off——"

Dane did whistle this time, softly. "Anybody else
interested in this jag of land?"

"Yeah—three-four big outfits interested. Pring,
for one, would like to get it, though I don't reckon
Pring will bid knowin' how bad I need it. Then
there's the Wagon Wheel, Straddle Bug, an' Blane's
Four Bars off the other side of New River. Them
three's pretty sure to bid——"

"Ain't you fellows worried some of these little
spreads'll be sendin' someone to file——"

"They'd do it quick enough if they dared," Kerwold said, "but they don't. We've got along all
right so far, but I guess they know how long they'd
last if they tried anything like that."

"Always the chance of real sod-busters turnin' up,
though, and——"

"I know that." Kerwold's voice showed his worry.

"How come you're wantin' this lease so bad?"
Dane asked and Kerwold told him.

" I'm sold too deep into next year's deliveries," he
said grimly. " I'm committed for a sight more Basin-
fed beef than I can show unless I get this Wildcat
land—— God damn it, Bufe! that country'll feed
more'n fifty head to the section."

"That good, eh?"

"You know it!"

"How does it happen you ain't wangled this——"

"Hell, it ain't been open till this month!"

"An' there's three more days before the bidding,
eh?"

Kerwold said "Yeah," morosely. "I tell you, Bufe——"

"That's the third time you've called me that in five minutes. For the love of God, Sam," Dane said sharply, "get a hobble on your jaw. I'll not be no use to you dead."

"Sorry." Kerwold's tone was short. He would have said more, it seemed, but Dane cut swiftly in:

"You haven't said yet what it is I'm supposed to do. You spoke of rustlers—got any idea who they are?"

Kerwold said almost inaudibly, "I couldn't prove anything——"

"But you've got a lot of ideas?"

Sam Kerwold said impatiently: "I got some notions. You better make your own mind up. On evidence got by yourself."

"Well, tell me this: Who you think's behind it?"

"Rather you'd find that out some place else, too."

Dane's eyes narrowed. He wished he could see Sam Kerwold's face, but this gloom was like a blanket. "You ain't givin' me much help."

Sam Kerwold's voice was reticent. "I know it. You'll have to work this out yourself—I know it sounds kinda lowdown-like, to bring a man three hundred miles to help you out of a jackpot an' then make him play it blind. But that's the way it's got to be."

There was a finality in the way he put it that precluded further argument. That was the proposition. Dane could take it or he could leave it.

He said dryly: "I always did do things the hard way. Would you mind tellin' me, Sam, what you're wantin' done with these fellows after I've spotted 'em?"

"I told you once I want the fear of God put into 'em!" The cattle baron said it harshly, smashed a fist against the porch rail. "I want that stealin' stopped—stopped permanent and pronto. How you do it's up to you."

CHAPTER VI

GRIM CHALLENGE

LONG moments after Kerwold wheeled away, Dane stood there in the porch gloom, silent, thoughtful. It was apparent enough from Kerwold's talk what was happening, or about to happen, here. An old familiar pattern, as familiar to Bufford Dane as the shiny creases of his saddle. Forces were at work here— greed and jealousy and fear. Someone had his knife out, someone determined to smash Sam Kerwold and everything he stood for. Flying K was headed out— unless drastic steps were taken. Only one thing could save it. Force must be met with force.

That Kerwold was feared and hated was not surprising to Bufford Dane; the surprise was that he'd got this far without somebody gunning him. There was nothing wrong with Kerwold—with what he'd thus far done; he was a part of the accepted system just as his enemies and what they aimed to do were part of that system. It was dog eat dog; rugged individualism; competition at its best. So long as competition endured, so long would these things happen. It was the way—the way of this time and place.

Bufford Dane was a man of few illusions, and what few he owned had long since been discarded. He saw things as they were—or most things. Sam Kerwold's problem was an open book, a thing he knew page for page. There were just two courses possible. No half-way measures counted; you must take the one or the other. You could fold your hands and do a lot of wishful thinking, or you could grab a gun and start smashing things.

Sam Kerwold had not called on him to sit with folded hands.

Jane Kerwold was playing the piano, the only one in the country. At considerable expense this instrument had come a weary way; it was a facet of Sam Kerwold's pride, like his daughter, like his ranch. He liked to hear it played and enjoyed watching others hear it. Jane Kerwold had a light, sure touch that made listening a pleasure.

Bufford Dane was probably the only one not affected by the music.

Holly, covertly eyeing him, was sure he did not hear it. The sombre look of his burnt-dark cheeks was not produced by Jane's melodies; it was the result—if Holly were any judge—of thinking, of a thinking wholly unpleasant.

His eyes veered, observed her interest; the dark cheeks locked his thoughts away. He said, calmly casual, "Been a long time since I heard that song," and shifted his regard to the ceiling.

But when Holly looked again she found him studying Safford. There was a darkness in his glance that set her own mind probing. Who was this Bufford Dane? She had asked herself that thing before. Where had he come from? What lay behind him that made his glance so wary?—his step so cat-soft quick?

There was a mystery about him that attracted her. His strong, dark, enigmatic face bespoke a man who did things—who had done some things, she guessed, which would not bear open talk about. The baffling blue of his eyes said so; the reticent slant of his cheeks.

She wished she could know his story. That somewhere along his backtrail that story had crossed Jane Kerwold's, Holly felt certain. She could not forget the girl's startled look—the stiffening of Dane's shoulders when Sam Kerwold had introduced them; that is to say, when they'd first taken stock of each other.

Holly's regard of Jane's back had something of envy in it. There was a look about Dane's features, about the set of his broad, sloped shoulders, that warned he was not a fit subject for trifling. Yet Jane must have trifled—or had she? What other interpretation could be put upon their silence regarding that undoubted previous acquaintance? That both regretted it was obvious; but whose had been the fault? *Had* Jane trifled with him, or——?

Holly looked at Dane again. His regard was on Jane Kerwold now, faintly aglint with a cold amusement; yet behind that sardonic look Holly thought to detect other and darker things—a bitter cynicism, surely.

And then her thoughts and reflections were shattered. A sharp hail rode the night; horse sound pounded the yard's adobe, cutting through Jane's playing, breaking it. There was an outside mutter of voices, booted feet thumped the porch boards and a hatless man came wild-eyed through the doorway, roved a stare while he caught his breath and said to

Kerwold hoarsely: "There's wagons on Wildcat Hill an' that fence we run below is ripped plumb out of the ground!"

CHAPTER VII

RUBBED OUT

"No man," Andy Cooper snarled, "can use me like Sam Kerwold has an' not git paid back for it!"

They were in a rear and private cubbyhole at Brill's; just the three of them, Brill, Andy Cooper and Topock. Topock's face was white. He was mad clean through. Not a hot, tumultuous anger that would spend itself in abuse or in some fierce exchange of blows, but a cold and deep, controlled kind of rage that put a chill up Brill's arched back.

He put the back against a wall. He wanted no trouble here, no grabbing after 'guns. "Now look——" he said. "Take it easy, boys; that ain't no way for you to talk. Two wrongs never made a right. Let's talk this o——"

Topock's voice went through that talk to strike at Cooper like weighted fists. "Never mind bringin' Kerwold in! We're talkin' about that switch you pulled. When I tell a man how to do a thing, that's the way I want it done, by God! What was the idea you bringin' them sod-busters in ahead of time?"

Cooper's bony face showed ugly. He made no reply, but sat there like a sullen lump and glared like he would put a curse on Topock.

Brill tried his hand again. "I think——"

Topock said: "Keep out of this, Brill!" and his black intolerant stare bludgeoned Cooper like a maul. Rage jerked at him, tore wild words from his mouth. The names he applied to Cooper were things no man would ordinarily take.

But Cooper took them, silently and sullenly. And when his pardner had run out of breath, Cooper thrust one chap-clad leg across the other and spat with a glance like agate.

"It seems to me," Brill mentioned dryly, "you're wastin' a lot of words on somethin' that ain't worth twenty. What difference does it make *when* your sod-busters get there, just so it's ahead of the bid-day?"

But Topock ignored him. He shoved his voice at Cooper wickedly. "There's just one boss to this outfit, hombre—just one, an' that one's *me*. Never do another thing without you ask me first. You hear?"

"I hear," Cooper said, and his lip curled as Safford's voice drew Topock's glance to the door.

Topock said "Well!" harshly as Safford closed the door. "Let's have it. What did Kerwold do to them wagons?"

Safford's wheeling glance was odd and he took plenty of time with his answer. He said softly, thoughtfully, "Kerwold hasn't touched the wagons, hasn't molested the homesteaders either. I can't think what's holdin' him. He told me he expected me to find out who was responsible for that mess someone made of his wire."

They stared at him blankly.

"Mean to tell me," Topock ripped out, "he's goin' to leave them wagons bedded down on Wildcat—that he aims to let them homesteaders *file* it?"

Safford nodded. "That's the way it looks."

"But—that's crazy, man! He *can't!* He'd never

dare to! It's a trick, I tell you—a damn trick to get you out of the way! He's *got* to have that lease to meet next year's commitments."

The marshal shrugged. "All I know is what I told you. He ain't botherin' the wagons."

"Not botherin' 'em now, mebbe," observed Brill thoughtfully, "but that ain't sayin' he won't—— You know well as I do, Lou, he's got to have that lease."

"I know he had some money comin' on that stage that got stuck up." Safford's stare was solidly on Cooper. "You didn't happen to work that, did you?"

"Sure," Cooper sneered. "With my ol' man's gun I did it!"

He chucked his chew in a corner, bit another from his plug. "What give you the idee *I* stuck it up?"

"That coffee-drummer's description——"

Cooper snorted. "How long you been a star-packer?"

"What's that got to do with it?"

"Nothin'—only you ort to know how reliable a eye-witness's guesswork is——"

"'F I thought you was tryin' to cut a rusty, I would sure eye-witness *you*," Safford said mighty quiet-like, and turned back to face Guy Topock. "No, the Ol' Man never s' much as put a finger on those wagons, Guy. Just sat there——"

"Mad, though, wasn't he?"

"He might of been," Safford said; "but if he was, he sure covered up good. Never made any threats——"

Brill said: "I bet Duarte Vargas did!"

The marshal nodded. "Yeah, he sounded off considerable. But when he got all through, Old Sam said, mighty earnest-like: 'No, you're not, boy—not

while you're roddin' *my* spread.'" Safford grinned.
" Vargas shut down like a grist mill."

Topock said: " What you figure on doin' about
Kerwold's wire? "

Safford puffed his cheeks out, hauled a stogy from
his pocket. As he bit the end from it, his eyes held a
dry kind of humour. " If I could guess," he said,
" who was responsible, I might figure to oblige Sam
by making an arrest. But shucks—ain't hardly a man
in this basin won't paw sod when you mention wire.
Be like hunting a needle in a haystack."

Cooper guffawed.

Brill, who was not a talking man, spoke then.
Mostly he kept his mouth shut and let his eyes reward
him, but the enigma of Kerwold's attitude for one
time bothered him out of this caution. He said with
his beefy jowls turned fretful: " What you s'pose
Sam's got up his sleeve? You don't reckon he *wants*
to see them homesteaders filin' Wildcat, do you? "

It was a new idea. The expressions of these others
showed it. Safford's chalk-pale face turned thoughtful
and Topock rolled his shoulders as he swung with a
sudden curse; but it was Cooper's tricky head that
grasped the implication first and he slammed off his
stool with twisted cheeks, smashed a hot wild look at
the others.

" By God, Brill's got it!" His fist struck the table
with a force that made the bottle jump. " It's plain
as paint—the slick ol' bastard!" He raked a stare at
Topock. " Know what he's goin' to do? By grab, *I'll*
tell you! He's goin' to let them weed-benders file an'
then get his lease from *them*!"

" You're loco!" Safford grunted.

Brill said bewilderedly, " But that's foolish, Andy.
He can't lease from them——"

" Why can't he? " Cooper's slitted stare was bright.
" Why can't he? " he repeated. Then harshly: " It's
the smartest thing he *can* do! It cuts out competition;
knocks that auction out of the picture—hell! *he can
lease that land from them homesteaders for half what
a bid will cost him.*"

A cold, grimly thoughtful silence clamped down
upon that cluttered room.

Safford's considering stare saw Topock's glance flick
across to Brill; saw Brill nod slowly. " It could be,"
Brill said uneasily. " What the devil we goin' to do? "

Topock said, " Them other boys will go hog wild
when they find what Kerwold's up to——"

" That ain't helpin' us! " Cooper snarled. " I
say——"

" Now wait," Topock said. " Keep your shirt-tail
in. Let's figure this out a bit. It might be we
could——"

" It looks," Safford dryly mentioned, " like bringing
those squatters in wasn't near as smart as you figured.
If this lease guess is right, Sam's got us blocked."

Bright flecks coalesced in Cooper's glare. He said
with a wild beast's anger: " By God, I'll lead the boys
on a raid that'll unblock us pronto! I'll——" He
broke off as cold air knifed the room, set the smoke
haze swirling bluely. Bony shoulders wheeling, he
looked toward the door.

Duarte Vargas stood in the opening with a hard grin
edging his features. There was an ironic glint in his
dour yellow stare as he closed the door behind him
softly.

A rope-calloused thumb stroked the mole on his
chin; the look of his eyes froze them rigid.

There was this moment of strained, brittle silence.
Then, " Spit it out, damn you! " Cooper shouted.

"They're gone."

"Who—who's gone?" Topock's eyes showed startled.

"Them precious nesters you brought in."

Cooper's jaw hung slack. Brill, too, showed disbelief.

Safford said: "You mean they've cleared out?"

"Lock, stock an' barrel. There ain't a wagon left on Wildcat Hill——"

"What the hell are you talkin' about?"

Cooper came cat-footed across the room, fists clenched, stare smashing at Vargas.

But Kerwold's foreman stood his ground. "Just what I said. Wheel an' hub. They've gone—there ain't a plough-chaser left on that lease."

The silence dried out, got sharp and hard.

Brill bewilderedly said: "Where've they gone to?"

Vargas shrugged. "Your guess is good as mine. The sign led toward the New River trail but——"

"Did Kerwold scare them out?"

"No, Lou, I don't reckon he did——"

Cooper scowled. "He bought 'em out, then!"

But Vargas shook his head. "I don't think Sam even spoke to them. They were there when the party broke up and they were there when the outfit turned in— scattered all across that slope. Must have been around twelve when I left Sam at the veranda. I turned in like the rest; but soon's I was sure they was all cuttin' wood, I slipped out an' saddled up——"

"What for?"

Vargas met Cooper's look with an easy grin. "Call it a hunch if you want. Anyway, I saddled up and went over there——"

"You was goin' to play 'em a tune on your mouth harp, mebbe?"

Topock said exasperated: " Shut up, Andy—let him get the thing told!" And to Vargas, "They was gone, eh?"

Vargas nodded.

"You were saying something about New River."

"Yeah. I was sayin', Lou, the sign appeared to point that way——"

"Appeared?" Brill said.

"Uh-huh. You see," Vargas smiled, "somebody had rubbed it out."

CHAPTER VIII

GUY TOPOCK

THERE was something wicked, something wild and ugly in the swing of Cooper's shoulders as he came round the table on cat-soft feet and started for the door.

"Where you goin'?" Topock glared.

"After them goddam squatters! I'm goin' to find out where they went an' I'm——"

"You're goin' to stay right where you are. Safford's the man to handle that——"

Cooper's uncharitable look raked Safford intolerantly. He said nothing. He was started for the door again when Topock's hand clamped hold of a shoulder, spun him round. "Get back on that stool an' stay there!"

Across three feet of piled-up silence the Texans eyed each other. Cooper's face was twisted, scowling;

Topock's stare was like spilled ink. Then abruptly Cooper wilted, went sulkily back to his stool.

There was a new respect in Safford's stare. Brill's looked odd, uncertain, nervous; the glint of Vargas' remained unchanged. Safford said, " You want me to——"

" I want you to get on the trail of those homesteaders pronto. I want to know where the hell they're goin'; or if they've got there, where they went." Rage still thickened Topock's talking. He drew a deep breath and said more quietly: " Don't ride up to 'em. Don't talk to them an' don't let them know you've followed 'em—don't let them see you at all. When you've found out where they're headed, come back an' tell me. Don't come back without you do."

Safford nodded, wheeled through the door. Kerwold's foreman closed it behind him.

Brill, troubled glance on Topock, said: " Think you ought to trust him that way? "

" I don't trust nobody," Topock said, and his look at Brill was a warning. He put that glance at Vargas then. " What's Gann got against Holcomb? "

Duarte Vargas' eyes showed a faint surprise. " How'd you know——? "

" I'm askin' the questions," Topock snapped. " What's he got against him? "

The expression of Vargas' cheeks changed subtly. " Goes a long way back," he said, and paused as though considering. " Gann used to be in the sheep business. Got to nursin' the idea once he'd like to see sheep in this basin; didn't figure he could cut it by himself, so he propositioned Holcomb—tried to get Straddle Bug's backing. Said they'd split profits fifty-fifty, him to furnish the sheep an' Holcomb to furnish assistance if the going got a little rough. Holcomb turned him down flat; said if he brought sheep into this country Straddle Bug would undertake to kill 'em off fast as they showed. Holcomb," Vargas added suggestively, " is one of the gents Sam Kerwold set up in business."

Topock stood silent a moment. " That all Gann's got against Holcomb? "

" Not quite. Short time after that some of Gann's best beef started takin' sick an' one night somebody fired his range, an' a little bit later two of his stacks was burned an' he come near losin' his buildin's. It's never been proved Holcomb had any part in it, but Gann's always blamed him for it."

" How did it get out Gann wanted to bring sheep into the country? "

" Holcomb told it—or one of Holcomb's outfit. I ain't sure which. Gann lays it to Holcomb. I know Holcomb offered to buy Gann out."

" Nothing come of it, eh? "

Duarte Vargas shrugged. The glint of his eyes turned ironic. " Three-four months after that, Holcomb found two of his water-holes poisoned. It got around his crew laid it on to Gann, but Holcomb never done nothing about it—never would talk about it, either. Fact is, he never talks much about anything. Got a rough lock on his jaw, I guess—lives all the time under his hat."

Topock said to Vargas: " Next time you run across Holcomb, mebbe you better let drop Gann's throwin' his jaw round about him. Spread it on thick, tell him Gann's talkin' about a shoot-out next time Holcomb crosses his track."

By the wall, Brill's glance went roundly inquiring. " You figurin' to start things between them two again? "

" Long as these outfits stand pat," Topock said,

"we can't do anything with them. Get 'em at each other's throats an' half our work's done for us." He looked Brill over thoughtfully. "You might start the word to circulatin' that Gann's talkin' sheep again. And next time Gann comes in here it might be a good idea for him to get the notion Holcomb's makin' war talk."

Vargas said with his eyes showing crafty, "Willow Creek Wally's a man you can use. He hates Ab Holcomb like castor oil—used to be Straddle Bug's foreman——"

Topock said: "This Wally's in your string, ain't he, Andy?" and Cooper nodded sullenly.

"What about Pring?" Brill said.

"I was comin' to that," Topock nodded. "You might sort of hint to Kerwold, Vargas, that Gus Pring's borrowin' heavy to get that Wildcat lease——"

Kerwold's foreman shook his head. "That's out. Sam won't listen to a thing against Pring——"

"Never mind. Mention you heard it, anyway. Suspicion's the best weapon we've got. Get enough of these outfits uneasy an' the rest'll be a cinch. The way to lick a game like this is to use every card you can get hold of."

Vargas' glance, while Topock was expounding this philosophy, showed far back in its depths the glint of a secret amusement. But his cheeks were darkly sober when he said, "What about this new man, Guy? You forgettin' him?"

"What new man?"

"That fella Dane I brought in last night."

"What about him?"

"I don't know." Vargas' tone was evasive. "Seemed like a pretty cool customer—I was sort of wonderin' if we could use him——"

"I'll take care of him," Topock answered flatly. "You mind what I told you. Get to work on Holcomb and Kerwold. Brill—you get Pecos Gann stirred up, and Andy," he said with a look at Cooper, "you go fetch Willow Creek Wally. Him an' me is due for a talk."

"Uh—just a minute," Brill said; "I thought——"

"Thinkin' ain't in your line, Brill. You just leave that chore to me. An' while I think of it," Topock said casually, "what's the total of them I.O.U.s you're holdin' on young Tim Ransome?"

"About eighteen hundred dollars——"

"All right. That's plenty—let's have 'em."

There was a visible reluctance in the way Brill got out his billfold, but he passed the papers over without remark and watched Topock button them into his shirt pocket.

Topock looked about with a cold, hard grin. "So Kerwold thinks I wouldn't do much in the cow business, does he?" His laugh was a soft thing, exultant. "Gents, in a month we'll be owning this country."

CHAPTER IX

NIGHT RIDERS

WHAT Duarte Vargas had said in Brill's back room concerning Sam Kerwold and the departure of the homesteaders' wagons from Wildcat Hill was not, strictly speaking, true—leastways it was not the whole truth. He had implied that Old Sam had not talked with the wagon men, whereas, as a matter of fact,

Kerwold had. With Vargas right at his side, Sam
Kerwold had ridden up to the homesteaders' camp.
His remarks, though brief, had been courteous and
not at all unfriendly. He mentioned admiring their
grit and fortitude, flattered their intelligence at
picking such good ground, and then, casually, had
expressed his surprise at their daring in thinking to
file on land so soon to be put up for lease at public
auction. "Of course," he said, "the land's open right
now to filing, but with all these womenfolks an' kids
along, I would think you'd rather pick land that—
even though it might not be so good as this—wouldn't
be so apt to cloud your horizon with gun-smoke."

The homesteaders eyed him with varying stages of
unease.

Old Sam explained. "You see, boys, this here's the
way the thing shapes up. Three-four big outfits is
after this lease; each one of them, I reckon, is figurin'
to bid it in—I understand there's considerable feelin'
about it. Fact is, I'd like to bid it in myself, as far
as that goes. But you folks are on it and I appreciate
your rights. Far as I'm concerned you can stay, an'
welcome. But some of these outfits ain't broad-minded
as I am; they'd call you 'weed-benders' an' figure you
got no more right to this land than plain squatters.
Some of 'em might get a little rough. Until right
lately this country has all been open range—free
grass, you understand; anybody's land for the grazin'.
Seein' your boys ploughin' it up is liable to make
some of these fellows pretty ringy. I don't know that
they'd actually molest you, but in my time I've seen
some pretty ugly things happen to folks that was
ploughin' up grass."

He paused a bit to let these words sink in a little;
and it was plain the wagon men were worried. "I'm

not tryin' to dictate to you fellows; I wouldn't undertake to say what you ought to do—that's one of the fine things about this country, a man does what he sees fit to do, the choice is strictly his own. But in your place," Kerwold said, and his tone was a little more sombre, " I think I'd hunt me a place with more elbow room, somewheres the cow outfits wasn't quite so big. It's not much pleasure," he went on, " puttin' your life savin's into a place and then have some damn cowman burn you out. Not much fun, either, gettin' up some morning to find your best saddlers hamstrung, your fences cut an' your stock run off or slaughtered. Things like that seem to happen round here and they don't much care who they happen to. My own wire was cut to-night—three miles of it slashed to ribbons, an' half the posts lugged off to feed somebody's cook-stove.

" Now there's some land over east of here—over by Yellow Jacket Spring; *good* land, too, an' never taken up, and no big cow outfits to bother you. I ain't sayin' you ought to go there, but in your place that's where I'd go. You do whatever you think is best for you—that's the nice part about this country; you got that privilege. Good night."

That was what Sam Kerwold told them, and two hours later they were gone. Not toward New River and the rest of the homestead outfits, as Vargas had suggested when relating their departure to Topock, but creaking and clanking eastward toward the Yellow Jacket and Methodist Mountain.

And there was one small other thing that Vargas had forgotten to mention. The sign had been rubbed out, he said—and it had, for two-three miles. But he had not seen fit to tell them he had rubbed the tracks out himself.

When Bufford Dane had said good night to Holly at the back door of the Ransome store building, she quite naturally had supposed that he was going to bed himself; and he did go into the store-room she had placed at his disposal, but he did not get into the bunk.

He sat down on its edge and pulled his boots off, dropped them noisily on the floor. Rising, then, he picked them up and, carrying them in his left hand, returned soundlessly to the porch. With his weight gingerly settled against the porch edge, he put the boots back on again and, quietly making his way to the stable, hoisted his gear to a shoulder and stealthily led the blue roan away. A quarter of a mile from Ransome's he put the animal under gear, stepped into the saddle and struck off south and east. Others besides Holly Ransome would have been startled had they known this; the thought put its own kind of smile across Dane's dark and wind-whipped cheeks.

Dane's glance went up to the stars. Be several hours till dawn. This country was unfamiliar to him and the moonless night disclosed few landmarks. He rode slowly, not so much confused as cautious. He had no wish to be discovered by chance wayfarers.

He kept an easy pace until, some half-hour later, he cut the trail he had been hunting. This he followed for three miles until certain his sign was lost among the tracks of other travellers. He swung then to the left, putting the blue roan's head dead east.

Near one he reached the footslopes leading up to Wildcat Hill. A gentle walk took him quartering through these rises. When he sighted the first of the wagons he stopped the horse and dismounted. Leading the animal, he inched forward slowly till he'd got the lay of things. Then into the saddle he went again; walked the horse grimly into the firelight.

There were startled exclamations, a smothered curse or two. Men came out of their blankets nervously; fire showed the glint of fear in their eyes. That stilled and watchful waiting showed the state of their unease.

Dane said: "Who's the leader of this outfit?"

A man came out of the shadows and stopped across the fire from Dane. He said reluctantly, "I am."

"Guess you understand," Dane said, "you're squattin' on a lease. Got anything to tell me why these wagons shouldn't be burned?"

Back in the shadows a woman gasped. A child started snivelling and was instantly hushed.

The wagon boss said, "That talk won't buy you nothin', mister. We know our rights. This land ain't leased—nor won't be if we file."

"That's right," Dane said, and let the stillness gather. There was in him a strong dislike for this chore, but his indebtedness to Sam Kerwold went back a long, long way. And he was a man who paid his debts.

The man before him shifted weight. He said a little harshly: "What are you here for, then?"

"There's one or two things," Dane said, "you'd better know before you file."

And when the quiet became again intolerable the wagon boss growled, "What are they?"

Dane took his time in answering and his look got wholly bleak. "First and foremost," he said then, "there's this to be considered. The cows are goin' to have this land whether you file on it or not. Past experience should tell you this—if it don't you can take my word for it. This is cattle country. It's goin' to stay cattle country no matter how many nesters get themselves killed, no matter how many wagons have to be burned. Why butt your heads against a damn stone wall? There's plenty good land to the east of here—land you can have an' welcome. But you can't have this . . . Understand me? This land belongs to the cows."

The wagon boss was rattled. Dane's words were having effect. Back in the shadows the child cried again and this time nobody stopped it. The wagon boss was badly placed. Pressure of opinion moved him to get out the makings with what was intended to be an appearance of unconcern. But he couldn't cut it. The shake of his hands spilled tobacco and with a sudden curse he flung the stuff away from him. Defiance edged his sullen stare and brashly, reckless, he snarled:

"All right. You've had your say—now I'll have mine! You damn cow wallopers think you own the earth——"

"Just a minute."

Dane's soft drawl was wholly quiet, yet it stopped the man in mid-sentence, stopped him with his mouth still open—left him that way, stiffly.

Into this quiet came a man's startled gasp. "My God! That's Bufe Telldane!"

They were like a wail, those nerve-jerked words that came from behind the wagon boss. They seemed to sear these homesteaders' minds with the scorch of a branding iron. Colour fled their cheeks and panic dropped their jaws. They stood behind their leader like a row of blasted trees, their features blank as pounded metal. The wagon boss's eyes seemed frozen as they stared in glassy fascination at the mounted man before him.

Such was the shocking power that lay in that dread name.

Dane, lounged loosely in the saddle, saw the consternation in their faces and knew that his work was done. There would be no wagons left on Wildcat Hill by dawn.

He nodded coldly. " Yes. I'm Bufe Telldane. Do you need any further reasons why you had better get off this lease? "

The wagon boss made some attempt at pulling himself together. There was no belligerence left in him now; only a marvelling kind of wonder. He seemed surprised to find himself still alive and capable of movement. He said huskily, " No—no, I reckon not. We—we'll get hitched up right away."

Dane nodded silently and backed his horse out of the light, and a few yards off watched patiently till, creaking and clanking, the wagons, got at last into line, rolled wearily off toward the east.

And still he sat there, dismally, loose-jointed in the saddle, chin on chest and thoughts gone bleak as any in the homesteaders' minds. He was not proud of this night's work; there was no satisfaction in him. He had achieved the object of his ride, and by that much had lessened Kerwold's hold on him. But he took no pleasure from the performance, nor from contemplation of it. If the fact that the homesteaders' moving had been accomplished without resort to gunplay were any consolation, his face did not reveal it.

He was still there in the saddle when wind brought new smell of dust to his nostrils, and a short time later his keen ears told him a ridden horse was mounting toward the hilltop. Afterwards he saw the rider come quartering out of the night and briefly stop, outlined in the dying embers' glow. He saw the man lean from his horse, watched him study the track-marked ground, and then, still watching, saw him canter across the broad plateau and vanish in the direction the wagons had gone.

He was still there, still later, when the man came back, leading his horse and with a jackpine's branch carefully wiping out the trail. The man's face wore a grin when, finally, by the fire he stopped and, satisfied, broke the branch to bits and flung them on the embers. There was a tiny blaze and by that light Dane saw his face.

The man was Kerwold's foreman, Vargas.

CHAPTER X

"MY GOD—TELLDANE!"

TELLDANE got down when the man had gone.

He stripped the gear from his roan, turned the animal loose on a picket-rope and then strode off a way and there threw his saddle down and, drawing a tarp up over him, put his head upon it and went to sleep.

He slept at once, for this was his will and he had trained himself to the habit. There were those who claimed that he never slept—that a man with his past could not. But these were wrong; he slept, and well; no ghosts could run Telldane's life.

His awakening, like all his acts, was sudden. One moment he lay sleeping, the next he was awake—completely so.

He let no sign betray it. His eyes stayed closed. He had not moved; his breathing continued natural. But all his faculties were alert and functioning. No sound had brought him out of sleep, no touch—nothing a man could lay hold of. Yet Telldane knew there was danger near; it was this sixth sense had roused him.

Something breathed near him and crack-like his closed eyes came open. Just the merest slit. Yet beneath the tarp that look promoted movement. His right hand moved—not quickly, not far; but when it stopped it had solid hold of a gun-butt.

The moon was up and by its light a figure showed grim-crouched above him. By his head it was. Squatted on its boot-heels with blurred face scant inches from Telldane's own.

Telldane's eyes came completely open. His left hand flung the tarp aside, his right hand brought the pistol up—straight up, cocked and levelled, muzzle gaping into the crouched man's face.

" Get back."

With a startled oath the man reared back on his boot-heels. Both hands jumped above his hat and a hoarse, scared squawk spilled out of him. " Don't shoot! Don't—— My God! *Telldane!* "

The moments crawled while Telldane watched him grimly. As the seconds passed, the silence thickened. A kind of shake got into the fellow's knees and he blurted with obvious sincerity, " God, Bufe—I hadn't no idear 'twas you . . ."

" I believe you," Telldane said, and a cold amusement edged his voice. Then the amusement was gone and the voice was only cold—an extreme cold that had unnerved tougher men than this one. " What are you doing here, Holcomb? "

Holcomb winced, but recovered quickly and said

with his cheeks wholly bland: "Why, I'm a rancher, Bufe—'member how I always het up to be one? Well, I am one now. Got a pretty fair outfit—Straddle Bug, up near Gone Wrong Canyon."

"You picked a good location," Telldane murmured. Then, more sharply: "But that's not answering my question. Hunkerin' over a sleeping man that way will one day get your face blown off."

"I can see that." Holcomb loosed a gusty breath. "God!"

"What were you up to? 'Fraid you'd miss if you didn't get real close, were you?"

Holcomb's face registered horrified denial. "You know I wouldn't go for to shoot you, Bufe——"

"Not if I saw you startin', you wouldn't. Now quit beatin' about the bush an' say quick what you were up to."

"Why—I—I wa'n't up to nothin', hardly. Honest, Bufe! Why, I ain't got no better friend in the whole wide world'n what you been——"

"Glad to see you appreciate it," Telldane said dryly. "Guess you were out huntin' strays or something— s'pose they're easier caught at night, aren't they?"

Holcomb was not confounded. The shine of sweat was on his face but he said doggedly: "Ha-ha! One of your little jokes, eh, Bufe? Recollect you allus was queer that way. Matter of fact, I *was* huntin' strays. Some of my fence got cut the other night an'——"

"Never mind improvin' on it." Derision curved Bufe Telldane's lips. Some remembered need then changed their slant abruptly. He said—and his tone was solemn: "I've got one word for you, Ab Holcomb. You can consider this a warning; and there won't be any more of them. You keep out of what's brewing in this basin, or——"

"God's sake, Bufe——"

"Never mind the protestations. An' you can tuck that paraded virtue back in the mothballs with your conscience. There's trouble—*bad* trouble—shaping up in these mountain meadows. See that you keep out of it."

Giving the man no time for jawing, Telldane turned and strode after his horse.

CHAPTER XI

THE BEST LAID PLANS——

FALSE dawn was shoving its first grey light across the basin when Bufe Telldane rode down from the hills and approached the Ransome store. As a rule, only members of the cow-punching clan were abroad at such an ungodly hour. Perhaps this thought had some part in the surprise that was slimming his glance as he eyed intently the three strange broncs loosely tied to the store-front's veranda.

Tossing his own reins over the rail, Telldane got thoughtfully out of the saddle. There was laughter inside and rough talk that he could not distinguish, nor could he make out Holly Ransome's voice—just man sound, and not particularly pleasant. He stood there moveless a moment, undecided. He hitched up his cartridge-belt and took a step toward the porch. He recalled then how the porch boards creaked, and with a tiny shake of the head he went around the place and entered from the rear.

The kitchen was empty, but voice sound was louder now, drifting back out of the store. He stopped by the door leading through, stood paused there an instant, considering. Something he heard then put a cold sensation along his back. He kicked the door wide open and stepped through with a gun in his hand.

He didn't speak. He didn't need to. The situation was plain all round. Ransome was in a chair and the girl, cheeks putty-white, was against the wall near by him. One man stood with his back to Telldane; he had a pointed gun on the Ransomes and his ribald talk was directed at Holly while his two companions were rifling the safe. The crash of Telldane's boot opening the door had pulled this fellow's head clear round. Before the safe his companions crouched like carven images. They wore no masks and their startled looks betrayed the state of their emotions.

"Drop it," Telldane said, and the man whose weapon had been menacing Holly and her father let go his pistol instantly. It struck the floor with a brittle clatter just as the front door was flung open by Topock who came wickedly in with a gun in each fist.

In that second of switched attention that Telldane's glance wheeled to find Guy Topock there was a crash of breaking glass and Bufe Telldane's back-flashing stare showed the men at the safe going through a window. He slammed one swift shot and was starting forward when the third man dived between Topock's knees and went skidding on to the porch. Telldane's charge was tripped by Topock's foot. Both men went down in a tangle. By the time they had extricated themselves and Telldane had reached the porch, the three erstwhile robbers were aboard their horses and quirting hard up the hillside.

Topock, diving for his horse, blocked Telldane's aim, and when the way lay clear again the robbers were beyond good pistol range. With tightening lips Telldane thrust the six-shoter back in his belt and grimly watched while Topock knocked dust from the hill with his rifle. But all three riders crossed the ridge and vanished and Topock, cursing, straightened and slammed the rifle back into its scabbard.

"Of all the rotten luck!" He wheeled abruptly, belligerently. "What the hell was goin' on here anyway?"

Telldane, without answering, was turning into the store when Topock's arm roughly flung him around. "By God, I asked you somethin', mister! I asked what was goin' on!"

His loud talk brought the Ransomes out. They watched by the door, still shaken, nervous. But Telldane didn't look at them. His glance met Topock's contemptuously. "Askin' *me*, are you?"

"Yes, I'm askin' you—an' I'll have an answer!"

"Sure you will, if you want one." Telldane's tone was level, his eyes still scornful. "There wasn't nothing happening, as you'd ought to know. Just a little grandstand play that kind of fizzled."

He smiled as Topock's face abruptly reddened, grew scarlet with rage and hate.

Then Topock was lunging forward, reaching for Telldane's shirt collar, snarling blasphemies and vileness. "You damn cow-flunky! Are you insinuatin'——"

"If the boot fits, pull it on."

Guy Topock swung then, a wild and rageful blow designed to catch Telldane unawares—to smash him reeling from the porch and drop him sprawling in the dust; and it probably would have, had it landed.

But Telldane leaned just then. Leaned forward and came swiftly up inside his guard with a teeth-jarring hook that lifted Topock off his boot-heels and set him dizzy against a post. His head rolled loosely and for that second it seemed like he would fall. Then with the roar of a bull his head came up; his right hand slapped his pistol's stock, had the weapon half out of leather when Telldane struck again. The cold fury of that blow exploded against the Texan's ear—against its lobe and the base of his jaw. It drove him stumbling from the porch. He struck the ground off balance and lurched three staggering, uncontrolled steps that caromed him solidly against the tie-rail and hung him there by an outflung arm among the snorting horses.

A malicious satisfaction sat the slant of Telldane's cheeks.

Holly looked from him to Topock with a startled wonder on her face, and when her eyes came back a kind of fear was in them; that and something else. The something else took over and she coldly turned and went inside the store.

But old Ransome's eyes were bright and round and the shape of his lips was wholly pleased. His hands were clenched and he kept mumbling over and over something that to Telldane sounded suspiciously unorthodox.

Telldane smiled a little wryly and stood gently rubbing his knuckles. But the bleakness of his stare remained intently, watchfully, on Topock.

The Texan stirred. He pulled the chin up off his chest and rolled bleared eyes about him dazedly. But there was no recognition in his face for what he saw. He was like some shanghaied sailor first awakening at sea. Then change rocked across his face, reshaping

c*

it to the malignant pattern of his bestial thoughts.

Dread edged Ransome's gaze as the Texan, groaning, got himself afoot and stood there, swaying groggily. His high roan colouring was gone; the bloated cheeks showed livid, mottled. There was something wild, abysmal, unreasoning, in the look he put on Telldane.

Telldane smiled remotely. " Got enough? "

Topock wheeled then, went lurching to his horse without reply. One shaking hand sought out the horn and he dragged himself into the saddle and rode directly off.

CHAPTER XII

A MAN DECIDES

TELLDANE saw very clearly what the Texan had been up to. Topock *himself* had planned the robbery, had hired those three to play their parts that he might appear in the nick of time to save the Ransomes' money and be deemed by them a hero. But luck had defeated him—the luck that had brought Telldane upon the scene to witness and to blast it. Telldane had guessed the thing was a put-up job the moment Topock came through the door; had been certain of it when the Texan twice had blocked his aim at the departing robbers and then, himself, had missed them. He wondered a little grimly if it had been Topock who had recently tried to bushwhack him. Though he'd said nothing about it, *someone* had tried to get him with a rifle. It was early this morning while he'd been riding to the store—just before he'd come out of the hills while the light was yet uncertain. It had been close the way that lead had viciously banged off the horn of his saddle.

Breakfast was eaten pretty much in silence. There was little talk, and this was mainly enthusiastic comment from old Ransome on the way Telldane had given ' that tough Texan what he's been asking for.' Holly listened in a scornful silence that soon choked off the old man's talk. He quit the table when he finished eating.

Telldane was amused at the way the girl ignored him. Her frozen courtesy did not bother him in the least. He cared nothing for her opinion—cared no more for what she thought of him than he would for a bullsnake's hissing. Both were harmless, beneath his notice. And he had learned by now that women were all alike. Put a sack over their heads and shake them up and you couldn't tell one from the other.

But he harked to what she was saying. Politeness demanded that.

"I suppose you feel real proud of yourself," she observed with a cold disdain.

The nod his head gave was not for her, but for the cherished conviction her tone and manner vindicated. She appeared blithely intent on proving his conception of women a just one. Shallow, empty-headed, selfish. She was like all the rest, he thought—deriving their greatest enjoyment when they were ripping some man to pieces. Oh, Telldane knew them! They liked to pose as demurely innocent while, cat-like, trying out their claws. Their chiefest sport was had in discovering and dissecting the varying degrees of passion they were able to rouse in a man. They were like black widow spiders; and he reflected with pitying condescension what great fools were men like Topock who sought to shackle them for parlour ornaments. Why, they'd safer coddle vipers!

He knew a second's regret for having exposed the Texan's hand. The punishment would have been as sure and a deal more fitting had he let the man's ruse succeed.

"Of course," Holly told him scornfully, "your intention was to make me believe that Guy Topock was back of that robbery—that he hired those men to rob us. I hope you realize your time was wasted——"

"Aren't good intentions always?"

"Oh!" she cried. "A philosopher, too!"

"Too?" he said incautiously. "What else am I discovered to be?"

"A drifting bravo, certainly. Gun-fighter is stamped all over you!" She said with curling lip: "Are you finding lots of bidders for your guns in Tonto Basin?"

He said a little grimly: "What give you the idea I was huntin' any?"

"Isn't that why you came here?"

His regard for her was reticent. His glance was resentful, hostile. She was like the rest of them—slick with her words; could flap her tongue any way she'd a mind to. There was no use arguing. No use trying to match them. A man was beat before he started.

Then a perverse humour seized him, a mood quite as contrary as her own. He said maliciously: "Yes, that's so. I picked the right spot for finding trouble. Why, only last night I run them crazy wagoners plumb off the Wildcat Hill——"

"Oh!" she cried, cheeks shading pale; and, holding aside her skirts as she passed him, got out of her chair and hastened off—no doubt to tell her father.

Well, let her tell him—let her tell the whole damn basin. By all means let her tell it! Give those bucks a thing or two to think about. He would like to see Guy Topock's face when the Texan finally heard it.

But he had plenty to think about himself—one thing especially; and his face grimed up as he thought of it. What bitter irony that the cause of his own downfall should be here in person to confound him! He had thought to have done with that, to have put its curse behind him. But three reckless years had not done this; it began to look as though three thousand wouldn't. He could not think of her calmly. The ignominious truth—though he denied it savagely—was that he was still fool enough to care for her. And now to find that she was here—that she was the daughter of old Sam Kerwold who held Bufe in his debt as result of past relations—this was the final straw!

With a muttered oath he crushed his smoke, grinding it bitterly into his plate. All the world must be bent in laughter at the luck of Bufe Telldane. That luck had once been a by-word. It bid fair to be again, he thought, and got wickedly to his feet, all the lines of his face made harsh by the rageful passion that rode him.

What were Kerwold's puny troubles when set beside his own? Why should Bufe Telldane risk his life (not that it was worth much!) and besmirch still further his already tarnished repute to help the father of the person who had spoiled that life in the first place?

By God, he would not!

To hell with them! Kerwold had brewed this

range war; let him stew in it! Let him hoard his water—let him grab his land and wire it! Let him fight his own damn battles! It was no skin off Bufe Telldane's nose!

And if Kerwold were licked, were humbled, then serve him right—serve that stuck-up filly of his right also! Maybe it would knock some of the damn pride out of her!

With the thought, Telldane slammed out of his chair. He would get on his horse and ride. Shake the dust of this feuding basin. Jane had made a fool of him once—she would not get that chance again! He'd been a fool, all right, and a soft-headed fool, but he'd not be one any longer!

Ransome called to him as he strode through the store, but the clack of Bufe's spurs was the only answer the old man got. Telldane was geared to getting out before the soft streak in him changed his mind again.

The mood shoved him round the house and headed him toward the stable. But half-way there he brought up with a snort. The roan was hitched to the rail out front. He retraced his steps, impatiently rounded the porch. Yes, the roan was tied there, head down, dozing. With his hand on the horn Telldane paused, harsh of eyes, grim-scowling. Sam, after his fashion, was a fine old man. Be pretty ornery, running out on him this way. Sam was depending on him—had every right to do so. That the obligation had been incurred without Telldane's sanction or approval was neither here nor there; that obligation existed. It was a just one. With every reason for standing pat— with none at all for helping him, Sam Kerwold three years back had saved Bufe's life, and it was Telldane's code that he must repay what the world—had it known

—would have regarded as a favour.

Bufe did some thinking, bitterly weighed the pros and cons. But it all came back to that. Kerwold had once risked much to save Bufe's life and Bufe was bound to square it.

Well, it would soon be over, one way or the other. And he needn't spend any time at Kerwold's—in fact, from every standpoint, the farther he stayed from Kerwold's, the better for all concerned. It would not be necessary to see Jane again—no one need know they had ever been acquainted. *He* wouldn't tell; and it was a lead-pipe *cinch* she wouldn't!

Yes, he'd stay a little longer. Till the Flying K was on safe footing; till he'd driven Sam's enemies out of the brush—or killed them. For it would probably come to that. Some way Topock had his knife out for Sam; and someone else, for a long time back, had been whetting up his cleaver. Bufe would take care of these birds, then drift, get out of the country.

Thus resolved, he was turning away from the blue roan's saddle when a bullet's whine drilled past his cheek and rifle's sound smashed challenge from the hills.

CHAPTER XIII

DUE WARNING

Topock had claimed he didn't trust anyone; yet all his plans were geared to and controlled by information Duarte Vargas had furnished.

Brill carried out his orders and started rumour circulating that Gann was talking sheep again and the word was spread with dispatch. To Holcomb, Brill said that Gann was tanking up these days and threatening to down Ab Holcomb on sight. Holcomb's cheeks got black with anger and he stamped from the place breathing brimstone. When Gann came, Brill mentioned casually that Holcomb was making war talk again, bringing up that forgotten business about his water-holes getting poisoned; and Gann, too, went away snarling oaths and curses. But to make sure the seed was planted on good ground, Topock sent Andy Cooper and his riders out one moonless night; and next day Holcomb was around with an outraged tale of gutted buildings and hamstrung horses, and Gann's friends heard of pulled down fences and dead, stampeded cattle.

It looked a heap like one more night would see red blood smeared across the moon.

Jesse Brill prepared for trouble.

His precautions were few and simple. He took all the cash from his safe and stuffed it in a money-belt which he strapped about his waist. He put his spare socks in his bedroll, and with that bulk across his left shoulder, was starting for the door when he remembered the cash in the till. He went and got it, cramming it in his pockets. He took one final look around. He glanced at the clock above the bar—3 p.m. of a hot afternoon; something warned him it would be a lot hotter by this time to-morrow.

He wheeled and was almost to the door again when it opened and a man came in—a stranger Brill had never seen before. But he knew who it was and that knowledge disturbed him, unsettled him. He took three more steps and stopped, rooted by a sudden fear.

There was nothing of menace in the stranger's pose. But Brill didn't like the smile on his lips—nor the cold, hard light of his stare.

Brill licked dry lips, at a loss to understand himself. Seemed like his blood had turned to water. He'd been hurrying, anxious to get out of this place, to get clear out of the country. Yet here he stood, motionless, speechless, bathed in an icy sweat.

The man by the door seemed to read his thoughts. The smile on his face grew wider. "Don't let me keep you, Brill. Run right along if you want to."

But Brill did not move. In an agony of fear and indecision he stood there gaping like a ninny. He wanted desperately to go, but something in that yonder man's stare kept him anchored in his tracks. He felt abruptly queer, light-headed: the place was hot as Egypt, yet there were cold chills crawling his back.

The stranger quit the door, came cat-footing forward a step or two. "Got a pencil, Brill? Got a paper handy?"

"You——" Brill moistened his lips again. "You mean a paper for writin' on?"

"I wasn't figuring to build no kite."

What hell's kind of talk was that? Brill didn't like the fellow's look—it was a sight too cold and watchful. Remindful of a spider with his eyes fixed on a fly.

Unaccountably Brill shivered and a shake got into his legs. He sought to pull himself together. "There's a pencil on the bar," he mumbled; and watched the stranger get it. A faint blur of motion then grabbed the turning tag-end of Brill's gaze, whipped it nervously round. From a corner of the window next the door Llano Tallbook's face stared in at him. *No!*—

that sly and malevolent gaze of Pecos Gann's wagon boss went beyond Brill—must be fixed upon the stranger.

Gone stiffly still as a statue, Brill saw jubilation suddenly brighten Tallbook's slitted stare; saw a gun-barrel come into sight beside the mask that was Llano's face—saw that cold tube shift and focus.

Gun's thunder shook the room, lashed the walls in shattered echoes. Llano's head fell away from the window with a blue hole through its forehead.

Brill whirled to find the stranger smiling, a smoking pistol in his hand. "Third time's a charm," the stranger drawled, and sheathing his gun, went across to a post and with a knife removed the tacks from a land bid notice and, reversing it, scrawled something on its back with the pencil he had picked up off the bar.

Still rooted, Brill watched him put it back on the post, drive the tacks in with his gun-butt. "Guess that'll do," he nodded, and with a hard look at Brill, went out.

Mechanically Brill walked up to the post. He stood there for a long time whitely eyeing the man's scrawled message. He braced himself against the post, went out of the place like a man gone blind.

Hours later Guy Topock came in. He stared around impatiently, several times shouting for Brill. He went behind the bar then and, thoughtfully, looked in the till. He scowled at the open safe, deep-frowning, finally helped himself from a bottle. He was lifting his glass when he saw the handwriting tacked to the post and crossed as Brill had crossed to stand and stare—but unlike Brill—very briefly.

"My God!" he said, and the glass fell out of his hand.

Completely absorbed he read again:

TO WHOM IT MAY CONCERN

By this writing due warning is served on all and
sundry that homesteaders, nesters or anyone else
caught squatting on the Wildcat lease lands will
be personally and speedily taken care of by

Yours truly,

BUFE TELLDANE.

With a curse, Topock ripped the warning from the
post and tore it into bits. Still swearing, and with a
face gone black as thunder, he went out of Brill's at
a wicked lope, flung himself into the saddle, and
an instant later was racing across the valley, spilling
blasphemies at every jolt.

CHAPTER XIV

AT HOLCOMB'S

AROUND eight o'clock of a bright crisp morning two
days later, Telldane rode down out of the pines and
into Ab Holcomb's ranch headquarters. He had been
doing a pile of thinking. What was going on was
obvious enough; how to prevent its continuing was
the thing that most was bothering him. It wasn't so
much Kerwold's lack of popularity among his neigh-
bours that was bringing this trouble to Flying K, as
it was some older, deeper-rooted score. Someone
wanted Flying K range or wanted Sam Kerwold
smashed. It was the only reasonable explanation for

what was building in this basin. *Why* was another matter; Telldane was not concerned with motives— not primarily, at least. His interest lay in blocking the things; in stopping it, thus easing himself out of Kerwold's debt that he might be free to ride.

He saw the man by the saddle-shed door—saw the rifle the man had hold of. But, ignoring them both, he stepped to the porch and knocked. Holcomb's heavy voice came at once the length of a hallway. "Gettin' goddam polite these days! Come in."

He found the Straddle Bug boss in an office at the back of the house. Holcomb's quick, upwheeling stare was one of surprise, Bufe thought; and of some-thing else—concern, maybe.

But the man had his wits about him. He said rumblingly: "Howdy, Bufe—been wonderin' when you'd drop around. Mindful of ol' times, ain't it— me an' you gettin' together this way? Sit down. What's under your hat?"

Telldane took off the hat and looked.

Holcomb forced another grin. "Same ol' Bufe." He said sententiously: "Nothin' ever changes, does it?"

"I been wonderin'," Telldane mentioned, and with a grim look peeled the gloves from his hands and laid them on the desk. "What do you know about Brill's killing?"

Holcomb looked nervous. He said vehemently: "'Fore God, Bufe, I had no hand in that!"

Sweat broke out on his forehead. He shifted under Telldane's stare; pounded the desk in protest. "God-damit, I wasn't even *near* the place!"

Telldane kept on looking at him.

Holcomb found the silence disturbing. He snarled: "Why pick on *me* ever' time somethin' happens?

You run me out of Texas—you goin' to run me out
of this place, too?"

"Depends," Bufe said. "What you got against
Pecos Gann?"

"Gann!" Holcomb hauled his boots down off the
desk angrily. "Who said——"

"It's common talk. What's back of it?"

"Ain't anything back of it. It's a damn malicious
lie! Dammit, all I *get* is trouble," he snarled resentfully. "Ain't nobody got a good word for me!"

"Kerwold ain't turned against you, has he?"

"What's the meanin' of that?"

"Gave you a start in the cow business, didn't he?"

With a bitter oath Holcomb surged from his chair.

"Sit down," Telldane said. "I ain't finished. The
story's goin' round that you and Gann had trouble
over sheep. That Gann came to you with a proposition; that you turned it down flat—said you'd kill
every sheep he brought in. It was right after that
someone burned his range. And then your water-
holes was poisoned . . ."

Telldane stopped at the look on Ab's wide face.
"What's the matter? Ain't that so?"

Holcomb was eyeing him queerly. "Some of it's so,
I guess—the part about the fire an' poisoned water-
holes. But you sure as hell got your signals mixed.
It was Pring—Gus Pring—Gann put that sheep deal
up to. Knew better'n to try that game on me. After
Pring turned him down, he come over here with
another bee in his bonnet—Gann, I'm talkin' of.
Wanted to throw his spread an' mine together, wanted
to start a syndicate—declared we could grab this
country—run the rest of 'em outa business." He
added virtuously: "I told him no—nothin' doin'. I
didn't want no part in it."

"Why's he threatening to gun you?"

"That squirt! Gun *me*? I could shoot the buttons off his pants any day he names!" The look Holcomb shoved at Telldane now was blackly edged with suspicion. "Where'd you get that, anyway?"

Telldane shrugged. "Then it isn't true?"

"It may be true, but it's goddam cock-eyed if it is! Gann might be wantin' like hell to see me planted— never was no love lost between us—but it sure ain't like him to go throwin' his jaw around that way. Somebody must be shovin' him."

The same thought had just struck Telldane. "Know who it would be?"

Holcomb shook his head. "He's seein' a lot of that new guy, Topock—leastways I've heard he is."

Telldane considered. "You think, then, someone's tryin' to set you two at each other's throats?"

"What else *can* I think?" Holcomb growled irritably: "There's somethin' goin' on round here that I ain't in on. Somethin' big! Cattle's bein' rustled wholesale——"

"You wouldn't know anything about *that*, of course." Telldane's grin flushed Holcomb darkly; brought him cursing from the chair to tower above Bufe, cocked and wicked.

Without alarm Telldane glanced up at the stocky man amusedly. "What's the matter, Ab? Conscience botherin' you?"

"I've had enough of your gab," Holcomb said, and his face was ugly. "I told you once I've quit all that. I'm goin' straight these days—you hear me? I'm a respectable rancher now an'——"

"Sure, sure," Telldane agreed; "you're a changed man, Ab—I can see it." He said soothingly, "Kerwold's been your friend, ain't he? Well, Sam's in

trouble now—bad trouble; an' it might be you could
help him."

Holcomb pondered that; eased off. "You workin'
for Sam?"

"Sam did me a favour once. I'm tryin' to repay
it. Thought mebbe you'd be wantin' to help Sam
too——"

"Would if I could——"

"Might be you can. You didn't drop Brill, did
you?"

Holcomb jerked back like a man slapped across the
face. His cheeks went darkly ruddy and he was lifting
clenched fists when Bufe said coolly:

"There, there; I was only askin'. *Somebody* killed
him. You never set fire to Gann's range—never tried
any tricks with Gann's cattle?"

Holcomb said darkly: "No!"

"An' you don't think he poisoned your water-
holes, set fire to your line-camps or hamstrung those
horses?"

"What's all that got to do with Kerwold?"

"I don't know. I'm tryin' to figure who's behind
this. You don't think it's Gann, eh?"

"Know damn well it ain't—you could shake Gann's
brains in a thimble an' never make ary a rattle. Look
here——" growled Holcomb abruptly, frankly. "You
can put that in the book. I ought to know. Guy
you're talkin' about's Gann Holcomb—my brother."

Telldane whistled.

"Surprises you, eh? Well, that ain't a patch to the
surprise I got when I heard he was braggin' to gun
me! I tell you, boy, there's somebody bigger'n him
behind this—somebody *really* big—somebody that's
got a think-box that would make yours an' mine look
puny. Who is it? What's he after?"

" That," Telldane nodded, " is what I'm tryin' to find out."

" Well, you won't find out from me. *I* don't know." Holcomb scowled about him irritably. " It's sure got *me* beat! "

" Who was it you were expectin' when you hollered for me to come in? "

Holcomb's look had been frank, had been keyed to a patent sincerity. But suddenly his eyes showed watchful and his roan cheeks were subtly altering to their sly, remembered slanting. All the lines of his face showed change and he said wonderingly: " Why —why, nobody, Bufe—I wasn't expectin' nobody——"

Boot sound, that moment striking echoes from the porch, came to interrupt him and a man's hail gave his words the lie. " You in there, Ab? I come over quick as I could, but——"

The voice, like its owner, stopped on the threshold.

Telldane grinned. " Come in, Pring. Never mind the apologies—better late than never, Ab always says."

CHAPTER XV

RIP-TIDE

SAM KERWOLD was leaving the harness-shed when the Flying K range boss stopped him at the door. " Guess Pring'll be sloshin' his hat on slanchways again, now Miz Jane's back home to roost fer a spell . . ."

At that point something in Kerwold's look stopped Vargas' flow of words. Quickened breathing stirred

his chest and the hands that had swung at his sides
came gingerly up to rest by hooked thumbs from his
gun-belt. He said apologetically: " 'Course you're
right. It ain't no skin off my nose. But a man can't
keep from wonderin' hardly, an' all hands know Gus
used to be thicker'n splatters round this outfit—over
here sittin' the bag 'bout every other night. 'Course,
I know he never had no more chance'n a stump-tail
bull at fly time, but——"

A dark flush worried Kerwold's cheeks and he said
harshly: " What the hell are you gettin' at, Vargas? "

The range boss moved the hands from his gun-belt,
spread them in a deprecatory gesture. " Well, I ain't
aimin' to be mindin' the other man's personal business, an' of course I don't rightly know how——"

" Never mind whittlin' all the bark off it. If you
got somethin' to say, get it said an' done with."

Vargas rubbed the mole on his chin; looked off
across the range for a bit. Bringing his glance at last
back to Kerwold, he said uneasily, " I just been kind
of wonderin', Sam, if you've heard—if you've heard
about the way Gus is borrowin' money——"

" Borrowin'? Who from? "

" Well, I don't rightly know. That partic'lar wa'n't
included in the rumour I got hold of. Point is what
he's borrowin' it *for*." He stopped and looked at
Kerwold brightly. " Like I said, he ain't been round
much in the last three years, but now Jane's back from
school again I note he's comin' over reg'lar——"

" By the everlastin'! " Kerwold swore. " Get to
the point, man, if you got one! "

" We-ell——" Vargas scowled off across the yard.
" I don't know's you're goin' to like this, Sam. But
from what I hear, he's borrowin' heavy—borrowin',
I been told, to bid in that Wildcat lease——"

Sam Kerwold's grip fastened hard on his shoulders. The old man's pale blue eyes were blazing. " You damn pup! " he stormed. " You mean to stan' there an' tell me Gus Pring—the best friend I ever had—is goin' behind my back to take that bid away from me! *Do you?* "

Vargas winced. He raised a warning hand. " Now wait a minute, Sam," he began, but Kerwold cut in savagely.

" Wait, *hell!* " he shouted. " You answer me yes or no, by Gawd! Now *do* you? "

" Well, all I know is . . . If you must—— Damn it, Sam! I hate like hell to tell you this, but the answer's *yes*—— "

" Where'd you hear this? "

" Got it from that new fella, Topock—— "

" Where'd he get it? "

" Says he got it straight from Flimpkin, cashier of that new bank at Globe—— "

Kerwold grabbed a rope down from a wall-peg, shoved Vargas out of his path and started hotfoot for the horse corral.

" Here—wait! " called Vargas. " Where the hell you goin', Sam? "

Kerwold made no answer. He yanked the corral gate open violently; swung and missed and swung again. Twelve seconds later he was in the saddle, ripping up dust on the trail to Pring's.

It would have been hard to say which showed the greater consternation—Holcomb or Gustave Pring. But Pring's was for that second only. He came with a cool smile into the room. " Hello. Aren't you the gent I met at Kerwold's?—fellow Sam was calling ' Dane '? "

Telldane's glance came abruptly vigilant. He sensed hidden things in the way Pring put that. He said, hardly smiling, " It ain't my name, but that's what I called myself. I'm Bufe Telldane—from Texas."

" Yes," Pring nodded. " I thought so. Remembered seein' your face on a dodger. Sam know who you are? "

" I haven't mentioned it to him."

" Notice you weren't at all bashful about slappin' it on that warning you stuck up at Brill's the other day. What were you tryin' to do there, anyway—scare somebody? Sam put you up to that? "

Telldane's opinion of Pring underwent change. The man was as sharp as a razor. He wondered what else Pring guessed. But instead of answering, Bufe just smiled.

The boss of Double Bar Circle was a broad-cheeked man, thick lipped and heavy featured. He had skin burnt dark as old leather and a hard, tough way with his eyes; they were odd eyes, palely yellow, lambent and confident—arrogant. He'd a chunky, blocklike figure and hair that was oily and black; it tufted the backs of his fingers and showed from the open neck of his shirt, which was neatly gaberdine and tan, matching well the burnt roan of his features.

" It's interestin'," Telldane said, " knowin' what people think of you." He fished out the makings. " Anything else you've noticed? "

Pring's cheeks were bland. " I've *heard* you're some kind of special ranger sent in here by the Governor—but, of course, I don't believe that. Ain't hardly likely, considering all the money Texas spent various times tryin' to apprehend you. I suppose you've cleared out of Texas for good? "

" You mean for the good of Texas? "

Pring smiled with his lips. " Got a sense of humour, eh? You're to be congratulated. You're the first outlaw I ever met that had."

" Your acquaintance with outlaws extensive? "

Pring's chuckle was a homey sound, quite comfortably carefree, easy. " As a matter of fact, you're the first one I've met—odd how a man'll say things that way. Are you the man we vote a medal for getting rid of Brill? "

" Afraid I can't claim that honour," Bufe said, and revised his estimation of the Double Bar Circle boss again. It had been a long time since anyone had slung such talk at Bufe Telldane; and while it warned him, it amused him also. He scratched a match on his Levis and lit the quirley he'd rolled. He lounged back in his chair, puffed contentedly. " Haven't seen Safford lately, have you? "

Pring shook his head. " I've too much to do to keep——"

" For a busy man," Bufe drawled, " I'd say you were pretty well informed. You knew about that warning I tacked up, yet only two men read it—Brill an' that Texan, Guy Topock. And Topock tore it up."

Pring's eyes showed a little narrow. He shrugged. " Things like that get around, Telldane."

Telldane said: " Evidently."

Ab Holcomb stared at them, scowling. " Crissakes! Talk American, can't you? "

But neither man so much as looked at him. Their looks were for each other; watchful, guarded, coolly smiling; they reminded Holcomb of a couple of beef contractors visiting the Indian Agent. They were that coldly civil, that blandly polite. Yet all the while danger's feel kept tightening. The rip-tide of unshown emotions wiped cold chills across his spine.

"Have you decided," Pring asked, "to take that job I offered?"

Telldane's teeth gleamed a smile of sorts. "I guess not——"

"I could raise——"

"'Fraid not. Don't believe you could borrow enough."

A frown got tangled in Pring's yellow eyes and he said, voice nettled: "Are you ins——"

"I mean," Telldane grinned coldly, "you couldn't corral money enough. My guns are not for hire."

A contemptuous grunt came out of Pring. "That's crazy! Every man's got a price——"

"That may be your philosophy . . ." Telldane stopped with head cocked—listening. Horse sound came and stopped at the porch. Boots struck gravel, crossed the porch, came echoing down the hall.

Sam Kerwold grimly entered the room and his raking stare found Pring.

CHAPTER XVI

GUS PRING

TOPOCK had no need to talk with old Ransome to know whose the hand that had driven Cooper's home-steaders off Wildcat Hill. He knew the moment he saw Bufe's notice. And he remembered where he had seen Bufe before—the man had been pointed out to him as Bufe Telldane that day in Roaring Fork when he had killed Dave Ruddabaugh.

A lot of things came clear to him then and he shivered as he remembered how twice he'd grabbed that gun-fighter's shoulder and roughly hauled him round. It was God's own mercy the man hadn't killed him!

But Topock's marvelling at this miracle was brief. Where another man—one less bold or less reckless— might have considered it as a 'stitch in time,' Topock's principal reaction as he considered the mauling he had got at Telldane's hands was one of vengeful animosity. His hatred for the gun-fighter mounted, and instead of considering ways of avoiding future conflict with the man, Topock's time for the next several hours was taken up with schemes for Telldane's undoing.

It did not prove a fruitful labour.

Still bitterly, wholly malevolent, he turned his attention to ways for keeping Kerwold from getting his hooks on the Wildcat lease lands. Apparently that damned Telldane was working for Flying K— else why had the gun-fighter made it his business to put Cooper's homesteaders off? He would have to reckon with Telldane; and he must reckon, too, with Cooper's notion that Sam Kerwold might attempt to lease from the squatters should they succeed in taking over the Wildcat lands. But *that* could be attended later. Right now it was urgent to remove those lands from public auction. There was one way that he could do it, and he grinned when the idea came to him. They'd slipped up on a bet that first time, but they wouldn't be slipping up this time. His black eyes glinted as he told Cooper what to do.

Kerwold's stare was bitter and angry. Without regard for the others, he said without preliminary: "You been borrowin' money, Gus?"

Pring's beefy cheeks got a little flushed. "Reckon I have. Nothing wrong with——"

"Borrow it from that bank at Globe?"

"Really, Sam, I don't see——"

"You don't need to! " Kerwold snapped. "All I want from you is a fair an' square answer—yes or no! Did you borrow with the idea of biddin' in that Wildcat lease? "

Kerwold's look was black and violent, but Gus Pring's gaze was cool, unflustered. He seemed quite at ease; a little puzzled certainly, but entirely free from shame or anxiety. He was much the coolest man in the room. His eyes showed the grave amusement with which some tolerant elder might have regarded a frantic child. He said smoothly:

"Hold on now, Sam; you're all afrother. 'F it comes to that, don't know as I much blame you. Where did you get this wild tale? From Flimpkin, at the bank?"

"Never mind where I got it," scowled Kerwold, the heady anger still travelling his cheeks. "All I want from you's an answer. Straight from the shoulder—yes or no?"

"Tut, tut! Of course the story's not true—I'm a little surprised you'd swallow such stuff. I suppose, in a way, though, the fault's really mine. I did borrow a bit the other day, and from Flimpkin at the First National. Got a few improvements about the place," he mentioned smoothly, "that I've been intending to get busy on. 'Course, I knew well enough the bank would never lend money on—— Well, the upshot was, I told Joe Flimpkin I was after the Wildcat lease an' he gave me the money."

Kerwold, under Pring's reproving look, showed a little sheepish. He cleared his throat two or three times embarrassedly; brought out his pipe, peered in its half-filled bowl and searched his pockets for a match. Pring handed him one, faintly smiling.

Old Sam puffed a moment, plainly without enthusiasm. Taking the pipe from his mouth, red-cheeked, uneasy, he said flustered: "Expect I've not done you much justice, Gus—suspicionin' you the way I been. But hearin' that yarn sudden like I done, kind of knocked me off my feed, I reckon." Backing up came hard to Kerwold, and Pring said, coming to his rescue:

"That's all right. Any buy's liable to cut his stick short when a man starts peddlin' loads of that kind." He said, eyes narrowing, "What I'd like to know is who brought up that bill of goods——"

"Seems like," Telldane drawled, interrupting, "you've forgot what brought you over here so early."

Pring, to whom the remark was addressed, affected not to notice. Still eyeing Kerwold, he said insistently: "Who was ladling that stuff, Sam?"

But Kerwold shook his head. "Best leave sleepin' dogs alone," he mumbled; and turned to look at Telldane as though only now realizing the stranger's presence. "What was that you was sayin', Dane?"

Telldane shrugged. "I was just commentin' on the tearin' rush with which brother Gus got off his horse this mornin'. Seemed like somethin' was botherin' him—mebbe it was findin' me here ahead of him."

Pring's hard, upwheeling stare was edged with anger, but his heavy lids concealed it quickly and some noted need adjusted his cheeks to an easy, jovial slanting. "No," he declared, "the strutting antics of casual gun-fighters have never managed to bother me much. But I have got news—it'll interest all of you —Mister *Dane-Telldane* particularly. There's a new batch of wagons on Wildcat this morning and "— looking regretfully at Kerwold—" I'm afraid they're here to stay."

Kerwold wheeled sharply.

Pring met his look with a shake of the head. "There's a fellow named Willow Creek Wally sort of bossing the outfit—maybe our friend, *Mister Dane* here, knows him—I'd say they might be lodge brothers. At all events, this Wally hombre took pains to tell me they've filed; that trespassers won't be welcome."

Ab Holcomb cursed. Kerwold's cheeks got darkly mottled.

Holcomb snarled explosively: "I fired that goddam range tramp once—thought he'd left the country! By——"

"Gus," asked Kerwold bitterly, "d'you s'pose he's tellin' it straight?"

"About filing?" The Double Bar Circle boss shrugged. "I see no reason to doubt it. Usually speaking, the word of fellows like this Wally ain't worth the amount of breath wasted; but in this instance I'm inclined to think the man's telling the truth. Easy enough to check——"

"No need of that," murmured Telldane. "I'll take care of these squatters."

Pring sneered. "Like you did that first batch? I'm afraid——"

"You needn't be. They'll be on their way before sundown."

"Oh—I see. That notice," Pring said. "Guess you feel it's your bounden duty——"

D

"We gun-fighters," Telldane drawled, "don't worry overmuch about duty. We're like some ranchers that way—obligations never weigh us down."

Pring's cheeks roaned up with anger. He said quickly, unthinkingly: "If that slap was aimed at me——"

Telldane grinned. "What's the matter? Conscience botherin' you? Tut, tut! Don't let it, Gus —'every man has his price.'"

The Double Bar Circle boss, abruptly remembering Kerwold, got a hold on his temper. He said stiffly: "I've no time to waste on riddles. If you're ridin', Sam, I'll go along with you."

Kerwold seemed not in any great hurry. His look was questioningly on Telldane. But Gus Pring had a way about him and that way took the old man out to his horse.

CHAPTER XVII

A MAN MUST FIGHT

THE sun was high in the afternoon sky when Bufe Telldane came in sight of the camp.

The wagons were there, all right. Drawn up in a circle, their formation a plain hint of expected trouble. They were not the wagons he'd sent rolling east; nor were these the men he had sent east with them.

A different outfit, this; one used to trouble—geared for it. With but two exceptions, all the men of that

cocked group were strangers. Hard-eyed, features im-
mobile as masks hacked out of wood. The exceptions
were Pecos Gann and young Tim Ransome—these
Bufe had met that first night at the store.

Riding up to them, he stopped the roan, lazily curling a knee around the horn. He nodded curtly.
"Howdy, Ransome. How come you're spendin' time
with these gophers?"

Young Ransome scowled, his stare gone sullen.

Gann said belligerently: "'Cause he's wantin' his
rightful share of this basin—same's the rest of us.
Any objections?"

Telldane's frosty eyes looked him over. "I can
think of some—from his angle. Lost all interest in
your health, kid?"

A flush stained the down on Ransome's cheeks.

"You're travellin' with the wrong crowd," Telldane
warned him. "Better——"

"Don't let that bastard scare you, Tim," sneered
Gann, eyeing Telldane toughly. "Best thing he does
is run sandys. That's Bufe Telldane—name the old
women in Texas use to scare their brats with. Ain't
nawthin' about him noways for a growed man to be
afeared of."

Telldane smiled amusedly. "Much obliged for the
introduction. Now that the pleasantries have been
attended to, I'd admire to know which one of you
wolves is roddin' this outfit."

"I am."

It was a gaunt man said it—a slat-built fellow in
bull-hide chaps.

Hired-gun hombre was stamped all over him; in
the crouch of his body, in the slitted stare—in the
long-fingered flexing of his hands. Telldane's glance
was edged with derision. "An' who are you?"

"Willow Creek Wally's my handle."

"All right, Willow Creek. Hitch up them wagons an' roll."

The gun-fighter's eyes showed a rush of temper. "Like hell!" He said loudly: "Who's figgerin' to make me?"

"The law would make you, I reckon—if I cared to wait that long. Since I don't, I expect likely I can make out to take care of the evacuation myself——"

"You can shout, too!" Gann snarled, cursing. "This here is all government land we're on! It's open to filin'——"

Telldane's teeth showed a cold white smile. "It was," he corrected gently.

Willow Creek Wally said: "That's right—it was. It ain't any more because we've filed on it."

"Someone around here needs glasses," Bufe drawled. "An' the someone ain't me. If you've filed on this strip, you've been wastin' your time—been plumb careless, too, I guess likely. I filed on this land three days ago. At that time, as Gann says, it was government property. But it ain't any more. It's mine. You might not have heard about it, but I posted a notice to that effect at Brill's right after I filed it. You're on the wrong foot, Mister. Hitch up an' roll."

"I guess not," Willow Creek said flatly. "We'll stick around a spell till——"

"Be a longer spell than you're bargainin' for."

A sulky brilliance got in Willow Creek's eyes and the hand that was by his holster spraddled.

"Better not," Bufe said; and some way all the hot colour washed out of Willow Creek's cheeks. He stood a moment that way, uncertain; then with a shrug and a sneer he wheeled away and, with a curt command

or the others, went angling off toward the horses being
held between stretched ropes.

"Well, by God! *Yellow!*" Gann cried; and with
a tight-snapped oath wheeled round to Telldane;
shook a fist at him, eyes bright with violence. "By
grab, you ain't runnin' *me* out, hombre! Not by a
jugful! I——"

"You'll be well advised," Telldane cut in, "—unless you're cravin' what Brill asked for—to hitch up
your team and get out."

Telldane's words, crystal clear, stopped every man
in his tracks. He had an instant's regret for the impulse that had made him drag Brill into this. He had
not shot Brill—had not tangled with him—and it was
a mistaken strategy, he realized now, to have intim-
ated that he had. These men were probably friends
of Brill's. Wild exultation suddenly brightened
Willow Creek's eyes. Telldane had precipitated—
was swiftly bringing on—the very violence his words
had been intended to avoid.

Gann's face was bloated, livid. Bufe saw how his
muscles leaped and stiffened; saw the lantern jaw with
its cud-bulged cheek jump forward.

He said: "Watch it, Gann!" and set himself there
solidly, with all his taut nerves screaming.

Gann may not have ranked high in the annals of
fast gun-throwing, but Telldane, aboard a horse, was
at a considerable disadvantage; and the glitter of his
smoky stare showed Gann to be aware of this. Cheeks
shaped to lines of cunning, a taunting grin curved the
sheepman's mouth. "Your talk is bigger'n Moses,"
he sneered, "but you're like all the rest of these gun-
yappers! Noisier'n hell on cart-wheels, but——"

Gann's talk abruptly quit. He went back a step
still crouched but with his eyes pin-pointed, frantic,

a corner of his mouth a-quiver, clawed hand spread
above gun-butt.

"Go on if you must," Telldane said. "Pull it."

But all Gann's courage had melted. He could feel
it leaking out of him, shrivelled in the blaze of Bufe's
wanton stare. The murderous impulse that had
shoved him into this—even the believed advantage
that had been his, was gone . . . washed away by the
easy confidence of Telldane's posture. Gann would
no more have touched his pistol now than he'd have
stooped to pat a rattlesnake. He could not think—
much less have moved—could only crouch there
frantic, paralysed; rooted by the knowledge that to
draw would be to die.

"Well, do *something*," Telldane snapped impatiently. "Drag your iron or drag your freight."

But still Gann did not move—he *could* not.

A moment longer Telldane waited. A mirthless
laugh came out of him then. With a shrug he kneed
the roan around.

That laugh, or that movement, broke the spell.

Wild rage in his face, Gann grabbed for his gun.
Willow Creek's eyes streaked a warning, but Gann
was beyond the reach of caution. Humiliated, boiling with anger and hatred, Gann's white-clamped fist
jerked the gun from leather—but the back he'd aimed
to salivate was no longer pointed toward him. The
big roan horse had wheeled clear around and Bufe
Telldane was facing him.

Too late Gann saw he'd been neatly tricked—saw
the gaping muzzle of Telldane's pistol. His own rising weapon was not quite level when Telldane's
roared—just once.

Gann's squat, crouched body jerked and buckled;
a reeling stagger spilled him into the dust where he

lay outsprawled, face down, unmoving.

"*Jeez!*" Tim Ransome's eyes were round.

Telldane drawled: "Any more drygulchers huntin' action?"

In that brittle silence no man moved. No man dared hardly loose a breath.

Telldane grinned at them, coldly mocking.

"Get hitched up an' drag it out of here—*an' don't come back*." His glance swung then in a slow half circle, seeming to memorize each touched face. It stopped with impact on the frozen pallor of Willow Creek's cheeks. "Tell Guy Topock I'm comin' after him—that he had better move fast if he expects to get clear."

CHAPTER XVIII

CATTLE BY NIGHT

RIDING back to the store at Ransome's Crossing, Telldane felt no regret for having killed Gann. The man had asked for what he got, and got exactly what his cowardly try had merited. Telldane, conscious only of a grim distaste for the entire business, shoved the man from his mind. He must keep alert, for by this shooting—and the proclamation that had brought it on—he had openly aligned himself with Flying K, and all the forces of wrath and greed and vengeance that were out to down Sam Kerwold would be focused on him. He had taken his stand and must abide by

it. There was no retreating possible now. Constant
vigilance must be the price he paid for life.

He rode with his Winchester across his lap and with
keen eyes searching the brushy slopes, seeking out
each covert—probing it, alert for the gleam of gun-
metal.

But with all this care his mind was not idle. It was
a time for thought, and Bufe thought hard. He
thought of things Ab Holcomb had told him—even
more about those Ab had left unsaid. And the controlled masklike countenance of the Double Bar Circle
boss frequently flashed across his mind. What hidden
thoughts and desires lay behind the man's suave and
inscrutable features? What deep purposes and dark
intentions lurked behind Pring's lambent stare? He
felt no trust of Pring and pondered long the scarce-
veiled belligerence of the man's remarks. Plainly
Pring was convinced Bufe was backing Kerwold—but
could that be a cause for hostility? According to
rumour, years back Pring had owed his start here to
the same generous hand that had backed Ab Holcomb;
Sam Kerwold had advanced the cash and cattle to
which the man's present standing was due. Too,
Telldane had heard that Pring was a candidate for
the prominence to be accorded Kerwold's son-in-law.
Pring had every reason, Telldane thought, to be backing Kerwold in this trouble that was brewing—had
every reason, yet Bufe was far from satisfied that he
was. And Holcomb—which side was Holcomb
favouring? Sam's? Or the side of Sam's enemies?

That Sam had enemies aplenty was quite apparent.
Topock, of course—and Cooper (Bufe had heard report of their embarrassing expedition to seek Sam's
backing). But this trouble went beyond that—had
been brewing for months before their coming. That

old framed business of Gann and Holcomb was proof
enough of this. What man or group in this basin
could have thought to profit by a feud between them?
And this guy, Willow Creek, whom Holcomb had last
year kicked off the Straddle Bug—where did *he* fit
into this? And Vargas? Telldane had not forgot
how Kerwold's foreman had met him on the night of
his arrival. Sam seemed sure of the man, of his loyalty
and straightness. But Telldane was not sure at all.
What had the man been doing in those trees that
night? For whom had Vargas been waiting? Not
for Bufe, certainly, because even had he knowledge
of Telldane's coming, he could not have known which
trail the man would take.

Who had cold-bloodedly murdered Brill upon the
trail to Payson? And why? Why and who had
murdered the old Dutch homesteader, Juke Ronstadt?
And where was Safford? Was he doing anything
to clear these mysteries up? From his words in
the store that night, Bufe thought it highly probable
that Lou Safford was aiming to throw his weight on
the side of Sam's enemies. If this surmise were right,
there was a pretty fair chance the marshal was crooked
—not that everyone opposed to Flying K was bound
to be, but because Guy Topock and his sidekick,
Cooper—who were heading at least one flank of the
opposition—were pretty obviously crooks and the
marshal had appeared to be on first-rate terms with
them.

Then there was that business of the stuck-up stage
which had taxed Sam Kerwold's pocket-book a couple
thousand dollars he could ill afford to lose.

All in all, it looked like the Tonto country was in
for a stretch of squally weather.

Pring had said there was a rumour loose to the

effect that Bufe was a special ranger sent in here by the Governor. If there was, it was the first that Bufe had heard of it. He could almost wish he *were* a ranger; his work would be so much simpler if he had a badge to back him—simpler, at least, so far as questions and answers were concerned. With a badge he could have cleared up some of these mysteries in pretty short order. But thought of the badge curled his lips derisively. It had been many a day since Bufe Telldane had packed a lawman's tin.

The thought turned his mind back on Kerwold—on the cause of his indebtedness to the grizzled boss of Flying K. Three years ago in Texas—three years almost to the night. He remembered the circumstances well—the Orient Hotel in Pecos—that smoke-fogged bar-room with its swinging lamps, the shouts and curses and . . . the sudden silence. He had been a stock detective then—three months on the trail of the McChandless gang and that night was to have furnished the final bit of evidence, the clinching proof that was to make his case complete. But somewhere along the line someone had talked. He was to have met Bob Brady, a ranger, in the bar that night and, together, grab the three McChandless boys and as many of the gang as they could manage. But Brady hadn't come and the McChandless boys were warned. Dode McChandless had stepped up to him as soon as he'd entered the bar. There'd been quick words, a blow. The din of bedlam filled the place as vengeful hands grabbed six-guns. Bufe hadn't had a chance—had been jammed against a wall with Dode McChandless' pistol toughly shoved against his belly, when Sam Kerwold, an utter stranger, had stepped through the lobby door. Bufe still thrilled to the remembered sound of Old Sam's voice dryly saying: " I guess the game is up, boys. Unless you gents are cravin' harps an' halos, don't so much as bat a eyelash. Jest hi'st them dewclaws an' grab for the rafters, an' what I mean—*grab quick!*"

Three years . . . It didn't seem so long.

Bufe sighed. 'Drag' Telldane they'd called him then, and the name had been a by-word, a scourge to long-loop hombres.

Bufe felt suddenly tired and old. The weight of all those yesterdays lay heavy on him now; their turbulence had gutted him, he was just a husk of the man who had made the victory of San Juan Hill that thing of glory the history books named it. Just the husk— the burnt-out husk; a man whose name to-day was steeped in calumny, anathema—a thing, as Gann had said, to scare bad children with.

Well, he had had his fun he supposed—most folks would say he had. He would lick this thing for Sam if he could and ride on over the hump. Somewhere, some place and time, perhaps, he would find the peace he craved; an end to all this turbulence. Some old. forgotten backwash where the name 'Telldane' had not been heard—where the man could unbuckle his gun-belt.

But he must square his debt with Kerwold first. . . .

The thought brought another sigh. So many loose ends were cluttering this; there was nothing for a man to bite down on. Stray threads, yes—God knew there were plenty of those! But try to catch one—ravel it; you found it torn from its moorings, lying useless in your hand. Take Guy Topock, for example. *He* was that way—a thread in point. He was mixed up in this, certainly—so was Holcomb, Pring, Duarte Vargas. So was Safford, seemed like. But *how?* Yes, that was it! What part were these fellows playing?

There was this rustling business, the original cause of Sam's letter. He believed he understood who was behind these wholesale cattle thefts. That had been Ab Holcomb's trade in Texas, and despite Ab's protestations, he saw no reason for believing the man had changed. And yet—he had always thought Ab grateful—a man who remembered favours. Certainly Sam's backing him to a new start here should come under that category.

Could it be . . .

The thought snapped off, Telldane going tense before the remembered need for vigilance. His cat-quick glance raked the surrounding shadows with a probing care. Dusk had gathered during his thinking and some way his horse had got off the trail.

He sat bolt upright in the saddle attempting to orient himself—striving to catch again what sound had snatched him from his ponderings. But in this thickening haze the wild tangle of surrounding crags and hillslopes seemed wrapped in the brooding hush of centuries. From the south a coyote's yammer rose and fell, a dropped and ululating sound, like a fragment of something long gone and forgotten, rolling farther, dimmer, drearily off into the vast immensity of space.

For its duration Telldane sat there, a hard, cocked shape in his stockman's saddle. A wide gulch fell away before him, broadening in this deepening haze into the dun expanse of a yonder desert that stretched —these shadows made it seem—illimitably away into a dark and far horizon.

With a shrug he was about to wheel the roan around with some vague thought of angling back, searching out some recognized landmark, when a random wind whirled up and struck him—rooting him moveless with its smell of dust. On its heels the sound came, faint and far, but unmistakable. The rumbling bawl of driven cattle.

It was more like a memory than actual sound, and Bufe, scabbarding his rifle, slipped from the saddle and, taking the scarf from about his throat, unloosed its knot and spread it flat against the ground. Then, lying full length, he put his ear to it and when he rose a remote smile faintly edged his cheeks and fatigue's dull weight was forgotten feeling.

Quickly, grimly, he swung to the saddle. Cogged rowels bit and the blue roan jumped.

Ten minutes' run put the gulch behind them, saw them travelling the desert floor. It was not, Bufe saw now, a desert, really, but a long wide-arching flat hock-deep in dust, drab-studded with burro brush and cholla, with now and again some greasewood clump lifting yellow flowers to the fading light. Across its reach Bufe's eyes were fixed on a low, dark blur that years of stock detecting told him was a driven mass of strung-out cattle.

He cut the flat at a racking tangent, drew up with an oath at the lip of a wash. Through the deepening haze his frowning glance picked out the gully's turn and wanderings; then, glance clearing, showing more hopeful, he urged the blue roan down its bank, went loping east along the bed's dry sand.

Turning, twisting, the wash led ever more steadily north. It was the way Bufe wanted to go and he was thankful he had had the wit to use it. The herd he'd seen was moving westward and sooner or later this wash would cross its path—unless it quit. And that was all right, too, he thought.

It was getting shallower fast now, and occasional

views above its eroded banks showed the dark blotch
of the herd much nearer; showed the drab expanse
of the dusty flat to be merging into the richer soil of
grazing lands. And suddenly Bufe saw against the
tangle of nearing hills an upthrust spire he recognized.
Apache Peak! The Fisk Mill road lay beyond it; and,
somewhat farther, off to the left, Skull Mesa reared its
table top. And at the top of Skull Mesa was Gann's
headquarters . . . *that herd was headed for the dead
man's ranch!*

Telldane knew in that moment the fate of Kerwold's vanishing cattle. The rustlers were using
Gann's spread in their relay; first stop on the out-trail
of Old Sam's cattle. They were held there probably
till the brands healed over; rested and fattened, then
drifted on, north and west, to New River. Sold there
in small lots, the rustlers would have a ready, cash
market. It was homesteader country; there'd be no
questions asked.

Still travelling fast, Bufe scanned his chances. Too
late now for help from Sam Kerwold; the Flying K
lay south and east. Far—too far. They might not
hold this bunch at Gann's—might drive straight
through. He couldn't risk it. A good-sized herd, that
one up ahead; all steers, very likely—cattle Sam
couldn't afford to lose. He had to keep on. If he
could stampede——

A sharp and upward slant of the ground took him
out of the wash. A stand of timber lay dead ahead,
perhaps three-quarters of a mile away; elsewhere all
was rolling, manzanita-cluttered rangeland. The
lancelike pole of a sentinel yucca rose straight as a
flagstaff off to the right and beyond it, not over a
hundred yards, came the first wall-eyed steers of the
bawling herd. The ground shook to their hooves and

the rattle of horns made incessant clatter. Above these sounds came a rider's voice:

" *Git on, y'u cow critters—hup thar! Hup—hup!* "

With the rider's shout still travelling the dust, Bufe jerked the slicker from behind his cantle. One flick of the wrist set its folds gyrating. Whirling it round and round his head and yelling like a Commanche, he yanked out his six-shooter and with flame bright-spurting from its sky-aimed barrel he drove the roan straight at the herd.

He was seen!

A shouted oath sailed through the dust. The leading steers snorted, swerved and split. A long halloo shrilled through the shadows; other guns took up Bufe's challenge and muzzle lights streaked the swirling murk. But the herd was split, spilling off in two directions—which was something, but not enough. Be too easy for this crew to round them up again come daylight.

Using his spurs and keeping the roan straight at them, Bufe shoved the six-gun back in his belt, and a quick jerk dragged the Winchester across his saddle-bow. Kicking his feet from the stirrups—still yelling —he dropped the tarp and, riding sharpshooter fashion, let drive three shots at the tangle of riders trying to force the cattle back in the trail.

One quick scream slid up a sobbing scale and choked. The frantic men before him melted, dividing pell-mell into the dust-streaked murk.

The cattle were definitely divided now—were scattering fast, breaking away in all directions; and he was almost on to them when the hatted head of a rider, then his shoulders—on Bufe's right—dimly cut the haze and sharpened. A lifted rifle jumped to his shoulder and the instant flame of it made a livid shaft reaching toward Bufe's saddle.

A stab of the rowels thrust the roan from its track. The close and flogging gait of horse-hoofs jerked Telldane's attention from the man to see five riders pounding in, low bent across their saddles, their spitting guns dull-thudding against the din.

A whistling something tugged his neckerchief. Shock jarred through him as one bullet solidly struck the saddle-horn. Then his lifted Winchester was barking answer and the nearest rider abruptly screeched and tumbled slantways off his horse's pastern. And one more sagged, wildly clutching at the horn, before the rest of them took fright and, cursing, spurred for the timber.

Then a close call laid its track against his teeth, its sound bursting from the right of him, recalling vividly that other and forgotten rider.

Without thought Bufe flung his body low against the roan's left side, and beneath its neck saw the man coming in full tilt and, dropping his empty rifle, fired the last shot from his pistol—and knew he missed.

Flame fanned from the rider's gun in triphammered bursts of sound that washed cold chills across Bufe's neck; and then the roan's stride faltered —broke, and desperately Bufe dragged his boots from the stirrups and threw himself clear as the animal, heels over head, went down in a crashing fall.

Bufe lit on his shoulder and the whole world spun as momentum rolled him over and over.

He stopped against a catclaw's thorns, jerked clear and whirled, the useless pistol still clutched in his hand, to see the rider reining his bronc around forty feet away—come loping back to make sure his job was a good one.

All fingers, bathed in cold sweat, Bufe thumbed

fresh loads from his belt. But knew before he got them loose he'd never fill the gun in time—and he didn't.

The rider, seeming to sense what Bufe was up to, loosed a mocking laugh and, stopping his bronc, drove three quick shots at point-blank range and watchfully sat his saddle long moments after Bufe had fallen, before at last, with a jeering laugh, he reined away, riding after his pardners into the timber.

That laugh rang long in Telldane's ears. Only that instinctive ruse had saved him—that thought to fall when the man's gun lifted. Not one of those shots had touched him; but they'd come close—almighty close, and his scalp still crawled to the feel of their passing.

It was a good five minutes after the man had left before Bufe, shakily, rose to his feet and went to see if the roan were dead. It was. And a probing glance showed no other animals in sight—showed nothing save an empty range, for the cattle long since had gone, stampeded, and the departing rustlers seemed to have taken with them the two men he had dropped. He was afoot with a long night walk ahead of him; and as he refilled his empty pistol, this night's need decided him that he'd pack two in future.

But it was not of pistols that he thought as he prowled looking for his rifle. There was no room in his mind for guns. He had done Ab Holcomb an injustice in suspecting the man to be behind Kerwold's cattle losses. He wasn't—or he had not, least-ways, been behind this attempt to-night.

That jeering laugh was still in Bufe's ears, still savaging his cheeks. In the gunflash of those final shots he had seen the face of the man who fired them.

Andy Cooper, the fellow called himself; but Telldane knew him by the name of Blevins—a renegade who'd departed Texas a half jump ahead of the sheriff.

Well, things were due to happen, looked like.

They were—but not even in his wildest dreams could Bufe have foreseen the queer, fantastic turn those things were building up to take.

CHAPTER XIX

FLAME OF DESIRE

DOG-WEARY and dead on his feet, Telldane at eleven-fifteen lurched stiffly down the final slope and came into the yard at Ransome's Crossing like a man dragged through a knothole. A four-hour trek lay behind him—four miserable hours in high-heeled boots to a man long used to a saddle. These things were not conducive to thought, and letdown from that fight on the flat had ridden him hard—unstrung him. All his nerves were jangling as he swayed there, one hand braced against the cottonwood's bole, stupidly eyeing the yellow bars of light coming out of the store-front windows.

Drained of emotion—physically and mentally exhausted as he was, habit still retained its hold on him. For three years he had been geared to the need for caution, and that need stayed with him now. He was doggedly bending his steps toward the door when that need stopped him, reawakened by sight of the horse that was hitched to the porch rail. A strange horse—a long-legged, jug-headed bay.

Bufe stood there shaking his head, trying to clear his mind of its cobwebs and, in some measure, he was successful.

Voice sound was coming from the store, low-held, an unintelligible mutter that yet held some odd cadence that tugged at Bufe's dulled memory. Man's talk it was; and he wondered who could be calling on the Ransomes at that hour. The thought came to him that he might go inside and see; and he was starting when the man's voice sharpened and hard on its heels there came a thud as of something falling and a quick, scared cry from Holly.

It was the last that roused him.

Stopping, he canted his head and listened. The man was speaking again, a wicked satisfaction in his tones—a kind of gloating. The sound of it grated across Bufe's nerves like a file, stiffening his shoulders and bringing him to a full awareness. The speaker was Topock—Cooper's pardner.

Weariness forgotten, Telldane's storeward progress was a smooth and soundless thing. The lines of his cheeks were couched in bleakness, and a cold, malicious purpose before he reached the steps moved him to briefly pause and inspect his loaded pistol. It was while he was engaged in this that Holly screamed; and, instantly, through that scream the laboured sound of struggling bodies came to clear his mind like magic.

Three strides took him raggedly across the porch and a blow from his boot flung back the door, banging it violently against the inside wall.

For all his avowed intention, Gus Pring did not

ride home with Kerwold. They had gone a bare two miles from Holcomb's spread when the Double Bar Circle boss pulled up with a cool apology. "Sorry, Sam, but I've got to go back. Some business I forgot to finish with Ab—a horse deal I better close before the fool changes his mind. Look—I'll see you later. Give Jane my regrets and tell her I'll drop by this evening."

Holcomb did not receive Pring's return with any great display of enthusiasm. "You played hell, you did, rubbin' salt into Telldane that way—far's that goes, you've fixed things all around. I'd just got through tellin' him I wa'n't expectin' nobody when you threw that bull shout down the hall——"

"To hell with that," Pring cut him off. "He ain't goin' to be botherin' us long——"

"I've heard that remark before. Been spoke by smarter guys'n you, too—but where are them guys now? By grab, I wisht I was out of this!"

"What's the matter—yellow?"

Holcomb gave him a long regard. "I guess you know better'n that, Gus. We been through enough tights together. But God knows——"

"You always was an old woman, Ab. Trouble with you is, you get the shakin' palsy every time that guy's name is mentioned. Fixed him up in Texas, didn't we?"

Holcomb shrugged, squatted down by the steps, made aimless curlicues in the dirt with a blunt and calloused index finger. He growled without looking up, "Was that what you borried that money for?"

"What are you off on now——"

"You know what I mean. Is it like Sam said— that you borried money from the bank to beat him outa Wildcat?"

Pring considered a moment. " An' what if it is? "

Holcomb made more marks. " I wouldn't of acked you in that, Gus. Sam's been a good friend o me—been a pretty good friend to you, too, if what 've heard is right. The bargain was, we was to leave 'lyin' K alone——"

The lines of Pring's big shoulders stiffened. A hange rode across his cheeks and he said bluntly: Get this straight. I've got nothing personal against am Kerwold or any other guy round here; but long's got a shot in the locker the plans we made are goin' head. The Boxed Double A Cattle Syndicate is goin' o control this country—from Long Valley clean on outh to Hell's Hip Pocket; and any spread that won't lay along with us is headin' for the skids! I've ounded Sam, an' talkin' to him about syndicates is ke red-flaggin' a bull. Sam's a dodder'n' old has-een—last bulwark of a gone-by era. Long as his ack-in-the-Beanstalk notions don't interfere with our usiness, he can go to Halifax for all of me. But the inute they do——"

Holcomb said protestingly: " But tryin' for Wild-at——"

" Tryin' for Wildcat is interference. Long as I saw ie chance, it was my intention to take Wildcat away om him——"

" I thought you was sweet on Sam's daughter——"

" We'll leave Jane out of this," Pring snapped; and hanged the subject. " Last time we talked together laid down certain lines for you to work on. One f 'em concerned that precious brother of yours—ave you found out where he stands? "

Ab Holcomb sighed. " I'm afraid he's swingin' vith Topock." He stared morosely at the marks he ad made in the dust. He said abruptly: " What

you figurin' to do now Topock's fixed it so them Wildcat lands——"

"Lease from the homesteaders."

"Maybe Topock won't——"

"Then Topock will have to go—like Sam or any
one else that gets in my way."

Holcomb shook his head. "You're bitin' off——'

"What I bite off I can chew," Pring said and
stepped up on the porch. "There's something on
your desk I——"

"Figure you can chew Telldane?"

"Bah!" Pring's shoulders stirred impatiently
"You got Telldane on the brain!"

"Guess I have. 'Nough to get on anyone's brain—
anyone that's got one."

There was something sinister, something wolfish
in the grin that tugged Pring's lips. "You can giv
the brain a rest," he said; "Bufe won't be botherin
us long."

Holcomb thought about it all the time Gus was in
the house; and when the man stepped out on the porch
again he was buttoning the gaberdine flap of hi
pocket. But Holcomb, still busy with his thoughts
didn't notice. That the thoughts held little of pleasur
was evidenced by the dissatisfied set of his cheeks. H
said uneasily: "Just the same, Gus, I'd feel bette
if you'd leave Sam out of this——"

"We're not going over that again."

Holcomb sighed. "I wisht," he said, "I'd know
all this——"

"You went into it with your eyes open—you kne
what the syndicate was formed for. You were a
keen——"

"I didn't know about Telldane then, an' I didn
suppose——"

"Too bad. Any time you don't see eye to eye with my plans and policies, you can pick up your blocks and go home."

Quietly spoken though they were, there was a crisp finality in Pring's words that stopped Ab Holcomb's protests. He'd encountered that finality before. In fact, there'd been many times since their secret partnership had been established that Holcomb Had wished himself out of it. But he could not get out—Pring had him, lock, stock and barrel. There was a clause in their agreement—like the death clause that was in it—that if for any reason either party tried to break himself out of the contract, all that party's property—livestock, land and buildings, went unequivocally to the surviving partner, and there'd been several occasions here of late that had made Ab wonder if he'd collect any profit at all.

With the dress half ripped from her shoulders, backed against the wall, with arms hard-braced against the Texan's chest, across Topock's shoulder as the door slammed back Holly saw the white clamped cheeks of Bufe Telldane.

The room gyrated wildly as Topock in a sweating haste roughly whirled her away from him as he spun to face the door. She reeled and stumbled, hearing him curse horribly. And when from hands and knees she looked up from the floor she found him crouched by the overturned cracker-box, face blanched, eyes bright with terror as they stared, uncontrollably fascinated, at the gun in Telldane's hand.

He was afraid of Bufe! His fear was unmistakable, laying sheer and stark in his widesprung eyes, in the cringing of his muscles, slack lips and stiffened figure.

She watched them breathless, looking first at one and then the other.

A malicious smile curved Telldane's lips, abruptly pulling them back from his teeth. There was hatred in that smile and a rage that was deep and bitter. He seemed plainly aware of Topock's terror; it deepened the contempt in his eyes and shaped the grimness of his cheeks to lines of cold derision.

He did not speak, just stood and looked, seeming to await some word from the burly Texan. Where was all Topock's courage now? All that reckless, swaggering bravado he displayed so readily to women? Where was all the confidence his former bold talk had indicated?

Perhaps Topock thought of this himself, for his shoulders straightened and he made some pretence of courage. He said, scowling: "What do *you* want— an' what's the idea of that gun? Tryin' to scare somebody?"

However he may have intended the words to sound, they succeeded only in being bombastic; and they did not fool the man in the door, and Topock could see they didn't. The knowledge did little to bolster the impression he sought to give; indeed, it seemed to Holly Ransome that his cheeks went even paler, if that were possible, than they had been before.

He cleared his throat, licked nervously at dry lips. "If this is a bluff——"

"It's no bluff, Topock. You've reached the end of your rope. If you got anything to say, you better say it quick."

It looked like Topock had a lot he wanted to say, but the words seemed to stick in his throat. His dry lips moved, but no sound came—no sound that was intelligible.

Telldane's smile was coldly derisive. "Time's up," he said. "You've got a gun on you—use it."

Silence, brittle and complete, shut down on the heels of his words. It was a horribly tense and terrifying interval during which the girl was gripped by the icy chill of paralysis. So, apparently, was Topock. He made a stiff and awkward shape, half crouched as he was; his mouth hung open, gaping, and the eyes seemed starting from his head.

"You—you—*I can't!*"

"What's the matter with you—crippled? You looked all right when I came in." Telldane said with curling lips: "Quite natural, in fact."

Holly found her voice. She said: "It—it's all right, Dane. He hasn't hurt me——"

"I'm glad to hear it."

He might have been—but you could not have proved it by that tone. Nor by the look of him, either. He did not take his eyes from Topock. He said with a bleakness not to be missed: "How long you been in this country, hombre?"

The Texan made three tries before he finally got his voice working. Even then it was just a mumble. "Three weeks——"

"Hmm. Been pretty busy, haven't you? Little *too* busy, I'd say, because it seems like you been overlooking something—something that's got considerable bearin' on the—er—state of your—ah—health."

"What's all that yap supposed to mean?" growled Topock, showing again some measure of his old belligerence. He seemed to have read into Telldane's delay some basis for relief; and with the relief came confidence. He said, sneering, "What'd I overlook?"

A corner of Telldane's mouth twitched as though a cold smile lurked just behind it. "Haven't you ever heard there's a code in this country, Topock?"

The Texan stiffened. Dull colour edged into his cheeks, bloating the jowls of him poisonously. "What are you talkin' about?" he snarled.

"The code of the Tonto, Topock—the unwritten laws of this country. There's one of 'em's got considerable bearin' on your conduct—on what's goin' to happen to you, likewise."

Topock went stock-still. The eyes in his stark white face were like burnt holes in a yellow blanket.

Holly, too, appeared to grasp the implication. Dread of what those words implied rushed her into headlong speech. "But he never touched me!" she protested. "I've *told* you! He hasn't done anything——"

Telldane paid no attention. He was watching Topock with a cold, banked interest; and the bleakness of that stare abruptly set the Texan shaking. He trembled like a gale-struck aspen and a great sweat clammed his forehead—stood in bright beads across his lips. A long, rattling breath rushed out of him and he quavered in abject terror: "Great Scot! I didn't mean nothin'—*honest to God I didn't!*"

And Holly stormed at Bufe desperately: "I forbid you to do this thing—I forbid you! Bufford Dane, do you *hear* me? I've not been hurt and you shan't use me as an excuse to do murder! Don't you *dare* to shoot him!"

Telldane turned then, swept her with a grim regard. The gleam of his eyes brought a crimson flush to her throat. As she went back a pace, his smile held a mocking malice. "I don't need any excuse for murder—I thought you knew that, ma'am. I——"

The look of her eyes must have warned him.

Mouth closing, he whirled to find Guy Topock with a lifted gun in his fist. White flame leaped out of its muzzle and from Telldane's hip an answering light burst raggedly. Two shots roared as one, shaking the walls with their tumultuous clamour; and the lamp-light, wildly flaring, showed the Texan with his wobbly knees buckling under him, pitching forward across the oiled floor.

They were like that, with the smoke still wreathing lazily from the barrel of Telldane's pistol, when from the open door behind them a cold voice said malevolently: "Don't move, Telldane—don't move at all. We've got you dead to rights this time!"

CHAPTER XX

LOU SAFFORD PLAYS HIS HAND

THE yard at Brill's was filled with riders—grim-eyed, muttering, angry men. Cooper's rustlers, just returned from the raid on Kerwold, the raid whose profits had been stampeded by Bufe Telldane. Cooper swung out of his saddle savagely. "Come inside, you!" he snarled at Tim Ransome, and clanked across Brill's creaking porch. At the door he paused, called over his shoulder: "Rest of you birds stay where you are. Keep your eyes peeled an' stay in the saddle; we'll be ridin' again in just a few minutes."

Tim Ransome followed him into the place, stood restless, uneasy, while Cooper lit the lamp. Then Cooper turned and his cheeks were wicked. "Don't know why in the hell I keep you on. You're no more

use'n a busted gut!   You know who it was stampeded
them cattle?"

"I—I guess it was Telldane, wasn't it?"

"You know it was Telldane, damn you!   Didn't
Topock tell you to get him?   Didn't he tell you he'd
cancel them I.O.U.s if you'd down Telldane?   Well,
why ain't you done it?   Eh?   Answer, you whelp!"

Ransome, shifting weight, nervously licked dry lips.
"I—I——"

"Ahr," Cooper snarled.   "If I'd no more sand in
my craw than you've got, I'd sure as hell cut my
throat!"

Ransome bridled.   He said defensively: "I ain't
no match for a——"

"Don't talk foolishness," Cooper snapped.   "Nobody asked you to go up against him—a shot from the
rimrock would've done the trick——"

"I tried that!" Ransome blurted.   "Twice I
tried——"

"Then you're a damn poor shot!"   Cooper scowled
malevolently.   "I'm goin' to give you one last
chance——"

"To hell with you!" Ransome threw back at him.
"You can shove them I.O.U.s up your pants-leg for
all of me—I'm through with this outfit!   *Through*—
do you hear?"

Cooper stared.   His laugh was ugly.   "Well, well,
well!   So you're through, are you?   Listen to me,
you spineless jackrabbit—there ain't *no*body bunch-
quittin' on me!   *Nobody!*"

Ransome glared back at him sulkily.   "I won't try
for Tell——"

"You won't need to.   Telldane's dead—I killed
him to-night.   Kerwold's the bird you're goin' to line
your sights on.   An' you better not do no more missin',

neither!" He grinned at the look on Ransome's blanched features.

"Kerwold!"

"You bet! It's high time——"

"Are you crazy?"

"Like a fox," Cooper sneered. "He's been messin' things up long enough—*too* long. You drop him to-morrow, or to-morrow night I'm puttin' a flea in Lou Safford's ear."

Ransome wiped his face on his sleeve; with a visible effort got hold of himself. "Lou Safford quit the basin a week ago——"

"You got a lot to learn," Cooper sneered. "Safford's been trackin' that first batch of homesteaders. He got back this morning . . ." Some thought scowled up his raw-boned cheeks and he snapped gruffly: "You get Duarte Vargas, too, while you're out there. That bastard's playin' some game of his own—the double-crossin' sneak rubbed out those tracks himself, an' by God he'll be paid for his antics. I don't know what his game is an' I don't give a damn; you get him an' get Sam Kerwold, an' don't come back till you do!"

Ransome began protestingly, "I——"

Cooper's fist lashed out, struck Ransome with a meaty impact that drove him reeling against the bar. With blood dripping off his chin he cowered there, shaking, whimpering.

"Get up on your feet, you drivellin' scissors-bill! What Topock ever roped you into this for—— More of his goddam smartness, I guess! You do what I tell you! Either you rub them two out or to-morrow night I tell Lou Safford you're boss of the night riders workin' these hills! Get out of here now—get over there an' get holed up where you can drop 'em first thing in the morning."

Recognition of that voice cocked Telldane's muscle
and left him stiff-placed, moveless. Behind him some
where stood Lou Safford. Lou Safford of the long
fingered hands and racking cough—Safford, the basi
marshal.

If Telldane realized the futility of action, if he cor
cluded from the other's words that he was trapped
his face, it must be admitted, did not publicize th
fact. His expression was wholly grave; but it wa
calm, too, unperturbed—almost tranquil, one migh
have said. No evidence of fear was in it. No worr
edged his cheeks.

He said, ignoring the ominous timbre of the other
voice, " Oh—— Hello, Lou," and sliding the bi
pistol into its sheath, stepped over against the counte
and, turning, put the flats of his hands upon it an
regarded the lawman with a composure that wa
baffling.

Safford glared. Blood suffused his neck abov
the string tie at his throat and, mounting, sprea
across his face in a swiftly darkening tide that di
not half do justice to his outraged sense of pr
priety. His black eyes snapped with anger an
he snarled, half choked, choleric: " Unbuckl
that belt and drop it! Telldane, you're unde
arrest! "

" For what? "

The marshal swore and the two men with hir
smiled thinly. " You got the gall to ask me that?
Lou Safford's cheeks were mottled.

Telldane said mildly, " If you mean for this "—an
he waved a hand round the room—" you're goin' o
half-cocked, I'm afraid. I didn't kill the old ma
there—I expect Guy Topock struck him with a gur
or maybe his fist. If you don't care to believe m

ask Miz Holly; an' anyhow he isn't dead. As for Topock——"

"Yes?" It was a sneer the way Lou said it.

Telldane grinned at him bleakly. "I sure killed *him* all right."

"Got an alibi all pat for that, too, have you?"

"You don't need an alibi for killin' a skunk."

Change ripped across Lou Safford's face. "Get peeled of that gun-belt an' hurry it up."

Bufe Telldane, without moving, drawled: "I'll have to know why I'm arrested first."

The marshal scowled at him wickedly, but Telldane, coolly indifferent, shrugged. "It'll save time, Lou, if you tell me."

One of the men with Safford growled. The other man spat and, shifting his cud, said belligerently: "Want we should bust 'im for you, Lou?"

It pulled Bufe's lips apart in a grin. He folded brown arms across his chest and leaned against the counter comfortably. Holly was on her knees near by, working over her father anxiously. But Telldane did not look at her; his regard stayed on the marshal coolly, and the blacker grew Lou Safford's cheeks, the more amused Bufe's smile became.

The affair was at a deadlock. There was a pistol ready in Safford's fist, but a certain gleam in Bufe's level eyes seemed to warn how far he could go with it. The men with the marshal stirred impatiently, but still Lou Safford stood and looked; angry, resentful, dark-scowling but cautious.

Bufe Telldane unfolded his arms. Hooking thumbs in gun-belt, he said: "Come, Lou—let's get this over an' done with. You figure to grab me for downin' Topock?"

But Safford, at last, seemed to have made up his

mind. "To hell with Topock," he ground out brashly. "You murdered Jess Brill an', by God, you'll swing for it!"

Marvellingly, Bufe Telldane swore. "So it's Brill you're after me for . . . Jess Brill! You're claimin' I murdered *Brill*?"

The marshal sneered and his men sneered with him. "Never mind the act! I know what I know—an' you know it, too! You was goddam careless *that* time, bucko; your gloves was found on the ground beside him!"

Telldane stared. "My gloves. . . ."

"Unbuckle that belt—*I'm no damn' fool!* Holcomb will swear to 'em. So will Pring. I guess you ain't callin' Gus Pring no liar!"

"He's the soul of honour," Bufe said sarcastically; and suddenly Safford went stiff and still and the two men with him stood rigid as statues at something they read in Bufe Telldane's stare.

He shoved free of the counter, stood tall and grim. "'Fraid I can't surrender to-night, Lou," he said. "Seems there's a couple loose chores I've forgot——"

"You bust out of here," the marshal snarled, "an' I'll get you outlawed for the rest of your life!"

Telldane's smile was a thing of the lips. "Be like old times—me ridin' the river. But," he said, soft-drawled, "I guess that's the way it'll have to be, Lou. Step over there——"

"*Get him, boys!*" Lou Safford cried and went for his gun, the other two with him.

White flame leaped twice from Telldane's hip. An oath, a screech, and the lamp snuffed out. Its last wild flare showed the marshal reeling. Then a thundering dark had the place in its grip—a blackness criss-crossed by the burst of burnt powder, alive with the whispering scream of thrown lead.

The place still throbbed with its crashing echoes when hoof sound flogged a rushed tattoo that beat swiftly upward, died away in the hills.

CHAPTER XXI

"THEN I'D CALL YOU TO YOUR FACE——"

FOR three solid weeks posses under Deputy Sheriff 'Deef' Smith scoured the basin country in search of Bufe Telldane. At times there were over half a hundred men out, prowling the crags and canyons, for Marshal Lou Safford was 'gone to his just rewards' and the county had offered a $2,000 bounty for the apprehension of his killer—who was also charged with the murders of Brill and Topock. Bufe Telldane was making history again; and Gila County aimed to do likewise if it could ever get its hands on him.

The deputy, Deef Smith—so called because of his unfailing habit of making you ask him everything twice before he would undertake to answer, was a tall man, built like a hitching-post and sporting floppy ears that stuck out from the sides of his head just like the ears of a donkey. In fact, everything about him seemed either to flop or to flap—the holster that was slung at his hip, the points of his pinto vest, the flaring flaps of his batwing chaps and the whang strings he had tied to him everywhere. His age was somewhere between fifty and sixty and he had the reputa-

E

tion of being a considerable sight more stubborn than a mule; and in the pursuit of Bufe Telldane he appeared doing his damnedest to prove it.

He had no business around Wildcat Hill, for it was fifteen miles into Maricopa, but he frequently showed there anyway, and the slant of his lantern jaw promised trouble if anyone looked like making something of it. Bob Lally, Maricopa's sheriff, just winked at folks that brought him this news. " Well, well! " he said, and that ended it.

So, all across that broken country, Smith drove his far-flung posses. Not once did they sight the fugitive or even so much as cut sign of him. Telldane had vanished. There was no getting round it; and finally, reluctantly, Smith disbanded his men. But he did not give up the hunt.

" He'll be back," he told inquirers; " an' when he comes back I'll git him! "

But if things stood still in the sheriffing business, no such impasse blocked the basin war. Raid and counter-raid followed each other in rapid succession. Kerwold was fighting back now, and every time one of his camps was raided, or more fence was destroyed, or more cattle stolen, dire consequences were attendant upon the property of some small cowman. Up-river, at Oak Spring Canyon, a squatter caught riding solo by a group of unidentified masked horsemen was promptly hoisted to a cottonwood limb and left dangling as a warning to others. South-east, below Bee Mountain, two masked riders shot a homesteader down on his doorstep and curtly told the widow to " load up your stuff an' git out of here! " Gann's ranch was fired, all its buildings burned to the ground; the corrals and pens and chutes were destroyed, and the bulk of Gann's stock was run off.

No man could say who had done it, but with Gann dead and no heir apparent, his riders—what were left of them—took the hint and departed. Young Tim Ransome, too, appeared to have quit the country; he had not been seen since the night of Guy Topock's killing. Considerable speculation was rife as to the cause of Topock's killing; and even Lou Safford's death was surrounded by an aura of mystery. True, his deputies swore that Telldane had yanked a gun and shot him while in the process of being apprehended for the cold-blooded murder of Brill. But the wise ones of the country shook their heads; and there were knowing glints in more than one pair of eyes. How come, the question was asked, that both Topock and Safford had been killed in the Ransome store? What had they been doing there that night? "You notice," folks pointed out, "them deputies ain't shootin' off their jaws none about why Telldane gunned Topock!" And this appeared cause for more head-shaking—as did the lack of all comment on the part of the Ransomes, father and daughter. There sure was a nigger in the woodpile some place!

But if there were, it stayed there. And after a time, for lack of fuel, most of the talk died out.

And then one night a solitary horseman rode down from the hills and knocked on the Kerwold door.

Jane Kerwold herself came to open it; and stepped back with a low, choked cry.

Bufe Telldane's bow was a brief, curt thing. The eyes in his gaunted face were bleak and the dust of long trails grimed his clothing. He said gruffly: "If Sam's around, I'd like to see him a minute."

She stood there, shrinking back from him, one hand at her throat, eyes dark and round and staring.

Some unknown thinking then worried her cheeks and she said breathlessly, almost anxiously: "Quick! Step in here out of the light!" and held the screen door open.

He stepped past her with curling lips, for he knew her anxiety was caused by fear that someone seeing him would lay the blame for his presence on Kerwold. He said with a sneer in his voice: "I won't be here but a minute. I don't reckon anyone's followed me."

She looked at him queerly, he thought—seemed about to say something. But she must have changed her mind, for, with a little nod, she hurried off; and pretty soon Old Sam's heavy step preceded him into the hall.

"By God, boy, I thought they'd run you out of the country," Sam said, and winked as he held out his hand.

"Listen," Bufe said, "put this in your safe—it's your lease for the Wildcat——"

Sam took it, dubiously eyeing him. "I'm obliged as hell," he said gruffly. "I realize it's entirely my fault you're——"

"You didn't have anything to do with it. I shot Guy Topock because he needed shooting, and I gunned Safford because he was trying to frame me—and there's one more guy I'm squaring up with before I take to the timber. You needn't feel responsible for my troubles at all. Now look—get your steers on to Wildcat right away an'——"

"Just a second," Sam said, and rasped a hand across his jowls reluctantly. "I hate to say it, an' I don't want you to figure I'm not appreciatin' what you've tried to do for me, but—the truth is, Bufe, I don't see how this lease of yours can do me a mite of good, now.

You've filed on it under the Homestead Act an' you've got to do your work on it in order to get your rights; an' how're you goin' to do that with half the country doggin' your sign? Hell, boy, they'll prob'ly cross your name off the books, now you been made a out-law." He stared at Telldane earnestly. "I hate like sin to say it, but I guess we've plumb lost Wildcat."

"You're still wanting that lease, ain't you?"

"Wantin' it? Hell, I got to *have* it if I——"

"O.K., then, get your cattle on to it. Until they scratch me off the books this paper covers you—an' beyond, I shouldn't wonder. With this paper in your hands you can tie Wildcat up in the courts for years if you got to."

"Yeah. . . . But you're forgettin' mebbe that there's a whole lot of other fellers needin' that land. Gosh, boy, I'd need an army to keep my cows in that grass!"

Bufe grinned across at him bleakly. "You get your critters on to it an' leave the rest up to me."

Kerwold stared, stepped back aghast. "My God! You ain't figurin' to stay on in this country, are you?"

"I'll stick as long as I can," Bufe said, and changed the subject. "Ever hear of an outfit called the Boxed Double A?"

Old Sam looked thoughtful; shook his head. "Located in this——"

Telldane nodded, darkly scowling. "The brand's listed in this county. I got an idee they been usin' Gann's place in their business. Look here——"

He crossed to Kerwold's desk, picked up a piece of paper and, with a stub of pencil dug from his pocket, swiftly made a couple of sketches. Sam's Flying K brand and, alongside of it, the imprint of the Boxed

Double A. He paused then, tipped his head, and looked at Sam Kerwold grimly.

Kerwold looked from Bufe to the brands and suddenly his eyes showed a bitter glint and his cheeks darkened up with anger. Telldane nodded. "Wouldn't take any great shucks with an iron to cover your brand with this one."

Kerwold said thickly : "Where's this outfit located?"

"They got a P.O. box at the county seat." Bufe's grin was hard and meaningful.

"Whose name's it in?"

"Same one that's listed in the brand book—Boxed Double A Cattle Syndicate."

"It's a goddam rustlers' brand!"

"Sure it is. Been started to take care of your surplus. S'pose it could be this fellow Cooper? Cooper an' Topock, mebbe?"

"But Topock's dead——"

"He wasn't when this brand was recorded."

They stared at each other thoughtfully. Bufe said: "I've been scoutin' round since I been on the dodge an' I've found out two or three things. It was Topock got your $2,000 off the stage that night. Turned most of it over to Cooper to pay off Cooper's night riders——"

"Raiders?" Sam said sharply.

Telldane nodded. "Cooper an' Topock may not have started this Boxed Double A—or, again, they may have. But one thing I can tell you certain: Cooper's bossin' a band of range roughers that are levyin' hard on your cattle—I caught 'em at it the night I killed Topock. They was headed for Gann's place when I stampeded 'em."

Kerwold stood a long while in thought. He said

looking up abruptly: "You the one that fired Gann's spread?"

Telldane grunted a negative. "I been wonderin' about that fire myself. Did you know Gann an' Holcomb was brothers?"

"Hell, no!"

"Well, they were," Bufe said, and told him of the conversation he'd had with Ab Holcomb. "I forgot an' left my gloves at his place that morning—don't suppose you recollect seein' 'em there, do you? I left them on Ab's desk, I think . . ."

But Kerwold shook his head. His mind seemed too filled with other things to be worried about Telldane's gloves. He said irritably: "I swear I'm so tangled in my mind I don't know up from down. But heavens an' earth! If Gann an' Holcomb was brothers, an' you caught Cooper's crowd drivin' some of my Flyin' K's towards Gann's Skull Mesa ranch, I'd say by God that the whole lousy bunch of 'em was ganged up to put me out of business!"

"It might be," Telldane admitted, "that they've all been workin' towards that end—it's a cinch Topock an' Cooper was the ones that got them homesteaders in here, an' that Gann was mixed up with them in that part of it, but . . . Well, frankly, Sam, I don't think Holcomb's connected with 'em."

He scowled at the desk-top frowningly. "That fellow Vargas round any place, Sam?"

Kerwold's look got intent, suspicious. "I told you once——"

Telldane waved it aside. "If he's round, suppose you call him in here——"

"Never mind——"

"As a favour, Sam," Telldane said gravely.

Kerwold eyed him stiffly, grimly. With a long hard

roll of the shoulders, he strode to the door, stepped out on the porch. Bufe heard his bull voice sail across the yard—heard somebody muttering an answer.

Sam came in and shut the door. Stood with his back against it, frowning.

"Not around, eh?" Telldane drawled. "I didn't think he would be. Find out where he's gone?"

There was a hard-held look to Kerwold's cheeks and his tone was flat, unconfiding. "Cook said he rode off some place after supper."

"Let's have the cook in here for a minute."

Sam yanked open the door and called him; and a few moments later the cook stepped in. His eyes sprang wide when he saw Telldane.

Bufe said: "That a habit of Vargas'—ridin' off after supper?"

The man's glance jumped to Kerwold. "Go ahead. Answer him," Sam said gruffly.

The cook still hesitated. He said nervously, "Well, uh . . . That is to say——"

"Is it or ain't it?"

"I ain't been payin' no special attention," the man said finally. "I got my own work to do an'——"

"Joe," Old Sam cut in harshly, "I got my back against the wall. Answer this fellow's question. If you've noticed anything—umm—*peculiar* about Vargas' actions, right now's a good time to mention it."

The cook's grizzled cheeks got a little pink. "I don't know's I have," he grumbled. "But some of the boys has been layin' bets lately about who Duarte's settin' the bag for. Seems they've noticed sev'ral mornin's late-like that that black geldin' of his has been showin' signs of night work——"

"I think that's all we want to know," Bufe said to

Kerwold; and Sam nodded to the cook who, still looking uncomfortable, forthwith departed.

Bufe said nothing. Kerwold, after a hard, bitter stare at him, growled: "Looks like you might be right about him at that. Mebbe I had better look into his doings a little——"

"Better watch your step if you do, Sam. The fellow's no Bible-tract salesman. Better take things easy—give him plenty of rope an' keep your eyes peeled. Be a good idea to find out what his game is before you jump him. . . . Well," he said with a shrug for the unconvinced look on Kerwold's face, "I guess I better be driftin'——"

"You're goin' to stick, then?"

"Long as I can."

"You watch out for Deef Smith, then—that guy's a hunter from who cocked the trigger—contrary as a mule an' stubborn as Job's boils. He'll hang to your tracks like glue, boy, an' if he ever sights you down a rifle——"

"I'll watch out for him."

He was climbing into the saddle when somebody stepped from the shadows, laid a detaining hand on his arm. Looking round, Bufe found Jane Kerwold facing him.

"Bufe——"

"Well?" Telldane said it coldly.

"Bufe, I——"

"All that's past," Bufe told her harshly, forestalling what she might have said. "Water under the bridge. You needn't worry—I'll keep my mouth shut."

The light was bad, but even so he could see how her shoulders stiffened. His words had hurt, and he had meant them to. She had tricked him once—

E*

played him for a sucker. He'd no intention of having the experience repeated. "If it's in your head I followed you here, you can get shut of that idea pronto—I'd never have come within miles of this place if I'd known you were Old Sam's daughter! "

" I believe you," she said quietly after a moment. " You *do* hate me, don't you? "

Bufe didn't bother answering that one.

" I suppose it would be useless for me to try to explain——"

" Complete waste of breath! "

Through the shadows he saw her shoulders droop, felt her hand withdrawn from his arm. But she did not go, not at once. She said, voice so low he scarce could hear her, " But it's so senseless, Bufe! If you'd only listen——"

" I've listened too long already," he sneered. " Nothing you could tell me would change my notions a fraction—I know what I know and that's the end of it. Do you think, after—after what I saw that night, that——"

" Not even if I said that I still loved you? That —that I had *always* loved you, and that what you——"

" What I inadvertently walked in on? " Bufe inquired sarcastically.

She half turned away and then her chin came up and she said determinedly: " Yes! That what you inadvertently walked in on had been deliberately pre——"

" Then I'd call you to your face what I've known you really are ever since that night—a lying, selfish, miserable little cheat! *Is that plain?* " Bufe's laugh was short, an ugly sound. He said, " Now get out of my way. I've got to ride and I'm in a hurry."

He did not wait for her to move aside but, swinging

into the saddle, he savagely wheeled the horse that
had been Lou Safford's, and feeding it steel, quit the
place at a hard fast run.

CHAPTER XXII

GUN THUNDER

QUITTING the Flying K yard, Telldane rode blindly,
giving the horse its way, his mind a seething mael-
strom of wild thoughts and tortuous imaginings.
Conflicting passions tore at him, and a cold sweat
clammed his brow as, furiously, he recognized what
an attraction the girl still had for him. This was the
truth—the bitter and humiliating truth. Despite all
he knew against her, despite all he'd suffered at her
hands, Jane Kerwold still had the power to move him,
to cause his pulses to leap and bound, to upset completely the traditionally cool and well-governed run
of his mind. A thousand thoughts besieged him, all
centring around the vital and compelling figure of
this girl, the purl of her voice—its husky cadence,
her ways—each manner and gesture, the cut of her
profile, the slant of her cheeks and the remembered
turquoise blue of her eyes—these, all these, were
before him, crystal clear with yesterday's poignance.
Three years he'd gone a headlong way trying to sear
these things from memory only to find, to-night, that
they were stronger, more compelling than ever before.

It was a curse laid on him for the turbulence he'd
embraced to forget them. He was like the man in the

poem, with the dead duck hung round his neck.

For he saw with a hateful clarity now that he was still in love; *in love*—God save the mark!—with a girl who had used him contemptibly—and seemed even now seeking so to use him again!

Where was his pride? he thought with blanching cheeks. God—had the world ever known such a fool as Bufe Telldane! Telldane, the man who had always prided himself on the steeled control of his emotions! In love with a girl who had cared so little as to make of his passion a mockery—a subject for hoots and scoffing!

He jeered at and berated himself; jeered at her, at what might have been. He sneered and cursed—consigned her to hell; but it made him feel little better. The truth was there to ridicule him, to flog and scourge and ride him. His passion burned with a bright white light. No abuse, no reviling, could quench it.

What a poor, puny husk of a man he was! To care with such undiminished passion—to *care at all* for one who could hold that regard in so low esteem. He must be soft in the head! He must——

Through his concerned absorption, scattering his disjointed reflections like chaff before a gale, came the flogged hoof sound of a horse that was running like mad. The racing pound of those hoofs bit through the night like a tocsin.

Head up, eyes narrowed to the warning of that sound, Telldane reined his horse from the trail. Wheeled into a thicket of squatting cedar, he crouched, forward-leaning from the saddle, waiting, with all his screaming nerves yanked tight, a pistol gripped in his hand.

Downslope tumbled echoes of that crashing gait

drove jouncing and bouncing—a roll of doom; un-reasoning, monstrous, a cacophony of sound.

Out of the darkness lunged a horse with nostrils flaring, ears flattened, foam flecked, its wild eyes glaring. Half out of the saddle—but clinging still with the clutch of death—showed its rider, hatless, hair flying, his whiskers whipped by that whirlwind pace, vest flapping, wind-bellied shirt all stains and tatters.

A name leaped stiff from Telldane's lips. *"Ab Holcomb!"* he cried, and spurred his horse after them.

But a frenzy of terror drove Holcomb's horse; and spur and quirt though Bufe would and did, nothing it seemed but miles could close that thundering gap between them. And then Holcomb fell—Bufe saw him go; out of the saddle and off the trail, over and over like a sack of spilled meal. Ab's body brought up in a greasewood clump; and then Bufe was down on a knee beside him.

The Straddle Bug boss was not dead nor out. A wan grin twisted the colourless lips; then a rasping, choking gasp—a cough rattled the breath hung up in his throat, and he shivered in Bufe's supporting grip. His head fell forward, chin digging his chest. But mumbled sound squeezed through his teeth and Bufe, bent close, caught the muttered words.

When he rose, sweat beaded the slant of Bufe's cheeks; they were white, stiff-clamped. His mouth was a gash. Ab Halcomb lay dead in the brush at his feet—but not in vain. His words rang like trumpets in Bufe's reeling brain. The truth—the staggering, ghastly truth—was his at last.

Duarte Vargas, at Flying K, got off his horse by

the pole corral and stood a moment in the pooled gloom, thinking. He knew the crew was out on the range, for he'd given the order himself, after supper. There'd be nobody round but the cook and Old Sam —and the girl, of course; but she didn't matter.

Duarte Vargas was a cold-blooded man; a thinking, scheming, far-sighted man who could see the main chance and had the wit to grab it. He was a close, tight-fisted man as well and had a goodly store of hard money laid by, the savings of fifteen years of ramrod's pay, augmented these last two years by the secret addition of cheques from a neighbour.

He had a laugh for the expression that must have stamped that neighbour's face could he have known what he, Duarte Vargas, was intending now. That man wanted power, the control of this basin; and for two years Vargas had taken pay for helping him. But he was through with that now. They had reached, this neighbour and Vargas, the parting of the ways. Vargas was through with helping someone else; from here on out he meant to help himself. The means and the reward lay right at hand.

He knotted the pony's reins to the corral's top bar, and straightened. Well pleased with his thoughts, he nodded and a cold smile curved his lips as he started for the house. Good! There was a light in Kerwold's office; and Jane would have gone to bed by now. And that was a good thing, too. What he had to say was between himself and Kerwold; and it would be just as well if there were no one else around.

Without bothering to knock he entered the house, stepped into Kerwold's office and closed the door.

Old Sam looked up with a scowl. " Where the hell you been? "

" Never mind that," Vargas said with a shrug. " I

want to talk to you. I've got aplenty to say an' you'd better listen——"

With an oath Old Sam slewed out of his chair, cheeks dark and neck muscles corded. "By God——" he began; but Vargas grinned at him.

"Sit down," he said, "before you fall down."

It was then Sam saw the gun—the sawed-off ·44 that was cocked and levelled from Vargas' fist.

"That's better," approved Vargas, chuckling, as Kerwold slumped back in his chair. "Nothin' like a good Colt gun for holdin' a fella's attention." He grinned at Sam wickedly. "Wonder what you'd say if Deef Smith was to learn you been aidin' an' abettin' the outlaw he's been three weeks tryin' to run down? Eh? What would you say if I was to tell him you not only been hidin' Telldane out, but was the fella that got him out here in the first place—the gent that's been hirin' him——"

"I'd say you was a goddam fool an' a liar!"

"Mebbe you would," Vargas grinned, "but you'd play hell provin' it! On the other hand, I could back up my remarks with concrete evidence— kind of evidence any jury in this land would pass on. I could show Smith that cave Telldane has been holed up in; I could show him the letter I got in my pocket that you sent Bufe, askin' him to come out here— surprises you, don't it? It surprised me, too, when I found it."

When Kerwold could trust himself to speak: "What are you after?" he growled thickly.

"Nothin' but a little land an' a deed from you in writin'," Vargas drawled. "I'm a modest man—you'd be surprised, Sam. All I want is that little jag of pasture above your north-west line-camp—up there by that corduroy road."

Kerwold's angry cheeks relaxed a little, showing some of the astonishment he felt. He tipped back his head and looked at his foreman oddly. "What in God's name do you want of *that* land?"

Vargas shrugged. "Just a quit-claim, or some kind of deed to it in writin', Sam. I've got a little money put by. Kind of figured mebbe I'd run me three-four cows an' mebbe a bull or two——"

Kerwold snorted. Then his anger seemed to get the better of him again and he banged a gnarled fist heavily on the desk top. "You damn' coyote! I never been blackmailed in my life——"

"Ssh! Not so loud," interrupted Vargas. "You're not talkin' to Deef Smith—yet." He chuckled silently, like an Indian, at the look on Kerwold's cheeks. Then he said slickly, in a tone as suave as velvet: "No sense usin' ugly words or callin' names in this business; if you want to start in heavin' names I can think of a few myself, an' the jail term for a guy that accessories outlaws . . . Shucks! What's the sense gettin' hot under the collar? You got plenty land—a sight more'n you'll know what to do with, now them Wildcat lands is filed on . . .

"Say!" Vargas exclaimed with suddenly narrowing stare, "Telldane ain't given you a lease on Wildcat, has he?" And, before the rancher could answer: "By God! I b'lieve he has! Well, well! Be kinda tough to go to jail now at last you got what you been fishin' for. Well, there's a way round it. Just git out a pen an'——"

"What's on that land?" Old Sam said, leaning forward.

"You write out that deed an' I'll tell you," Vargas murmured agreeably; but the glitter of his eyes did not change by the slightest fraction. "But you better

write it quick—I'm gettin' awful nervous, Sam. I
got a bad itch in my trigger finger——"

Abruptly Kerwold chuckled. Leaning back in his
chair he crossed his arms and stared at Vargas mock-
ingly. "You been readin' too much Buntline, boy.
Go ahead an' yap to Smith—this ain't my signin'
night."

The grin fell off Duarte Vargas' face. "What's
that?" he gasped, jaw sagging. It was not the smartest
of answers, but this unexpected independence had
thrown his whole plan off gear.

Kerwold jeered at him, laughed aloud. He said
contemptuously: "Go have your talk with Smith. Be
amusin' to see how far this pipe dream'll get you——"

"But—but that letter . . ." Vargas faltered. "That
letter you wrote Telldane——"

"I'll tell Smith it's a forgery——"

"You'll—— By God, you'll shout, too!" Vargas
struck the desk with a force that shook the room. The
fingers of his other hand clamped white about the gun,
and his furious face was bloated, was horribly twisted
with a wild and raging malevolence. "You'll write
that deed an' write it quick, or I'll blow your goddam
guts out!"

Kerwold paled, but he kept his arms crossed
stubbornly.

"Blow ahead," he said; and Vargas shook with
anger.

"You goddam fool!" he snarled. "You think I'm
scared to kill you? You never been more mistaken
in your life!" He thrust his fury-ridden face within
short inches of Kerwold's own. "I been away all
evenin'—cook'll swear to it. I'll tell Deef Smith I come
home an' found Telldane rushin' away from here—
I'll say I found you groanin' on the floor, all blood—

that you swore Telldane had done it!" His eyes glared
at Kerwold balefully. "You goin' to write——"

Whatever else he'd been going to say was lost in
gun sound—shattered. He clawed frantically at his
chest, spun half around and, mouth sprung wide in a
soundless screech, crashed sideways into the desk—slid
soggily off it on to the floor.

Through the spraddled fingers of an upthrust arm,
Sam Kerwold saw flame belch again from the hip of
the man stiff-crouched in the door.

And that was all. The world pinched out in a howl-
ing black. His body jack-knifed from the chair, fell
forward in a crumpled heap beside the dead Duarte
Vargas.

CHAPTER XXIII

"—AN' SHE SCREECHIN' LIKE A TOMCAT!"

FOR long moments Telldane stood above Ab Holcomb's body—stood sombrely; rooted there by the ugly
pattern he had put together from the dead man's
words. So many of his preconceived notions had been
wrong, had been utterly haywire. He had to fight in
those first moments to give Holcomb's story credence.
Slowly, then ever more quickly, the picture grew clear
and sharpened to a steel-point focus as the dead man's
story threw its light into long-dark corners. It was
simple—so bitterly simple. The wonder was that he
had not guessed these things before. Every edge of it

dovetailed neatly; all the pieces dropped into place—
almost all of them anyway.

A little over three years back—just before Telldane
had met Jane Kerwold—Gus Pring had come to Holcomb with a proposition. Both men had been Texans,
each had known the other by repute; Holcomb had
been a rustler, Gus Pring—under another name—
had been an absconding West Texas banker. They
had, Pring said, considerable in common. It was his
suggestion that they combine their spreads and form
a syndicate. Holcomb had thought well of the idea,
and so the Boxed Double A Cattle Syndicate came into
being.

But Holcomb had dealt with too many slippery
customers in his time to trust any man very far. Pring
might be sincere, but Holcomb was not going to bank
on it. He insisted on keeping his property separate
and under his own control; but had, under pressure,
signed a contract which provided that, in the event
of either one should chance to die before the other,
the surviving partner was to fall heir to the entire
combined properties.

About the time Telldane had first met up with Jane
Kerwold (near Ballinger, this had been, where the
girl had been spending a part of her college vacation
with her Great-uncle Harold) business interests had
happened, one day, to take Pring and Holcomb into
Ballinger. Pring had met Jane on the street and had
been asked to the uncle's house for supper. During
the course of that evening Telldane's name had
bobbed up frequently and when Pring had suggested
a date for the following evening, Jane had expressed
her regrets, informing him that she had a previous
engagement. Suspecting it was with Telldane, Pring
had ascertained the time and, taking Uncle Harold

and his wife to see a play-acting troupe to get them out of the way, had left a stage all set for Telldane's special benefit. Pring's melodrama had proved all he could have hoped for. Telldane had arrived at Uncle Harold's to find the woman he was engaged to clasped in the ardent embrace of a tall and florid gentleman togged out in gambler's clothes.

And Telldane—poor fool—had jumped to the hasty and entirely erroneous conclusion it had been intended that he should. Even now his jaw-muscles corded as he recalled the leering grin with which the fellow had sped his departure.

Pring had made a fool of him, all right.

Telldane acknowledged it. He'd deserved all Pring had dealt him for the brash, fine-gentleman manner with which he'd waved aside Jane's attempted explanations, declaring that his eyes had already told him all he cared to know of the business. And that very night he'd got out of Texas and had not gone back there since.

Oh, yes, Pring had made a fool of him—but there was going to be an accounting . . .

He forced his mind back to the rest of Holcomb's story. With Telldane thus satisfactorily disposed of, Pring had expected soon to hear the sound of wedding-bells. Unaccountably, however, Jane would seem to have turned against him. She'd avoided him for the rest of that summer; and now that she was home again seemed still to be avoiding him, and what times that she couldn't, was casually cool and impersonal.

Pring had been forced to believe at last that Kerwold's Flying K—via wedding-bells—was not for him and, without consulting Holcomb, had cast about for other and speedier means of getting his hands on the property. But with Kerwold's visit the other morning and disclosure of the Globe bank deal, all Holcomb's original distrust and suspicion of Pring had been roused again. Little things were remembered; small troubles and minor mysteries assumed their proper perspective—he and Pring had quarrelled. Not too bitterly, of course, but enough to set Ab's wits to work. He'd decided Pring needed watching.

But Pring had proved much smarter than Holcomb thought him. Pring had been having Holcomb watched; had learned of Holcomb's activity and had led him into a trap.

To-night Holcomb, watching Pring's place, had seen the Double Bar Circle boss ride off into the hills and had followed. Pring had gone to a rendezvous with Duarte Vargas, the Kerwold foreman. What they talked about, Holcomb had been too far off to hear; but the fact that they'd talked, off to themselves this way, had been enough to show him that Pring was up to some more slick work that was not being shared with his partner. Seething with rage and resentment, Holcomb had set out to dog Pring's sign after Pring and Vargas had parted. He had still been following Pring when a rifle, from point-blank range, had begun ripping up the echoes. Every shot had struck Holcomb, had swept him from the saddle and left him dying in the trail—he'd been dying, but still was conscious, when Willow Creek Wally rode out of the thicket and jogged off after Gus Pring. After what had seemed to him an endless time, Holcomb had some way managed to catch his horse and climb into the saddle. He had known that he was dying. His thought had been to reach Sam Kerwold and warn him—to foil Gus Pring if it was the last thing he did on earth.

Well, he'd foiled him—or Telldane would.

Telldane examined his six-guns—he was packing two these days—and swung grimly into the saddle. He had lost Jane Kerwold, that was certain. No girl could overlook the things he'd said to her, much less the high-handed way he'd used her. She might forgive, but she could not forget. It was not in human nature to forget such treatment as that. His lack of faith, his intolerant and bigoted certainties, had placed her beyond his reach.

But Pring was not beyond his reach. Pring had sown the wind—let him beware the pending harvest.

Deputy Sheriff Deef Smith was sitting up late; he was at his desk in the two-by-four office darkly brooding over a handful of yellowing dodgers he had dug three weeks ago from his files. The face of Bufe Telldane stared back at him from them—not a good likeness, but good enough. These were old Texas handbills offering rewards for Telldane's apprehension on charges since dismissed. Considering them was heaping coals on the fire of Deef Smith's hatred—a personal animosity he held toward every law-breaker. Undoubtedly Telldane had perpetrated the things described in these dodgers, and just as undoubtedly the things had since been forgiven him by a bunch of soft-headed nitwits in recognition of the man's once-splendid record—as if past virtues excused him!

It always made Smith's blood boil to see an outlaw pardoned. Once an outlaw, always an outlaw! It was Smith's unswervable conviction that the only good outlaws were dead ones; and if he had his way they'd all be dead, or safely caged behind bars.

It was gall and bitter wormwood to him to realize that for three long arduous weeks Bufe Telldane had been laughing at him—at the impotence of Smith's man-hunt.

Smith crumpled the dodgers in a savage fist and flung them into a corner. "Goddam fools!" he swore, thinking of the men responsible for Telldane's Texas pardon. "The mealy-mouthed, apron-stringed petticoats! By God, he'll get no pardon here! Just let me get my hands on him! Just——"

It was then he heard the hoof-beats. They brought him grim-lipped out of his chair. And he was that way, one hand reaching for his rifle, when the door was flung open and a white-faced man burst into the room, dust covered, horse lather flecking the knees of his Levis.

It was the Kerwold cook, Bide Jonathan.

Bide said: "Great Gawd A'mighty, Sheriff! Come out to our place quick! I never in my born——"

"What's up?" Smith's voice rode through the words sharply. He caught Bide Jonathan's shoulder. "Never mind the build-up! What the bloody hell's happened?"

"Murder—cold-blooded murder! I swear to Pete, I——"

"I'll swear, too, in a minute! Who's murdered? Who done it?"

"I'm a-tellin' you, ain't I? Telldane—that's who! Come in there like a——"

"*Telldane!* Telldane's *murdered?*" Deef Smith gasped.

"Hell, no! He's murdered Vargas! Vargas an' Kerwold, too, I guess—leastways Sam——",

Wrathful, exasperated, Smith shook the cook without gentleness. "Never mind the frills, you nitwit! Tell me straight out what's happened. When'd it happen? What started it? Tell me all you know about it an' never mind your savin' soul! "

He got the story finally. Telldane, according to Bide Jonathan, had come out to the ranch that evening. Answering Kerwold's hail, Jonathan had entered the old man's office, going on ten o'clock, to find him closeted with Bufe Telldane. They had wanted to see Vargas about something—no, Jonathan didn't know what. Vargas hadn't been round; had left right after supper. After learning this much Kerwold had sent the cook back to his shanty, and a short time later, from that shanty, he had seen Telldane ride off.

"But he musta come back—snuk back, I guess likely, 'cause round eleven o'clock—I'd gone to bed— I heard shots." Springing to the window he had seen that big bay of Lou Safford's—the one Telldane had been riding—hitched before the porch. Alarmed, he'd jumped into his boots and gone pelting for the house. He'd got hardly half across the yard when Telldane came running out. Telldane had seen him, had flung two quick shots at him, vaulted into the saddle and gone hell-bending off toward the hills.

Entering the house he'd found a bloody sight awaiting him in Kerwold's office. Vargas lay sprawled in a pool of blood—dead; shot through the back. And across the room Sam Kerwold—all blood, too—had lain, crumpled, beside his overturned chair.

At this point Smith had broken in to ask where Kerwold's daughter was.

"Jane? My savin' soul! Didn't I tell you? Great bulls of Bashan! She was *with* him—with *Telldane*. He come outa that house luggin' her under one arm —an' she screechin' like a tom-cat! She was kickin' an' scratchin' an' poundin' him with her helpless little fists—but he was hangin' right on to her like she wasn't no bigger'n a baby——"

"You mean to say he carried her off——"

"I'm tellin' you, ain't I? 'Course he carried her off—took her up in the hills with him . . ."

Deef Smith didn't hear any more. He wasn't listening. He was busy cramming rifle shells into his pocket. And there was a cold, bright glint in his eye.

CHAPTER XXIV

APACHES!

It was close to daylight when Bufe Telldane sighted the headquarters buildings of Pring's Double Bar Circle outfit. In the flat grey haze preceding dawn the place looked gauntly drab, deserted. But Bufe was not dismayed for there were horses in the big corral. His natural inclination was to ride straight over to the house, get Pring out of bed and have it out with him; but natural inclinations, he was beginning to learn, were damned expensive luxuries. Pring was a feud style fighter, deadly as a sidewinder. Twice already Bufe had under-estimated the man, and a third time might prove the last. Pring, if he were but half as slick as Holcomb claimed, would not be passing up any bets; he would have considered the possibility of Telldane's coming and have prepared for it.

A creek's twisting course wound a short way back of the harness-shed, and from its eroded lip the ground pitched gently upward toward a low-crowned knoll, or miniature butte that was topped by a stand of timber. Bufe, riding in among those trees, dismounted. He looped the reins of Safford's horse about a juniper's gnarled branch and, easing the marshal's Winchester from beneath the stirrup fender, crept forward to the edge of brush. That vantage afforded him a pretty fair view of the yard below, and he hunkered there on his boot-heels with a rifle across his knees, prepared to wait day's coming. If Pring had readied a trap for him, he meant to know it before going down there.

His wind-scoured cheeks were bleakly slanted and the roll of his lips showed bitter—but not one half so bitter as the thoughts that ranged his mind. He watched, but hardly saw the grey yard spread below him; Jane Kerwold's features were before his vision and he could not get them out of it. No pleasant thoughts were these that were tumbling through his head as, with the outward patience of an Indian, he sat watching the false dawn fade from the east. Once he groaned aloud, remembering the words he'd used last night on Jane when by the porch she'd tried to talk with him. He had lost her, irrevocably and finally. By his own acts, by the brutal things he'd said to her, he had scattered the last cold ash of their departed romance.

Day dawned beyond the eastward mountains, the sun's new glory gilding the western bastions, lining with purest gold the far-away peaks of the eastern slopes. Morning came rocking its way across the valley, but nothing stirred in the yard below—nothing human, leastways. The horses in the big corral let out a few desultory whinnies, stretched and peered hungrily across the bars; but that was all.

Telldane watched for another half-hour then stiffly rose and climbed into the saddle. He sent the gelding at a slow walk toward the creek, reached it, splashed across, and quartered past the harness-shed. Still no sign of movement; nothing to show there were men around.

Odd—uncommon odd.

No smoke came from the cook-shack chimney; no sound emanated from the bunk-house's chinked, log walls. No movement anywhere save that created by the restless broncs in the pole corral.

He got down before the ranch-house porch, climbed its steps and crossed its sun-warped planking to pound the butt of his six-gun against the door. Hollow echoes mocked that thumping.

Something was plain enough to Telldane then. Pring was gone. The ranch was deserted.

He stood a moment scowling, then yanked the screen door open and strode inside. Through room after empty room he tramped with scowl growing blacker and blacker. He stood upon the porch again and stared across the yard, bleak gaze roving the horses in the enclosure. Crowbaits. There was not one sound horse there.

Where had Gus Pring gone—and *why*?

What new devilment was the fellow up to that had taken all hands away from this spread? Pring had not quit the country; that much was certain. He had come too close to victory to be pulling a fade-out now; there was no sense to it—no need that Telldane knew of. Pring could not have known that Willow Creek's job was a botched one; it was not likely that Willow Creek himself suspected it. They believed Ab Holcomb dead—as dead as Brill and Ronstadt.

Only one thing could have pulled that outfit away from this spread—more devilment.

Jaw muscles corded, Telldane swung into the saddle. They were some place in this basin and he would find them.

A wild, forbidding stretch of country, this land
below the Mogollon Rim; timbered slopes and dust
strewn deserts, a place of lofty peaks and sunken
broiling, rock-choked wastes and gulches. By ten
o'clock these flats were stifling and what fitful wind
was shouldered off the mesas was furnace-hot. Every
bit of metal about Bufe's gear was scorching to the
touch and his eyes were red with the glare.

It was in his mind that Pring and his outfit might
be trailing stolen Kerwold cattle. Now that Topock
was dead, Andy Cooper, he thought, might have cast
his lot with Pring; for certainly Pring would have
been cognizant of their activities. It was in the cards
he might have made a deal with Cooper just as he
had with Willow Creek Wally and—yes, as quite
probably he had with Vargas. All along, ever since
first meeting the man that night when he'd come from
the trees by the corduroy road, Telldane had felt
Duarte Vargas was playing a double game. Kerwold
had scoffed at the notion, but Kerwold's enemies were
out to smash him, and where could an agent of those
enemies be better placed than right in Kerwold's out
fit?

He left off thinking abruptly, narrowed eyes in
tently staring, body stiffened in the saddle. From the
tip of Humbolt Mountain, far ahead to the north,
smoke was rising straight into the sky; and Bufe's
raking glance flashing eastward across the hazed
horizon found others. Saddle Mountain—Cypress
Peak—Four Peaks Mountain—Sugarloaf! From each
of those crests smoke thrust its grey tail into the sky
and Telldane was seized with a sudden conviction
Someone was keeping tabs on him, signalling his
whereabouts, smoke-talking about his progress and
direction!

He reined up with cheeks gone sober. It would hardly be Pring who was so interested in his actions, for every contact he had had with the man had advertised Pring's opinion. Pring was not only unafraid of Telldane; he was contemptuous of him. Having framed him so neatly once, the boss of Double Bar Circle would surely never consider it necessary to camp all these scouts on Bufe's trail.

It was a time for thought and Bufe thought hard. And the upshot of that thinking was remembrance of the deputy—Deef Smith. Bufe's dust-streaked face kicked a twisted grin. Yes, that would be Smith. The man had spent three bitter weeks savagely casting for Telldane's sign, trying to run Telldane to earth. The futility of those efforts must have pricked the deputy's ego like the stabs of a Spanish dagger. Deef Smith—in Smith's opinion—was no safe man to trifle with; and Bufe, knowing something of the lawman's reputation, could see how Deef Smith would be wild to get him. He had thought the man would have given up, but it was plain now that he hadn't.

And then Bufe's roving glance crossed something that sprang his eyes wide open; and he leaned forward, startled, amazedly staring at the ground. There in the dust of the trail before him was a track. A moccasin track—the clear-cut shape of a buckskin-covered foot!

Apaches!

There was no doubt in Bufe's active mind as to the meaning of those smokes now. Deef Smith, determined to get him, was employing Apache scouts!

Even as the realization clutched him the hot sand bulged beside the track, dust geysered suddenly from and the sharp flat crack of a rifle kicked across the stifling silence.

Telldane's spurs flashed wickedly. Safford's hors
lunged forward with a rushed, hip-jolting violenc
and settled to a flogging run with Telldane, ridin
Indian fashion, hanging on by a knee and an arm.

CHAPTER XXV

" YOU CAN CROSS TELLDANE OFF THE BOOKS!"

JANE KERWOLD, following Bufe Telldane's departur
did not go at once to bed. Re-entering the house an
retiring to the privacy of her room, she sat for a lon
time by the window thinking. She sat with dark blu
eyes, widely wistful, regarding the play of light an
shadow, watching it build and break its patterns i
the empty yard outside. Like life those patterns wer
she thought; and sighed now and again as win
whipped lonely anthems from the dusty foliage of th
trees.

She saw Duarte Vargas by the moon's cool light ri
into the yard and leave his horse by the big corral. Sh
wondered idly where he'd been then heard his ste
upon the porch, heard the screen door close behir
him, and found herself reflecting this was the fir
time she could remember that he had not let it sla

Some fifteen minutes later another horse came in
the yard—came so quietly that it was there in th
cottonwoods' shadows before she became aware of i
and even then she was not sure until it crossed a pat
of moonlight and she saw it plainly, briefly, and reco
nized its rider.

Gus Pring.

It looked like Gus. The man had Gus' way of sitting a saddle.

Again she sighed, and hoped she was no part of whatever reason had brought him here at this late hour. And that was queer, when she stopped to think of it, for there had been a time when knowledge of Gus' presence would have been a welcome thing— indeed it *had* been, many times. But that had been before she'd met grim, taciturn Bufe Telldane.

She was still there by the window, absorbed with thoughts of Bufe Telldane, when gun sound jerked her from the chair. Jerked her upright, frightened, trembling, startled eyes fixed on the door. She sprang toward it, wrenched it open, went down the hall in quick alarm.

For a moment, coming in from the dark, the light in Kerwold's office blinded her; and then, turned sick with horror, sight returned and the room in ghastly focus sprang clear before her eyes. There lay Vargas in grotesque posture, glazed eyes staring, beside the desk. His twisted mouth hung open; blood was bright upon his shirt. And there, just beyond, face down, was sprawled her father; and above him, smoking pistol still in hand, was crouched Gus Pring.

"*Gus!*"

The choked cry spun Pring round.

Jane screamed when she saw the look of him. With blazing eyes, he sprang for her. Terrified, Jane whirled, tried to reach the hall. But he was too quick for her. She tripped, was falling when she felt herself yanked backward, felt his arms close round her. A rough hand then cut short her screams and everything went black.

She was jarred awake by an agonizing sense of movement. Every tortured muscle ached, her nerves were screaming and her wrists and ankles felt as though they were being cut in two. Her jerked-open eyes found a world still dark; a creaking, thumping, jangling world that would not hold still for a second. Then awareness came that she was on a horse, was tied face down across a saddle; her wrists and ankles were tightly lashed beneath the animal's belly.

Consciousness must have left her then, for next time she opened her eyes things seemed lighter, a sort of leprous grey colour as though mist-blotched and barnacled. All her weight was against the cantle and her wrists and ankles felt as though they were about to be twisted off her. The horrible, blinding pain of it all was enough to make her faint. But she did not faint; not then, at least. And, presently, her reeling senses discovered that the horse was climbing a hill. Gravity it was that kept her weight so hard against the cantle. Perhaps it was gravity that made her head throb so; seemed as though in another moment it must surely burst. As something to get her mind off it she tried to identify her surroundings. But hanging butchered-steer fashion, head down from a saddle, was not conducive to great feats of observation. All she could see through the swirling dust were occasional patches of sand and sliding rubble.

But she was not alone. That much was plain. There was a deal too much noise—not to mention the dust, to be made by one lone horse.

She tried to cry out, to attract attention. But couldn't. There was a lump in her mouth and her cramped tongue was dry as cotton. She tried to waggle it round. The strange lump gave a little, soggily; but it would not go away and she could not —though she tried—spit it out. It came to her then what it was. It was cloth—she was gagged!

Trussed up and gagged, lashed fast to somebody's saddle!

It was not the sort of knowledge from which great comforts are taken. She must be a prisoner—a captive possibly, or hostage. The knowledge was not conducive to any tremendous satisfaction, either. While she was pondering it, remembrance came with all its resurrected horror. The recollections overwhelmed her.

When her reeling senses became again cognizant of the things immediately about her, the jar of motion seemed to have stopped. Her limbs were numb and useless and her head was a blinding torture. Through the pulsing, throbbing agony of it came knowledge of another's presence close by. No—that was wrong; there must be *several* men about her. She could hear their grumbling voices. Then someone was cutting her ropes away. Someone else lifted her out of the saddle; but when they set her down she crumpled miserably in a heap. Her legs—coming back to life— stung as though skewered by hatpins; but they would not hold her up—not even with the aid of the big rough hand that, vicelike, gripped her shoulder. They buckled again, futilely, and somebody close by swore.

Then a lantern abruptly was thrust in her face, and by its flare she saw the lower half of one side of a vest, a dark, indiscriminate patch of shirt, the flaring wings of bull-hide chaps; but of their wearer's face she saw nothing at all. The lantern light did not strike it.

Then a voice said gruffly: "Bring her along," and another voice said maliciously: "I'd give somethin' to see Telldane's mug when he finds out this dame is missin'!"

Cooper's voice, that last. She was certain.

F

The first speaker laughed. "Prob'ly won't be hearin' about it—I've an idea he's goin' to be busy. The cook's been greased an' he's gone to town with a tale for Deef Smith's ear. Unless Smith's changed, you can cross Telldane off the books."

CHAPTER XXVI

COOPER LAYS PIPE

COOPER had not, as Topock had supposed, killed Ronstadt, the Buck Basin homesteader. But Cooper had been well suited to let his erstwhile pardner believe he had; that belief had eliminated possibly embarrassing questions. As a matter of fact, it had been Vargas who had killed Juke Ronstadt. Cooper had seen him do it and had determined to find out why. And he had, at last, but it had not been easy. Vargas was a canny customer with an ingrained habit of caution. That habit, on Cooper's part, had occasioned a good many oaths. Indirectly it had brought about Vargas' death; for had Kerwold's double-crossing foreman not been attempting to make doubly sure a matter already certain, he would not have been round at the time of Pring's visit and would have been, therefore, quite probably still numbered among the quick.

But Cooper was satisfied to have him out of the way; he had learned why the man had killed Ronstadt. The knowledge was not an unmixed blessing and he'd shared it for quite some time. Ronstadt had been killed because, inadvertently, he had stumbled

across a secret—Vargas' secret; and now Mr. Cooper
had discovered it, with all its attendant risks and
worries. And the risks were there, and the worries,
too. For the substance of Duarte Vargas' secret was
cached on Kerwold land.

It was this knowledge that finally had swung
Cooper over to Pring. He had early sensed that the
Double Bar Circle boss was far from the disinterested
spectator that he would have other folks believe.
Cooper had watched Gus Pring as he'd watched
Duarte Vargas, patiently and assiduously; and the
watching had borne fruit. Vargas was mixed in the
valley's turbulence in the hope of grabbing on to that
precious find; a something Vargas wanted but had not
the guts to file on while Sam Kerwold lived to exact
vengeance. But Gus Pring's purpose in smashing
Kerwold was of larger, more far-seeing scope; this
basin was a paradise for cow raisers—a veritable cattle
empire, but Gus Pring could not grab it so long as
Kerwold lived and prospered. Therefore, both to
Pring and to Vargas, as Cooper saw it, Sam Kerwold
was a barrier, an obstruction to be removed.

To Cooper, the removal of all three of these
hombres was a prime and urgent necessity. But first,
he'd told himself, give Pring and Vargas rope—give
them all the rope they wanted; and after that . . .
his turn would come.

And now that turn was coming.

Cooper, knowing it, chuckled. For *he'd* ambition,
also. His craving for power and opulence had been
as great as any man's. Nor was he averse to a good-
looking wife.

His recipe was comprehensive.

And it was working—oh, so beautifully!

Already Sam Kerwold was out of the saddle, mur-

dered last night by Gus Pring. Ab Holcomb and
other lesser lights—they'd been taken care of, too.
There was not a homesteader left in the country.
Except Telldane, of course, who had filed on Wildcat.
And *he'd* not be around long. Pring, slick fellow,
had framed Telldane for Kerwold's murder, and that
guy, Deef Smith, would finish him. Telldane, once
had risen from the dead; but he'd pull no rise act this
time! And Vargas was dead, and his secret safe; and
as for calico—— Well, Cooper had kind of taken a
shine to Jane Kerwold. And here she was, put right
in his hands by Pring, locked up in that yonder cabin.

Again Cooper chuckled. Things were shaping up
pretty nice—pretty damned nice! There was only
one fly in the ointment—Pring himself; and maybe . .

He took Willow Creek Wally aside, well out of the
other boys' hearing. "Well?" Willow Creek eyed
him wonderingly.

"No," Cooper said, "it ain't. In fact, I don't mind
tellin' you it's pretty damn bad. I don't like the look
of things at all."

"What you mean, don't like the look of 'em?"

"Just that. All this killin' an' girl-snatchin'!"

Willow Creek shrugged. "No skin off my nose—
yours either. Gus Pring's the one that's done it. An'
you got to hand it to him——"

"You sure have," Cooper said dryly. "He's
slicker'n slobbers——"

"What's up your sleeve?" Willow Creek said.
"What you drivin' at?"

"Ain't sure I know myself, but I'm gettin' goddam
suspicious. I dunno what he's got in mind for me,
but he's sure as hell got you down for a first-class
necktie party."

Willow Creek's face showed the hoped-for reaction.

his growl was a proper-pitched sound. " By God, if
you——"

" Shh! you fool! Not so loud," Cooper snarled,
with a quick glance across at the men. " It may be
I'm wrong. I hope I am, but—— Well, it's this way,
Wally. I overheard Gus tellin' off a couple boys to
swear your neck into hemp. They're to push the
word around that you an' Telldane is pardners——"

" Pardners! " Willow Creek exploded. " *Me* an'
Bufe Telldane? Why——"

" I know—I know," Cooper cut in suavely, " but
that don't make no never-mind. The idea is for these
two fellas—soon's Smith's got Telldane's light blown
out—to come forward an' swear they seen you waitin'
for Bufe in the timber last night; that when you
parted he went one way an' you, takin' the girl, went
another. Fixes it pretty neat, don't it, why Telldane
ain't got the girl he's s'posed to've run off with? "
He showed a sympathy for Willow Creek's emotion,
adding pointedly: " It also gets you out of the way
for when it's time to count up the profits. 'Course,
I may be mistaken, you know. *Mebbe* I misunder-
stood what I heard; but I figured you'd ought to know
about it."

CHAPTER XXVII

LOST TIMBERS

WHEN Bufe Telldane again swung upright in the
saddle he was a good many miles from where the unknown marksman had let drive at him with a rifle

from the rimrock. He'd cleared out of that place in a hurry, but his mind had not been idle. The chances were it was one of Deef Smith's Indians who had cut loose at him back there. But it might have been the deputy himself and Bufe wasn't taking any chances. For the time being, at any rate, he aimed to put himself out of reach. Time enough to get on Pring's trail after Smith had been shaken off his own trail.

So he headed for the Verde River.

He rode hard and fast, and when he reached the broken ground along it he sent Safford's horse between red bluffs and went angling down a wash that took him into the bottoms and along these, skirting the river, he rode north at an easier pace. Deef Smith's scouts, so long as he kept below the rim, would have considerable difficulty keeping track of his progress.

He stopped at noon in a kind of cove, unsaddled and staked his horse to graze. In the shade of a desert willow he lay down and drowsed for two or three hours; after which, with a smoke between his lips, he considered the situation.

Had something new happened to cause Deef Smith to get those Apaches after him? Or was it accumulated gall and spite on the deputy's part that had brought him to their hire? Smith was a go-getter, it was both his record and his boast. He had a reputation for getting his man, and it was plain he aimed to get Bufe. So far as Telldane had ever heard, Deef Smith was honest, played a straight game. No holds were barred when he got on the trail, but he didn't go out of his way to hound a man just because a man had a bad name.

Smith must, therefore, believe that Telldane had murdered Brill. He must believe Telldane had shot

and killed Safford because Safford had got the goods
on him with regard to Brill's killing. Still and all, in
the three weeks Smith had been hunting him he had
not before employed Indians.

Telldane considered this, grimly thoughtful.

He considered some other things as well. He considered, for instance, Ab Holcomb and Holcomb's
story; he considered Duarte Vargas and Pecos Gann.
Holcomb, of course, had known him at once—as soon
as he'd first laid eyes on him; for Telldane had been
the reason for Holcomb's migration from Texas
where Ab had been doing a profitable business rustling other people's steers. Telldane had been a stock
detective then and had let Holcomb get away; in fact,
he had warned the man he had *better* haul freight if
he put any value on freedom. There was a chance,
he had thought, Holcomb might go straight . . . The
point was, Holcomb—when Bufe had come into this
basin—had known him. It was Telldane's belief that
Gann and Vargas had also known him, or had pretty
well guessed who he was. There was, contributory to
this notion, that scene in Ransome's store on the night
of Bufe's arrival when Pecos Gann, crying " Jeez!
D'you know——" had jumped a blurred hand for his
gun.

Yes, it seemed pretty certain that Gann and Vargas
had known him. It had been Vargas, riding out of
the trees, who'd suggested his going to the store.
Vargas must have known that Sam had written Bufe
. . . Each must have feared Bufe's coming—but why?

True, Gann had been mixed up with Topock—
might even have been taking pay from Pring. But
Vargas . . . Where did Kerwold's foreman come in?
Had he, like others in this basin, been working all
along for Pring? Holcomb had said last night he'd

trailed Gus Pring to a rendezvous with Vargas . . .

Telldane gave it up for the time. The whole damn thing was so mixed up, it made him dizzy to think of it. For one reason or another practically every man of importance in this country was out to down Sam Kerwold. All of them were Kerwold's enemies, which was all Bufe needed to know. Their various motives weren't important. It *was* important to see that their schemes bore no fruit. That was why Kerwold had got him here.

Bufe picked up his rifle and prowled along the bottoms, finally rousting out a jackrabbit which he shot and promptly cleaned. Building a tiny fire then, he cooked and ate it. And then took another nap.

It was dark when he woke up.

He saddled Safford's horse and rode north along the river in the direction of distant Ashfork. When he reached the big bend east of Saint Clair Mountain, he climbed up out of the bottoms and took the road from Davenport Wash and followed it leisurely south-west till it reached Camp Creek. Hoof sound then drove him off the trail. With a clamping hand across the gelding's nostrils, he waited in the brush by its side.

There were six riders in the party; two whites and four breech-clouted bucks. They weren't picking any posies, either, but despite the speed with which they passed Bufe's covert, the moonlight showed him Deef Smith's face, and its expression made him glad he'd wheeled from the trail. They were hunting him, no doubt of that!

He waited another ten minutes and was just swinging into the trail when he heard them coming back again—leastways, someone was coming—several some-ones, by the sound. What had happened? Not that it made much difference. He could see what would happen all right if they caught sight of him.

He put Safford's horse into the creek's dry bed and quietly eased him south. It did not take him long, however, to realize the futility of quiet. Smith's crowd had stopped back there in the trail; tiny bursts of light suggested they were striking matches, and he remembered then the flattened calk on the off rear shoe of Safford's horse.

He abandoned quiet and spurred for speed. This was no time for stealth or parley. Contact with Smith and those Indians with him could have but one result —gunplay. There'd been too much of that already.

Coming out of the creek bed half an hour later, he cut through the timber for higher ground. Smith's crowd, like hell emigrating on cart-wheels, was coming fast, not far behind.

Telldane pulled up on a little knoll, keening the south-flung reaches spread below in the moon's pale light. Yonder line was Kerwold's ripped-up fence. Off there was Wildcat Hill. Smith's bunch, by the sound, had reached the place where he'd left the creek —were making quite a commotion. He could hear Smith's voice, keyed tight with rage, snapping commands like a whip-lash. He was spreading them out, going to beat the timber.

Bufe's glance swept the shadows with a risen vigilance as he kneed Safford's horse off the knoll. He sent it quietly downward, angling toward the demolished line-fence, veering sharply back into the timber when he realized that boundary's lack of cover.

A challenge slammed after him through the gloom. "You, over there, headin' west! Who are you? Sing out, goddam——"

Telldane sank his spurs. The gelding lunged for the open. A rifle cracked through the hoof-pound

F*

sharply, twice. The first shot withered past Telldane on the left; the second kicked splintered bark from a tree bole just ahead of him, and then all the rifles behind him let go in a solid blast of sound. A branch above his head cracked off. With twigs falling all around him Telldane put his bronc across the fence. Three long jumps it made, and staggered. The horse was done. Bufe left the saddle—lit on braking boot-heels, skidded, and went plunging for a clump of young elder with the whine of lead tearing whistles of sound all about him.

Across his shoulder as he crashed through the thicket, Wildcat Hill reared bleakly black against the north-west stars. The base of that long slope was bathed in moonlight, devoid of cover. That way was out; he must go some other. His raking glance zig-zagged the shadows. Straight west, south of and paralleling the torn-up fence, was a scrub-oak stand, its pooled gloom promising the only shelter he could see.

Pistol in hand he lunged from the thicket, low-crouched, heart pumping fiercely. They hadn't seen him; the elder thicket cut off their view—they were still tunnelling it with their lead, their noise drowning out the sound of his running.

He was almost into the scrub-oak stand when a man's voice bit from its shadows.

"Hold it!"

Telldane, gathering his muscles, sprang. Not aside, but straight ahead, straight at the point where the voice had come from. He had to get into that scrub-oak or die. A gun's flame burst in his face as the momentum of his drive brought him square against the hidden man, carrying him backward, shoulder hard against the fellow's chest. The gun went off again, that flash of light showing Willow Creek's face. Then they were down in a tangle of thrashing arms and legs. Shock hammered Telldane's ribs to the muffled explosion of Willow Creek's gun; then his own gun-barrel struck Willow Creek's head and the man went limp as a meal-sack.

Breathing hard, Bufe reached his feet. A back-flung glance showed Smith's bunch breaking from the elder. He hammered two shots, heard a man's strangled yell and, without waiting to see more, dashed west through the trees.

Five minutes' hard running brought him to their edge. He pulled up, trying to throttle his laboured breathing to hear if they were coming. They were.

Dead ahead, beyond the fringe of trees, lay the corduroy road. Here was where he'd met Duarte Vargas the night he had come into this country.

The rotten timbers of that road would leave no track—very little sound. He moved on to it, still running, and struck south. Its course was angling. The old road curled and twisted through the trees. Behind him Deef Smith's riders left the oak; they'd not know which way he'd gone—would have to spread out.

Bufe left the road, swinging east. The brush grew thicker, impeding progress, making stealth impossible. He was cursing his luck when something tripped him, hurled him heavily through the brush. The ground gave way beneath his weight and dropped him, rolling, frantically clawing, sharply downward. He stopped suddenly, brought up in a choking cloud of dust.

It was dark—pitch dark, and he'd lost his gun. He sat cat-still, intently listening. Sound of the posse reached him dimly, became vaguer with distance and finally quiet.

He got to his feet then, striking a match. His glance, whipped around, sprang suddenly wide. The walls of this hole were of rotten timber. Man-laid timber—he was in a shaft! The shaft of some old, long-forgotten mine!

In the east wall a tunnel led off into Stygian gloom. And there at its mouth, aglint in the light, lay his pistol. He stooped to retrieve it, went still with an oath. The dust was laced with the tracks of boots, and not all of them old ones—not by a jugful!

He picked up his gun and went into the tunnel. He dropped his match and struck another, coming presently to where some recent working had widened the passage. Against the near wall was a pick and a powder-keg; the opposite wall was piled high with filled sacks. He examined the side where the pick had been used and soundlessly whistled beneath his breath.

He saw the answer to several things now—saw plainly what Duarte Vargas had been doing up there by the road the night he'd arrived—Vargas had probably just left this place. Kerwold's foreman had apparently found what its owners had given up searching for. Gold! That whole blame wall was lousy with it!

Bufe had just made this discovery when voice sound grabbed him, pulled him upright.

Deef Smith was coming back.

CHAPTER XXVIII

SKULL MESA

THE creak of saddle-gear, the jingle and clank of spur and bridle-chains, drew nearer and stopped. Telldane, stiff-crouched in the tunnel, could hear quite plainly the savage growl of Deef Smith's voice. They must, he thought, be halted some place almighty close to the shaft top.

Deef Smith was laying the law down. "Makes no damn diff'rence!" he snapped. "Unless he's growed wings he's hid out around here somewheres, an' by grab he'll stay bottled up here till I can git men enough to roust him out! Keller, you take these bucks an' string 'em out where they can watch this whole smear of country. There'll be a thousan' bucks in it, hard money, for the gent that brings him down. Now git on an'—— Never mind that! I'm goin' to poke around some more over to Kerwold's—might find somethin' that cook overlooked . . . You told Ed Cranton to get them bodies, didn't you?"

That was all Bufe heard just then; he was too startled by the implication in Deef Smith's reference to Cranton to bother with the rest of it. Cranton was the Ashfork undertaker—what bodies was he supposed to have been told about? Telldane did not care for that talk of bodies—not even a little bit. Something had been happening; a whole and ornery lot by the sound, and . . .

He pulled up again, listening. The sound of hoofs was dying out, being swallowed up by distance as the scouts moved off, again to take up their vigil. They—but all of them weren't gone! There was horse sound right above him now!

Bufe made his mind up pronto.

This tunnel must lead out of here. . . .

It did. Parting a mesquite's branches he saw the shine of stars again; and there on a crest by the old-timbered road, sharp-cut against the moon glare, showed the stiff, cocked shape of a horseman—*Smith!*

Deef Smith it certainly was. Equally obvious was the fact that Smith, with that rifle across his knees, was lingering in the hope that his quarry, thinking him departed with the rest, would come cat-footing from his hide-out. What Smith meant to do in that case was plain as paint on a pot lid!

Smith was less than twenty yards off and was facing the other way. But he faced round quick enough when a voice said softly: "Grab a cloud an' hang on to it, hombre." He faced round with an oath, gun lifted to shoot—but there was nothing in sight for target.

Telldane said: "I'll not ask again," and, cursing, Smith put his hands up.

"Let go of that gun an' ride straight south—ride *slow!* That's fine. Pull up."

Telldane stepped out of the branches, six-shooter cocked and levelled. "Slide down, an' do it careful. I'd just as lief shoot as not," he said. "Now tie that nag so he won't wander off." And, when Smith had done so, Telldane relieved him of his belted gun and prodded him through the branches.

"What the hell is this——"

"Tunnel," Bufe said succinctly. "Strike a match an' lead the way."

"You goddam fool!" Smith snarled. "You'll never cut it! I've got——"

"Just let me worry about that. Get movin'!"

When they reached the wide place where the sacks were piled, Bufe said: "There's a candle stump. Light it—that's fine. Now sit down an' get the weight off your heels. Whose bodies was Cranton supposed to get?"

Smith was staring round curiously.

"Vargas' secret mine," Bufe said. "C'mon now, answer my question."

"Whose bodies," Smith mocked: "that's rich, that is! You lousy back-shootin' killer! Where've you got that girl?"

"What girl?"

"Jane Kerwol—*Tey!*"

Telldane took his grip from Smith's throat and stepped back, cheeks white, eyes blazing. His voice was bleak, repressed, hard-held. "Talk," he said, "and talk fast!"

Smith did. Sullenly, with lips peeled back, he told the story Kerwold's cook had brought him; told how he'd gone to the Flying K, of what he'd found when he got there. "I suppose," he sneered when he finished, "you'll tell me somebody's framed you."

Telldane told him nothing of the kind. "I've got to borrow your horse——"

"You crazy loon! You can't git away! I've——"

"I've no intention of getting away. I'm goin' after that girl," Bufe said coldly. "Peel off that belt and put your hands behi——"

"Like h——" Smith's bluster died at the look of Telldane's face; he grudgingly did as ordered. "But you——"

"For your information," Bufe cut in, "it's Pring

that's behind all this—wake up an' get your eyes
open! It's Pring that's got Jane Kerwold, too—the
man's hog-wild for power! Gone to his head; he's
tryin' to grab this entire valley. The fool's gone mad
as a hatter! For God's sake, use your head, Smith!
Can't you *see* it?"

"I can see you swingin' at a rope!" Smith snarled;
but Bufe paid no attention.

"He's bribed Sam's cook, that's plain enough—
probably killed him by now to shut his mouth. It's a
cinch he knows about this mine—that's why he killed
Vargas; one of his reasons anyway. Pretty slick of him
framin' me for Sam's murder—but he's pulled that
trick once too often."

Bufe paused, then added grimly: "Look here,
Smith; you ought to be able to see this much——"

"I can see your face when they kick the trap out
from under you!" Smith jeered. "You might's well
surrender now an' save yourself some trouble. You'll
never get——"

"Listen, you damn fool!" Telldane gritted.
"Can't you see what's goin' to happen to that girl?
She must have seen him—recognized him; elseways,
why would he have carried her off? Do you think
you'll ever see her again? You won't if I can't stop
him! He——"

But Smith was grinning at him sourly. "'F I had
your talkin' talents——"

Bufe saw there was no use arguing with him; nothing could change him. He was convinced of Telldane's guilt and would consider no alternative. Bufe
dared waste no further time. He tied Smith up and
left him. He knew the man would get loose of that
belt, but it would serve till Bufe got clear.

Well, Pring had bested him again—but he'd not

have long to brag of it! Meantime, Bufe must ride;
and fast. There was one slender chance Jane was still
alive. . . .

Telldane knew that soon as he struck open country
Smith's Apache scouts would spot him; and they did.
Rifles opened up from the rim-rock and the scream of
lead was all about him. Crouched low above Smith's
saddle he urged the game horse on with quirt and
spur; and, ears laid flat, it flew like a rocket, straight
out from under the Indian guns, a silver streak in the
moonlight. But one chance shot, or a gopher hole,
Bufe knew, would send them crashing, and he prayed
for luck as much as for speed; he would need luck this
night—plenty of it.

The Indian yells dimmed out behind; the crack of
Indian rifles. But these would follow—even now,
Bufe guessed, Smith's scouts would be catching up
horses. And Smith himself, directed by those shots,
would soon be dogging the trail. But that was all
right. Let him keep his lead and the whole damn
country could follow! What he aimed to do would
not take long—just the time for squeezing a trigger.
After that they could have him, he guessed; he hadn't
very much to live for.

For he was not fooled. Knowledge—that knowledge
recently acquired from Holcomb—that Jane had not
been the capricious, perfidious cheat he had supposed,
did not excuse the supposition. He had thought her
one and called her one—only last night he had said to
her face, things no woman could ever excuse. No,
those fond hopes were done with—as dead as they'd
been three years ago—deader; blasted by scorn and
mockery, destroyed by lack of faith. But, even if they
hadn't been, the knowledge of his turbulent years, of

the things he'd done in this valley, would have driven her from him in repugnance. Proclaimed an outlaw from Usery Pass to the Limestone Hills, Telldane's future was sealed—sealed with blood and dishonour; tied with calumny, like the rope Smith would put round his neck.

But before they closed the books on him, there was one more chore for his guns. If he could, he must save Jane Kerwold and send Gus Pring to hell.

From time to time backward looks were flung across his shoulder, and each time his head twisted front again, his mouth showed tighter, more cracklike.

They were coming all right. Smith and his yelling Indians were not a mile behind him; not gaining, thank God! but holding even, holding the pace like hounds. One false step on his bronc's part though——

He prayed—and prayed again. Not for greater speed, but for his horse's safe arrival at the ranch at the top of Skull Mesa. And Bufe prayed thoroughly; not with lips alone, but with soul and heart—with every last energy in him.

For he was sure that Gann's gutted ranch, or its vicinity, was where Pring had taken Jane. Obviously Gann, all along and unknown to Ab Holcomb, had been working in Gus Pring's interests. It was the only explanation that would fit Gann into things. He had, of course, allowed Cooper and Topock to use his place as a relay stop in their stealing of Kerwold's cattle; but Bufe greatly doubted if Topock or Cooper, either, had yet taken a cent of profit. Gus Pring would have seen to that; they'd have been stalled off with some fancy tale—slick talking was Gus Pring's strong point. But now that Pring's game was cut-and-run, what better place could he run to? What place was less apt of suspicion? He would keep out of reach till Telldane was done, till something happened to Smith.

It was after midnight when Bufe sighted Gann's gutted buildings. He did not stop but slewed a circle round them and cut for Gann's north line-camp. That place, he knew, was still intact. There was a tank there and a tumbledown shack, a horse corral and cattle-pens; and there—God granting him luck— he would find Jane Kerwold, a prisoner.

Then, as the breakneck pace of Smith's roan gelding whipped him across a ridge, he saw it—a dark, devil's pattern of upthrust blocks against the mouth of a draw. Saw the horses—six of them, saddled and hitched by the big corral.

Clickety-clack, clickety-clack. The wind-brought sound of the clattering mill was abruptly stilled, lost and flattened in the pounding crash of exploding guns. Flame blossomed from the cabin wall in lurid streaks. The rip and thump of lead—the whine of its passing, was a risen wail in Telldane's brain as, low across the roan's stretched neck, he spurred straight on without pausing or swerving.

Smith's horse was used to the screech of lead and, with ears laid back, it gave all it had.

Two hundred, one-fifty—eighty yards; that near they had got when Bufe jerked the rifle from under his leg and drove its last shot at the huddle of horses. Like a dynamited hill that group split apart. One reared straight up and fell backwards screaming; two more were down in thrashing heaps—a fourth was pitching. The final pair broke anchorage, took the top bar with them. From the cabin door two men lunged toward them.

Bufe dropped the rifle and snatched out a pistol.

Three times its fanning hammer fell. One man's white face twisted clear around. Plain in the moonlight. Willow Creek Wally. He went toppling backward like a pole-axed steer.

The other man made a saddle—slashed wildly with a ten-inch blade at the reins still tied to the dragging-bar. He had nearly cut them when Bufe's shot took him, smashing him slantways from the squealing bronc.

But this was passing turmoil. Bufe had not stopped. Smith's horse still was carrying him straight for the cabin. Guns winked light from door and window; but panic, desperation, had unsteadied their aim. He was twenty yards off when they scored their hit. They must have fired together. A deafening blast rocked across the yard. Bufe felt it strike. Its travel came up the gelding's legs.

The horse was going. Bufe kicked free of the stirrups as its head went down. The uprearing saddle hurled him forward. He struck on his chest and ploughed five feet through choking dust. He came out of it on one knee and an elbow, the pistol still savagely clenched in his fist. There were two shots left. He used them, drove them both at the dark crouched shape that bulked in the door—saw it fall.

The flash of his gun briefly lit the cabin. The sight inside sent his heart to his boots; hung him breathless and frozen, just short of the door.

There were two men inside—two men and Jane Kerwold; those exploding shells had shown her face, chalk white, twisted toward him from where she struggled in the grip of Pring's arm. But Pring had her fast and was safe behind her; he laughed as his free hand brought up a gun—laughed deeply, exultantly, triumphant and mocking. "Go on," he jeered, "shoot!"

And somebody did—but it wasn't Telldane.

It was Cooper.

His shape showed, crouched, across the room Bufe saw the leaping flame that left it. He was to the side of, slightly back of, Pring; and his shot took the rancher beneath the left arm where his clutch of the girl exposed his ribs. Jane fell free as he staggered back; and a swift lunge took Bufe through the door in a long, low dive that ended at Cooper. Cooper's shot ripped its track across Bufe's cheek. Then Bufe's arms locked hard round Cooper's legs and carried him crashing against the wall.

The gun went skittering from Cooper's grasp. Bufe's own, shot empty, had been dropped before he sprang. But Cooper had a knife and meant to use it. Bufe caught the glint of it just in time and flung himself backward.

Rage ripped from Cooper in a snarl of breath. In the powder-fumed murk he was just a black shape, but Bufe saw it coming and again lurched aside. The blade thwunked wickedly into the wall. Before Cooper could jerk it free, a voice snapped harshly: 'Hold it! First guy moves gets tunnelled!" and a match burst redly from the pooled gloom of the doorway.

It threw weird light across and showed Cooper crouched and glaring; showed Deef Smith well into the room with a six-shooter gripped in each fist and the look on his face a dire warning. Showed the crowded bucks stolid-cheeked round the door, every man of them packing a rifle. The man with the match lit a lamp on the wall and shifted his rifle suggestively.

"All right, Cooper," Smith said. "Get away from

that knife. I've got him covered——"

"Got *him* covered!" Jane cried hysterically.
"You'd better cover *Cooper*!"

Smith's eyes raked her briefly, returned to the scowling Cooper. "Why should I cover Cooper?"

"Because," Jane cried, "he was Pring's chief gun
boss—it was Pring that's been behind all this——'

"Now that's damn foolishness," Smith growled
testily. "I know you're upset an' all that—willin' to
make allowance for it. But it's Bufe Telldane that's
behind this trouble, an'll swing for it, too, by god
freys!" He said to Cooper: "Who killed Gus?"

A crafty look edged Cooper's cheeks. An out-flung
arm pointed square at Telldane. "Him—the god
dam loafer-wolf!"

"That's a lie!" Jane blazed. "Don't let him
wriggle clear of this," she said, flinging round on
Smith.

"What's she talkin' about?" Cooper snapped, with
a show of surprised resentment. "You'd think we
hadn't saved her, t' listen to her yap——"

"Don't you dare stand there and lie—it won't do
you a bit of good now, anyway." She said to Smith.
"I've got the cook's signed statement—got it right
here in my blouse. Bufe hadn't a thing to do with
those murders, or with my being here, either. He
saw what you hadn't the *wit* to see and came over
here trying to rescue me—and he's done it, too! The
man you——"

"Hell, I heard enough o' this!" Cooper snarled,
starting for the door.

"Just a minute," said Deef Smith softly. "I think
we'll look into this—keep him covered, boys." And
to Jane: "You say Gus Pring——"

"Of course!" Jane said more calmly. "Gus was

trying to grab this basin and I think my father caught on to him. At any rate——" And she told Deef Smith the story; all of it that she knew; about going into the office last night and finding Pring, gun in hand. "He bribed the cook to ride in and tell those lies," she said; "and afterward, when the cook joined us here, Gus killed him—but he didn't die right off; he managed to give me a paper, and it tells the truth!"

She started toward Bufe, but Smith's arm stopped her. "Hold still a bit. I want to get this straight in my mind. You say Gus Pring killed your father and Vargas? That Cooper here's been workin' for Gus——"

"Yes, and so was Vargas and Willow Creek, who used to be Holcomb's range boss, and that fellow, Guy Topock, that was Cooper's pardner. They've been stealing our cattle and pulling all these raids—— Oh, I've heard plenty since I've been here. I—I think they intended to kill me."

But Smith was no longer listening; he was staring hard at Cooper. "What you got to say to that?"

"I wouldn't waste my breath," Cooper snarled, "tryin' to——"

"It would *be* a waste of breath," Jane agreed, "because——"

"Well, I think I'll take both of you in," Smith scowled at Bufe and Cooper. "Telldane's wanted for the murder of Brill and——"

"But he didn't murder Brill—he hasn't murdered *anyone*," Jane flashed. "Andy Cooper murdered Brill; killed him for his money-belt—he told me so himself—thought it was a great joke that you were fixed to pin it on Bufe. And Guy Topock robbed the stage——"

"You certainly know all the answers," Smith scowled.

"Of course! Don't you *understand?* Gus Pring intended to—to murder me—they didn't care how they talked. Why, Vargas discovered gold on Father's land—an old mine or something that's been closed for years. He was going to double-cross Gus, but Gus found out about it."

"I guess you better unlimber some talk," Deef Smith told Cooper grimly. And finally, sullenly, Cooper did, confirming Jane's declarations. He must have realized there was no way out; and a little later, handcuffed, Smith took him off to town.

And when they were gone, Bufe said to Jane: "Words ain't much use at a time like this. I reckon I owe you——"

"Nonsense! You owe me nothing—the owing is all on my side. Father told me how you came out here because he asked you to—of all you've been doing to help him. Poor Dad. It hurt him pretty bad to find how Gus had taken him in—I guess Gus took about everyone in. I——" She broke off and Bufe saw tears in her eyes; knew she was thinking of her father.

He stood there, twisting his hat, trying to think of something to say. But words seemed puny things to console the loss of a father. What he finally did say was, "I—— Well—I guess I better be shovin' on. Things'll be quietin' down round here; won't be much work for a gun-fighter. Expect I'll drift on over the hump . . . I—uh—Jane, I'm mighty sorry I've been such a fool—such a miserable——"

"Shh!" Jane wiped a sleeve across her cheeks. "You've——"

"No. I been a fool. No faith nor charity nor anything else. Just a gun-fighter, an' I guess that's all I ever *will* be. I—I want you to know I realize it; that I'm sorry for the things I've thought of you an' called you—that I ain't blamin' you at all for throwin' me over. I—— Well, good-bye——"

"You—you're not really leaving?"

Bufe nodded. He smiled sourly. "I expect things'll quiet down better if I'm off some place else —things usually do, I've noticed."

"But—but I've been kind of hoping you'd take over the Flying K and——"

"Nope—— 'Fraid not." The prospect of being around where he would see her every day, where he could realize more keenly—if that were possible—the things that might have been, held no allurement.

"But, Bufe—I *want* you to!"

He stared, amazed. His cheeks wrinkled up in puzzlement. "You—— Say! I don't get this——"

"Don't—don't you care for me any more?"

"*Care* for you! Great grief! Why—— But shucks; you can't mean——"

She nodded, smiling through her tears. "Of course. I've always loved you, Bufe—even when— when you acted so mannishly obstinate and mean, I—— Oh! my dear!"